HOLLY A. KELLISON

# COMPROMISED
*Boundaries*

BOOK II of
the Boundaries Within Series

authorHOUSE®

*AuthorHouse™*
*1663 Liberty Drive*
*Bloomington, IN 47403*
*www.authorhouse.com*
*Phone: 1 (800) 839-8640*

© *2018 Holly A. Kellison. All rights reserved.*

*No part of this book may be reproduced, stored in a retrieval system, or transmitted by any means without the written permission of the author.*

*Published by AuthorHouse 02/01/2018*

*ISBN: 978-1-5462-2602-4 (sc)*
*ISBN: 978-1-5462-2601-7 (hc)*
*ISBN: 978-1-5462-2603-1 (e)*

*Library of Congress Control Number: 2018901049*

*Print information available on the last page.*

*Any people depicted in stock imagery provided by Thinkstock are models, and such images are being used for illustrative purposes only. Certain stock imagery © Thinkstock.*

*This book is printed on acid-free paper.*

*Because of the dynamic nature of the Internet, any web addresses or links contained in this book may have changed since publication and may no longer be valid. The views expressed in this work are solely those of the author and do not necessarily reflect the views of the publisher, and the publisher hereby disclaims any responsibility for them.*

Dedicated to *my* Parents
(Yes, sibs, I'll claim them this round)
Thanks for always supporting my adventures,
even when you don't agree with me!

# Contents

## Book III

### Boundaries Within; The Series

# Prologue

J ames walked up to the house and knocked on the door. Grey was at the bottom of the steps, and two other members of his team were at opposite ends of the home. James always liked to be prepared. A man opened the door and eyed James, shaking his head. Stepping back, he gestured for him to come in, alone.

"Do you realize how inappropriate it is for you to just show up at my home like this?" Brian walked him into the dining room, and they sat across from each other.

"Do you realize I don't care?" James said. "That family has been through hell the last couple of months."

"Tess is okay? She made it out of the hospital with the babies doing well?"

"Of course." James grinned. "You know who she had fighting for her."

"And the rest of the family?" Brian asked.

"Sort of fine. You know who called the mark?" James asked.

Brian shook his head. "We didn't get to talk much that night. I only had time to back off the local PD and organize a small team to clean up that mess."

"I know. That's why I'm here. It was Taryn, her twin," James said. "She's the one who shot her in Chicago and started this whole damn thing. This is the part you'll love—it was all over a man. Robert Monroe was the festering wound, and then it was Colin McGowan."

"Colin?" Brian was shocked. "I know all about Robert, but Colin?"

"Colin kept her as his little dish on the side for years until he married Tess," James explained. "He still supported her, but he didn't see her again. The last time he was with Taryn, she got pregnant with his son. Now Taryn is dead, and Tess is alive. All the parties that were after the bounty were taken out as well. Tess is free."

"I know you didn't fly up here to tell me all that," Brian said. "What's on your mind?"

James looked around the meticulous room. "Dominic Markenna."

"I knew there was something bothering you. He hasn't surfaced in years." Brian shrugged.

"Are you positive he was involved?" James asked.

Brian took a deep breath. "His name hasn't come up since he sold his company. I'm going to leave a little room for possible misinterpretation, but he is a smart man. His father is a manipulative bastard—even from prison. One of my friends in the Justice Department, Meagan Trask, stood up for him when I arrested him after the incident with Tess. I cannot give you a definitive answer."

"Markenna is at Jonathan's home as we speak," James said. "They won't let me touch him. I just don't trust him. I've worked the list with precision. If he's not supposed to be on it, you've got to tell me because I'm almost done."

"Where's Jonathan?" Brian asked.

"In Savannah," James answered.

"I'll fly down tomorrow and talk with him," Brian said.

"I will be there until Jack gets back. Half of my men will stay close until I feel comfortable enough to release them."

"Where's Jack?" Brain wondered, knowing he never took vacations.

"Taking a much-needed vacation with Harper." James grinned.

"What's he doing? He figured he couldn't have Tess so he'd take the next-best sister?" Brian laughed.

"Something like that," James said. "My team and I are heading out tonight to follow a lead on a few people from the list. I should be back in Savannah tomorrow morning. I want an answer tomorrow—or I will put a bullet in his head regardless of his connection to the McGowan family."

"Fair enough," Brian said. "I'll wait for your return."

## Chapter 1

James took a quiet, deep breath, releasing it slowly as he watched through the scope on his rifle. There were four men that they needed to eliminate in this town, and two of them were standing about two hundred yards from his position. The only thing he was waiting for were a couple of his men to be in a position so all four men could be taken down at the same time. The idea was to make the four shots sound like one to bring less attention to the area. They were on the east side of a small town south of the border, where authority was feared because of corruption.

"One copy."

"Copy," James said softly, knowing the voice of each member on his team.

"Target in range."

"Copy," James replied, still looking through his scope.

"Target two in range," another team member stated.

"Copy that," James responded. Looking to his right, James got the nod from Wes that his target was in line as well.

"On my count of three, two, one," James said through his radio, and all four men pulled off one shot, dropping their targets in perfect synchronization.

James put his head back against the seat and closed his eyes. The events of the night played through his mind. The conversation he had with Brian was the memory that replayed the most. Since Dominic had resurfaced at the McGowan home, James barely said five words to him, but his observation was consistent. James always had someone watching him.

Glancing around the cabin, he watched his men talking and laughing. The comradery on his team was unmatched anywhere else in the world. They were all friends outside of the jobs they did with James, but James kept a certain distance, as he needed to be their leader. With his position, he had a responsibility for their safety and refused to fluctuate. Their lives wouldn't be risked because of a breakdown in authority.

Closing his eyes, he pictured Wes as he lay down on his stomach with his rifle looking through the scope at his target. Wes was a friend of Jack's, and they were stationed together overseas while they were in the service. Wes, like all his men, was an expert marksman and head of Jonathan's security team at his house in Savannah, with Jack as his boss. The convenient part of this setup was that Jack knew Wes's position with his team, so whenever James needed him for a job, he could always leave.

A few of his men were married, but most remained single like himself. It was difficult to find a woman that would accept the type of work they did without judgment. Their work didn't have a set schedule, and jobs were random. That was one of the reasons he liked Tess so much. With a couple of exceptions, like the work she did on Dominic Markenna, her mentality was like his own. James preferred the jobs where he and his team could get in and get out in less than twenty-four hours. He didn't like jobs lingering or security stints for adults. When those jobs came around, he subcontracted to a couple members on the team that didn't mind doing security for individuals on a short-term basis.

The job with Tess dragged out much longer than he anticipated. In the past, he'd put people under for a month, maybe two, but never three years. Selfishly, he prolonged her case, especially the first year. The time they spent together was etched carefully into his memory. The last time they were together physically was just before she got married. He knew that would be the last time, as he was heading out of the country to work on the list. Their time together was short, but he had loved her dearly since she was sixteen. The look on her face the night he killed her parents would never leave his memory. There was a moment of undeniable fear, but when she realized he wasn't going to hurt her, there was relief.

The one scene that played over and over in his mind, nearly as often as Dominic, was when they walked into the rambling shack only to find three men inside abusing the children as if they were rag dolls. After lining the three men up against a wall, James had his men take the children to the plane as he remained inside with his top team member and friend, Grey.

With a deep sigh, James eyed each one of the men slowly. "What would you do to live?" James asked the one in the middle as he pointed his weapon at him.

"Doesn't matter," the man answered with a shrug. "You're going to kill us anyway. Just do it and move on because you have a lot more of these wretched children to try and save."

"Wretched." James repeated his word as he pondered. "The only thing wretched is the men like you beating and abusing these children. So, if I must spend the rest of my life hunting down men like you, so be it." With a quick pull of his trigger, James shot the man in the abdomen and smiled.

The man slumped down in pain but wasn't dead. "Couldn't even shoot me in the head, you fuck."

Kneeling, James used the end of the barrel to make the man look at him. "No. I want you to die slowly, and that will be a slow and very painful death." Standing, James shot the man on the right in the head, then turned his attention to the man on the left.

"I have money, lots of money. You can have it if you let me go. I will not talk to anyone, I swear. Just please let me go."

"Hmm ... money I don't need. But what I am going to do is fly you back to the States, where you will share information with my friend. Then you'll be locked up in some super-max prison away from the general population. But here is the kicker." James grinned, glanced at Grey, then looked back at this man. "If you don't tell my friend everything you know, that he wants to know, I will make one phone call and make sure you are put in gen pop and the other inmates know exactly why you are there. They will do to you what you have done to these children, but they won't kill you. They will give you a few days to recover, then do it all over again. This cycle will repeat for the rest of your pathetic life. Do keep in mind it will be your money that these inmates are paid with."

"Time to roll," Grey simply told James.

"Bag him," James told Grey. "We'll put him in the cage in the cargo hold."

"Yes, sir."

James gazed out the window of his plane as his mind jumped to Tess, wondering what she was doing. Was she sleeping? Or did she wake up already? His thoughts were interrupted when one of his men took a seat by him.

"James," one of his top men, Rick, said.

"Yes?"

"Some of us are getting breakfast after we land. Do you want to join us?"

"I'm supposed to meet with Brian and Jonathan after we land about another name on the list," James apprised him. "The children will be dropped off in Savannah. I told Brian to arrange transportation for them."

"How many are left on the list?"

"Eighteen, and seven of those are Markennas." James informed him.

"One of those Dominic?"

"Yep." James nodded. "That is the conversation I'm having with Brian."

"I'm sure that thrills Tess."

"Tess and Matthew." James shook his head. "Matt won't let me touch him."

"Of course not; it's his brother. I'll touch if need be. You can keep your hands clean on this one. Just give me the word."

James grinned with a single nod as he went back to his seat. "I'll keep that in mind. Thanks."

Wes came back next and joined James.

"What's on your mind?" James asked.

"I know what I'm about to ask is against all of the rules, but ..." Wes looked James straight in the eyes. "Two of these kids are twins. The two little seven-year-olds sharing the front seat. Their names are Micah and Danni. What do I have to do to adopt them?"

James raised his eyebrows, surprised by this question. "We can ask Brian. But I've got to ask, Why?"

"Callie and I have talked about this work that we've been doing, and we would like to give one or two of these kids a better life. You know we have the capability to do that."

"Are you sure? You know the kids we save need lifelong therapy."

"Yes, sir, I'm aware." Wes nodded. "Those two kids are it. My gut has said that ever since we plucked them out of that rat hole."

"Do they remember their parents at all?" Rick asked.

"Nope." He shook his head.

James took out his phone and called Brian. While speaking, he glanced around the cabin at the children that were quietly sitting or sleeping. Most of them wore tattered clothing and looked as if they hadn't bathed in weeks. Once they were in the air, his men fed them and tended to any cuts and scrapes. Then they gave each a toothbrush and toothpaste, allowing them to brush their teeth after months of neglect. After a brief conversation, he ended the call and looked at Wes.

"Here's what you need to do." James smiled. "Wait until they take the other children off the plane and leave. Then you can take the twins. We will let Adam do an identification process, our way. If we don't get any hits, we'll make it so you and Callie can keep the kids. But, Wes, if we do find their biological parents and they're not strung out on drugs, the kids will go back to them. They must go to a therapist, other than Callie. Understand?"

"Yes." Wes nodded.

"Well then, I would call your wife and let her know you're fostering a couple children for a while." James smiled.

"Thanks, boss." Wes shook his hand and pulled out his phone as he walked to the front of the plane.

James watched Wes take a seat and decided to make another call. "Hey," he said when he heard her voice, watching his men feed the children more snacks.

"Hey, yourself," Tess replied in a soft voice.

"What are you doing?" James asked as he looked out the small window at the sunrise.

"Making a cup of tea for myself and coffee for everyone else," Tess answered. "It's early. Where are you at?"

"Heading back over the border. Less than two hours out from you. I was hoping you were awake."

"What's on your mind?" Tess leaned against the counter as the coffee brewed, knowing something was wrong with him.

"I need you," he said softly.

"Okay." Her voice was understanding. "I will be here when you get back. I'll meet you at the air strip."

"Thank you, Tess." James ended the call and closed his eyes.

Chapter 2

T he jet touched down an hour and a half later. Tess was waiting for him by the private hangar. There were government people around to take the children and another specialized unit to take the prisoner. So, she hung back and waited for all that chaos to finish before she walked over to James. Seeing him dressed in his brown fatigues made her grin, missing those days. As he walked up to her, he dropped his duffel on the ground and hugged her tightly for a few minutes.

Tess knew a few of his men saw them, but she didn't care. If James needed her, she was there for him. When he finally released his grip around her waist, she looked up at him and smiled. "Go ahead and do it," she said, still smiling as he brought his lips to hers.

James kissed her softly, deeply, as he needed the touch and feel of a woman, and Tess was it. When he pulled back, he caressed her cheek softly, and Tess slowly opened her eyes as she moistened her lips with her tongue.

"I needed that." He grinned at her.

"If that's all you need, I can help you." She gently touched his cheek.

"What I really want is to put you on the plane and fly up to Maine and spend the day with you there." James picked up his duffel, took her hand, and walked over to her car. "Remember that day after Jack left, and we went to dinner and just talked for hours?"

Tess nodded, remembering that time with explicit detail.

"It was relaxing, calm, transparent." He sighed and released his breath slowly. "Other than Carina, you are the only woman who knows my true self and is good with that."

"You do bad things to very bad people." Tess shrugged. "I don't see a problem with that. You are their karma."

"I suppose." James watched Brian's people put the children into a couple of vans and drive away. Then he watched a unit take out the prisoner from the cargo hold. They left his head covered with the black cloth.

"Are you going to tell me what's wrong?" she asked, leaning against her car.

"I can't tell you something I don't know." He leaned on the car beside her and watched Wes come off the plane with the twins. "Wes and Callie want to adopt those two kids," James said as they both watched them.

"That's admirable," Tess stated, void of emotion. "Are they doing it the legal way or kidnapping them?"

James laughed a little. "Brian said that we could let the kids go home with Wes and we could run the ID process. Wes knows that he and Callie are foster parents for the time being. So, yes, we are sort of doing this the legal way."

"Is that Wes's wife over there?" Tess nodded toward another SUV parked behind the government vehicles.

"Yes," he answered, watching the blonde-haired woman meet Wes halfway. "Look at how she interacts with those kids."

"What about it?"

"I like how she knelt to their level to be less intimidating. These kids don't trust adults as it is, with what they've been through. I like her approach."

"You want a wife and children," Tess simply stated, taking his hand and holding it.

"No." He shook his head.

"Yes." She nodded.

"Why do you say that?"

"Because, that's what's wrong with you."

"I was fine until … you happened. You are the only one who makes me look at the world from different eyes. I didn't want children until I met you. I didn't want a wife, family … none of that crap. I was happy just being me and taking care of Carina. Damn it, Tess." James eyed her with an underlying grin. "You made me feel, and feeling makes me vulnerable."

"What was that phrase you said to me that one time at Carina's?" She smiled at him, knowing he knew.

"Turn it off." James shook his head with a grin.

"As Colin reminds me regularly, emotions suck sometimes, but you've got to have them to remind you that you're alive." She sighed, looking at the jet.

"When did he get philosophical?" James brought her hand to his lips, kissing it softly.

"There's a side to him that no one else has ever seen."

"Where is that husband of yours anyway? He's usually stalking you in some capacity," James mocked.

"At the house with the kids," she answered. "You know he has always watched me. As soon as we met, I would catch him just watching me with whatever I was doing, whether it be reading a book, cooking, or kissing Jack. I used to think it was strange, but I've learned that it's simply his observation of me, or rather women in general. It's through observation that he learned how to be so charming with women."

"I detect a little sarcasm in there," James noted.

"Sometimes he's a bit too good with his psychology bullshit. Could you imagine if he would have been a psychologist instead of what he is today?"

"Heaven help the world." James rolled his eyes. "He'd be a good politician."

Tess laughed. "Too many skeletons in his closet."

"His business reputation is pristine. Did you know that?" James eyed her.

"No. I know he's very good at what he does, but I don't pay attention to that part of his reputation. It's his home reputation that I have to deal with the most."

"There's a lot of women that would like to be in your shoes." James raised his eyebrows.

"True. But there's a lot of men who would like to be in his. And he seems to forget that every now and then."

James laughed. "Absolutely, and I am one of those men."

Tess gave him a grin with a small laugh.

"Is Brian at the house yet?"

"Yes." She nodded. "He dropped in about twenty minutes before you. His government ride is over there."

Tess pointed to the private jet that was at the end of the runway. It was smaller than his, but then again, James hauled twelve to fifteen men around the world in it. As they watched Wes take the children away, James heard the engines start on his plane again. Adam, who was also his computer guy, was dropping off a couple of his men in the surrounding states and wouldn't be back until the afternoon.

James sighed deeply as he stretched. "Let's head back to the house, unless you're willing to have a quickie in the hangar."

Tess looked up at him smiling as she shook her head. "You know you're wrong about Dominic."

James looked at her from across the roof of the vehicle. "I hope so, for your sake."

"Why do you have to be like that?" she asked as they got in the car.

"It's male dominance." He grinned. "You're my territory, not his."

Tess laughed. "I'm territory now?"

"Yes, ma'am."

Tess grinned, starting the car.

"How are you doing with the whole thing that shook down with your husband?" James asked, knowing that he slept with another woman right after Taryn was killed.

"He's still alive." She glanced at James, straight faced. "And only by the grace of God."

"You cheated on him," James simply stated a fact. "How can you judge him for the same thing?"

"Did I?" Tess cocked her head. "The only thing I'm guilty of is kissing Dominic that night Colin didn't come home. We didn't have sex. He wanted to, but it didn't happen. I know you saw me come out of that room with him that night, but don't jump to that conclusion because you're assuming the worst. There's only one man that I would break my marriage vows for, but it hasn't happened."

"Jack?" James was curious.

"No!" Tess scrunched her forehead. "I would never do that to my sister. Besides, I love Jack, but it's not like it used to be."

"Well, who the hell's left?" James was thinking through the few men Tess had been with in her life. The list was very short but entirely too closely related, unbeknownst to her at the time.

"Doesn't matter. Not happening. Even if it did, I wouldn't tell you." Tess flashed him a wicked smile.

"Fine." James eyed her. "I'll figure it out. Back to your husband. How are you doing with that?"

"Hmm." Tess pursed her lips together as she looked down the strip of the runway. "I'll feel better once I find the whore and have my revenge, just like I did with Taryn. I wanted him to be present when that bullet shot through her head, and I wanted him to witness it. I will do the exact same thing, again."

"You're vengeful." He eyed her. James remembered walking in on Tess and Grey as they spoke about Taryn and how to handle the situation. Tess didn't trust Colin to deal with her the proper way, so she collaborated with Grey to have him take her out, but she wanted Colin, front row, to witness the death. James wasn't given a say-so in the matter and was warned to not interfere, and he didn't.

"He made me who I am. All of you did. And this is the result when one of you hurt me." Tess knew the cold side of Morgan, her work alias, was very present in her attitude. The tears had been cried out. All that was left was the anger and bitterness.

"Did I ever hurt you?"

Tess turned to him, and with her soft but deadly hand, she caressed his cheek. "No. You can't hurt me. When you laid out the, what shall we call it, terms of our relationship, I conditioned my emotions for exactly that. You can never hurt me the way he has. I love you very, very much. You've become one of my best friends, and I hope I never lose you. And I will always be there for you, anytime and anyplace."

"Would you ever marry me if something happened to your husband?"

"Matthew has first dibs." She smiled.

James grinned. "Matthew is the one you'd break your vows for."

Tess smiled but didn't say a word.

"So, I would have to kill the brothers to have you?"

"Yes."

"You know Colin wouldn't be a problem, but Matthew?" James shook his head. "He's like a brother to me. Why did you choose Colin over him?"

"I always choose Colin over anybody else. Sometimes I wish I didn't love him like I do."

Impulsively, James slipped his hand behind her neck, bringing her lips to his. Colin didn't deserve her. Everyone knew that except Tess.

"Sometimes I wonder what my life would be like had we met before Colin."

"We would have had a great life." James kissed her slowly. "You two will work through this shit, and you'll be fine."

"I love you," she whispered.

"I love you too, Mama T." James rested his forehead on hers as his hand lay gently on her stomach. "The babies are doing well?"

"Yes," she answered, looking at his hand on her tummy.

"Are you about twenty weeks now?" he asked as she rested her hand on his.

"I think so." She smiled. "All I know is that I am twice the size as I was with Savannah, and there is no way I'm carrying these two for nine full months. Thirty-six weeks max."

"You're beautiful," James stated with a soft smile.

Tess gave him one more kiss on the cheek, then headed back to the house. Pulling up in front, they noted Jonathan and Brian chatting on the porch. She covered James's hand, prompting him to look at her. "You know I fully support you with almost everything except hurting him."

James nodded. "I know. Thanks for meeting me at the airstrip. Sometimes I just need …"

As his voice drifted off, Tess ran her soft hand over his cheek. "I know. You don't have to explain anything to me. I know."

"Let's do this." He sighed, and they both got out of the car.

"James." Jonathan McGowan gave him a nod. "How was your trip?"

James nodded at the patriarch of the McGowan family. "Productive. Four more off the list, and seventeen children saved. That leaves eighteen, and seven of those are Markennas. One of them being Dominic. Verdict?"

"I think he is clean," Jonathan stated, knowing James didn't want to hear this. "With all the conversations that I've had with him since he showed up, my gut tells me that he is being honest with me about everything. He said he sold his company after he found out about the people laundering money through it. Dominic is willing to cooperate with Brian in any way that he can."

James shook his head. "Why are all of you so protective of him? I don't understand."

"I've taken into consideration all of your concerns," Jonathan began, spotting Dominic walking over to them. "I've not discounted any of them, but I haven't found anything to discredit what he says."

James sighed, dissatisfied with this determination.

"What concerns you the most about him?" Brian asked.

"I just keep thinking he is going to gain everyone's trust here and then strike." James shrugged and looked at Jonathan. "You took Tess away from him. If that was me, I'd have killed you by now. I don't even want to leave here, because I don't trust him. It would be devastating to me if he hurt anyone here."

Tess touched his arm. "James, what would make you feel better?"

James stood and just stared at her for a long minute. Then he shook his head, catching a glimpse of Dominic about four yards from him. Knowing he could hear the conversation, James continued, "I don't want him being around you. You've been through enough. I don't want you to have to worry about anyone trying to hurt you ever again."

Tess smiled lovingly at him.

"Tess," he said softly. "That would rock my world, and not in a good way."

"Nothing's going to happen to me," she assured him. "Dominic is not a threat to any of us. Besides, Colin doesn't even let me be in the same room as Dominic by myself, if you haven't noticed that already. I think it's more of a jealousy thing than a safety thing. Regardless, it's quite annoying."

"Keep it that way, please." He leaned down, kissing her forehead as he eyed Dominic.

"I will," she stated. "But, I promise, he won't hurt any of us here, or anyone else for that matter. He's not that kind of a man."

"So you say." James shifted his eyes from Tess to Dominic. "You knew Taryn was putting together her little army to kill her sister and anybody else who got in her way. Why didn't you contact Jonathan? Or better yet, your brother, Matthew? Instead you show up the night all that shit goes down and we're supposed to trust you?"

"I thought I could talk her out of it." Dominic shrugged. "I guess my power of persuasion isn't as good as yours."

"I think you were hoping Colin would've died in all that fucking chaos, but he didn't. So, you still don't get the girl."

"No, I don't get the girl. And it sucks, but I got something better, my brother and Jonathan. You have not walked a moment in my shoes, so fuck you and your judgment of me." With that said, Dominic turned to walk away as the front door opened and Colin stepped out.

"Damn! It is tense out here." Colin chuckled a little, having no idea what was going on. "Baby, we need to go."

"Okay." Tess nodded, taking his hand.

"Where are you two off to?" Jonathan asked.

"Hospital," Colin answered. "The surgeon wants to check up on her. I have a call from Ben Walker being forwarded to you from my assistant. He is ready to diversify his investments a bit more. I don't like to take these calls when I'm not in front of a screen. Do you mind?"

"Not at all," Jonathan answered. He had turned over most of the day-to-day operations of the investment firm to his son but still helped Colin as needed.

"Thanks."

Jonathan went to Tess. Gently, he hugged her, kissing her cheek as he stepped back holding her hands. He smiled as he looked at her for a moment. "Daughter," he said softly. "You glow. Gina and I will watch the children if you and Colin want to go spend some time together today."

"Thank you." She kissed his cheek. "But it's not—"

"Sounds great, Father," Colin interjected, taking her hand back. "I would love to take my wife out to lunch, alone."

Tess touched James's shoulder briefly before walking off the porch to leave.

James paced, shaking his head with frustration. With a sigh, he turned back to Jonathan. "For the sake of this family, I hope you're right about him." James pursed his lips.

"I'm going to have a friend of mine call you," Brian said. "Her name is Meagan Trask, and she runs a special task force regarding the Markenna family. Let me put it this way: she helped put that list together with me years ago, but she has always supported Dominic's innocence in this whole thing. Regardless, if anyone knows the Markenna family, it's Meagan. She's tracked their business dealings from the heart of their home in South America to every other point globally. I think she could give you the insight that I may be lacking."

"Fine." James shook his head, frustrated. "In my opinion, the world would be better off with all the Markennas dead—all of them."

Picking up his bag, he tossed it in the back of the SUV, got in the driver's seat, and headed out the main gate. There was no destination in his mind; he just wanted to drive, clear his head. Perhaps he was overthinking all of this with Dominic, but what if he wasn't? Why didn't he trust him? Was it because of his personal involvement with Tess? Or did he just not like him in general? Matthew seemed to have no problem with him, which he found unusual because Matthew's mind worked a lot like his own. They both took situations and processed them from every angle to avoid unnecessary errors. Mindlessly, he continued to process everything he knew about Dominic as he drove.

With Dominic on his mind, it quickly detoured to Tess, wondering how she could be with a man like Dominic and then himself. They were complete opposites, with nothing in common. With his mind wandering back several years, he thought of the weeks after Tess had been shot in Chicago.

It was a full two weeks before the hospital released her with strict discharge instructions. She wasn't allowed to travel until her next checkup with the surgeon, but that wasn't for three weeks. With orders like that, James and Colin moved her to his home on the outskirts of Chicago. It was the safest place for her to recover, and no one would even know where she was. As she recovered the first couple of weeks at his home, James devised a plan with Colin and Jonathan for her continued recovery after he put her under an alias. Colin would rotate work from the Portland office to Atlanta every two weeks. Eventually, after enough time had passed to make it look less suspicious, Colin would make a full-time move to Portland. James's number-one man in the field, Greyson Parker, would stay with her while Colin was away every two weeks.

The plan seemed a bit sketchy at first, he thought, but it obviously worked out perfectly. No one ever located her, and she maintained her relationship with Colin.

"Hey, Tess." James sat down on his bed. She had been sleeping in it for the last four weeks.

"Hmm?" She turned her head to look at him as she woke up.

"Baby, you need to wake up." He ran his hand softly over her knee that was poked outside of the blankets. "It's traveling day. How are you feeling?"

"I'm okay." She sighed, not wanting to travel.

"Pain? I can go get you some of your pain meds if you need them." He looked at her for a response.

"I feel okay right now." She took a slow, deep breath until her lungs reminded her that they were still healing. "Can you help me upright, please?"

"Yep." He stood as she pushed the blankets off and carefully turned her body so her legs dangled off the edge. When she put her hands up, James gently took them and pulled her up.

Tess felt a little lightheaded but shook it off.

"You okay?"

"Yes." She nodded. "Do I have time for a shower before we go?"

"Of course." He walked her over to the master bath. "We just need to get on the road before one o'clock. That way, we can easily keep the schedule that I set up."

James turned on the shower, put out a couple of towels, and turned back to Tess, who leaned against the sink.

"All set up," he told her. "You got it from here?"

Tess nodded, looking in the mirror as he left the room. As she unbuttoned his shirt, slipping it off her shoulders, she looked at the red scar on her chest between her breasts. The doctor said it would fade over the years, but it was a scar and would always be there. Tess just saw it as a reminder that someone wanted her dead.

"James," she called softly to him as she opened the bathroom door.

Turning away from his packing, he glanced to see what she wanted.

"Can you take the bandage off my back, please?" she asked. His shirt was off her shoulders but covering her breasts.

"Of course." He nodded. "I forgot about that."

Walking over, Tess turned her back to him, and she could feel him gently pull the bandage from the entrance wound. "How does it look?"

"Not too bad," he answered, resting his hands on her shoulders. "It's healed a lot. After you get out of the shower, I'll check it again. But I'm thinking you won't need to bandage it anymore."

"Okay." She nodded, turning to him. As they stood within inches of each other, Tess just stared at him without speaking.

"Damn it, Tess." He released a slow breath. "You make this so hard."

"Shower with me?" she suggested.

"No." He shook his head. "You're with Colin. Remember him?"

"I wonder how long it will take him to become engrossed in his work again and forget about me."

James slipped his hands just below her ears, cupping her head. Slowly, he leaned in, kissing her softly, lips barely touching. "He's not going to forget about you." He rested his forehead on hers. "And I'm not interested in just having an affair. I would want more, and we both know that's not happening unless he's dead. So, take your pick."

James remembered their time together very well. Each moment was etched deeply into his mind. As a man, he could only fight off the physical urge for so long. And without her even realizing it, every day they spent together, his wall dropped lower and lower until he had no defenses against her anymore. When he finally gave in to her on the West Coast, the only regret he had was not doing it sooner.

To his surprise, he pulled up to the bar that Jesse Anders worked at around eleven thirty. He sat in his car for a few minutes, asking himself what he was doing and how he ended up there. This wasn't on the schedule for today, but here he was. A smile emerged from his lips as he saw her walking up to the entrance. Quickly, he got out of his car to catch her before she walked in. "Jesse!" he called out.

Jesse turned around when she heard her name being called. For the slightest moment, the despair of her past crept upon her, but when she noticed it was the handsome man with the charming smile from a few weeks ago, she relaxed. She did wonder if this was coincidence or if Colin McGowan didn't keep his promise to be quiet about their unexpected two-day fling last weekend, and this man would think she was easy. "Hello," she said as he stood before her. "What brings you here?"

"Honestly …" He sighed. "I was a little frustrated with my work, so I got in the car for a drive and ended up here. There's a reason I ended up here. I'm certain of it, as I don't believe in coincidence. How are you?"

"I'm fine." She grinned. "Want to come in or just stand out here and talk?"

"Are you working? Can you take a break and have cup of coffee or lunch with me?"

"I don't start for about forty-five minutes," she told him. "Coffee?"

"Yes." He nodded. "That would be great. Where would you like to go?"

"We can go just down the street a block or so," she told him. "There's a coffee shop down there. We can walk. It's not that far."

"Okay." He casually observed his surroundings. "Sounds good."

"What brought you back here? I know this town isn't high on the list for tourism."

"You," he replied without hesitation. "I can't get you out of my mind."

Uncertain of how to respond, Jesse simply smiled.

"How's your life here?"

"Why do you ask?"

James reminded himself that she didn't know him or who he was and needed to go slow. "Quaint seaside town."

"In other words, not much here." Jesse cocked her head toward him as they continued walking.

"That would sum it up." James grinned, feeling guilty for thinking that way.

"I really can't complain," she finally answered. "I have a small cottage a block from the beach. It's a small town, so everyone knows everyone … and it just makes me feel … safe. Life's been hard. I'm happy to just feel safe."

"You've had a hell of a life."

Jesse stopped walking and looked at him, unsure if he was guessing or if he knew something—or if Colin talked. It would be so disappointing if this man had been sent to beat her like Dimitri did.

"I saw you talking to Taryn when we were here before. What did she tell you about me, or rather, all of us?" It would be easier to face this head-on instead of dancing around the subject.

"She said the one you walked in with was her brother-in-law, but then I saw them kissing." She scrunched her forehead. "That was weird."

"Yes," James agreed with a short laugh. "That little duo was weird."

"The other one that came in later, with her, was a bodyguard." Jesse bit on her lower lip. "And you are a contract killer."

James grinned, shaking his head. *Damn Taryn.*

"Is it true?" Jesse asked.

"I prefer the term contract specialist." Shrugging it off as if it was no big deal, James continued, "I have a team that does extractions and some specialized work that leaves very bad people dead."

"Oh." Jesse suddenly felt nervous, and her heart began to physically hurt. The pain was coming again. Marcos Markenna had found her, and the beatings would begin, again.

James noted the tense look that rolled down her body from her head to her toes, and her eyes diverted away from his. Knowing he needed to reassure her at this moment or this was going nowhere, he took a breath and continued. "Does who I am bother you?" James asked as her eyes came back to his.

"Only if you were sent to beat me like the other," she answered honestly in a soft, meek voice.

"Never." The word was firm as he shook his head, knowing he would find out about this beating that she feared. "I liked you the first moment I saw you. Please understand, being who I am, I must know who I'm with and around. And we did a thorough background on you."

"And you're still here." Feeling her heart calm, she grinned.

"Yes, ma'am. You couldn't be safer with anyone else. I promise you." He smiled as they walked into the coffee shop.

James spent the next half hour talking with her over two cups of coffee, and they split a turkey sandwich. He found her to be kind, simple, and easygoing but very cautious of her surroundings. She was beautiful in a simple way, and he swore her misty green eyes put a spell on him.

Walking back to the bar, he slipped her hand into his. "Do you mind?"

Jesse smiled, shaking her head. "It's weird but a good weird."

Stopping to face her just before they reached the bar, James spoke. "Dinner, Saturday?"

"I work until seven," she told him. "After?"

"Okay." He nodded, knowing he was going to change that somehow. "I will pick you up here."

"Okay." As she tried to tame the grin on her lips, she nodded, and the feeling of small butterflies began to swirl in her stomach, wondering if he was going to kiss her.

James leaned down, slowly bringing his lips to hers for a soft kiss. It wasn't too long, but it wasn't quick either. It was perfect for a first kiss. Her lips were soft, warm, and inviting. "Okay." He took a deep breath as he pulled back, feeling like a sixteen-year-old boy kissing a girl for the first time. "I will be here Saturday at seven."

"Okay." She nodded with a smile as he slowly began to walk away, and their hands touched until the very last moment.

"Damn it," James muttered, turning back to her. Cupping her face, he kissed her deeply.

Jesse didn't protest as she kissed him back. Her hands rested on his hips, feeling the undeniable warmth of this man's body beneath her fingers as she was easily lost in the passion of the kiss.

James wasn't sure how much time passed when they pulled back slightly. His hands were still softly on her cheeks as he gazed into her eyes. "It's going to be a long few days."

Jesse smiled in agreement.

"Do you have a cell phone?"

"Yes." She nodded, unable to take her eyes off his handsome face.

"Let me give you my number," he stated as she took her phone from her back pocket. James rattled off his cell number, and she gave him hers. "I will be calling you." He smiled, walking her to the front entrance.

"I hope so," she answered.

"You can call me anytime. Even if you work until midnight."

"Are you sure?"

"Absolutely. I would love your voice to be the last one I hear before I sleep."

Jesse smiled. "Okay, I'll call you when I'm off shift tonight."

"Perfect." He leaned over, giving her one last kiss. "I'll be waiting."

"You have to go." She couldn't contain the smile on her lips. "Or I'm never going to go to work."

"Okay." He brought her hand up, kissing her knuckles. "Have a good day and be safe."

"I will." She nodded and watched him gently let her hand go and walk over to his SUV before she went into the bar.

As James drove back to Jonathan's, he couldn't help but smile, even if it was to himself. Jesse Anders was going to be the best thing that ever happened to him. Undoubtedly, she took his mind off Markenna and Tess and the whole family. Maybe this was what he needed, to detach himself somehow from Tess, because Tess was the source that kept him tethered to this family. Maybe he was getting closer to breaking that line. Then again, maybe not.

# Chapter 3

Meagan Trask walked into the kitchen to find that her six-year-old daughter, Aria, had made herself breakfast already. Surprisingly, there wasn't any spilled milk or cereal. Smiling, Meagan walked over and kissed her child on the top of her head. "Good job," Meagan stated.

"Now I can make you breakfast, Mommy." Aria beamed, very proud of herself.

"Yes, you can." Meagan poured herself a cup of coffee and sat at the table with Aria. "Let's plan that this weekend. Who's picking you up today?"

"Mrs. Milner," Aria answered and continued eating.

"And do you get into cars with anyone you don't know?" Meagan asked, although she had been repeating this to her daughter since she was three.

"No, Mommy," she answered.

"'I just want to keep you safe, my beautiful girl." Meagan looked at Aria; the resemblance to her father was uncanny. With dark hair and stunning green eyes, there was no denying who her father was.

Every single day, Aria reminded her of the man she walked away from for her job. There were more days than not that she regretted her decision, but by the time she realized it, three years had gone by, and she was certain he had moved on. She was positive because of the surveillance photos of him with another woman. A beautiful, classy woman who was her opposite. Well, at least that was her opinion.

When Meagan heard her phone ring, she pulled it out of her pocket to see Brian was calling. "Hey, Brian." She walked over to the kitchen window.

"Good morning, Meagan." Brian smiled to himself. "How's Aria?"

"Wonderful," she answered. "How's Elle and the girls?"

"Very good, thank you."

"You never call me this early unless it's something important," she reminded him.

"I know, sorry. I was just wanting you to call James Cordello and have a conversation with him about the Markennas."

"James Cordello?" This was a bit surprising, she thought. "As in the mercenary James Cordello?"

"Yes." He laughed a little. "He's working on the list, and I told him Dominic shouldn't really be on there anymore, and I just want you to confirm. Currently, Dominic is back in with the McGowans and is there now."

"Wait, wait, Jonathan McGowan, Dominic's stepfather from when he was a baby?"

"Yes," Brian confirmed. "You know how intricate that family is, so trust me when I say it's become more intricate—if that's possible."

"You'll have to help me update that family tree," Meagan noted.

"Oh, yes," Brain agreed. "Colin McGowan married Tess."

"Well, if anyone could keep him in line, it would be Tess, or as I know her, Morgan." Meagan thought back on the pictures of Dominic Markenna with Tess McGowan at some gala event years ago. Morgan Kellas was part of a little trio that she wasn't allowed to touch years before. Knowing James Cordello subcontracted out to them put her off limits by Brian. Her thought was interrupted when there was a knock at her door. "I have someone at my door. Stay on the phone with me. I don't usually have visitors."

"Okay." Brian easily agreed.

"Aria." Meagan scooted her daughter into the mudroom after putting her dish in the sink. "You know the rules. Stay here until I come and get you. Don't come out if you hear anything bad. Okay?"

"Yes, Mommy." The child nodded. "I know."

"I love you," Meagan told her as Aria tucked herself into a closet, hiding.

"Brian," Meagan began as she walked to the front door. "You know what to do if something ever happens to me?"

"I know, I know," he assured her. "I will take Aria, pull her birth certificate, and find her father. If he's an ass, I'm keeping her."

Meagan grinned to herself, thankful to have Brian as a friend. When she reached the door, she went to peep through the hole, but it was kicked in just as she put her face close to it. The impact threw her across the foyer, with the cell phone flying out of her hand and under a small table in the hallway. She was stunned speechless as she tried to get her bearing back. Opening her eyes, she saw four men walk into her home.

"Meagan Trask." The older man looked down at her with a snippy attitude. "Pleasant to see you again."

"Get the hell out of my home," she stated, trying to get back up, but he used his foot and pushed her down again.

"I'm certain you remember me." He smiled viciously.

"Marcos Markenna," she stated. "Aren't you supposed to be in prison?"

"Everybody has their price." He grinned, and his attention went back to his men as they finished searching her home for anyone else.

Meagan held her breath, hoping Aria was still hidden.

"Clear," each one of the men stated to Marcos.

"Where's your daughter?"

"Not here." She shrugged, and his fist came down, hitting her hard in the face.

"You sure that's your answer?" he asked for clarification.

"Fuck you," she stated, and another fist struck, knocking her out.

"Pick her up," he instructed his men. "Let's go. I'm sure her house has some sort of alarm on it. I'll get answers out of her on the road because I want to know where my son and daughter are."

"She's a federal agent," one of the men stated to Marcos. "Are you sure you want to jump in this arena?"

"Yep," he told the man. He snapped his fingers, and two other the men picked her up and took her to the SUV in the driveway.

Brian grabbed his coat and was shouting out orders on his way out of the building. The local police could get to Meagan's house faster than he could, and he made sure they were dispatched immediately. Meagan's home was about a thirty-minute drive normally, but he made it in fifteen. By the time he arrived, her home was surrounded by police cars.

Running across the yard, he asked if they had her daughter, but no one answered, and they looked completely dumbfounded. Jetting through the front door, down a hallway to the mudroom in the back of the house, he stopped a moment, caught his breath, and released it slowly.

"Aria, it's Brian," he called out in the room, not wanting to scare the little girl. "Do you remember me? I work with your mommy. It is safe to come out. I know the safety word is marshmallows."

Aria came out of a small cubby behind some coats and shoes. She moved slowly, cautiously, which told Brian that the child was mortified.

"There you are." Kneeling to her level, he gave a soft smile. "I'm going to take care of you for a bit, okay?"

"Where's Mommy?" Small tears rolled down her cheeks.

"Mommy …" His voice trailed off, unsure of what to tell this little girl. "Mommy had to go help get rid of some really bad people, and she asked me to take care of you while she was gone. Are you okay with that?"

Aria looked around the room as she nodded her head slowly. Her eyes went from Brian to the two other officers in the room. When Brian put his hands out for her, she carefully walked over, allowing him to pick her up.

"Okay." Brian sighed, relieved. "It will be okay, sweetie. I'll take very good care of you until Mommy comes back."

"The man with the dark hair said to stay in the closet where it was safe." Aria opened her tiny hand, showing Brian a small medal. "He gave me this and said it would help keep me safe."

"A man talked to you?" Brian's heart beat a little faster as Aria nodded. Taking the coin-sized medal from her hand, Brian realized it was the patron Saint Michael, and it was for protection.

"I think you should hold on to this." Brian put the medal back in her hand. "The man was right. This will keep you safe."

The child simply nodded as Brian gently wiped away her tears.

"It's okay." His voice soothed her. "I'll keep you safe too."

# Chapter 4

Jesse walked into her bathroom to put her hair up. As she braided the long ponytail, she looked at herself in the mirror. All she saw was a woman who wanted to embrace life and not be afraid of anything anymore. Working at the bar and grill toughened her up a little bit, but so did the gym and the boxing lessons that she had been taking since she was about twenty-seven. If someone was going to try to physically hurt her now, she was ready. Being thirty-four, all she wanted was to have a man love her and know her past and her fears and not exploit them.

Colin McGowan was the first man she had ever shared her story with, a week ago. Before that, she never spoke of her true history. If she wanted to maintain her identity, she couldn't share her past, but Colin McGowan made her trust him just as he trusted her with his secrets. Thinking back, she berated herself for stepping into that arena with him, but the sexual desire was intense. Before Colin, she couldn't remember the last time she felt that need, that craving for a man.

Unexpectedly, James showed up in her life. Maybe he would be the one to love her. However, before she let herself fall into romance with this man, she needed to know just how much of her past he knew about. This would be something she would ask him tonight, in person.

Knowing she was thinking too much, her mind wandered off James to Marcos. If he died, would she finally be free, or would one of his men continue to kill anyone she cared about? Was this torture something his last son would inherent and continue? Admittedly, she had only met one of his sons, Dimitri, and he was worse than his father. She remembered his fist very clearly as it connected with her face during one of the many beatings she'd received over the years.

Remembering back, it was her twenty-fifth birthday. She had not celebrated her birthday since her grandmother died. She didn't celebrate anything anymore. Her days simply rolled into each other, with nothing much to look forward to. It was easy to pick up a minimum-wage job here and there. Although it wasn't much money, it kept her fed and clothed and a tiny roof over her head. The thought of going to college had crossed her mind once or twice, but she didn't know how to balance a full-time job and a college curriculum. So, in her free time, she went to the public library and educated herself. In the last couple of years, she read about world religions, philosophy, and criminal justice.

Being Louisiana born and raised until she was twelve, she found Arizona to be hot and dry and a place where people went to die. No young person in their right mind would purposely want to live there. Admittedly, she did visit the Grand Canyon and found the sheer magnitude and depth amazing. Pictures didn't come close to what it was like physically being there. Then there was the Petrified Forest. She had saved enough money to take a privately guided tour. The forest proved to be another one of nature's amazing feats. To have artifacts that were thirteen thousand years old still amazed her.

Having the day off, she decided to get all her errands done early, so she could lay by the pool in her apartment complex. And then she had a date tonight. Being that it was her first date ever with a man, she was nervous. She had no girlfriends to chat with about this, to help her decide what to wear and what to do with her hair. She never let anyone close. In her mind, she had to lie about her life, and who would want to be friends with a liar? The thought of cancelling her date tonight crossed her mind constantly. His name was Todd, and he was one of the cooks at the restaurant she worked at. He was easy to look at and made her laugh all the time. Just thinking about him made her smile.

It took him months of asking her out before she finally said yes. She never told him that it was her birthday; she didn't want him to feel as if he had to do anything extra special because she certainly never did. He was in his fourth year at the nearby university and worked part-time for the extra money. His study was in geology with a minor in botanical science.

Jesse's thoughts were interrupted when there was a knock at the door. With a grin on her face, she opened it. Before her stood two men, and she knew in the pit of her stomach that this wasn't good. Without saying a word, one man pushed her back, and they both walked in.

"Who are you?" Her cracked voice as her heart raced.

"My name is Dimitri Markenna." The man came within inches of her face. "I'm Marcos's son, and I'm here to let you know that you can't hide from me. I will always find you. And my father wanted me to let you know that you will be alone for the rest of your life, just as he is in his cell because of you. When he is free, you will be free."

And that was when the first fist struck her across the face. It felt like a boulder hit her straight on. She weighed no more than 130 pounds, so her body flew backward with the impact of his fist. She lost track of how many punches she endured before she was close to unconscious. At one point, she felt him pick her up and toss her on the bed and begin to take off her clothes, and she vaguely remembered some other man stopping him, saying they needed to go, as the sirens in the distance were getting closer.

After that last thought, she passed out and didn't wake up for three days. Thankfully, she was in the hospital. As her eyes slowly wandered the room, they stopped when a woman stood up from the chair in the corner. She was around her own height and had dark hair and an athletic body. But it was her sympathetic smile that calmed her.

"Hi, I'm Meagan with the Justice Department," she said with a soft yet raspy voice. "You're my ... for a lack of a better word ... my case now. I figured after everything you've been through, you could use a female friend and confidante."

"Hi," Jesse said barely above a whisper. "It was his son."

"I figured." Meagan sat on the edge of the bed. "Dimitri? Because there are two of them. The other one hasn't displayed any violent tendencies ... yet."

Tears fell from her eyes. "Did he rape me?"

"No," Meagan assured her. "He just beat you something terrible. We're looking, but we can't locate him. You're going to be in my protective custody when you get released, and we'll find you a safe place one way or another. The doctors want to keep you here for another five days or so. He broke your collarbone and cracked your eye socket. You had internal bleeding, but the doctors fixed you all up. I'm so sorry this happened to you."

That was the first beating. There were several more, before she was brave enough to ask Meagan to press charges. She was willing to be in public and testify against him if it would stop the beatings. Meagan supported her every step of the way and became the only friend that she ever had. She vividly remembered walking out of the courthouse in Virginia with her two government bodyguards and passing a man who looked similar to Dimitri but was more refined. Their eyes connected on the steps as they passed each other, and she wondered if that was the other son.

The last four years of her life had been quiet. No threats, no visits, and no reminders had come. When Meagan told her that Dimitri had been killed, a huge weight was lifted even though the threats could continue; at least it wouldn't be Dimitri beating her.

Meagan had found this very small, one-bedroom eight-hundred-square-foot home that was close to the beach for Jesse. She told Jesse that she needed something that had a perk, considering all she'd been through since she was a child. It was on the outskirts of town and only a block from the beach. She loved it. Every day, she would walk to the beach, lay in the sun, or go swimming. Her skin was golden from all her time outside, and her dark brown hair had natural highlights from the sun. Her green eyes stood out amongst her tan skin. Many men that went to the bar complimented her on her eyes, and it seemed to give her great tips.

Meagan visited her every six months or so even after her promotion. It was a welcome sight the first time Meagan visited her with baby Aria. She was a beautiful little girl that resembled her mother. Jesse found it interesting that Meagan never spoke of the father. She always told her it was an unexpected relationship that ended when she was promoted, and she never told the father. Jesse remembered that time well, as Meagan was torn between her job and Aria's father's job. She didn't want him to sell his business, but she didn't want to walk away from her position, and they couldn't raise a child from different states.

After putting on her tennis shoes, she glanced in the full-length mirror to make sure everything looked just right before walking to work. She had the early shift today, which meant a few less tips, but she would get home before two in the morning. And then there was James, who would be picking her up for dinner. He was certainly something to look forward to after her shift today. With a smile, she headed out the door to get the next eight hours over with.

**✳✳✳✳✳✳✳✳✳✳✳✳✳✳**

James was in his room getting ready. He took a deep breath as he checked himself in the mirror. Admittedly, he couldn't remember the last time that he cared about what he looked like. This was different. This was going to change his life, so everything, including his look, had to be perfect. Besides, the last time she saw him, he was wearing his brown fatigues with a T-shirt of the same color. When there was a knock at the door, he stopped staring at himself.

"Come in," he called out.

"Hey," Tess said, standing in the doorway. "You sure are taking a long time getting ready."

"I know." He turned back to the mirror. "I want to look … perfect. I don't want her to have a reason to not like me."

"Women don't care if you look perfect," Tess assured him. "We just care that there is that physical attraction and you kiss well and are good in bed—and in that order. Intelligence is a plus, especially if we want a relationship."

"Seriously?" He wasn't certain if she was lying or being honest.

"True story." She held up her hands in defense. "At least for me. And I happen to know, firsthand, that you pass all of the above."

James grinned, shaking his head as he tied his tie.

"And your money doesn't matter." Tess walked over and took the tie from his hands and began tying it herself. "Especially to a minimum-wage, independent, working girl like her. You'll probably blow her away with what you have planned, but that's not what's going to snag her on your line."

"What's going to snag her?" he asked, watching her eyes on his tie.

"There's this thing about you." She tilted her head. "You make me feel safe and protected. And having heard a little about her past, that is what will hook her to your line. She needs to feel safe with you. Besides, who could resist that handsome face and this well-chiseled body that you have?"

"You. If you would leave your husband," he said, his voice low, "I wouldn't have to be doing this."

Tess smiled, shaking her head. "You know that's never going to happen. There, it's perfect."

James looked in the mirror at her work. "Nice. I imagine that talent came from your husband?"

"Of course," she answered. "I have been with him for a very long time. Besides, the tie works well when tying a man up."

James looked at her curiously. "Are you talking in bed or on a job?"

Tess grinned. "Both ways work well."

"Why didn't you ever do that with me?" James sighed, feeling he had missed a sexy moment with her.

"You never wore a tie when we were together."

"I could've changed that had I known." His hand slipped to the side of her neck.

"No. That is something between Colin and me. Don't you have little things that you just want to keep between you and one other person?"

James thought back to his walks along the river in Portland with Tess. That was his time with her, never to be shared with anyone else. "I do, and most have been with you."

Tess looked up, and their eyes caught and held. There were no words needed to understand what was captured in his eyes.

"I love you, Mama T. I'd wait forever if I knew there was a chance of spending my life with you." His thumb caressed her cheek. "But my gut is telling me that there will never be that opportunity because if you're not with Colin, you will be with Matthew, and I want my own, and I want it now. And my gut tells me Jesse is meant for me."

Tess nodded in agreement. "She better be extraordinary. You deserve nothing less than that."

James kissed her forehead. "No one will ever be you, but I think Jess is meant to be in my life."

"I want nothing but the best for you." Tess slipped her hands around his waist, giving him a long hug.

Wrapping his arms around her shoulders, James kissed the top of her head. "Have you talked to Harper yet?"

"No, she was gone by the time I got out of the hospital, and I really don't want to bother her and Jack." Tess sighed. "When was the last time Jack took a vacation?"

James cupped her face. "Well, she's still with Jack, so that's a good sign."

"I suppose." She noted the mischievous grin on James's face turn. "Don't give me that look."

"Where's your husband?" he asked her softly.

"I like how he's Colin when you're friends and my husband when you want to kiss me." Her voice was barely above a whisper. "You may not have a wife yet, but I do have a husband."

"You can make me feel so good and so bad in one simple sentence." He pulled her to him, hugging tightly. "I love you."

"I know you do." Her finger traced his lip. "You don't realize how much I want to kiss you and spend the day in bed with you like we used to do."

"Oh, but I do." He took her hand and kissed her fingers.

They both closed their eyes for a moment, taking in the simple touch of each other.

"Colin's waiting for you," she finally said, breaking the silence.

"Dare I ask why?"

Tess simply shrugged with a smile.

"Okay then." He walked her over to the door. "Let's go."

Tess walked with James down the stairs to the living room where Colin was on the phone. When he saw them, he cut it short. Work could wait; besides, it was Saturday.

"Damn, look at you," Colin said, walking over to him.

"Think this is suitable?" James asked him. Knowing the reputation the McGowan men had with women, James would value this one opinion from Colin.

"Yep." He nodded with approval. "If she doesn't like this, she's not suitable for you."

Tess walked over to Colin, taking his hand that he had put out for her. Softly he kissed her head, running his hand nonchalantly over her stomach.

"When are Matthew and Dominic bringing Savannah and Connor back?" James asked.

"Wednesday," Colin stated. "Jack is supposed to be back tomorrow. We'll be fine. Just relax and enjoy the company of a beautiful woman."

"I do, every day I hang out with your wife." James smiled.

"You need to get your own. Here." Colin shook his head, handing him a set of keys.

"What's this for?"

"Tess's car." Colin raised his eyebrows with a grin. "Remember the 911 turbo I was telling you about?"

James nodded.

"It's waiting for you out front."

"I haven't done something like this in years," James confided.

"Are you nervous?" Colin asked with a surprised smile.

"Maybe a little." He turned back to the mirror just to make sure everything was good. "This whole dating thing sucks. Can I just have your wife, please?"

Colin laughed. "No, that's not happening. You'll do fine with Jesse. If not, you know how to get rid of bodies."

James thought for a moment. "Hmmm, should I warn her in advance that it is in her best interest to like me?"

Colin shook his head as James grinned and headed out the door. Turning back to Tess, he was concerned, as she looked tired. "Are you okay?" he asked, sitting beside her.

"I'm fine, just tired. I feel like I'm tired all the time."

"Baby, you had a bullet lodged in your skull. Let your body heal. It was a traumatic experience. Does your head hurt at all?" Knowing she had not been her normal self since she was released from the hospital, he worried.

"Not much. Can we just go for a drive or something simple? I need to get out of the house."

"Want to drive to Atlanta?" he suggested. "We haven't been to our house there in years. We could stay a few nights and come back before Matthew brings the kids back."

"Yes, let's do that. I just need a change of scenery."

"Let's go pack a few things." He helped her to her feet. "When James gets back, we'll take your car. Our days are numbered in the sports car."

31

# Chapter 5

Jesse came around the corner with a smile when she saw him standing casually at the end of the bar. James was an incredibly handsome man. With dark blond hair cut down to half an inch on the sides and an inch on top, she could envision running her fingers through it. With dominant brown eyes, she wondered if that came from his father or mother. Then there were his perfect lips. All she wanted was to be kissed by those soft lips. Walking over, she still wondered why he would even be interested in a woman like her. She was a bartender in a small hick town south of nowhere. However, their conversations the last few nights on the phone told her that he really liked her, and she knew she liked him.

"Hi," she said, smiling. "You're about five hours early."

"Hi." James grinned. "I know. I don't like to be late."

Jesse leaned against the bar, unable to take her eyes from him. "Are you going to torture me for the rest of my shift by being here?"

"Torture you?" James cocked a mischievous grin.

"You know what I'm talking about." Jesse watched him lift her hand to his mouth, kissing it softly as his eyes held hers.

"Is that what you're talking about?"

Jesse nodded, unable to tame the grin.

"Can you come around the bar?" James asked.

Jesse nodded again as she came around the bar to stand before him. "Is this better?"

"Yes." He nodded, slipping his hand behind her neck. "I've wanted to kiss you since the other day."

Jesse smiled as he brought his lips to hers for another soft, perfect kiss like their first one. A few minutes passed before they were interrupted by her boss.

"Hey, Jesse." A stout woman stood on the other side of the bar. "Why don't you get out of here ... for like a week?"

"Excuse me?" Jesse was stunned, thinking she was in trouble.

"You work your ass off for me and haven't taken much time off in the last few years," she stated. "So, you get a week, with pay, starting right now."

"But ..." Jesse couldn't imagine not working for a week.

"No butts." Her boss shook her head as she gave James a wink. "Go."

Jesse turned back to James with a grin. "You have something to do with this, don't you?"

"Maybe a little." He shrugged. "Come on."

Jesse grabbed her wallet from under the register. Outside, he held the door open for her on a stunning sports car. The only time she had ever seen a car that nice was on television.

"This is different than the one the other day," she noted. "Is this supposed to make me in awe of you?"

"I hope not." He tilted his head. "It's not even mine. You're supposed to be in awe of me because I certainly am with you."

"Maybe I am ... a little." Still looking at him, she sighed. "I barely know you, so why do I feel like I can trust you?"

"Because you are going off your gut instinct." He tilted his head up a bit. "And your gut instinct is damn near always right. And I'm not saying that to get you into the car. I say that because that is the only thing I trust."

"Hmm," Jesse mumbled as he brought his lips to hers.

The kiss was soft, thought out. Their lips came together as if meant to be. Everything in the world disappeared the moment his lips touched hers. Neither had any idea how much time passed before each pulled back slightly.

"That's going to happen often," James stated as his thumb caressed her lower lip. "Let's get out of here."

Jesse nodded in agreement as he opened the door for her. After she sat down, he went around and got in the driver's side. When he started the car, the engine purred so softly, if he didn't know better, he would think it hadn't started yet.

"Where are we going?" Jesse asked as his hand covered hers on her lap.

"Your place," he answered honestly. "I would ask for directions, but I already know where you live."

"Of course, you do." Jesse had to remind herself that he was a mercenary and they knew everything about people.

"First, let me tell you that I will never lie to you, unless it is to keep you safe." He turned down a small graveled road. "And second, remember the background that I did? In the business I am in, I must know who I am around because if anything happens, I need to trust who I am with just as much as they need to trust me."

"How thorough was that background anyway?" she asked.

James stopped the car in front of her tiny house and turned toward her. "If the DOJ is going to give people new identities, they need to learn how to not leave gaps."

"Ugh." She sighed.

"Jesse." He took her hand again. "Are you afraid of me?"

"No," she said without hesitation. "Which is really unusual, given my past."

"Good. You shouldn't be," he assured her.

"I just don't want you to end up being that man that was sent here to remind me," she stated honestly.

"Remind you?" He was confused.

"The man I testified against sent his son a few times to remind me that they always knew where I was and could get to me whenever they wanted," she told him.

"What did he do to you?" He wanted to know because he was killing someone, preferably named Markenna.

Jesse looked away from him for a moment and fought back the tears. "Dimitri would beat me," she said softly.

James brought her hand gently to his lips, placing a small kiss on her palm. "I'm so sorry. If he wasn't dead already, I'd kill him. For the record, nobody could pay me enough to harm you in any way. I liked you from the moment I saw you that night. If I didn't have the family to deal with for the last month, I would have come back sooner. I have this amazing pull toward you, and I have to find out why." James got out, shut his door, and walked around the car to open her door. After she stepped out, he followed her to the porch.

"Okay." Jesse turned to face him. "What's the plan?"

"Without giving away too much, because I would like some of this to be a surprise, you should prepare for a very romantic dinner at a seaside restaurant. And pack a bag for the week—jeans, shorts maybe a sweater, as the nights can get cold. Casual clothes, and bring a bikini. You'll have your own room. Unless you want to share." He smiled, raising his eyebrows. "If you decide at any time that you don't like me, I will bring you home, my promise to you."

Jesse smiled, as this was going to be exciting, but she was a little nervous too. "Come on in." She unlocked the door, and he followed her in. "Am I on a time frame?"

James thought for a moment. "To make the reservations at six thirty, we need to be at the airstrip at four, and it will take us an hour and a half to get from here to the airstrip. So, you have one hour to get ready."

"Airstrip?" she inquired.

James smiled. "Yes, ma'am."

Jesse motioned for him to follow her into her bedroom. "Did you know I have never flown before? Have a seat on the bed. We can talk while I get ready."

James sat on the bed, getting comfortable. "That I didn't know."

"Yep." She pulled out a large duffel bag and started putting clothes in it.

"Well, be glad it's a private plane." He watched her move gracefully around the room. "I'm not a fan of commercial airports or customs."

"Private plane?" She stopped what she was doing to look at him again. "Is it like those small four-seater things?"

James laughed, shaking his head. "No, ma'am. It's an eighteen-person jet. Very nice, very comfortable."

"Wow." She smiled. "This will be kind of exciting."

Jesse pulled two dresses from the closet and held them up for him. "Which one is appropriate for tonight?"

"Hmm." James looked at the little black one. It was simple, short, but still respectable. The other was a dark midnight blue, longer, but sleeveless. "The black one would probably look better with this."

James stood up and pulled a small, long box from his inside jacket pocket. Jesse walked over to him, and he opened it. He watched her eyes grow big when she saw the diamond bracelet, then a smile formed.

"That's beautiful." She moved her finger over the diamonds as she spoke softly.

"Get dressed, and I will put it on you," he told her, loving the genuine smile on her face.

Jesse took the dress into the bathroom and closed the door. Fifteen minutes later, she reappeared with her body nicely fitted into the black dress. She had taken her hair out of the braid, and it lay softly down her back, nearly to her waist. James didn't even realize how long her hair was. He noticed she had put on a little bit of makeup but not much. It reminded him of Tess, simple and elegant. She brought a small bag with her and tucked it in the duffel. James figured it was all the little stuff that women must have.

"Well?" she asked, spinning slowly for him. "Suitable, I hope."

"Absolutely stunning." He walked over to her with the bracelet in his hand. After he hooked it on her wrist, he gazed upon her mystic green eyes. They stood out next to her tanned skin and dark hair. "You are very beautiful."

Jesse looked shyly away. "No, just like all the rest."

"No." James took her hands in his. "You're not or I wouldn't be here." James leaned in, kissing her softly. It was slow and tender as his hands left hers and slipped behind her neck, controlling the kiss. The feel of her hands, first on his chest then slipping down to his waist and around to his back, made a deep, passionate desire prevalent throughout his body. After a couple of minutes, he reluctantly raised his lips off hers. "I could do that all night with you," he told her with a smile. "But we need to get moving."

"Mmm," Jesse said, thinking the same thing. "Let me throw a few more things in my bag, grab my shoes, and I'll be ready."

James looked at his watch, noting they had another twenty minutes before they needed to leave. "What can I help you with?"

"Nothing. I am almost ready."

James watched her tuck a few more things into the duffel. Then she went into the closet and brought out a pair of black heels. She sat on the bed beside him, taking off the price tag.

"I bought these two years ago." She laughed a little as she slipped one on each foot. "I don't get out much." Jesse stood, making a crooked face.

"What's wrong?" he asked, looking at her from head to toe, thinking she looked perfect.

"I don't know how women wear shoes like this." She shook her head. "I'm usually barefoot."

James stood, placed his hands on her hips, and nipped at her bottom lip. "You can take them off whenever you want."

"Do you always go to these great lengths for dates?" Her arms rounded his broad shoulders.

"The last time I was on a date with a woman that I truly liked, I think I was in college. And I didn't have the means to plan out a date like this before."

Jesse smiled, kissing him this time. There was something about this man that she already loved.

"We need to go," he said, releasing her from his grip. He reached over and grabbed her duffel as she took her wallet and house keys. "Whatever you need that you may have forgotten, I will pick up for you."

"Okay," she said, locking the door behind them. Having taken care of herself for her entire adult life, it was odd to have someone else offer to buy her something.

"It's the least I can do since I barely gave you any notice," he simply stated.

As she made sure her car was locked, James put the duffel behind the seat and opened the door for her. "Nice car." He noted the new dealership tags on it.

"Thank you." She glanced over at the SUV Colin bought nearly a week before.

The ride to Jonathan's private airstrip went by fast, as their conversation was continuous and effortless. There was never an awkward moment of silence. They had talked many times over the past few days. Sometimes it was a quick conversation, but late at night, it was always for a couple of hours. James enjoyed hearing her laugh and seeing her smile, knowing her past was tough. It was nice to not have to hide who he was. She seemed to accept him just as he did her.

James pulled the car near the hangar where his plane was prepped and waiting for them. "You ready?" He smiled, giving her hand a slight squeeze.

Jesse nodded with a big smile. As they got out of the car, Jesse felt her heart nearly stop beating when Colin McGowan walked over to them. Nervousness engulfed her entire body, as she didn't want James to know about her indiscretion with this man.

"Thank you for the car." James handed Colin the keys.

"Of course. Tess and I are heading into Atlanta until Tuesday, and we're going to drive her car. Figured we might as well use it while we can."

"Yep, not sure how you would fit four car seats in there."

"Four?" Jesse looked surprised but knew the truth.

"They have a set of twins and another set on the way," James told her and glanced at Colin.

"Oh my, that's a lot of children." Jesse grinned at Colin as she instinctively ran her hand over her stomach, knowing he wanted to know if she was carrying his child or not.

"By the way, it's nice to see you again." Colin directed his attention to Jesse.

"You too." She smiled kindly as a flash of waking up beside him crossed her mind.

Jesse woke early—well, ten in the morning really wasn't early, but it was for her. It was the morning after their first night together. Colin had her facing him, wrapped up in his arms. Her hand was draped around his waist as he continued to sleep. Looking at him, he was very handsome, she thought, and he kissed well, just like every woman's dream. Sliding her hand slowly over his shoulder to his waist again, she was a little surprised when he kissed her forehead.

"Thought you were asleep," she whispered.

"No." He kissed her lips this time as he brought her leg over his hip. "I was just waiting for you to wake up."

Jesse caught her breath as she felt him find his way inside of her. As her eyes closed with the intense feeling, his lips continued to kiss her, with his hips keeping a steady, slow motion.

Jolted back to reality, her heart was beating a bit fast as she pretended to be listening to the two men.

"Tess confirmed your reservation for you." Colin looked back at James. "So, get the hell out of here. I don't want to see you for a while. Bullets tend to fly around you."

James laughed, nodding his head. "Okay, okay."

Colin patted James on the shoulder and then went to Jesse. "Be good to him. He's a good man." He gave her a hug, whispering something in her ear.

Jesse followed James up the steps on the plane. Inside, Thomas greeted them, then verified the destination, closed the door, and took his seat at the controls. James put her bag on the couch and guided her to one of the comfortable chairs in the middle. Sitting beside her, they buckled in, and he carefully watched her as the plane began to ascend. The moment the wheels left the ground, he was certain she stopped breathing momentarily. Reassuringly, he held her hand even as she squeezed it.

Once the plane leveled out, she released her breath and looked at him. "That was kind of scary," she admitted.

"I was flying planes by the time I was twenty. Sometimes it feels like I am in a plane more than a car."

"That's weird to me. You told me about your cousins, Jack and Harrison, but what about your parents?" Jesse asked.

"My father took off when I was a kid. Jack and Harrison's father died in a car accident when they were around nine and ten. Our mothers, who were sisters, moved in with their mother, Carina. We were raised in the same household for the most part."

"Where's your mom?"

"She died when I was twenty-three, from a boating accident." He brought her hand to his lips and kissed it. "You won't see me on a boat too much."

"I'm so sorry." Jesse unfastened her seat belt so she could turn and face him better.

"There was this perpetual void in my life for a few years. That was when I started to seriously train for my career and learned to control my emotions. I missed her so much that I just *hurt* inside. I don't know." James sighed as he caressed her cheek. "It was a dark time in my life because we were close. But at least I didn't see her murdered in front of me."

Jesse nodded, pursing her lips together. "It was terrible for an eleven-year-old to see that. And since that event dictated my life, I can never put it to rest. There are constant repercussions if I do the wrong thing, lower my guard, trust the wrong person. I'm exhausted from all of it. I want a normal life where I don't have to lie about anything to anyone."

James gave a half grin, knowing he could help her, but that was not why he wanted to meet her. There was an instant attraction when they first met, and he had to get to know her better because he saw a future with her. Never had this vision been so clear, not even with Tess. There were rules with his work, but he knew if he fell in love with this woman, the rules would be broken. Was that a danger he was willing to risk?

"Regardless of how things go between us, I will help you deal with the people you hide from. No one should have to live the way you do. You need to be free and happy. Life is too short to have it any other way."

"Just so we're clear, I'm not going on this date so you can deal with my baggage. It's mine. I've dealt with it thus far."

"I understand." James nodded, knowing she didn't realize who he truly was. There was no way he would be with a woman who had a Markenna trying to kill her. Every single one of them would die. Maybe he could give that to her as a wedding present. Laughing to himself, he shook his head slightly, knowing he was getting ahead of himself again. *Reel it back in*, he told himself.

"How do you and Colin know each other?" Jesse wanted a change of subject.

"That's a very long story." He sighed, not even knowing where to begin. "I guess it started when my cousin Jack and Colin became best friends in high school, and they have been ever since. I never really liked the man until his wife, Tess, was shot and he called me for help. He went through a lot and almost lost her. Long story short, we became friends working through that for a few years. Tess I've known forever, as her older brother and I have been good friends since college."

"I have a feeling there are lots of side stories to all of this." She watched him slip her hand into his.

"Many. Should you find me tolerable, all the stories will come out eventually." James unbuckled his seat belt, leaned over, and kissed her lips. It was nice to finally kiss a woman who didn't belong to another man. He'd been exclusive with Tess far too long and almost forgot what it felt like to be with an unmarried woman. He managed through slow moves to get her out of her seat and onto his lap. His hand rested on her thigh on top of her hem line as his other hand roamed her back. They were lost in each other until Thomas came over the speaker to let James know they were beginning their decent.

Jesse stood up and looked back down at James with a smile. James rose from his seat as well, taking her hands in his.

James's eyes looked down for a moment before meeting hers again. "I want to be fair in telling you that I … I'm falling in love with you."

Jesse sucked in her bottom lip, released it, leaned up, and kissed his lips softly. "You should know you're not alone in that feeling."

James wrapped his arms around her, hugging her tightly. Was she the one he'd been waiting for all these years?

# Chapter 6

They were on the ground in fifteen minutes. James had a hangar at the small, private airport, as he shared his time equally between Maine and Chicago. Inside was his black SUV. He moved her bag to the back seat and opened the passenger door for her. As he drove, he gave her a brief history of the area, as this was where he spent much of his younger years. It only took twenty minutes to drive to the restaurant. James pulled up front and parked. The valet opened Jesse's door as James came around to take her hand.

"Good evening, Mr. Cordello," the young man said as James handed him the keys.

"Good evening, Daniel." James shook his hand. "How is your father?"

"Well prepared for you, sir." Daniel gave him a slight grin.

James smiled back, holding his arm out for Jesse. She slipped her hand on the inside of his elbow and let him lead her inside. The seafood restaurant was very cozy, and dimmed lighting made the enormous fireplace in the far corner stand out beautifully.

"James," Jesse whispered to him. "Where are all the people?"

"I reserved the restaurant," he whispered back.

"Oh," she said, looking around as an older looking gentleman walked up to them.

"James." Oscar shook his hand. "How have you been? And who might this beautiful young lady be?"

"Oscar, this is Jesse." James said. "Jesse this is Oscar, Daniel's father and the owner of this wonderful restaurant."

"Pleasure to meet you, Ms. Jesse." Oscar kindly took her hand with a warm shake. "Your table is this way."

Oscar seated them near the fireplace, and another server came over with a bottle of wine.

"Compliments of Jonathan McGowan," Oscar told James with a grin as he poured him a glass.

James lifted the glass and took a sip, knowing it would be very good. Jonathan didn't do anything short of top of the line. He nodded his head once, and Oscar poured Jesse a glass.

"Your appetizers will be served shortly," Oscar informed James. "Let me know if you need anything in the meantime."

"Thank you, Oscar." James gave him a nod and focused his attention back to Jesse.

"I feel like I don't belong here," she told him softly.

"You do with me, so get used to it."

Jesse smiled, shaking her head.

"I want to make a toast." He lifted his wine glass, and she did the same. "To finally finding you in the most off-the-wall town on a very unusual day."

Their glasses lightly tapped together, and they each took a sip. James reached across the table, interlocking his fingers with hers. They talked for the next few hours about the countries he had traveled to and the hunting trips he took with Adam. Jesse talked about her father before he was murdered and how he taught her how to fish and shoot a gun when she was only eight. Their conversation continued throughout the four-course meal. It was easy conversation to make. They both laughed often and finished off the bottle of wine and started on another.

"This was wonderful, James," Jesse told him as the dessert plates were removed. "Thank you so much."

"We're not done." He smiled, looking at his watch. It was nine thirty. "Let's head out."

James walked her to the door, then excused himself for a moment and went over to Oscar. "Everything was exceptional, Oscar." James shook his hand. "Thank you." Taking an envelope from inside his jacket, James went to hand it to him.

"Already taken care of." Oscar smiled, patting his shoulder.

"You closed the restaurant for me. Please," James insisted.

"I was told that if you argued with me about this to remind you that you saved her life and she just wanted to do something nice for you. Tess's way of saying thank you." Oscar grinned, pushing the envelope back to James. "She already paid and with a healthy tip. Go and enjoy the rest of your life with that beautiful woman. I want a wedding photo."

James smiled and thanked him again. When Daniel pulled the car around, James opened the door for Jesse. He closed her door and walked to the driver's side where Daniel was holding the keys for him.

"Was everything to your liking, Mr. Cordello?" Daniel asked.

James grinned, pulling the envelope from his inside pocket. "Everything was perfect. Here. Take this and put it in your college fund."

Daniel smiled. "Thank you, sir. I promise, I will."

"You know what we say about a promise in my family?" James asked, and the young man shook his head. "Sometimes it's the only thing you've got. You make a promise, you keep it, or you die trying. Make sure you go to college. And rest assure, I will know if you don't."

Daniel nodded as James got in the SUV. "Thank you, Mr. Cordello."

The drive to the next destination took about a half hour. It was dark, so Jesse didn't get to see much of the scenery. Every now and then, there was a glimpse of the ocean that would shine off the light from the lighthouse. Tranquility engulfed her. She felt safe and content for the first time in her entire life.

The ride was exactly thirty minutes. James pulled into a circular driveway and stopped under a covered entrance. Opening her door, he held out his hand. Jesse stepped from the car and looked up the side of the two-story home. It was rustic but well maintained.

The light on the porch was softly lit, and just before James opened the door himself, a sprite, elderly woman with a warm smile greeted them.

"James." She hugged him tightly. "I was hoping you would make it."

"One way or another, I was coming home." James smiled, taking Jesse's hand. "Jesse, this is my grandmother, Carina."

"You are a like a breath of fresh air, beautiful," Carina said, giving Jesse a hug. "Please come in. I'm so happy to meet you. James called a few days ago to say he might bring someone home with him. I had no idea it would be such a beautiful young lady."

"Gran, you don't have to tell her everything I told you." James closed the door behind them.

"Oh, but I do." Carina gave him a wink as he took his jacket off Jesse's shoulders and hung it in the hall closet. "He's never brought a woman here before. So, that tells me there is something special about you."

"Really?" Jesse wanted to hear more.

"Take off your shoes and stay awhile," Carina told her. "Besides, your feet ought to be killing you by now. Your impression has been made. Be comfortable."

"Thank you." Jesse sighed, slipping the heels off. "My feet aren't used to heels. They prefer sandals or nothing at all."

"I was making my last cup of tea before bed. Would you like some, dear?" Carina smiled warmly.

"No, thank you." Jesse nodded. "I'm fine."

"James, take her in and relax." Carina excused herself.

"The impression from the outside is nothing like the inside," Jesse told James as he took her hand and showed her around. "This is amazing."

It was a lodge style, nine bedrooms, six baths. Fully restored and updated. There were two decks that spanned the length of the home on the back side that had a magnificent view of the harbor for a backyard.

"This is your grandmother's house?" Jesse asked after they finished the tour of the main level.

"No, it's mine. She loves it here. So, I fixed up the place, and she uses it as a B&B during the summer. She loves hosting people." James was very humble about his home.

"I thought you said you lived in a farmhouse?" She was confused.

"I do." He smiled with a nod. "It's twenty minutes out of Chicago. I like that place too. This is Gran's place. I just help her maintain the lifestyle she loves."

Jesse walked across the vast living room to the windows that were two stories high. "I can't wait to see this view tomorrow." She glanced over her shoulder at James, who was seated on the corner of the couch watching her. "Why are you staring?"

"Because I can," he told her as she walked over to him. Reaching out his hand, she took it, and he pulled her on the couch beside him. "How are your feet?"

"Happy they're barefoot." She leaned her head against his shoulder and watched the fire burning. "Does anybody else see this side of you?"

"Gran and my cousins." He kissed her temple, deciding to leave Tess off that list. "I'm very selective."

Looking at her hand wrapped in his, she gave a slight smile. "Colin was right; you are a good man."

Carina walked back in and gave James's hand a squeeze. "I am going to turn in. Everything is locked up, and the alarm is on. We can catch up in the morning."

James and Jesse stood, and he gave Carina a hug. "Sounds good. I love you."

"I love you too." Carina went to Jesse, giving her a hug as well. "Wonderful to meet you. Tomorrow we will spend some time getting to know each other. Sleep well, dear."

"Thank you, and you too."

They watched Carina walk off, and then James turned to Jesse. "Another glass of wine?" She nodded, and he went off to the kitchen.

Jesse walked over to the fireplace. Her hand ran across the river rock that formed the entire fireplace to the ceiling, at least two stories high. It was an amazing room, like an old-style lodge. Places like this only existed in magazines, she thought. It was out of her league, but this man was such a perfect fit.

James walked back in the room, finding her before the fireplace, looking at the pictures. He liked her barefoot and smiled at the thought. She was incredibly beautiful. He tried to think of another word to describe her; perhaps exotic was second best.

"You're staring again," she noted, walking over to him.

"I can't help it." With a smile, he handed her a glass of red wine.

They sat and talked for a couple more hours. The conversation came easily. At one point, Jesse told him about the night she saw Marcos kill her father and mother in a few brief sentences. James could tell she had turned off her emotions toward the entire ordeal. It had happened, and she managed to come out on the other side, still alive. It wasn't until she yawned that James looked at his watch, noting it was after midnight.

"Want to see your room?" he asked, and she nodded.

James took her upstairs to the right, giving her the room next to his. It had a four-poster bed and its own bath. Jesse walked over to the window, wishing it was daytime so she could see the view. She peeked into the bathroom and noticed the claw tub that was in the corner.

"Can I take a bath?"

"Of course." He laughed a little. "You can do whatever you want, except leave. The alarm is obnoxiously loud."

"My feet will love it," she told him.

"Let me go get your bag," he said, leaving the room.

Jesse walked around the room. It was beautiful, just like the rest of the house. The bed was a dark oak with white linens, with a white lamp on the nightstand. The dresser was opposite the bed, with the same dark oak, six drawers, and a large mirror above it. By the window was a white chaise with a light blue blanket folded neatly at the end. She felt incredibly spoiled.

James came back with her bag in hand, and after setting it on the dresser, he walked over to her. His hand slipped around her neck, gently pulling her mouth to his, with his other hand on her hip. Lips soft, warm, and wanting. He let the kiss linger as if time didn't matter, and in his world, it didn't. He felt her hand on his chest and the other on his waist. Her lips parted, allowing him to taste more of her. A few minutes passed, before he pulled back slightly. "I need to go before I don't." He rested his forehead on hers.

Jesse lifted her lips to his again; she wanted more of that. His body felt strong under her hands, and his kisses made her knees weak. She could explore this man's body all night long. "Okay," she said, blinking her eyes open. "You're right. You need to go, or I won't let you."

James smiled, pulling her in for a hug. His hands ran through her hair and across her shoulders as he kissed the top of her head.

"James," she called to him softly before he walked out the door. "Thank you for an amazing evening."

"You're welcome," he replied. "Thank you for trusting me."

Jesse smiled as he walked out the door and turned left down the hallway.

Once in his room, he slipped off his shoes, put them in the closet, took off his clothes, and hung them on a hanger. Then he took a cool shower. Standing with his eyes closed, the water streamed down his chest. It was easy to imagine spending the rest of his life with her. Conversation between them was easy. There was a trust that he usually didn't feel with too many people, but he felt it with her. He liked the fact that Jesse was average height, at least five seven, and built like Harper, soft but firm, not too athletic. Jesse was a perfect fit. She had long, dark brown hair that was highlighted with light golden streaks from the sun. The bottle-green eyes popped next to her tanned skin.

After a good five minutes of standing there thinking about her, he washed up and got out. He put on his dark lounge pants, cracked open a window, opened his door halfway, and lay back on the bed. In the distance, he could hear the waves crashing on the rocky shoreline. It relaxed and comforted him. When he was here, he didn't have to watch his back. He knew it was safe. All the bad things he did out there were left at the town's border. Here he was known as Carina's grandson who came often to help and visit. He liked having that image, but, admittedly, he also liked his professional image.

After tossing and turning for an hour, unable to sleep, he got out of bed and quietly walked down the hall to Jesse's room. He knocked softly, so that if she was asleep it wouldn't wake her, but if she was awake, she would hear it. He waited a few moments, then headed for the stairs. A smile came to his lips when he heard her door click open.

"Hey," Jesse said with a smile. "What are you up to?"

"Seeing if you were awake." He leaned against the door frame.

"Yep, come in." She held the door open for him.

"Damn," he mumbled under his breath when he saw her in a tank and tiny, nothing much to them, shorts.

"What?"

"You look incredibly sexy." James grinned as she smiled and took his hands in hers.

"Hmm." Jesse licked her lips as her eyes wandered over his chest. "Do you always walk around shirtless? Because that is like a small form of torture to me when you have a body like this."

James's turn to smile. "Good. Now you know how I feel."

"Oh, really?" Her eyes went from his chest to his eyes.

James nodded, bringing his lip to hers. That seemed to be the only place they wanted to be. "Put on your bikini. I'll be back in two minutes for you."

James went back to his room, put on his shorts, and went back to Jesse's room. She was trying to tie the back of her bathing suit when he walked right up, took the two pieces from her hands, and tied it for her.

"Thank you," she said, turning around to him. "Don't tell me we are going to swim in the ocean because you would have to throw me in. It's so cold out there."

James laughed, took her hand, and walked down to the lower level. "How about an indoor heated pool and Jacuzzi?" He opened the door leading into a large room. It had a huge lap pool in the center. To the left was a Jacuzzi, and to the right was workout equipment. The far wall was nothing but windows.

"During the summer, all of those windows slide open to the deck. There's a fire pit and the trail that leads to the boat house."

"Is this all your design?" Jesse was curious.

James simply nodded.

"I can only imagine what your version of a farmhouse is."

James laughed a little. "Trust me, it's not as extravagant as this home. The farmhouse is more isolated for privacy, as it's the main base for my work."

Jesse glanced up at him as he brought her hand to his lips, kissing the palm. With ease, his arm came around her hips, picking her up. With her arms draped perfectly around his shoulders, she smiled as his lips went straight for hers again. As he occupied her lips, he walked to the edge of the pool and jumped in. As they swam up to the surface, Jesse was laughing. James saw genuine laughter, which reminded him that Adam told him he could make her life better. At that moment, he was succeeding.

# Chapter 7

J ames woke and for a moment forgot where he was and who he was with. As everything from the night before rushed back to his mind, he remembered they were in Jesse's, or as he would prefer to use her real name, Emma's room. He smiled, as Emma's body was aligned perfectly with his. Her head rested on his arm, and his hand draped over her waist. The memories of the night played through his mind—the swimming, the Jacuzzi, and then the kissing, touching, the positions, and the orgasms. Just thinking about it began to arouse sexual feelings again. Without conscious awareness, his hand slowly caressed down her waist and over her hip to her thigh and back up again. The move was slow but enough to rouse her from the sexually intoxicated slumber.

"Mmm," she mumbled without opening her eyes.

James kissed her shoulder as his hand slipped between her legs, easily finding that place of pleasure for her. His other arm that was under her neck wrapped around her body, holding her tightly against his chest. With her eyes closed, he could feel her body tense.

"James," she breathed out as the feeling intensified.

Kissing her neck, he whispered in her ear, "Come for me, Em."

Emma's hand grabbed his bare hip as he brought her to the edge and took her over. James kissed her neck again, moved his lips to her shoulder, then rolled her onto her back so he could kiss her wanting lips. She was very receptive, with her hands roaming his body as his did hers. When he was directly above her, she spread her legs and took him in.

"Emma." His voice was barely audible as he kissed her.

"James." Her hands came around his shoulders and up his neck. "Let me be on top."

James held her against him as they rolled over, changing positions.

Emma found that place that felt just right and smiled at James as she slowly moved her hips. Her hands rested on his stomach as his moved from her breast to her hips. When her eyes closed as she got close, she felt his hands grasp her hips tightly as they came together. She didn't move off him but smiled as she looked down at him.

"I want to wake up like this every day," she stated.

James pulled her mouth down to his. "Me too. Life would be so much better."

"Indeed."

"Come on." He rolled both them over to the edge of the bed, sitting up with her still in his arms. "I want you to see the sunrise."

"Okay," she said, standing up. "Give me a sec." She went into the bathroom to straighten up a bit and put on her button-down shirt.

James put his lounge pants on but stayed shirtless. She walked to the window, opening the drapes, but James took her hand and shook his head with a smile. He led her down the hall to his room. They walked past the bed into a sitting room that was nearly as big as the bedroom area. The sitting room had a sofa, recliner, and some tables. James took the remote, pressed one button, and the blinds lifted, revealing floor-to-ceiling windows with a set of French doors that led to a balcony.

"Hang on," he said, going back into his bed to grab a blanket. "It's going to be cold out there."

As James opened the door, a cold breeze hit them. Emma shivered, wrapping her arms around herself. Closing the door behind them, he took her over to a double lounge chair with big, soft cushions. He sat down and had her sit next to him, draping her legs over his. Then he covered them up with the blanket, drawing her close.

"It is beautiful out here," she softly said, looking out across the coast line as the sun was getting ready to make its daily appearance. Her head rested on his shoulder, and he kissed her forehead.

"I've wanted to share this with someone for a long time," he said, watching the sky change colors.

Emma raised her head to look at him. His hand came up, caressing her cheek as he kissed her. As the sun began its ascent, they could feel its warmth on their faces. Emma broke the kiss to look at it. James watched her smile in the early dawn. It was as if she was seeing the sun rise for the first time.

"Thank you." She grinned after the sun was in full force.

"You should know that I am going to marry you," he simply stated. "I know you're thinking something like *yeah, right,* but three things I just love about you. First your tank top that night that said, 'This girl is made of gunpowder and lead.' I would have taken you then if Colin wasn't with me. Second, you're not afraid to take control." He grinned at her, knowing she knew what he was talking about.

"I was glad you were okay with that." Emma kissed him. "What's the third thing?"

"The look on your face as the sun rose." A seriousness crossed his face. "It was as if you had never seen a sunrise before."

"I don't …" Emma looked down then back to him. "I don't know how to do this."

"Do what?" he asked, raising her chin so he could see her face.

"Love. I've been alone so long because every time I love someone, they're killed," she said. "I want this as much as you, but I don't want you hurt."

James kissed her lips slowly, softly. "Trust me?"

"I'm not good at that," she reminded him.

"I know." He nodded. "But you're going to have to practice trusting me. You've got to start somewhere; start with me. I'm never going to hurt you, and I won't let anyone else hurt you."

Emma wanted to believe him, but she had always been precautious, especially with her heart. She nodded as her eyes filled a little.

"I'm falling in love with you, Emma." His voice was soft. "I promise to keep you safe and unharmed even if I have to utilize every resource I have. And I have a lot of resources."

Emma grinned. "I like it when you use my real name."

"I will call you that if you prefer," he stated.

Emma nodded. "Just not in public until I don't have to be Jesse Anders anymore."

"As you wish, Emma." He kissed her softly.

"I'm falling in love with you too." Her voice was barely above a whisper.

"Let's go back inside," he suggested. "It's freezing out here."

# Chapter 8

Dominic stood at the edge of the patio looking out over the lake, but his mind was far from the beauty of this place that Jonathan welcomed him to. He needed to figure out what he wanted to do with the rest of his life, as he was almost forty-three, single, childless, and, lest he forget, jobless. Did it count that he had money in the bank? He wondered but then shrugged it off because he didn't care; there was no ambition, no motivation, nothing. Taryn chose the path that ended her life instead of working through the predicaments that she caused herself. He would have stood by her through all of it—the good, the bad, dealing with Colin in the custody of Connor. He would have helped her through everything, but she chose death instead. Then there was Connor. The love he felt for that little boy was beyond a comprehension he could understand until he called him daddy.

"Dominic."

Jolted from his thought, he turned his head. "Yes?" he answered as his brother walked toward him.

"You okay?" Matthew asked, standing before him.

"Fine." He shrugged. "I'm just trying to figure out what to do with the rest of my life. It's like starting over again."

Matthew nodded, understanding the loss that Dominic had suffered in the last few weeks. "Father and I were just talking about this." Matthew raised his brow. "Want to come in and talk business?"

"I don't want a handout," Dominic reminded him. "I don't need it, and you know that."

"Our father doesn't give handouts," Matthew stated. "But he won't let a good investor go to waste either. You're educated, and your company was very successful. You just had some poor clientele. We don't. All our clients get a thorough background before we sign them on. Dad wants to offer you a job in the Atlanta office."

"Doing what?" Admittedly, he was a little bit curious.

"Running the day-to-day operations with Harper so Dad can step back a little more." Matthew gave a half grin. "Harper is good but very green. You have the experience in management that she lacks. Father knows that Harper, although she works now, one day will want the whole family thing and not a career. Besides, Harper doesn't want to manage. Colin and I will be in Portland working that office, and he wants someone he can trust in Atlanta."

"Your brother doesn't like me," Dominic reminded him. "Do you really think putting me in the Atlanta office, with a position of authority and control, where I would have to deal with him on a daily basis is a good idea?"

Matthew smiled. "I think it's a great idea."

"I don't know." Dominic sighed, turning back around to look at the lake. "If I took the job, your brother would think I did it just to piss him off. I don't want any more animosity in my life."

Matthew stood beside him, placing his hand on his shoulder. "It's not all about my brother."

"She's happy with him, isn't she?" Dominic asked.

"Very." Matthew nodded.

"How do you … do it?"

"Do what?" Matthew didn't quite understand his question.

"Be around her without being able to … be with her?"

"It's not always easy, but it is what it is. We have Savannah between us, and she looks so much like our mother. Did you notice that?"

"After I saw the pictures in Jonathan's office, yes." He sighed deeply. "I miss our mother. Life just wasn't the same without her."

"I don't remember her that much." Matthew shrugged. "I grew up with just my dad and brother. I don't even remember Colin's mother much. When Gina came into our life, I was in college."

"All I had was Dimitri's mother." Dominic shook his head at the thought of her. "She had no backbone, unlike the women here. He would yell and beat her regularly until one day he hit her so hard it caused a hematoma on the brain, and she died. After that, it was just whores who liked the money he spent on them. He was a great example of what I didn't want to be."

"Did he ever hit you?"

Dominic laughed a little and eyed his brother. "When I was little, no, but I knew the day was coming. When I was about fourteen or fifteen, I started working out, taking boxing classes after school. And the day he went to hit me, I ducked and came back up and beat the crap out of him. I packed my bags and Dimitri's, told him to stay the hell out of our life and moved to the States. I was only seventeen, but over the years, I had taken fifty thousand from him and stashed it. Because I knew one day I would have to leave in a hurry. Got to the States, rented a tiny apartment, and when I turned eighteen, I became a citizen, went to college and graduate school, and here I am today."

"What's the story with your bother?" Matthew was curious.

"I should have left him with his father." Dominic shook his head. "He was constantly in trouble; if it was illegal, he was doing it. I bailed him out of jail so many times I lost count. There was a point when Father came to the States and got him to work for him doing the dirty work. It was frustrating because he could have had a better life than what we grew up with, and he chose poorly. Happiest day of my life was when that young girl testified at his trial for the murder of her father. I was balancing graduate school and my company that had just reached its seven-figure profit goal and heard about the arrest and conviction—twenty-five years. That was when Dimitri decided to take care of things on the outside for dear old Dad. The girl that testified against Marcos had been put in the witness relocation thing. Well, Dimitri found her and beat her badly, so they moved her again, and he did the same thing. The last time, the girl pressed charges and got him four years for assault. He did two years and couldn't find her again, so he started making drugs instead. I saw that girl at the courthouse. He beat her bad, just like our father. She was so thin and frail … and sad. I felt so bad for her. So, you know what I did?"

"Do tell," Matthew prompted.

"I found the woman who oversaw her case, Maggie." Dominic smiled, remembering the first time he kissed her. "I explained who I was and all that good stuff, and I apologized for my family's behavior. My company was posting great profits, so I had a little extra money, and I asked Maggie to give the girl something … nice. She came up with a home—somewhere, they wouldn't tell me—which I understand, and Maggie said that is wasn't big, but it was perfect, and she loved it. I paid for the home, and she has a trust set up that pays for the home's expenses."

"And you never met her?" Matthew was sort of surprised, as it wasn't common for a Markenna to be generous.

Dominic smiled. "Nope. I used my money to buy the home. When Father was incarcerated, I took most of his money and put it in the trust. And when Dimitri died, I took all his money and put it in the trust for her also. She will get the full cash value when she turns thirty-five. She's a rich woman and has no idea."

Matthew grinned. "I can totally see how we're brothers."

Dominic laughed as he nodded. "You hold her trust fund."

"What's her name?" Matthew asked, not realizing this.

"Her real name is Emma Anderson," Dominic stated. "I don't know the name she's under right now."

"How are we supposed to release the funds to her if we don't know the name she's using?" Matthew was thinking aloud rather than asking the question.

"Meagan Trask." Dominic sighed, thinking of her smile. "She knows the name. Mags works for the Justice Department."

"That'll be easy enough then." Matthew nodded. "Where's your father?"

"Louisiana state pen." He brightened up. "Every single time he is up for parole, I go and remind the panel why he's in there and why he needs to stay in there. He ever gets out, I'm as good as dead."

"We do have people who can take care of that," Matthew reminded him.

"I hope so." Dominic grinned. "Let's go talk to Jonathan."

# Chapter 9

Meagan woke, looking cautiously around the room, not knowing where she was or how much time had gone by. With her hands and feet bound, she winced as a sharp pain shot through her jaw. The memories of Marcos Markenna breaking into her house were clear in her mind.

*Aria.*

Thinking back, she remembered the other men stating they didn't find anyone else in the home, it was clear. Aria should be safe, she told herself, easing the anxiety that was building in her mind. Brian was on the phone when it all happened, and he would know to find Aria. He would know what happened, as she purposely said Markenna's name. Her daughter would be fine, but she wasn't too sure about herself. Knowing Marcos Markenna's reputation, she would be lucky to survive this ordeal. Then Brian would find out who Aria's father was, and she wondered if he would tell him or keep Aria with his family. Either way, Meagan knew Aria would be safe.

Hearing a door open, she didn't move.

"Ms. Trask?" a man's voice softly said.

Meagan opened her eyes slowly, knowing it wasn't Marcos. Before her was a man that looked like Dominic. The genes in the Markenna family were strong and dominant.

"I figured you were awake. I'm Antoine Markenna. I'm sure you know who I am, as I know the research you do on our family. I'm not going to hurt you, but I can't guarantee that my uncle won't. Don't talk back, and he won't hit you. I found your daughter hiding."

Meagan's eyes went wide with fear.

"I told her to stay hidden until we were gone. There was no way I was going to let him harm that child too. He's a bastard of a man and has threatened the life of my son if I don't help him. I do what I must. I will try my best to keep him from hurting you, but please don't antagonize him."

"Let me go, please?" Meagan pleaded.

"I can't," he answered, shaking his head. "I'll do what I can when I can for you, but he can't know. I'm sorry, but my son's life trumps all others."

Tears filled Meagan's eyes as she nodded. She understood his position, as she would do that same thing for her daughter. "What does he want with me?"

"Emiliana and Dominic."

"They can never be free, can they?"

Antoine shook his head. Hearing the door open, he stood up as his uncle walked into the room.

"Ah, good, she is awake." Marcos walked over to Meagan.

Meagan cringed at the sound of his voice and the accent that rolled off his tongue. The memory of Dominic's voice came to mind. It was exactly the same, with a twist of passion. Marcos's voice only had passion for death.

"I heard that your daughter was in the house, hidden. My men must've not searched well enough or just didn't tell me." Marcos eyed his nephew, knowing he would be one to betray him. "But no matter, I will find my children first, then pick up my granddaughter. Sit her up."

Antoine sat Meagan upright on the bed.

"Now, Ms. Trask, where's my daughter?"

"On the coast," Meagan stated, knowing she was going to have to give the location away.

"A little more specific because I don't have my tracking device for her yet."

Meagan looked at him for a moment without speaking. How would he have a tracker on Emma? Was that how he kept finding her all those years? Glancing at Antoine, he glared at her to tell him. "I'll tell you, but what tracking device?"

Marcos grinned with a slight raise of his eyebrow. "I'm surprised you didn't figure it out years ago. How do you think Dimitri kept finding her?"

With a shake of her head, Meagan closed her eyes for a moment. "Of course, we should have known."

"Location?"

"Mason Bluff. I'll take you there," Meagan lied, at least a little. Emma wasn't there, but Marcos didn't know that. It was a safe house Meagan put her in before relocating her to the last home. It was set up to make it look lived in, just for incidents like this.

"Good girl." Marcos smiled, touching her bruised cheek. "Antoine, leave us."

Antoine knew what was coming next. He didn't want to walk out of the room, but he didn't know how to save Meagan from his uncle. "If she'll take us there, let's go."

"I said leave us." Marcos eyed his nephew, daring retribution.

"Very well." Antoine shook his head slightly as Meagan's eyes pleaded with him to not leave her alone with this monster.

When Antoine closed the door behind him, Marcos moved his hand over Meagan's thigh. "I've been locked up a very long time because of you and my daughter. And now it's time for you to start paying me back. I'm just not certain as to how that will be yet."

Meagan's heart pounded with fear. When he pushed his way into her home, she knew that one of two things would be happening. First thing she knew, Marcos would put a bullet in her head. The second thing would make her wish for the bullet.

# Chapter 10

Six days had passed. They walked hand in hand through the little Maine town. James enjoyed watching Carina get along with Emma. The two women had a continuous game of Scrabble going on at the kitchen table. It was working out just as he'd hoped it would. He took Emma all over the area, pointing out different places that he remembered while growing up. It was as if they'd been together for years. He knew when he met her that there was something about her that he loved, and his gut was right again.

Emma stopped walking and turned to him with a smile.

"What?" He eyed her with a grin.

"I'm ..." She hesitated a moment. "Happy."

"Are you sure? Because there was a little hesitation there." His hands rested on her shoulders.

"I was just thinking if I said it, I might jinx it." She tilted her head with a shrug.

"Superstitious. I see." He kissed her forehead. "You make me happy, and it's been a long time since I've been happy." Leaning over, he kissed her lips softly. "I'm in love with you, Emma," he whispered into her ear as he kissed her lobe gently.

"You don't have a single doubt?"

"Nope." He smiled, shaking his head. "I need you to quit your job so we can ... move on."

"And where are we moving on to?" she asked.

"To begin our life together." His finger caressed the hairline on her forehead.

"Okay." Without hesitation, she nodded. "I'll call my boss later today, but I still need some more clothes from my house."

"That's fine. We can go tomorrow. We'll need to head to the farmhouse after. I need to finish up a to-do list I'm working on."

"A list?"

"Yes." He raised his eyebrows. "A list. I will explain it to you in more detail at home. No one can listen to us there."

"I love you," she said softly. "I didn't think I could fall in love with someone in such a short time, but I did, and I am."

"Good, because I love you too." James leaned over, kissing her again.

"So, where will we live? My place would fit in your kitchen."

James smiled as his hands ran up and down her arms. "Home base is the farmhouse in Illinois. I come to Gran's as often as I can, and I will stay for a couple of weeks at a time. As she gets older, I like spending as much time here as possible. Plus, I do the maintenance as well. Do not discount your place. I like it. It's cozy."

"Cozy is code for small." Emma raised her brows with a smile. "I don't own it."

"Do you want to?"

"If I didn't have to be relocated again, I would love to own that little place."

"Then we'll make it happen." James ran his hand over her shoulders. "We have to have a financial conversation at some point."

"I'll get a job if we're living here or wherever we go. I'm not afraid to work. I'll pull my own." Emma had always supported herself and had never depended on anyone else.

James chuckled a little, shaking his head. "That's not what I meant."

"Oh." She was confused.

"You don't have to work. I have plenty to support us for several lifetimes. Further down the road, we'll talk about finances. I need to have someone that I trust to take care of everything if something should happen to me. You know the work I do. And even though everything is well planned, things happen out there. They've dug a bullet out of me three times. I don't want you left high and dry if I die. I don't think Gran would do that to you anyway."

"I like your grandmother." Emma smiled. "She's super sweet, and I love her cooking. Maybe she'll teach me how to cook."

"If you ask, she will." James hugged her again, kissing the top of her head.

As they began to walk, hand in hand, he heard the familiar pop of a shot, then another. Knowing in the pit of his stomach that she'd been shot without seeing the blood, he wrapped his arm around her body, pulling her to him as one more shot rang out. Feeling the familiar burning sensation rip through his shoulder, he dropped them to the ground in an instant. With cover from a planter box, he could hear people screaming on the streets before everything was nothing more than a muffled sound in the background.

"Emma." He looked down at her in his arms.

"What is happening?" With a shaky voice, she barely spoke above a whisper. "Something hit my chest. It burns."

James pulled open her jacket and could see the blood stain spreading on her upper left side. Turning her over, he checked her back to see if it went through. Evidently, the bullet went straight through, as there was another blood stain forming on her upper back.

"Is it difficult to breathe?"

"No, it just burns really bad." Her eyes pleaded for him to save her.

When she turned her head slightly, he could see where another bullet grazed the lower part of her cheek. That was a little too close for his comfort zone.

Then the sirens sounded. He wasn't moving them until the police were here. With Emma wrapped up in one arm, he pulled out his phone and called Jack.

"James," Jack said, instantly knowing something was wrong.

"We were shot. I'm up at Carina's, and someone shot Emma and me. Call Colin and Matthew so they are aware that maybe we pissed somebody off."

"On it," Jack stated. "Harper and I will head back within the hour. We're in Miami. I'll call Wes and have him round up a couple of your men. Be careful."

"Thanks," James said, hanging up as the police rushed over to them.

"James!" It was one of the local policemen that he knew. "I have an ambulance dispatched."

James nodded and stayed down. The pain in his shoulder was intense as he watched the officer apply pressure to Emma's wound.

The police played the scene just as James wanted. Once they were safely in the hospital, James wouldn't let anybody touch him until they took care of Emma. He stayed in the room with her as they cleaned the bullet wound and stitched her up. It was located just a couple inches to the left of her spine and down from her neck. It missed everything vital. He watched the doctor push a little sedation just before they cleaned it out. The wound was nearly in the same place as Tess's a couple months before.

"She is good. You're next." The doctor was firm.

"A local only. I don't want to be sedated." James was insistent before he would let the doctor touch him.

The doctor pulled the bullet from his shoulder and stitched him up. James needed to have a clear head. While the doctor worked on him, a nurse cleaned up Emma's cheek where the bullet grazed, but it didn't require any stitches, just a couple butterfly bandages. James lay there for a few minutes after the doctor finished, wondering who it could possibly have been. Who would have the shrewdness to try to kill him in his safe zone? He pulled out his phone and called Jack again.

"How are you?" Jack asked.

"Fine." James shook his head, clearly irritated. "What did we miss?"

"I don't know. Harper and I are on the plane. Colin and Tess are headed toward you now. Are you at Gran's?" Jack wondered.

"No, hospital still. I'll call Colin and ask him to swing by and pick us up. That will give Jesse a little bit of time to sleep."

"We'll figure it out," Jack told him. "We always do."

"Okay. I'll see you later tonight." James sighed, ending the conversation. Then he called Colin.

"Hey, man," Colin said, surprised to hear from him so soon. "How are the two of you?"

"Crappy. When you land, will you swing by the hospital and pick us up?" James asked.

"Yep, we are about an hour out still, but that will be our first stop. Hang in there," Colin stated.

"Thanks. I hope you have guns." James grinned.

Colin laughed. "Tess and I, we travel for a war. We protect our own."

"Good," James said, ending the call. As he sat up, another doctor came in. This one he knew from years of living there.

"James." Dr. Jenny Rue gave him a warm smile as she touched his arm softly. "I heard you were brought in with your wife?"

Jenny had gone to high school with him. After, like most graduates, they took off for college in different directions. Jenny was the first girl he ever kissed.

"It's been quite a while since I've seen you." Jenny cupped his cheek as she looked in his eyes.

"I know," he replied, taking her hand from his face, giving it a comforting squeeze. "I've been working quite a bit."

"Still doing the work you can't talk about?" she asked as she looked over at Jesse laying on the bed sleeping.

"Yes, ma'am."

"She's a beautiful woman," Jenny stated, looking back at James.

James simply nodded, wanting this uncomfortable moment to end.

"How long have you been married?" Jenny asked, walking back to him.

"Just a year," he lied. "How about you? Have you found a Mr. Jenny Rue yet?"

Jenny grinned, shaking her head. "I work twelve-hour shifts here, five sometimes six days a week. That doesn't leave much time for a personal life. I liked what we had. It was perfect. You'd come into town for a few weeks, the sex was great, then we'd go do our thing. No expectations. It's hard to find a man who's good with that nowadays."

"And that is why I don't have a job like yours." James leaned against the bed. "I like doing a job and not working for a month or two or three. It works for me having Carina here."

"You and your cousins are good to Carina." She smiled. "She's very lucky to have all of you boys take care of her like you do. I see her in the clinic every six months. She's a healthy woman. She never said anything about you being married."

"You know how I don't like my personal life being public information," he reminded her.

"I know. I didn't realize I got tossed into that category." Jenny smiled as she stood upright. "I need to get back to my patients. It was good seeing you—and congratulations."

"Thank you, Jen." James kissed her cheek and gave her a hug before she walked out of the room. James sighed deeply after Jenny left the room. Rolling his eyes, he went over to Emma's bedside. Running his hand softly down her arm to her hand, he was surprised when she took his hand in hers.

"How long have I been out?" she asked when she opened her eyes. "I didn't realize we'd been married for a year. Please tell me it was a great year."

"The best." He smiled as he leaned over, kissing her softly. "Sorry you had to hear all of that. Jen was my first girlfriend in high school. When it was time to go off to college, we broke up. Then it was casual sex off and on for years after. No big deal."

"Am I no big deal?" Emma began to doubt their relationship for no good reason.

"You, Emma, are the biggest deal of my life. You're not casual sex; you are the only woman that I want to make love to for the rest of my life. I love you." James cupped her cheeks gently and kissed her softly.

Emma grinned; she loved hearing those words from him. The thought that a man loved her this way was still perplexing, but it felt good. "I love you too."

"You better." He kissed her forehead. "Scoot over. We're going to be here for another hour or so. Colin and Tess are on their way to pick us up."

"What?" She wasn't sure if she heard him correctly.

"They're flying up, and on their way to Gran's, they're picking us up from here." He had a weird feeling about the way she asked why. "We have to figure out who the shooter was—if it was from the job we just finished or something else, or just completely random. But I don't think it was random. A shooter doesn't aim three times at the same subject unless that's the target."

"Oh, okay." Emma suddenly felt very nervous. She didn't want to see Colin McGowan, much less his wife.

# Chapter 11

C olin and Tess stood at the end of the hospital bed, hand in hand, looking at James and Emma sleeping.

"I almost hate to wake them," Tess said softly.

Colin nodded in agreement. "I know, but they don't look comfortable. You know James will want his own bed."

"True. Emma is beautiful. What in the hell was she doing working in a bar? She could be one of those exotic models."

"She is pretty." Colin turned to his wife, caressing her cheek. "But I am kind of partial to my wife."

Tess leaned up, kissing him. "I do love you."

"Good thing since I feel the same way." Colin kissed her.

"My God, listening to you two almost makes me want to be drugged." James sat up, looking at them. "Thank you for coming."

"Of course," Tess said as Colin smiled. "It's the least we could do."

"I told them that my personal physician was coming." James smiled, standing up. "Which one of you wants that part?"

"Colin, you should take that. You know more medical jargon than I." Tess shrugged. "I'll play your assistant."

"Mmm." He gave her the eye. "My sexy assistant."

"Seriously?" James looked at them. "Have you been married for like two days?"

Both laughed a little as Colin's arm wrapped around her shoulder and he kissed her temple.

"Get us out of here, please?" James asked Colin.

"It's already done," Colin stated. "Papers are signed, bill is paid, a nice donation has been made to the hospital fund, courtesy of McGowan

Industries. You two are free. We do have a script for pain meds, but we have some of Harper's ...stuff."

"Here." Tess handed him one of Colin's button-up shirts. "It's not exactly warm outside."

"How are you doing, little mama?" James asked her as he put the shirt on.

"Growing bigger every day." She smiled, placing her hand on her stomach. "Come here."

James walked over, and she took his hand, placing it on her stomach. It amazed him that he could feel the distinct roundness of her stomach already, but she was in the second trimester now.

"I'm certain Colin gave you a lecture already on being safe?"

"I don't need a lecture on how to keep my children safe," Tess reminded him.

"I still gave her a lecture." Colin laughed, then went completely straight faced. "She is to stay in the house with Carina and Emma, never in the line of fire. She can help with research, and that is it. She can carry her 9 mm but better hope to hell she's not in a position to use it. And she is not allowed to shoot any of the family members without consulting me first."

"Perfect." James kissed her on top of the head. "Let's go."

Colin scooped up Emma, and they walked out of the hospital.

They arrived at Carina's home just before dark. Colin carried Emma, taking her straight upstairs. Tess grabbed her backpack and walked in behind James.

Colin laid Emma down on James's bed. He slipped off her shoes and tucked a blanket around her. When he pulled it to her shoulders, his hand softly caressed her cheek as she opened her eyes.

"Don't let him find out." Emma grabbed his arm tightly.

Colin simply grinned.

"I've never regretted something so much in my life as I regret that weekend with you." Tears began to fill her eyes.

"You only regret it because James came along," he stated with full confidence. "Otherwise, you would want more, and we both know it."

"No," she said with a timid voice.

"Deny all you want." Colin smiled. "Your facial expression speaks louder than the words from your mouth." Leaning close again, he brought his face within inches of her, and she put her fingers over his mouth. Kissing her fingers softly, she pulled back but only after a few moments had passed.

"Don't, please," Emma begged him one last time.

"Sweet Emma. You couldn't deny me even with your morals and some integrity, but now you've seen my beautiful wife. I'd be crazy to mess that up and risk losing her. Besides, I made a promise, and I don't break my promises." Colin caressed her head gently. When he heard James coming up the stairs, he pulled away. "I told you bullets fly around him."

"Yes, you did." She nodded as James walked in.

"Need anything before I leave?" he asked her as James sat down, taking off his shoes.

"No, thank you."

Colin smiled, giving her hand a squeeze, and went over to James. "What can I get you?"

"Nothing," James responded. "Actually, ibuprofen. It's in the drawer in the bathroom. My head is pounding."

Colin walked into the bathroom and was surprised by the sheer size. The setup was perfect with a walk-in shower and a huge soaking tub. His first thought was how much Tess would like that. Dual sinks were in the center with beautiful granite throughout the room. After pulling open a couple of drawers, he finally found the ibuprofen. "How many?" he called out to James.

"Five," he answered.

Colin came back, handing him five pills and a glass of water. James popped them into his mouth, took a swig of water, and handed the glass back.

"Thank you," James said, standing back up.

"You're welcome," Colin replied. "Do you have your cell?"

James nodded.

"Call me if you need anything else," Colin told him. "Tess will be up in a bit with some of Harper's stuff."

"Okay." James nodded again and shook his hand before Colin left the room.

Downstairs, Colin found his wife and Carina chatting away.

"It's been years, Tess." Carina stood with her hands cupping Tess's face. "And you are glowing. How far along?"

"Twenty weeks and five days," Colin answered for her, picking up their bags from the foyer. "You are supposed to be on bed rest for another two days. Don't push it."

"I know." She nodded at Colin as he took the bags up the stairs, then hugged Carina again. "I've missed you so much."

"I've missed you too." Carina hugged her one more time. "Come on. Make yourself at home."

Inside, Tess stopped for a moment, soaking in the beauty of this home. She loved coming here with Jack back in the day. When Colin came up behind her a few minutes later, his arms wrapped around her waist, resting his hands on her stomach. He kissed her neck softly and looked out the windows, as she did, at the magnificent view.

Tess turned in his arms, putting her hands on his shoulders. "Kiss me."

Colin did as she asked, then rested his forehead on hers. "I love you. Be extra cautious, please, and get off your feet."

Tess's hands reached up to his face, cupping it, and she kissed him deeply. "I love you too, and I will."

Colin hugged her tightly. "I told James you'd be up with Harper's stuff in a bit."

"Okay."

Going upstairs, Tess pulled out the jar with some greenish-looking paste that Harper had used a couple of weeks ago. She walked down the long hall to James's room, and with a soft knock, she walked in.

"Hey." James glanced in her direction as he was changing.

"I can come back," she said, as he was down to his underwear.

James shook his head. "Please, you've seen me naked. I don't care."

"True, and you look really good naked."

"What is it with you and ex-girlfriends today?" Emma asked him as she tried to get in a more comfortable position.

James looked over his shoulder and smiled at Emma, then Tess. He pulled on his lounge pants and walked over to her, shirtless. "Just one of those day, I guess." Taking Emma's hand, he kissed it softly. "Emma, this is Tess. Tess, this is Emma."

"Well, these aren't the best circumstances to be meeting you." Tess eyed James, then gave that sassy smile to Emma. "Hello, Emma. Just to set the record straight, I'm not an ex-girlfriend. We are very good friends. I love him dearly. Do not hurt him."

"Okay, Mama T." James directed her attention back to him. "I think your mother instincts are taking over. Be nice."

"Are you always this mean to people you just meet?" Emma propped herself up on her elbow, knowing they weren't going to be best friends.

"Oh good God." James rolled his eyes. Picking up his phone, he buzzed Colin as Emma and Tess exchanged un-pleasantries. In less than twenty seconds, Colin was in his room.

"Tess, come on." He put his hands on her shoulders, speaking softly as he guided her out of the bedroom. "Stop tormenting a girl you've never met before. They were just shot. Compassion."

"Fuck compassion." Tess scrunched her forehead. "I don't think I like her."

"Ah, my sweet, sweet wife. You just don't like women—period." Colin kissed her forehead, took her hand, and walked back down the stairs.

"That was fun," Emma said sarcastically after Colin and Tess left the bedroom.

"You have nothing to fear from Tess." James put his arm around her as she rested her head on his shoulder. "Tess is … I don't know … just Tess."

"Why is she like that?"

"She went through a lot in her younger years. That, along with her profession, has shaped her into the person she is today," James explained.

"What kind of things?"

"Her stepfather abused her and her twin. It was a bad household." James was vague, knowing Tess didn't like anyone knowing about her past.

"What did her mother say?" Emma was rather shocked.

"Her mom didn't care. She was spun on drugs and alcohol, very self-absorbed. Once they were killed, Jonathan McGowan, Colin's father, took the twins and Harper in and finished raising them with Gina. Tess didn't meet Colin until her last year of college. After she graduated, she started working the jobs with Jack and Colin. Jack trained her to fight, shoot, and kill, and she's very good at it. Morgan's reputation is …" James took a moment, as he had never admitted this before. "Her reputation is close to mine."

"How do they even get jobs? It's not like it's posted in the 'help wanted' section of the paper."

James laughed a little. "No. The jobs Jack did with Tess and Colin were ones that I gave him. I'd get some extra work and subcontract to Jack."

"Oh," she said, not getting the answer she was looking for.

"I can't tell you who hires me," he began, knowing this was the answer she was wanting. "And it's not because I don't want to; it's just a matter of safety for you. I don't tell anyone who my job source is. I've never shared it, and I probably never will."

"Okay. I understand." Emma yawned.

"That's the story of Tess." James kissed her head.

"And what's the story with her and you?"

"Damn." He chuckled a little to himself. "You really want to hear about another woman today? That will be two."

"Yep," she answered.

"Tess is one of my best friends." He began with his voice low. "There was a time when she and I were sleeping together. But that part of our relationship never evolved, couldn't evolve. Tess has skills that Jack taught her that work on men, damn near 100 percent of the time. If Tess wants something or someone, she will get it, and you can't stop her. It doesn't matter if you're single or married. If she wants you, she's going to have you. And, admittedly, she got me. And if she wants you dead, you will be dead."

"Why couldn't it evolve?"

James sighed, thinking back. "Tess and Colin have this thing, and they will never be with anyone else. They put each other through hell, but at the end of the day, they will defend each other until their dying breath. Tess knew Colin had cheated on her, not too long ago, before he came clean about it. As soon as she finds out who it was, she will kill her, no doubt in my mind. On the other side, Colin knows Tess has had a few indiscretions herself. But here they are, together. They're meant for each other."

Emma didn't reply as guilt traveled through her body.

"You have nothing to worry about with her and me." He noted that Emma was too quiet about this. "Tess and I are like family now. I would never sleep with her again, as we are in a place beyond that desire, that need with each other. I do love and care about her. But, Em, I'm in love with you."

Emma looked up, meeting his eyes with hers. "I'm in love with you too," she said softly.

# Chapter 12

Matthew walked into his father's house with Savannah in his arms and Dominic and Connor in tow. They had just flown back from Chicago and missed Colin and Tess by mere hours, but he completely understood why they had to go. Being a father was something that came naturally, and he loved it. There wasn't a moment's hesitation when Tess asked if he would mind watching Savannah and Connor for a few more days while they helped James.

"Daddy." Savannah had her head resting on Matthew's shoulder as she played with the button on his collar. "I'm hungry."

Matthew looked over at Dominic and smiled, as that was the first time she called him daddy. "Let's go see what Grandma has cooking," he said as he gently rubbed her back.

"I think they're going to fall asleep early tonight," Dominic noted as they walked into the kitchen.

"That'll give me some time to review some figures for the merge." Matthew sighed as he put Savannah down.

Connor had his arms hooked tightly around Dominic's neck; he wasn't letting go.

"Hey, buddy." Dominic tried to loosen his grip. "Don't you want to get down and play and stretch your legs?"

"No." He just held on tighter. "I miss Mommy. When is Mommy coming home?"

Dominic looked over at Matthew, shaking his head. "Couple days, and you can see her, or I will take you to her. Okay?" His face was within inches of his as the little boy had tears falling. "Don't cry. I'm here with you. I won't leave you."

Connor nodded and rested his head on Dominic's shoulder.

Savannah pulled on Matthew's shirt shyly, and he knelt to her level. "What, sweetheart?"

"Why is Connor crying?" she asked with a soft voice.

"He misses Mommy," he told her.

"I miss Mommy too," she said, touching Matthew's face. "Will Connor play with me?"

"Let's ask." Matthew glanced up at Dominic with a grin. "Connor, would you like to go play with Savannah?"

Dominic turned so Matthew could see the little boy's face. When he nodded, he put him down, and the two kids went into the family room. Gina had a small trunk that she had filled with toys for them weeks ago.

"How's parenthood working out for you two?" Gina asked, coming around the counter.

Dominic sighed, shaking his head. "Connor needs Tess around … bad. Taryn was gone so much the last few months. I had him all the time, took him everywhere with me. Even did his doctor appointments."

"I know this is a difficult transition for you." Gina rested her hand on Dominic's forearm. "If you ever need to just talk, I'm here for you."

Dominic nodded as she hugged him. "Thank you, Gina."

"Let's get Tess online," Gina suggested. "Do a little FaceTime for the kids."

Matthew took the tablet from the kitchen table and buzzed Tess. It only took a few seconds, and she appeared on the screen.

"Hi," she said with a big smile. "How are the kids?"

"Tess." Matthew walked down the hallway for a little privacy. "Connor is having a hard time without his mother. He needs you. I know you're not her, but you need be now. I also know you're still trying to heal, but he's just a two-year-old, and you know I'm out of my league with this."

Tess smiled. "It's okay. I understand. I will fly back tonight if you think I should."

"No, although I would love to have you in my bed again." Matthew gave her a mischievous grin, knowing that would remind her of the night Colin took off after Taryn was killed.

"That had been coming for a while." Tess nodded.

"I agree," Matthew replied as a memory flashed of his hand caressing her hip. "James and Emma were shot. Just figure it out quickly."

"Give me a couple days, and if it's going to take longer, we'll move the party back down to Savannah. Or if it's safe, maybe we can bring the kids here." She ran her hand through her hair. "Why don't I chat with them?"

"Of course. Actually, that's why I called." He nodded and walked back to the family room. Kneeling before the two children, he turned the tablet so Tess faced them. "Hey, it's Mommy."

The children beamed seeing her, and both began talking at the same time. Matthew laughed at how excited they were to chat with her. It was amazing how Tess could make two children so happy by just talking to them. She chatted with them for over twenty minutes before Savannah wanted to go back to playing. Connor wanted to keep talking. Tess gave him one-on-one conversation until he decided he was done and wanted to go play again. Matthew handed the tablet over to Dominic afterward to talk with Tess.

"Thank you," he told her. "He's been wanting you all day. Taryn was gone too much, and I know he's feeling some sense of abandonment. I just don't feel like I'm enough for him."

"He's doing fine," Tess assured him. "And you're doing fine with him. I told Matthew to just give me a couple more days to help James, and then I will either come back or we can bring the kids here. Just remember that he's only two, and they are very resilient. He won't remember any of this stuff that he's going through right now. But you are there for him, and you are his solid, consistent parent that he's known all his little life. I promise things will calm down, and Colin and I will get the kids into a nice, normal routine when we get back to Portland. Savannah had it, and we'll incorporate Connor into the same routine. I promise it will get better."

"You're a good mother," he told her with a smile.

"I try my best," she replied. "I know I've been lacking since I got out of the hospital, but I just haven't felt great."

"Please, Tess, you don't have to explain to me." He shook his head. "You were shot in the head. I think you get a pass for a few weeks."

"I'm going to go lay down before Colin finds me still up." She smiled. "Give them hugs for me."

"Will do." He grinned.

"Love you, and we'll see you soon."

Dominic was speechless as she disconnected the call.

# Chapter 13

Tess walked into the kitchen and took a seat beside Colin as Carina was cooking on the other side. Looking at Colin, she grinned as he kissed her forehead. "I just talked with the kids. We need to get them home and back into a normal routine."

"I know," he agreed. "Let's deal with this. Then we'll head home. You didn't have any problems flying up here, so you should be able to do the flight home."

"That's what I was thinking."

"How's it going taking care of your sister's child?" Carina inquired.

"It's fine. Connor is a good little boy. Very sweet. I'm thinking it's been Dominic's influence, not Taryn's."

"Maybe it's part of his DNA design." Colin eyed Tess.

"Maybe." Tess shrugged, knowing he didn't like Dominic having any input in Connor's life. "But I'm still leaning toward Dominic."

Colin shook his head, bringing her hand to his lips for a soft kiss.

"Well, I'm certain the two of you will be wonderful parents to him." Carina caught the slight irritation in Colin's voice with Tess.

"Yes, we will." Tess grinned, resting her head on his shoulder.

"Do you need to go lie down?"

"I think so," she agreed. "I'm just going to go lay on the couch for now. I love that room."

Colin kissed her on the head and watched her walk off to the living room.

"She's been through a lot," Carina stated, noticing the concern on Colin's face.

"I worry about her. She's tired all the time. I don't remember it being like this when she was pregnant with Savannah. I'm just hoping it's all from the pregnancy and not the head injury."

Carina grinned, reaching over she covered his hand with hers. "She's carrying twin boys. That alone would be exhausting, and they aren't even born. Let her rest tonight, and I will give her something that will help with the exhaustion tomorrow."

"How do you know they're boys?" he queried with a smile fixed on his lips.

"Trust me. I know."

Colin stayed with Carina in the kitchen as she baked a few things. Admittedly, it had been years since he'd visited. The home was beautiful, he always thought, and he had no idea that James owned it until recently. But it made sense, as James was rather humble looking on the outside, but preferred the finer things on the inside. Colin preferred all the finer things and had no problem letting people know.

When Carina looked over at the clock on the wall and it was nine thirty, she smiled at Colin.

"What?" he asked, looking up from the computer.

"Harrison should be arriving at any moment." She grinned. "Do you two still not like each other?"

Colin closed his eyes, shaking his head. "Seriously? He's coming?"

"It's the second weekend of the month," she said.

"Honestly, I haven't spoken to him in years."

The distinct sound of keys rustling around by the front door alerted them that Harrison was there.

Putting his bag down so he could hang his coat in the hall closet, Harrison glanced in the living room at the body lying on the couch. "Oh my goodness." He couldn't believe his eyes when he realized it was Tess. Running his hand softly over her head, she stirred.

Tess's eyes blinked open, and when they focused, a big smiled crossed her lips. "Harrison." She sat up and hugged him tightly. "My favorite attorney."

"Tess, my favorite little assassin." He helped her upright. "You're pregnant and more beautiful than ever."

Tess smiled. "Yep."

"Crazy," he stated. "I saw Matthew couple days ago with your daughter. She's adorable. I was very surprised when I walked into his office and saw her with him."

"She's a good little girl."

"He said you got married." His hand held hers as he looked at the ring on her finger.

"I did—Colin." She smiled.

"I could tell by the size of the ring. Besides, it's about damn time," he stated. "Not sure what the hell he was waiting for all these years. You are a rare woman, and that son of a bitch is so lucky to have you."

"Be nice, Harrison." She ran her hand over his cheek. "I love him very much."

"I'll be nice for you." He kissed her forehead. "Where have you been all these years? James wouldn't tell me, and Jack didn't know."

"Portland. It was good for Colin and me to be displaced from the family and Georgia."

"Matthew told me a little bit of what happened. I'm very happy that you're alive and well. How's that hole in your noggin?"

"It's fine."

"And you're having twins?"

"Matthew didn't hold anything back." Tess grinned as he hugged her again.

"Matthew and I go way back. How long are you here for?"

Tess furrowed her brow, unsure of the information Harrison had, if any. "We came to help James and Jess."

"Why and who's Jess?"

"Jess is his girlfriend, and they were shot in town today. They're upstairs sleeping. After everything that just happened with me, we're hoping to find the connection or something to make sure it doesn't happen again. You know how our work goes."

"Yes, I'm well versed in the work you guys do."

"I know you don't like it, Harrison, but this is the career choice that was made. James has eliminated a lot of bad people and saved so many. You can't fault him."

Harrison simply looked at her, shaking his head. "I never wanted it brought here. I don't want anything to happen to Carina or my family. We're very limited, as you know."

Tess smiled. "Why aren't you expanding it?"

With a soft chuckle, he shook his head. "I'm … possibly … working on it. I just have to get out of my own head."

"I know you've always been worried about the financial aspect of it. So, here's my one bit of advice that you didn't ask for. Take half of what you have and move it offshore. That way you always have something to fall back on in case it goes bad."

"You're going to tell me you and Colin have done this with your own money?"

"Colin and I have an understanding. All the money I made before is invested, as is his, and we live off his current income. We'll never divorce, so the conversation is irrelevant."

"How do you know you'll never divorce?" Harrison was curious because this was his fear.

"Because we put each other through hell, but at the end of the day, I can't imagine being with anyone else." Her mind quickly thought of Matthew.

"I've missed you." Harrison gave her a long hug before they both stood.

"I've missed you too." Tess gave him a soft kiss on his cheek, then took his hand as they walked into the kitchen.

Harrison was the epitome of an attorney. Clean shaven, hair cut perfectly short, his suits were top of the line, and even his skin was as smooth as his attitude. To Tess, Jack looked just like his brother when he cleaned up and wore a suit, but it wasn't often that Jack put on a suit and tie. Both brothers had the same dark caramel skin tone as Carina. Tess imagined it came from their mother, whom she'd never met before she passed away. With their mother being Hispanic and their father of African American decent, Tess always admired their perfect skin tone.

In the kitchen, Tess walked over to Colin as Harrison gave his grandmother a kiss on the cheek and a hug. Then he turned to Colin. With a smartass grin, Harrison gave him a nod.

"Colin McGowan." Harrison cocked his head sideways. "It's been a long time."

"Never long enough though." Colin stood and shook Harrison's hand.

"That is certainly the truth." Harrison chuckled a little.

"At some point, you two need to draw a truce," Carina said. "The only reason you don't like each other is because you are both so much alike."

"Gran." Harrison shook his head. "I think you're becoming delusional."

Carina snickered as Harrison joked with her. "I'm right, and you know it."

Colin didn't say anything, as it wasn't worth getting into a fight with Harrison. With Harrison being an attorney, he loved to debate issues, and Colin never liked to be wrong.

"How are you feeling?" he asked Tess, running his hand over her cheek.

"Okay." She rested her head in the nape of his neck.

"We should put you to bed. You still have another day of bed rest."

"That's such a waste of my time." She sighed but knew he was right.

"I'm still surprised by what happened," Harrison said, popping a strawberry in his mouth.

"The bullet actually went through Jack's shoulder first. Did he even tell you?" Colin glanced at him.

"No, and I talked to him a week ago." Harrison shook his head, irritated with his brother. "Why doesn't he ever tell me things like that?" Glancing at Carina, she understood.

"I didn't know either," Carina remarked. "Just wait until I see that grandson of mine."

Colin's phone vibrated on the counter beside the laptop. With Tess still snuggled up to him, he picked it up with his free hand. "Speaking of that grandson, Jackson," he said, recognizing the number.

"How's everything there?" Jack asked, knowing it should be okay for the moment.

"Quiet," Colin answered. "House alarm is on. Everything is locked up tight. James has Harper's miracle goop on him, so he should be great tomorrow. Your brother is here."

"Harrison?" Jack thought for a moment. "Damn, I forgot it's the second weekend of the month."

"Yep." Colin sounded thrilled.

"You must be loving this." Jack smiled.

"About as much as I love being shot at." Colin grinned. "I think you're in a bit of trouble with him and Carina."

"Why?"

"Something about being shot and not telling them."

"Great—another fight today. I had my first fight with Harper."

Colin chuckled a bit. "And that surprises you? She is my sister after all."

"I didn't realize how damn stubborn she was."

Colin simply laughed. "Do I need to pick you up at the airport?"

"No, I have a vehicle waiting. I have four of James's men and Harper." Jack took Harper's hand in his. "We should roll in within the hour."

"See you in a bit." Colin ended the call and looked at Harrison. "Your brother sends his love."

Harrison simply grinned.

"I'm going to go put her to bed," Colin announced, standing up. "Come on, honey."

Harrison watched them walk out of the kitchen, then turned to his grandmother, shaking his head.

"I honestly never thought he would figure that one out."

"It's easier standing on the outside looking in on a relationship." Carina patted him on the shoulder. "Speaking of relationships, how's Elizabeth? And why didn't you bring her?"

Harrison grinned. "Elizabeth is well. She sends her love to you."

"When are you going to marry that girl?" Carina asked.

"Gran, we aren't …" Harrison was stumbling over his words, as this sort of talk made him nervous.

"Harrison Carter Keene." Carina gave him a stern look. "It's not a we; it's a you. Stop being afraid of the commitment of marriage. Elizabeth is a good woman. And you are a good man. You're successful and have a solid family base with your brother, James, and me."

"I'm tainted by all the divorces that have come through my firm," he admitted to his grandmother.

"I know you are." She rested a hand on his shoulder.

"In my head, marriage is being in love with someone so much you can't imagine life without them. I don't want to have a prenup. That's setting yourself up for failure before you even say, 'I do.' But I want to protect myself financially." Harrison shrugged. It was only with his grandmother that he could be completely honest.

"Harrison, forget about the money. Don't you think the benefit outweighs the risk? It's not like both of you are twenty years old and getting married because you need to. You're a smart man. Stop overthinking this. Do you love her?"

"Yes." He nodded.

"Then make sure you don't lose her." Carina gave his hand a squeeze. "She won't wait forever."

Harrison nodded, knowing Carina was right and he needed to deal with this fear that he had.

"You should go check on James for me," Carina said as she wiped down a counter.

"Tess told me what happened. Are you in danger here?"

"I don't know," she answered. "Jack will be here soon, and he's bringing some of his men to make sure we're fine."

Harrison hugged her tightly. "I will hurt him badly if something happens to you because of whatever he's involved in."

"Harrison." Carina stood back, eyed him, and reminded him of one thing. "Compassion."

Harrison walked upstairs after checking the alarm even though Colin had done it before. At the top of the stairs, he looked to the right. James's room was at the end. Seeing the door halfway open, he sighed and walked into the room. A light was on in the far corner, enabling him to see his cousin and the woman sleeping beside him.

Rarely did he see James sleeping, much less with a woman. He was always on the move. His life took him all over the world, into many dangerous situations. Harrison worried about him but never let him know. Now this fight was brought here, the place he went to get away from everything. He trusted his brother and his cousin. They each excelled in their professions, just as he did. But he never wanted their work to be brought here. Making sure the doors were locked in the sitting room, he started out but then stopped when James put his hand out.

"Hey," Harrison said softly. "How are you doing?"

"Okay," James mumbled.

"I was just making sure the doors were locked in here. I will let you sleep. Do you need anything before I go?" Harrison asked.

"More ibuprofen please," James said as he sat up. "It's in the drawer in the bathroom."

"Okay." Harrison got him five and a glass of water. "Here you go."

James took them all at once and then drank all the water, just like before.

"Has Emma woken at all?" James asked.

"Not that I know of." Harrison shook his head.

"Jack here yet?" James looked around for the time, then took his phone off the nightstand.

"Colin said he would be here at midnight or something. He seems to be all over it. You should just sleep."

"Harrison, is that concern in your voice?"

"Just a bit." He smiled. "Don't get used to it."

James stood up slowly. He wanted to stretch but didn't dare. "I'm starving. Did Gran make anything for dinner?"

"Yes, of course," Harrison stated. "She left it in the fridge for whoever gets to it first."

"Nice." James took a button-down shirt from the closet and put it on but didn't button it. He walked over to Emma's side of the bed. She was still on her stomach, sleeping soundly. He kissed her on the head, pulled the covers up a little, and headed to the kitchen with Harrison.

"Tess okay? She wasn't supposed to fly yet," James said as he sat at the counter. Harrison pulled the food out and began to reheat it.

"I guess." Harrison shot a quick glance over at James. "I can't believe what she's been through, and she's still alive. She's my favorite woman in this world, and the fact that her sister called a mark on her blows my mind. When did you finally meet her?"

"Four years ago, here." James smiled, remembering. "She was here with Jack."

Harrison had a confused look.

"Yes, Jack was with her for a while." James nodded. "It didn't end well. He left her, saying she belonged with Colin, blah, blah, and she lost the baby, and it was just all around not a good time back then."

"She miscarried Jack's baby?" Harrison brought a plate of food over to him.

"It seems that way."

"Jack never said anything." Harrison poured himself a glass of wine. "Was he okay?"

"When he left, he went straight into the overseas mission he did with Gina and Harper." James shrugged. "After some of the things that just went down, I don't think he took it well."

"I should've known." He shook his head, irritated with himself.

"Harrison, I only knew because I was here with her when it happened." He sighed. "Jack doesn't talk about it. He never talks about things like that."

"So now what's he doing?"

James smiled. "He's still working for MGI, running security for the company and Jonathan's home in Savannah. And he's with Harper. He'll marry her."

"I've actually never met the other sister." Harrison sipped his wine.

"Harper is very book smart, very business savvy, very quiet, and very innocent." Guiltily, he grinned. "Let me put it this way: she waited for Jack."

"Seriously?" Harrison grinned. "Damn, so she loves him then?"

"Yes. Those two will get married." James took another bite. "The only unfortunate thing that's happened is she didn't know about Jack and Tess until Taryn blurted it out the last night, and Harper hasn't talked to Tess since then."

"That's immature." Harrison shook his head.

James nodded. "By the time Tess got out of the hospital, Jack and Harper had left town. It weighs heavily on Tess. I'm hoping Jack was able to get Harper to stop being a bitch to Tess. She doesn't need that now."

"Great female drama." He shook his head. "Speaking of females, who's Jesse or Emma? You called her that. What's up with the name thing?"

James put down his fork and smiled, looking at him. "Emma is her real name. She's been in witness relocation most of her life. She is ... mine. The first time I saw her, I knew. I couldn't get back to her until last week, and we've been together since, and I'm keeping her."

"That sounds like you found a stray puppy." Harrison cocked his head.

"She's intoxicatingly beautiful. Wait until you see her. She's had a hard life, Harrison. She testified against Marcos Markenna for killing her father and mother."

"Is that Dominic Markenna's father?" he asked.

"How'd you know that?" James was curious.

"I met him with Matthew earlier this week," he stated. "Matt's merging his company with his father's and moving to Portland. He wants me to take care of the legal end and keep my firm on retainer for his division."

James nodded, knowing Matthew would do something to be in his child's life daily.

"You know what's given him the business reputation that he has?"

Harrison asked, and James shook his head. "He's always been fair. And given his position and knowledge in his industry, that's rare. I admire him for that. Tess should have married him."

James laughed, shaking his head. "Colin's not that bad. He's grown on me over the years. He and Tess have this … unbreakable bond between them. It's interesting, to say the least. Tess was well within her right to leave him when she found out he was sleeping with her twin and had his son, but she didn't. They love each other like nothing I've ever seen."

Colin walked into the kitchen just as James finished his sentence and grinned. "James, you're giving away our secrets."

"I know." James raised his eyebrows.

"How come she stayed with you after finding out you have a kid with her sister?" Harrison asked, astonished.

Colin shook his head, still amazed. "So, Harrison, now that you know what you know, does your firm have a division that could take care of the legal stuff involving my son and the custody?"

"I do, but you have an army of attorneys. Use one of them."

"They're all corporate." Colin shook his head. "They're not well versed in family law. I want the best dealing with this legal custody issue with my son."

"What do you think the issue will be?" Harrison was curious.

"My name is not on his birth certificate. In her trust, she named Dominic as his guardian. Can you believe she named a fucking Markenna as guardian for my child?"

"I see your dislike for the Markennas is on my level." James grinned with a quick raise of his brows.

"Can't stand them."

"You seem to tolerate Dominic well."

"Only because of my brother. I have an excellent game face." Colin chuckled a little.

"I'll have Elizabeth get in touch with you." Harrison pulled out his phone to text her as he was talking. "She's head of the family law division. You tell her what you want, and she will make it happen."

"Thanks, Harrison."

"I got a question for you." James cocked his head at Colin. "If you have such a dislike for Dominic, why did you let Tess get so close?"

Colin gave a little laugh. "He was a job. I was still seeing Taryn when that job was taking place. Tess did what she needed to achieve her objective. Besides, she was with Jack more than me back then."

"How were you able to share her? I could never do that with Elizabeth. I do not understand the three of you."

Colin grinned, knowing it was very uncommon to share a woman like he and Jack did. "I did it for her. You know what she came from and how long it took for her to let herself be with me. I could tell she wanted to explore that sexual realm with others. There's no one I would trust with her more than Jack. I knew he wouldn't hurt her in any way. Besides that, there was this chemistry brewing between them back then that needed to be unleashed."

"I know you had an underlying motive." James raised a brow.

Colin laughed with a slight nod. "Less guilt for seeing Taryn. Tess knows all of this. I've told her. We've talked. What none of you realize it that no matter how dysfunctional Tess and I seem to all of you, she gets me, and I get her. At the end of the day, she's the one I want in my bed every night, she's the one I want raising our children, she's the one I will love until I stop breathing."

"You cheated on her," James stated.

"And she's cheated on me. Besides, it's just sex, nothing more. Tess is love, nothing less."

"James," Emma's soft voice sounded from the kitchen entry.

"Emma." He smiled and waved her over. "Come meet my cousin."

Colin eyed Emma as she glanced his direction. He could tell that she'd heard what he said, but he didn't care. When it came to mind control and the manipulation of others, Colin knew he was the master. Emma didn't have a chance against him. Even if she told James, it wouldn't matter; his wife would never leave him, and James would find a way to make peace because he loved Tess too much to be completely out of her life. Emma, regardless of her beauty, would always play a second to Tess.

Emma walked in wearing one of James's oversized flannel shirts that she found in the closet. It came down to her midthigh, so she figured everything was modestly covered. She walked straight over, taking his hand as she stood right beside him.

"How are you feeling?" James asked, running his hand softly over her back.

"Hungry." She smiled, looking at his plate of food.

"I will heat you up Gran's leftovers," Harrison stated. "I'm Harrison, by the way."

Emma smiled. "Hi. Emma—wait, I mean Jesse." Looking at James for confirmation that she didn't truly mess this up, she sighed when he simply gave a nod.

James explained to Harrison, "At home, she's Emma, and out there, she's Jesse. But just for the time being."

"Got it." Harrison nodded to Emma.

"Hey, I brought down Harper's stuff," Colin stated, looking at James. "Do you two need some?"

"Oh, yeah." James nodded. "Turn around, Em."

Emma turned around, and James gently brought the shirt off her shoulder so he could see the exit to her wound. He motioned for Colin to come over and look.

"Doesn't it look like the stitch is pulling out?" James asked him.

Colin got up and walked to Emma, then turned her so the light was better. "Yes." Taking the jar from James, he opened it. "I'll just put on a little, and when Jack and Harper get here, one of them can stitch her back up."

Colin finished applying the goo and then handed the jar to Emma. "You can put this on him."

"But ..." James gave him a sad look.

"Nope." Colin shook his head. "If you were dying in the field, there would be no hesitation, but you're not."

James smiled, knowing very well Colin would take care of him in the field. Emma moved his shirt off his shoulder and applied the paste. When finished, she handed the jar to Colin and washed her hands.

Harrison had her plate heated up and waiting on the counter for her when she was done.

"Thank you," she told him and began to eat.

Harrison watched her and had to agree with James that she was very pretty, and these green eyes were hypnotic. Her hair was a mess on top of her head, and he noticed she did have a lot of it.

"Are you going to be up for a while?" Colin asked James.

"At least until Jack gets here," he told him.

"Here." Colin handed him his .357. "I'm going to head up. Call if you need anything."

Colin got up, and James reached over, putting his hand out. Colin shook it.

"Thank you for coming," James said with all sincerity. "I appreciate it."

"After what you've done for Tess and Sav, anytime."

James smiled as Colin nodded and walked off.

"I'm going to turn in as well," Harrison told him. "Gran is already in bed, so it just leaves you two. Everything is locked up, and the alarm is on. Call if you need anything."

"Thank you, Harrison." James got up and gave him an easy hug.

"It was nice to meet you," Emma said, standing as well.

Harrison walked over to her, placing his hands on her shoulders. "I'm not hugging you for obvious reasons, but it was nice to meet you too." He gave her a kiss on the cheek, nodded to James, and headed upstairs.

"That was good," she told him after she finished. "I was so hungry."

"Me too," he said, walking around the counter to her. He turned her seat around to face him. With a soft smile, he gently caressed her cheek that wasn't hurt. Their eyes held as his fingers unbuttoned a few buttons on the shirt she was wearing.

"Kiss me." Emma's voice was barely above a whisper.

James tilted his head down, kissing her as his hand slipped inside the shirt, brushing lightly over her breast. He heard her take a deep breath with the touch. Bringing his hand up, he cupped her cheek, kissing her lips again. "Come on," he said as she hopped off the barstool and took his hand.

James dimmed the lights in the room and guided her through a door off to the right. Inside was a sunroom that was very dark, as there was no moonlight to shine through. There was a sofa and a couple rocking chairs and a table. James sat on the sofa and pulled her onto his lap. He continued to kiss her as his hands unbuttoned the shirt all the way down. Caressing her shoulders, his mouth dropped to her breast, taking each one in his mouth, sucking, kissing. Emma could feel him harden between her legs. Her head dropped back with the sexual sensation he was giving. Easily, they came together as one. Her hips rolled in a slow motion, and his lips met up with hers.

"Emma," he said between kisses. "You feel so good."

"You do too," she breathed out, her hands on his collar.

"Tell me if we need to stop," he whispered in her ear.

"No." Emma kissed him just below his earlobe. "I'm fine."

Neither knew how much time had passed before the intense heightened moment came. Emma closed her eyes as James cupped her cheeks and kissed her forehead before resting her head on his shoulder. Bringing his hands around her body, he held her close for a while.

"I'm sorry this happened, Em," he said softly.

Emma sat up, and her hand caressed his cheek. "There was no way to know."

"I should have known," he stated. "This is what I do for a living. I hung around in Savannah an extra week just to make sure everything was good, that there was no one lurking around, and I didn't even see this coming."

Emma got up and started buttoning her shirt. "Don't, just don't. You didn't miss anything." With a deep breath, she rested her hands on her hips. "I should have told you this sooner. Marcos Markenna made a promise to me when he received twenty to life. He said anyone I get close to or love, he would kill. And it didn't matter that he was in prison; he had many friends inside and out. So far, he has held true to his promise. He killed my grandmother, then a boyfriend. I had made friends with this girl, Mandy, and he had her killed too. Therefore, I don't let myself get close, and I don't let myself love because he always takes it away. I should have never let you in because he will kill you too, and all your family. I am unlovable." Ashamed of the trouble she caused, she turned away from him.

"Emma." James's voice was soft. "Will you look at me please?"

Slowly, she turned around to face him as tears cascaded down her cheeks. "I'm sorry I brought this here." She shook her head, crying. "It's not yours to deal with; it's mine. I will go."

James quickly grabbed her by the arm when she turned to leave. "No." He shook his head this time. "You don't get to walk out on me because something in your life is difficult or has brought problems. That is not how this works, especially with me."

"Somehow he kills every person that I get close to." She had a scared look in her eyes. "I won't. I can't let him hurt you and your family. He would have Tess killed without a moment's hesitation, and she's pregnant. I'm going to leave."

Emma slipped out of his grasp and headed upstairs to change. She was nearly running, double stepping the stairs to his room. She was slipping into a pair of jeans when he walked in and shut the door behind him.

"You can't make me stay," she stated, grabbing her wallet and heading for the door.

"Wanna make a bet?" he said with anger in his eyes.

"Please," she begged, walking up to him. "I love you. I don't want them to kill you. I couldn't live with that. Don't you understand?"

James's phone vibrated. He didn't want to look, but he knew he had to. "Don't move," he warned as he went to the nightstand to grab his phone. Jack had texted him that he was outside. When he turned around, Emma was gone. So James called Jack. "There's a girl that is going to be coming out the front door," he began. "Don't let her off the property. Bring her back for me, please."

"You got it," Jack replied as his men and Harper piled out of the SUV.

# Chapter 14

Grey opened the back and pulled out two duffel bags with guns and other weapons and handed one to Thomas and another to Smith. Harper grabbed her bag and headed for the front door. She was stunned when it opened suddenly, and a woman nearly ran her over.

"I'm so sorry," Emma said as she continued to head past the SUV.

"Wait ... who ..." Harper called to her, but she was out of sight.

Jack popped out from the backside of the SUV with a gun in hand pointed directly at Emma. When she saw it, he noted she nearly stopped breathing as her running ceased.

"Please don't shoot me." Emma's eyes were huge with fear, and her hands were up in a poor attempt to get this man to stop pointing a gun at her. She couldn't see the man's face, and he wore a knit hat on his head.

Jack didn't say anything as he walked up to her. He saw Grey from the corner of his eye walking to the back side of this woman. Jack kept the gun pointed at her, knowing he wouldn't pull the trigger, and besides, the safety was on. "What's your name?" Jack finally asked.

"Jesse," she said softly. "Just let me go. I won't come back. Please don't hurt him."

"Hurt who?"

"James." She swallowed the lump in her throat.

Jack smiled and nearly laughed. "He is exactly who I came here for."

"Please?" Emma had tears flowing, and she instinctively stepped backward, running into a person. When she turned to look at this man, her eyes grew even bigger. "I'm sorry. Please don't hurt me."

"That's not really ..." Grey was cut off when Harper stormed toward them.

"I know you," Emma said, tilting her head, looking at Grey then Jack.

When she realized it was the other men who came into the bar that night, her heart calmed somewhat.

"Jack! I swear we are about to have another fight." Harper walked over to the girl, taking her hand in reassurance.

"Oh, Harper." Jack holstered his gun and walked closer. "I wasn't going to hurt her."

Emma's eyes went from Jack to Harper, unsure of who this woman was. Then she saw James standing a few feet behind them with his arms crossed.

"This is a great first impression," Grey stated, not moving from his position until James gave him the nod.

"Come on." Harper nudged her to follow. "Jack isn't going to hurt you or James. They're cousins."

Emma let Harper walk her back to the house, exactly where she didn't want to go. "I need to leave," Emma told her before they walked through the door. "He will get killed because of me, and I don't want that to happen. I love him."

Harper took Emma's hands in hers. "So, leaving the world's best assassin is your answer?"

"Yes," Emma stated, not thinking of the question Harper actually asked.

Harper looked over at James, shaking her head, then back at Emma. "I'm Harper McGowan. If I wasn't marrying Jack, I would marry James. He rocks, he's hot, and he has lots of guns. If you love him, you don't leave him. That's not how relationships work. Did Tess put the green stuff on your wound?"

"Colin did," Emma answered.

"Of course my brother did. He's a player. Don't let his charm seduce you. However, I must have accidentally added an herb that impairs good judgment." Harper smiled. "I had my first fight with Jack today. It was big, but I won. I fought to be here, and I will be damned if you're leaving. Get your butt in there."

Emma felt scolded by an Ivy League princess. Giving Harper an odd look, she walked in the opposite direction of the house to James, who was simply leaning against the SUV, listening to Harper. She walked straight into his arms as she cried.

Harper looked at James with a smile, picked up her bags, and walked into the house.

"You need to be inside," Jack told James.

"I know." James nodded, still holding onto Emma. "Just give us a minute."

"I would love to say sure—but no, James." Jack shook his head. "It's unsecure out here. Move it inside." Jack waited for James to go in before he would.

James's hand ran up Emma's back and hit dampness. He pulled his hand away only to find blood all over it. "Em," he said, pulling her away slightly. "You're bleeding. Let's go fix you up."

"Jam ..." Her voice trailed off as her body wavered a bit, and her eyes closed, then opened, then closed again.

Jack didn't even hesitate. As soon as he saw her off balance, he scooped her up in his arms and took her inside.

"Take her to my room," James told him as they went inside. "Harper!"

"What?" Innocently, she popped her head around the corner from the kitchen.

"Can you check out Emma please?" James was following Jack up the stairs. "She passed out."

"Probably from dealing with you two," Harper mumbled. Grabbing her medical bag, she followed them upstairs. "Emma? I thought her name was Jesse."

"Witness relocation," James explained. "Real name Emma. Jesse was a front."

"Why can't you find a normal woman?" Harper asked.

"Emma is somewhat normal," James defended.

Harper couldn't help but laugh. "Sure, that's normal because most people are put in witness relocation programs. I think you've been doing your job too much. None of this is normal."

James stopped on the stairs, turning to Harper. "You'd marry me?"

"No." Harper grinned. "I'm completely in love with Jack."

"If Jack wasn't around?"

"We wouldn't have met if Jack wasn't around."

"I beg to differ. Your brother is my best friend."

"Differ all you want. *We* would have never happened. I'm not the type of woman that men like you fall in love with."

"Why do you say that? I think you're beautiful, smart, funny, and a bit eccentric."

"You're dangerous."

"Jack is too. He's done the same work as me. What's different?" James was very curious, as Harper's mind perplexed him.

"Jack has a sensitive side, and he's not afraid to show it." Harper placed her hand on James's heart. "The things you've seen and done have hardened you on the inside. You keep the emotional side of you tucked so far away in your soul sometimes you have a difficult time finding compassion. Emma is going to change that."

"Your brain boggles my mind." James grinned. "I can't get a read on you. And yet that's what I've done all my life is read people, take them apart to see what they're made of, how they tick, and then kill them."

"You're like my brother, Colin." Harper smiled, knowing he didn't want to be compared to Colin. "Smart man, but he hides an emotional side of himself, like you."

"Emotions get you killed." James sat on the stair. "I can't have that, given my career choice."

"I know." Harper knelt before him. Gently, she rested her hands on his knees. "Emma's a learning curve for you. You and Tess had a contract, literally, to not get emotionally involved. It was just sex and perhaps friendship. But with Emma, it will be a love that runs deep in your soul, and the emotions that you've hidden will be pushed aside for this love that she's going to fill you with. This will change everything in your life."

James stared at Harper, comprehending her words. "I like my life."

Harper smiled again. "It's going to get better. Trust me."

"Are you two coming in here or what?" Jack hollered from James's room.

"Oh, yes," James answered. Before standing up, he pulled Harper into his arms after kissing her forehead. "You're like this weird little sister I never had."

"I know. Let's go help Jack."

Jack laid Emma on James's bed and took off the shirt that was blood stained. The front of the wound was still covered with a bandage, and there was no blood seeping through. Carefully, he rolled her over to fix the exit wound. After getting a warm, damp towel, he cleaned the blood from her back, allowing him to see where the stitch pulled out. Thankfully, the bleeding had eased a bit.

"Harp, could you apply a little pressure?" Jack asked as she walked into the room with James.

"Of course." Harper walked over, took a piece of gauze, and applied direct pressure to the wound as Jack pulled out the suture kit.

"Anything I can do?" James asked.

"Don't fight with her," Jack responded. "She needs to stay down and heal."

"I wasn't trying to fight with her," James defended.

Jack looked at his cousin. "She needs to stay down. Want me to drug her?"

The first thought to come to James's mind was Taryn and the way Jack drugged her as they tried to figure out how to handle the situation. "No, she'll stay down. Don't drug her."

Jack glanced at his cousin, hoping he was right. As he put in a couple of stitches, James lay down beside Emma, taking her hand in his as her eyes fluttered open.

"Jack's suturing the exit wound," James explained as she lay perfectly still. "It busted open and was bleeding."

"I'm sorry," she whispered as tears filled her eyes.

James ran his hand softly over her cheek. "You need to stay in bed for a day or two. Take it easy and rest."

"Okay." With a nod, she agreed.

Jack put in three stitches and let Harper put some of her pasty mixture on the wound before covering it with a large bandage.

"Okay." Harper stepped back with Jack. "Keep her down, please. I'll be downstairs if you need me. She may want a couple ibuprofen if it hurts at all, but there is an analgesic in the herbs to numb it so there won't be much pain."

"I've got a terrible headache, and the ibuprofen is not touching it," James told Jack. "Do you have something in your miracle medical bag?"

"Yes, but it will make you sleep. I know you don't like that." Jack eyed him to see if he wanted to move forward on this.

James nodded. "Just make sure you position everyone, the house is secure, and Emma doesn't take off."

"I'll take care of it all for you." Jack looked at Harper, glanced at Emma then back, and raised two fingers up.

Harper prepared a needle and handed it to Jack. After giving his cousin the shot for pain, Harper handed him another needle. Without hesitation, Jack gave Emma a shot as well before James could stop him.

"I thought I said no," James reminded Jack.

"I'm not chasing her ass if she takes off." Jack handed the needles to Harper to dispose of. "You sleep, she'll sleep. The house is secure. Your men are working out their positions. It's all good. Trust me."

Jack picked up Harper's medical bag, and they walked out of the room.

James dimmed the lights, helped Emma out of her jeans, and crawled back into bed beside her. Gently, she lay in the crook of his arm, her head resting on his shoulder.

"Don't walk out on me again," he softly told her, feeling the effect of the shot. "Unless it's because you don't love me."

"I won't," she told him. "I'm sorry."

James repositioned his body to face her. "I will take care of whoever is trying to hurt you. This is what I do. But you have to trust me to do this and know that it's not something that happens in a day or two."

She nodded. "I know. It's just been a very long time since I had someone to trust."

He ran his hand through her hair and kissed her. "Will you just trust me please to fix this for you?"

"I will try harder," she whispered as her eyes drooped. "You need to understand that it is my natural instinct to run when trouble comes; otherwise, I will be killed. And I don't want to die."

"When I say I love you, that means I want to spend the rest of our lives together. We can't do that if you're dead. Start trusting me."

Without any more conversation, they both fell asleep.

\*\*\*\*\*\*\*\*\*\*\*\*\*\*

Jack stopped Harper in the hallway, turning her toward him. His hand reached behind her back, pulling her close, kissing her softly. "I love you, Harp."

"I love you too," she responded, wrapping her hands around his shoulders. "I'm sorry we fought."

"Me too, but I just want you safe."

"I know." She gave a small smile. "But I just want to be with you."

95

"Let me position the men and run through the security around here. Then we can make up." He grinned.

"Okay," she replied. They kissed one more time and then went in separate directions.

Harper went down the hallway to Jack's room and was walking in when Colin opened his door across from her.

"Hey, Harp, everything okay out there?" he asked, having heard some loud noises.

"Yeah." She nodded, setting her bag inside the bedroom door. "Is Tess asleep?"

"No, not at the moment," he answered, wondering why she wanted to know.

"Oh," she said, looking down.

Colin walked into the hallway closer to Harper. "Are you done punishing her yet?"

"Are you done cheating on her?" Harper threw back.

Colin sharply glared at his sister. "How do you know that happened?"

"Seriously? Colin, everybody knows."

"Well, that's not going to ever happen again," Colin defended.

"Better not or I'll tell James who the other woman is and let him kill her." Harper shocked herself with those words.

"Damn, Harp, did you really just say that? How do you know who it is?" Colin was amazed.

"Oh my gosh." She closed her eyes. "All of you are rubbing off on me. I don't know who it is."

"I made a mistake," he said, resting a hand on her shoulder. "It won't happen again."

"Promise me?"

"I promise you." Colin kissed her forehead. "Now it's your turn."

"Ugh." She sighed deeply and nodded as tears filled her eyes.

"Don't cry, Harp. Just go talk with her. I'll go talk with Jack. And, Harp, she can't have any stress, please."

"I know," she said, furrowing her forehead.

When Harper walked into Tess's room, Colin walked off down the stairs. She noticed a small lamp glowing in the corner on the nightstand, and Tess was lying on her side, almost in the middle of the bed. When

Harper walk in, she went to get up, but Harper told her not to. Instead, she kicked off her shoes and climbed in bed with her so they faced each other.

"I'm so sorry, Harper." Tess touched her hand that rested between them. "I never meant to hurt you."

"No, Tess." Harper had tears in her eyes. "I'm sorry. I knew you and Jack had something between you. I just didn't realize how serious it was, and he told me about the baby. I acted like such a spoiled brat. Please forgive me."

"Nothing to forgive." Tess ran her hand over her cheek. "I should have told you. I just never talked about my relationships with anyone before. I've never been good at doing that. Jack and Colin have always known me best, and I did love him very much at one point. And can I just say how lucky you are to have him love you? When he told me how he felt about you, I knew he would love you forever."

"I love him so much." Harper wiped a tear away. "I want to be with him all the time."

Tess smiled. "That's how I feel with Colin. Even though we've been married for three years, I want to be with him all the time. He's my everything."

Harper smiled. "I can actually say that I know what you mean. How are you feeling?"

"Better now."

"Can I feel the babies?"

"Of course." Tess grinned, taking Harper's hand and placing it on her stomach.

"It's so cool," she stated. "I'm so excited to see you grow with these babies this time. I can't wait to get married and have my own."

"I want you to be around more, if you can," Tess told her. "I know we'll be in Portland most of the time, especially having Savannah and Connor. But I really want you to come visit often."

"I will. Tess, I'm sorry for what Taryn put you through. That was unbelievably bad of her."

"Thanks, Harp." Tess held her hand in hers. "I don't think I will ever understand. Colin blames himself, but she and I fought since we were teenagers. It's just going to be one of those things I won't get an answer to."

"How do you feel about being a mom to her son?" she asked.

"He's just a little boy." Tess shrugged. "It's not his fault his mother was a bitch. I won't make him pay for it. I will love him like my own."

"I admire you for that," Harper admitted. "Colin's lucky to have you still."

"I put him through a lot of stuff before we got married." Tess smiled. "I can handle this."

"I should let you sleep." Harper gave her a hug. "I love you, Tessy."

"You haven't called me that in years." Tess smiled. "I love you too."

"I'll let Colin know he can come back." Harper raised her eyebrows as she headed out the door.

# Chapter 15

Marcos Markenna stood on the porch of the little house by the beach. Taking a deep breath, he smelled the salt air and smiled. It had been too many years since that scent penetrated his sense of smell. The musty stench of the Louisiana penitentiary still lingered in the back of his mind. Seventeen years in that hell made him truly appreciate being on the outside of those walls. It took a while, but he finally found a member of the parole board that he could pay off to get his release. With it being kept quiet, his son had no idea he was out. If Dominic knew, he would certainly raise some sort of hell to make them keep him in, as he had done in the past.

Taking a seat on the porch bench, he sat back, just enjoying this moment as he thought about the ruining of Jesse Ander's life. Would he be ruining it or saving her? That was a question that he asked himself constantly. One would be thankful that she didn't have to hide out constantly and be afraid of their own identity. A woman like her should be proud of her blood line. Instead, she was a weak, timid girl. Very disappointed, Marcos knew he could change that. Emiliana's only brave moment, he thought, was testifying against him and then his son, but she cost him seventeen years of his life.

When he heard about the death of his son, he was devastated. Yes, Dimitri did dabble in some illegal things, but he was a true Markenna. Next item on his list was to pay his respects to his son. Admittedly, he was surprised Dominic had any type of service for him, as Dimitri was a constant disappointment to his elder son.

He sighed, leaning back with his arm stretched across the back of the bench. He smiled, looking to his right at Meagan, Emiliana's main contact at the witness protection division. Her hands were bound, as were her feet.

He left her mouth free, as he gave her a choice when she was first taken: she could keep her mouth shut and only speak when spoken to, or he could tape it shut. Her choice. So far, she had behaved very well. His finger ran over the bruise on the side of her face where he hit her when they first met. Instinctively, she shied away from him, afraid.

"You don't have to be afraid." He eyed her. "Simply behave as a woman should. I won't hit you."

Meagan didn't speak and barely breathed. She knew the kind of man he was, and she was as good as dead at this point. There was relief when they arrived and Emma was gone. The safe house was three houses down from Emma's real home, and Meagan knew Emma wasn't there. This was a decoy. The only thing Meagan ever asked of Emma was to keep this home looking like she lived there, just in case of an event like this. She only hoped the girl stayed away or was with someone who could help her, because this wasn't going to end well. That poor girl had already been through hell with this man, and she deserved to be left alone, but men like Markenna never forgot the ones who betrayed them.

"When was the last time you spoke with Emiliana?" Marcos asked her.

"It's been years," she lied. "Once I moved her here, things quieted down."

"Hmm." He looked away from her. "Well that's already changed for her. She's in Maine for the moment, with some man. One of my guys shot her, but she's still alive. Definitely a resilient woman."

"If you knew where she was, why did you make me tell you about this place?"

"I wanted to see where she'd been living all these years. See what my money paid for."

"Don't you mean Dominic's money?" Meagan eyed him.

Marcos laughed. "That little shit son of mine drained most of my accounts when I was incarcerated. His company was doing good but not good enough to buy this place and both of his."

"Both?" Meagan only knew of the place in Virginia.

"You don't know him as well as you thought you did. He has a place in Virginia, but he also has a place in Peru. Don't you find it interesting that he has a home so close to his roots?" Marcos thought he would let her ponder that one a little bit and draw her own conclusions.

Meagan was quiet for a minute as she processed this bit of information.

Did she believe him? Or was he just trying to turn her on Dominic? She thought back on all her conversations with Dominic, and not once could she recall him telling her about a place in Peru. Instant doubt filled her mind. Was he really like the rest of his family? Nothing in her time with Dominic made her doubt his honesty with her. Marcos had to be lying.

Meagan finally spoke. "Why are you trying to kill your children?"

"Who said I wanted them dead?" Marcos pitched a look her way.

"Don't you?"

Marcos gave her a wicked half grin. "No. I love my children, regardless of what they've done in the past. Emiliana was tainted against me since she was born. I didn't even know about her until a week before I went to confront her mother. All I wanted was to see my daughter, and Mia wouldn't let me. I don't know how things got so out of control. But that is the past. I want to move forward."

"Do you think you can just round up all your children and become one big, happy family again?"

"Is it so bad for an old man to hope?" Marcos grinned.

"You disgust me, old man." Meagan turned away from him.

Marcos eyed her when she looked back at him. "Keep running your mouth and …"

"Uncle." Antoine walked onto the porch. "How long are we staying here?"

"I need to find Dominic," Domingo told him. "Then I'll finish with Emiliana."

"Dominic dropped off the face of the earth," Antoine told him. "He sold his company, his house in Virginia has been empty for a couple years, and there's been no activity with his name anywhere."

"Find where he put his money," he told his nephew. "We'll start there."

"He invested the money from the sale with a company called Taylor Enterprises," he said. "There's been no activity on those accounts in four years or so."

"Someone at that company has to know how to reach him. Find that person—or even better, find the owner and ask him."

"Will do," Antoine stated. "Will you be staying here, or do you want to go back to the hotel?"

"I think …" He sighed. "I'll stay here for a little bit with our friend Meagan." Marcos glanced at Meagan with a smile.

Meagan tried to separate her mind from the abuse that Marcos continually hand-delivered. The punches she took from him thus far were mind numbing. The upper strength that he possessed was from prison. Typically, most inmates had strong upper bodies, as that was all they worked on. Being around Marcos and his thick accent reminded her of Dominic and their time together. They had a strong, intimate relationship, not just with their bodies but with their minds too. It was effortless for them to talk into the early morning hours. Everything with Dominic was simple, natural. Maybe that was why she never really moved on after their relationship ended; deep inside she knew she would never connect with another man the way she did with Dominic. Only God knew how much she missed him and how she regretted every decision that took her away from him. If the opportunity ever arose for her to see Dominic, much less be with him again, she would take it faster than a blink.

# Chapter 16

Several days passed. Emma stood by the window in the living room, staring out at the view but not enjoying it much. Her wound felt much better and was healing quickly, but Marcos Markenna weighed heavily on her mind. She wondered if she should call Meagan and let her know what happened. But she still wasn't certain if it was Markenna or maybe someone from James's past. All she knew was that there was a bad feeling in the pit of her stomach, and it scared her to death.

"Hey," James said, walking up behind her, putting his hands around her waist as he rested his chin on her shoulder. "What's on your mind?"

"I feel like Atlas, carrying the weight of the world on my shoulders," she told him. "But I know there's other people out there who have it much worse than I."

James kissed her cheek, keeping her tightly in his arms.

"Should I call Meagan?" she asked, needing some sort of advice.

"Who's Meagan?" The only Meagan he knew was the one Brian spoke of at Jonathan's, Meagan Trask.

"Meagan is my ..." Emma thought for a moment. "I'm not sure what I'm supposed to call her. But she's the one who relocates me and gives me a new identity."

"Do you know her last name?"

"Trask," she answered.

"This world keeps getting smaller." He stepped away from Emma, running his hands through his hair as he thought.

"Why do you say that? Do you know Meagan?" Emma asked.

"The day I randomly showed up and we had lunch, I had met with Brian from the Bureau, and he was going to have Meagan Trask call me about Dominic because she has been tracking the Markennas all over the world with their business transactions, if you know what I mean. She was supposed to give me insight on Dominic and why he shouldn't be on my list anymore. But I never got a call from her."

"What's this list you talk about?"

"Brian left a list." James lowered his voice out of habit. "One day after a meeting we had, this list he left was a rather lengthy list of 128 marks that had something to do with the human trafficking trade. It had financiers, the people who provide the transportation, and even the ones who run the brothels and the child laborers. I started working the list about two and half years ago, taking out one person at a time. I'm down to eighteen, with seven of them being Markennas, and Dominic is one of those. Brian thinks he should be removed from the list, and Meagan was going to confirm with me."

Emma stood with a blank stare as she comprehended what his work entailed. Taking his hands, she turned them over, looking at them curiously. These were hands that truly killed, not just once or twice but hundreds of times. These were the same hands that had touched her body, caressed her skin gently.

"What's going on in that head of yours?" James asked, knowing something was clicking around in her brain.

"How many people have you killed with your hands?" As she asked, her eyes slowly drifted up to his.

"I have no idea," he answered with a shrug.

"Thousands?"

"No." He shook his head. "More like hundreds."

Emma stared into his dark brown eyes without speaking as her mind processed her life in a flash.

"Emma." James wasn't certain as to her odd behavior.

"It's weird to think that these hands that touch me so gently have squeezed the life from others."

James had an odd feeling, unsure if this was an acceptable thing that she could live with or not. "Emma, you know this. Why are you acting like it's the first time you've heard what I do?"

Taking a deep breath, her eyes connected with his again. "This is something I would watch on TV or the news. Never, ever would I have imagined being with a man that ..." Her voice wavered. "A man that has actually killed another human. And what's odd, I don't even care that you do that because you understand me, my fears, my shitty life, and you love me anyway."

James nodded his head slowly. "I do. Are you afraid of me?"

Emma shook her head in the same slow fashion. "I'm in love with you."

James reached down, picking her up so her legs wrapped around his waist. With one hand holding her, the other slipped behind her neck, bringing her lips to his. Their kiss was deep and demanding. Emma's hands enveloped his shoulders as her legs tightened around his hips.

Jack walked into the room with Harper beside him. Seeing his cousin and Emma in a very heated, passionate moment, he glanced at Harper with a grin.

"Maybe we should come back in a bit?" Harper whispered to Jack. "But I have to ask if you could pick me up like that. That's kind of hot and sexy."

Jack looked at her sideways. "You just keep surprising me, don't you?"

Harper simply shrugged with an innocent grin as Jack slipped his arm around her waist.

"I love you." Jack's words were as tender as his love for her.

"I love you too." Harper smiled, kissing him softly.

"And I do believe I picked you up like that." Jack apparently needed to remind her. "You were completely naked and seducing me."

"Ahhh." Harper remembered their first intimate moment. "I do remember that."

"We'll do it again, just to complete the memory that's forming in your mind."

James heard voices across the room, and he stopped kissing Emma but held on to her.

Emma opened her eyes when his lips pulled back, as she didn't want the moment to end yet. "What's wrong?" she asked softly.

"We have company," he replied as they both looked to the foyer at Jack and Harper.

"Oh." Emma smiled. "Perhaps you should put me down?"

James smiled. "I don't want to, but this was a great precursor to what's coming later."

"Mmm." She kissed him. "I can't wait."

With that said, James put her down but kept a hand on the back side of her neck as Jack and Harper walked over.

"Sorry to interrupt," Jack began. "We need to have a conversation."

"In private?" James asked his cousin.

"Yes," he answered. "Harper wants to check Emma's wound anyway. So, let's … walk."

Jack and James walked down to the dock, leaving Emma in Harper's capable hands. Being who they were, both carried handguns and stood before each other with their hands on their hips and not in their pockets in case they needed to pull their weapon quickly.

"What did you find?" James asked him.

"Markenna was released a month ago," Jack began. "He paid off one of the men on the parole board. He never checked in with his parole officer, which is no surprise, and he is off the radar. I called Dominic to see if he was aware of this, and he had no idea. And let me tell you Dominic is a little more than worried, as he testified at a couple parole hearings so they would keep him behind the bars. He says his father will come after him. Matthew is dealing with that end, but they are bringing the kids here. Rick is flying in with them, and he said he was bringing a couple of your other men as well. You'll have to touch base with him on that. We need to find him before he gets here."

James turned to face the bay as his mind processed the information. "I don't know if it's a good idea to bring the kids here," James stated.

"I don't have the manpower in Savannah like I did for Tess," Jack told him. "All the ones I brought in scattered after the job was done. I don't have just twelve professional men like you do. Your men are experts with this. Don't you think they will be safer here than there, if we're up here?"

James nodded. "Yes, just like before when I told Tess to keep Savannah close instead of sending her away. Harrison will kill us if anything happens to Gran."

Jack grinned with a nod.

James took out his phone and called Wes.

"Yes, sir?" Wes always answered his phone this way when James called.

"I need you to up security at the McGowans'. Add in Adrian and Javier. We're dealing with the Markenna clan. Everyone needs to up their game and be aware of every person that comes into contact at the McGowans.

I will inform Jonathan. Adam will do roll call in twenty-four hours and update the team."

"Got it. I'll call you if anything unusual happens."

"Perfect." James ended the call looking back at Jack. "That's dealt with. Emma has to tell us everything about her involvement with Markenna," James said. "She doesn't realize that the simplest thing could be what helps us. She isn't going to like this at all."

"Want me to talk to her?" Jack offered.

A sly smile crossed James's lips, and he shook his head. "No, let's have Colin talk to her. She likes him, trusts him for some weird reason. He can get her to talk and share those deep, dark secrets with his psychology bullshit."

"You're trusting him with your girlfriend." Jack laughed a little, knowing his friend's reputation.

"I'll hang out with Tess while he's talking to Emma." James grinned back.

✳✳✳✳✳✳✳✳✳✳✳✳✳✳

Colin rounded the corner into the kitchen. James said Emma was there with Gran, but Carina would excuse herself when he came in to leave them time to talk. "Hello, ladies," Colin said, taking a bottle of water from the fridge. Carina smiled and said hello, and Emma did the same.

"I need to go answer some emails," Carina said, excusing herself from the room.

Colin stood on the opposite side of the counter from Emma, trying to figure out a way to start this conversation. The conversation he wanted to have wasn't the conversation that James wanted him to have.

"Colin, you're staring." Emma raised her eyebrows. "What's up?"

"Do you know yet?" He knew she was aware of what he was asking.

Emma brought her eyes to his and held them for a couple minutes before she shook her head.

"How do you think this is going to work out if you are pregnant?" he asked with his voice low.

"I'll tell you how it's going to work out," she began with her voice soft. "If I am, I don't even know if it's yours or James's. So, the best thing to do is hope that I'm not, because if I am, I'm going to let James think it's his because I don't know. Besides, you're fucking married. What are you going to do? Leave her, because I'm pregnant with a baby that may or may not be yours? She is an assassin and can kill me in my sleep, spike my food, whatever. Don't even bring it up anymore because I won't even tell you."

Colin grinned, loving her feistiness. "The more I think about it, the more I realize we don't need to be having a kid between us. I have no intentions of telling anyone or ruining anything you have with James, but we will do a DNA test if you are, because I do need to know for my own piece of mind. I love my wife, and she needs to remain oblivious to you, or you're right—you will die by her hand."

"There were two of us there. I didn't do this by myself."

"Doesn't matter. You would die before she leaves me." Colin was sure of himself. Besides, he wouldn't let Tess leave him.

"Do I mean that little to you?"

Colin eyed her momentarily before answering. "It doesn't matter what you mean to me. Emotions are irrelevant here."

"Wow. You're an asshole," Emma said, rather shocked by the lack of emotion.

Colin grinned again, as it didn't bother him one bit. People either loved him or hated him; either way, he slept soundly at night. "You don't realize the family you've gotten involved with."

"I'm involved with James and his family, not yours."

"James is still in love with my wife. And he is considered part of the family because my father thinks of him as a son. Emma, this is a very powerful family. Be careful. I do care what happens to you."

"Don't lie to me. I'm simply another playing piece in your life. I'm in love with him." Emma had tears forming. "I don't want to lose him."

Colin nodded his head, placing his hand upon hers. "I know. Don't ever let him know about us."

Emma bit on her lower lip, nodding.

"You do realize it's going to happen again?" He raised his eyebrow.

"No, it won't."

Colin smiled. "Oh, but, Emma Grace, it will. If I want you, I will have you."

Emma shook her head. "What about everything you just said?"

"Just means no one can find out. You loved the way I made you feel, the way I touched your body, the orgasms I gave you. I liked it best with you on top, fucking me. Does James make you feel the same way I did?" Colin loved messing with people's heads. He had no intention of ever sleeping with her again, but he wanted to see her reaction.

"Stop," Emma warned, feeling something weird deep inside.

"When we're done, you're going to find James and fuck him because that desire is beginning to burn inside of you right about now." Colin's mouth curved slightly.

"Shut up, Colin." Emma hated the fact that he was right.

"You're breathing gives it away." Colin stood. "Learn to control your breathing. Learn to be emotionless. It's easier to manipulate people that way. Come on, let's do this."

"What the hell was that?" Emma asked, confused by this man.

"That put your guard down so I can hop into your head easier."

Emma sucked in her bottom lip. "You were the first man I was ever honest with. I felt safe with you. It had been a long, long time since I trusted a man enough to … you know."

"I know." He nodded. "Emma, it was just sex, not a lifetime commitment. Move on, forget about it. I know you've done that with other men. I'm no different."

"You're married. None of the others were married. I know better, but I gave into that animalistic behavior anyway. I'm so ashamed."

"Emma, I promise that I won't mess up anything you have with James." He looked down for a moment, took a deep breath, and looked back up. "I need to know, but I don't want any ties."

She nodded. "Fine. But he can't know."

"That's fine." He sighed and grinned. "I'm very good at paying people off to shut up and lose information."

"That's good because financially I'm at the mercy of James right now."

Colin smiled, looking guilty.

"What?"

"There is an account set up." He pulled out his wallet and thumbed through a couple bank cards. "Here."

Emma took the card from him, looking at it.

"There's fifty thousand to start," he began. "Every three months, I'll put in another twenty thousand for a year."

"No, why?" she asked, not wanting his money. "And how does your wife not know?"

"That isn't a concern of yours," he stated. "The pin is my birthday. Never feel trapped or stuck in something you don't want to be in because of a lack of money. Think of it as a payoff."

"You're such an asshole. I don't want this." She tried to give it back, and he shook his head. "Damn you."

Colin grinned. "Em, my net worth is over eight figures. And if you need more, call me. It's not a big deal."

"Damn you're stubborn." She slipped the card in her back pocket.

"We've already determined that I'm an asshole. Let's move on to your daddy."

"I've told James everything that I know." She shook her head. "What else do you want?"

"You know something, and we need to extract it out of that brain of yours," he stated. "There's little things that you don't even realize you know that you've suppressed. I'm going to help you remember those things."

"I …" She shook her head. "I worked a long time to forget the bad things … I don't wanna … remember them." She shook her head and sucked in her bottom lip to ward off crying.

"Emma." Colin reached over, covering her hand. "This isn't a question as to whether you want to or not."

Her face went straight as her heart pounded. "Please don't make me," she said softly.

Colin tilted his head, confused as he walked around the counter to sit facing her. He took both her hands in his and brought them to his lips, kissing her knuckles softly as he watched her eyes. Knowing that threw her off, his hand slid to the side of her neck just below the ear. "I can make you forget after were done," he said softly.

"Can you really?" she asked, barely above a whisper.

"Yes." He nodded. "You just have to tell me that's what you want, and I will."

"I don't know." She shrugged her shoulder. "Let's get this over with."

"Let's go over to the sunroom. If you decide later that you want to forget, we can do it then also. It doesn't have to be right now."

Emma followed him out of the kitchen and into the small room to the right. Last time she was in there with James, they had sex on the sofa. A smile crossed her lips as that memory replayed in her mind. The touch of his tongue on her breast and the feel of him.

"Em." Colin looked at her with a smile. "What are you grinning about?"

"Last time I was in this room." She smiled guiltily. "I was with James. He was sitting on the sofa like you are now." And her mind drifted again to his lips on her neck.

Colin's lip twisted up as he thought of her straddling him right now. Then his mind wandered back to talking with her that first night after Taryn was killed. Seeing her die before his eyes left him distraught in a way he'd only experienced once before, when Tess was shot in Chicago. Emma was the only person who came to his mind to talk to. As a bartender, she should be used to people wanting to spill their woes.

Colin remembered sitting on Emma's couch. It was after midnight, and he was getting tired. They had been talking for the past six hours. He told her everything about himself, every secret, every love, every kill. By the time he was done talking, Emma had enough information to either shoot him herself or turn him in. Instead of her being afraid of a man like him, she told him her secret. Having heard a bit about her past from Adam, Colin was rather surprised that James would still be interested in this woman, given her family tree. But even if James wasn't, he certainly was.

"Colin." Emma reached over, touching his arm. "You look like you're going to fall asleep. Let me go get you a blanket and pillow."

Colin nodded as Emma got up and went to the other room. Standing, he stretched as she walked back in. As she stood before him, she handed him a pillow and blanket. Colin simply put them on the couch and turned his attention to her.

"Thank you." He reached his hand out, caressing her cheek. "And thank you for listening and letting me trust you."

Emma held her breath when he touched her. It had been years since she let a man touch her. And just the simple warmth of his fingers made her entire body tingle.

Colin caught the simple look on her face and the way she tried to control her breathing. And for the first time since he was married, he didn't care if he broke his vow. Instantly, he wanted Emma more than anything or anyone else in the world. Slowly, he moved his other hand to her cheek, cupping her face softly, noting her eyes close with a slow release of her breath. When he brought his lips to hers, he carefully kissed her, knowing he would stop immediately if she didn't reciprocate.

But she did.

"You're married," she whispered, but they kept kissing.

"Shhh." And he kissed her with a little more passionate depth.

"I can't stop you." Her hand rounded his shoulders. "'I've longed for the touch of a man. I just haven't trusted anyone in a very long time."

"You can trust me." His hands slid down her back side, resting on her hips.

"I do trust you." She sighed when his lips moved to her neck.

"I won't hurt you." Colin stopped kissing her to look in her eyes. "My promise to you. But you have to promise me something."

"What?"

"No one can know about this." His eyes looked at her lips then back to her green eyes. "You know what my family is made of."

"I know." She nodded.

"And you can stop me, anytime." He cupped her face again. "Just say the word."

"I don't want to stop you." Her voice was barely audible.

Colin held her beautiful eyes for a moment longer before kissing her full lips again.

"Colin." Emma sat on the edge of the sofa and shook his knee as his mind was somewhere else.

"Oh, yes?" He laughed a little. "You made my mind wander. Remember that first night? I promised you I would never hurt you, and I won't. Don't forget that. I hold true to my words. I always have."

"I do trust you."

"Even though I'm an asshole?"

Emma nodded.

With confliction in his heart, Colin would never let her know how he truly felt. "Just know that I will always be here for you. Anytime, anyplace. You need me, just call."

"Thank you." Her forehead creased a little. "I haven't had that in my life much. First you, then James. Sometimes I wonder when I'm going to wake up."

"You are awake." Colin sighed. "And he loves you very much."

Emma nodded, knowing this, but it was also nice to hear some reassurance that it wasn't just a fantasy in her head.

"Let's do this," he stated.

"Do what?" She completely forgot the original intent.

"Fix your memory." He smiled, sitting up. "Sit back on the couch and relax. Fully relax, close your eyes, take a deep breath, and slowly release it. You're going to listen to my voice as you feel your body calm, knowing you're in a safe place. We're going to start with the night you saw your father murdered."

Emma instantly woke up as she heard yelling downstairs. It was late, and she knew if her mother caught her up, she would get in trouble. But the yelling was loud, and there was a voice she didn't recognize. Curious, as young minds are, she quietly walked over to the stairs. With the hallway dark, no one could see her peeking through the rails, watching.

Seeing her father on his knees as some strange man pointed a gun at his head made her eyes grow wide with fear. It was her mother who was yelling at the man with the gun.

"Please, Marcos," her mother begged. "Don't hurt him. He's done nothing to you."

"Mia." The dark-haired man spoke calmly. "You let another man raise my daughter, Emiliana. Did you think I would never find out?"

"You left me," she reminded him. "You left and didn't come back. Did you expect me to wait all these years for you?"

"Allow me a moment to refresh your memory. You left me. Walked out, knowing you were carrying my child."

"I couldn't bring a child into that world we were living in. It wasn't fair. And you did leave with that woman."

"Don't you think I would've changed a few things had I known you were pregnant? You were my wife, Mia! A child would have changed everything."

"Your life wasn't changing because of a baby."

"I guess we'll never know now, will we?"

"Marcos, please, just tell me what you want," Mia pleaded.

"I want my wife and my daughter," Marcos stated, turning his attention to Seth. "Thank you for taking care of my child all these years. I want you to know that I'm grateful to you. I also want you to know that it is Mia's fault what is about to happen." Marcos cocked the gun, placing the barrel on Seth's forehead.

"No, no. Please just stop," Mia pleaded to no avail. "I'll give you anything. Please don't kill him."

Marcos raised his eyes to Mia's as if in slow motion and pulled the trigger.

Emma gasped as her father dropped to the floor. Covering her mouth with her hand, tears filled her eyes as her body began to quake uncontrollably.

Mia cried out as she dropped to the floor beside her husband. Knowing he was dead, she simply cradled his head in her arms, sobbing.

"Where's my daughter, Mia?" Marcos asked in a calm voice.

"She's not here," Mia cried.

"Then I guess I don't need you anymore." Marcos aimed the gun at Mia and shot her in the head.

Emma watched the man a moment longer as he took out his phone. When he began talking, she quietly snuck back to her room, hiding behind the wall paneling like her dad showed her years before.

Through the night, she heard footsteps all over in their home. Knowing it wasn't the police, she stayed tucked away. It was as if the man was searching for something. Or perhaps he was searching for her, but he never called her name. That was the longest night of her life. In the late morning, her grandmother found her, as she had known about the hiding place for years.

Colin started with the terrible memory that Emma had tucked deep within. The story she told him, a few weeks before, didn't come close to the details that she shared while in the hypnotic state. Over two hours had passed, and he had a very detailed picture of her entire life. The interesting part was she didn't even realize the information that she gave him. Kneeling before her, he placed his hands on her knees as her eyes were still closed in her trance state. He had a couple more questions to ask her before he brought her back to reality.

"Tell me about James," he said to her, and a smile crossed her lips as James walked into the room.

"I'm in love with him," she said. "But I'm not good enough for a man like him."

Colin stood up, glancing at James leaning against the doorway.

"Ask her why she would feel that way," James told Colin.

Kneeling, Colin took a breath and asked Emma why she felt that way.

"He's educated, traveled the world, speaks three different languages," she said with a solemn voice. "I'm none of that. My education came from the streets. The farthest I've traveled is Arizona."

Colin looked up at James with a sigh. "Do you want to do this?"

"I've never done this before." James shook his head.

"Seriously?" Colin looked at him sideways.

"I shoot people in the head." He shrugged. "I don't play in there."

"Do you want to?" he asked.

"Is she going to remember any of this?" James was a little curious.

"Not really." He smiled.

"No," James said after a few moments of hesitation. "I can't. That wouldn't be right. But I don't want her to feel inadequate."

Colin knelt before her again, taking her hands in his. "Emma, I'm going to count back from three, and on one, I want you to wake up. But when I do, I want you to realize that you are good enough for a man like James. It doesn't matter what's happened in your past. James loves you, and you love him. That's all you need." Colin looked over at James, who nodded. "Three ... two ... one."

Emma opened her eyes and looked around as if she'd been asleep for hours. When James sat beside her, she smiled. "Well?" she asked them as Colin stood back up.

Colin smiled. "You are in love with James. So I guess we can't have a sultry affair." Colin winked at her and left the room to go find his wife. She wasn't too far away, sitting in the living room with Carina and Harper. He took a seat beside her, kissing her hand.

"How was it?" Tess asked.

"Fine." He shrugged. "She has some serious confidence issues."

"I'm sure it has nothing to do with the shitty life she's had." Tess raised her eyebrows and looked over at the front door as it opened and Jack walked in. Behind him were Matthew and Dominic, each with a child in their arms. A huge smile emerged on her lips, seeing the children.

"Mommy!" they both cried at the same time.

The two men set them down, and they ran over to Tess and Colin. With arms wide and smiles wider, they hopped up onto her and Colin's lap, and the chatting began. Everyone watched them with the kids for a few minutes until they calmed.

Colin was the first to stand with Savannah in his arms. He walked over to Matthew and Dominic. "Thank you for taking care of them."

"Not a problem," Matthew answered.

"And how's Connor doing?" Colin asked Dominic.

"Better." He nodded. "Every time he talked with Tess, he was fine afterward. I'm glad we could bring them up to you two."

"Well, thank you and welcome to Carina's house." Colin gestured over to Carina, who stood up to greet the new family that walked in.

"Matthew." She went to him first with a hug. "I can't remember the last time I saw you. Very happy to have you here. Now introduce me to your other brother."

"Carina, this is Dominic." Matthew looked from her to him.

"Pleasure to meet you," she said kindly, giving him a hug. "And welcome. Make yourself at home. I was so happy to hear that you found your way back to Jonathan. He's a wonderful father."

"Thank you." Dominic grinned, loving this old woman already. She was the grandmother that he never had. "Your home is beautiful. Thank you for having me."

"You're part of the family and welcome anytime." Carina patted his hand with a smile.

James walked into the room with Emma's hand in his. As they glanced around to see who showed up, James smiled, and Emma froze, dropping his hand. "Emma?" James caught her stare at Dominic. "Do you two know each other?"

"I don't think we've ever met," Dominic simply stated. "I would remember a woman with those … oh my God." Dominic took a step toward her, and she took a step back and then another.

"Stop." James held his hand up to Dominic, not sure of what was happening here.

"This is the girl, Emma Anderson. The one at the courthouse that testified against my father and my brother." Dominic looked at Matthew, as he knew the story.

James was confused. "Explain."

"Please don't ..." Her voice trailed off, and it felt like she couldn't breathe as tears filled her eyes. "Pease don't hurt me."

"I would never." Dominic shook his head. "Never. I am not my brother."

Emma turned, running out of the room as James eyed Dominic for the story behind her behavior.

"Don't move." James pointed to Dominic as he pulled out his radio to his men. "Who's up top?"

"Seven on top," Smith answered.

"Emma may be on foot outside," James stated. "Don't let her out of your sight, but don't detain."

"Seven, copy," Smith replied.

James directed his attention back to Dominic. "Okay, CliffsNotes version."

Dominic told James how he knew Emma in as few sentences as possible. And for the first time since he met him, James believed Dominic wouldn't hurt her.

"Thanks," James said with a pat on his shoulder as he ran out of the room. Outside, James radioed Smith. "Status?"

"She's walking down the road about three hundred yards south. I'm going to lose sight in about another hundred yards or so where the road turns and there's those big-ass boulders."

"Copy seven," James replied. "Who's on ground?"

"That would be nine," Rick replied as James came upon him off the shoulder of the road.

"Just follow," James asked. "Stay about fifty yards or so behind us."

"Will do." Rick nodded as James began a fast walk down the road to catch up with Emma.

In less than ten minutes, James reached her. He didn't speak, nor did Emma; they just walked together. Casually, he slipped her hand into his as they continued their saunter down the road.

A solid five minutes passed before Emma stopped, turning toward James. With a slight smile, she looked up at him. "I love you" was all she said.

James reached his hand out, caressing her cheek softly with a nod. "So, where are we headed to?" he asked, looking around, hoping his men had them covered thoroughly.

"Georgia," she replied.

James nodded again, took a deep breath, and began walking with her. "I wonder how long it would take to walk that far. How are your feet doing?"

Emma looked down at her bare feet, wishing she had grabbed some shoes on the way out. "They're fine." She shrugged. "I'll mug someone and steal their shoes."

"Why would you mug someone?"

"I didn't bring my wallet."

"Okay." He nodded as they continued to walk.

James was thankful it wasn't raining, but in the far east, the clouds were brewing for another storm. With the rocky shoreline on their left and the forest on their right, he wasn't feeling too comfortable being out in the open like they were. This was a dangerous situation to be in. Then she stopped walking again.

"James." She looked at him. "Is there—"

She was cut off when Seven came over his radio. "One sec, Em," he said, listening to Smith.

"Drop behind the rocks," Smith told James. "There's a lock on you."

James scooped up Emma, taking her off the main road and hiding behind the rocks on the shoreline. He tucked them down between two large boulders before replying to Smith.

"What've you got, Seven?" James asked, keeping his arm around Emma in a very protective manner.

"I have a man about fifty yards south from your location with a scope on you," Smith answered. "Which happens to be attached to his 6.5 Saum."

James laughed a little. "Glad you can see the model of his rifle. Tree line or shoreline?"

"Shoreline," Smith answered. "Want me to disable the Saum?"

"Please," James stated, then looked at Emma as he listened to the shot fill the air.

"What is going on?" she asked.

"There was a sniper about fifty yards from us," James explained. "Smith just took him out. We'll wait a few minutes to make sure there's no one else. Then we'll head over to see who it was."

"Oh," she simply replied.

James sat down in the sand. "So, Dominic."

"That's Dimitri's brother." She shook her head. "I saw him at the courthouse. How and why is he here?"

James took a breath. "He's Matthew's half brother. Their mother was Isobelle Markenna. She was married to Marcos, fled while she was pregnant with Dominic, met Jonathan and married him. She was killed in a car accident when Dominic was five or six, and Marcos kidnapped his own kid, taking him back down to South America. You have no reason to fear Dominic."

"Does he know who I am?" she asked.

"I'm sure Matthew's told him." James shrugged. "But I haven't said anything. I don't really know him, and I've put no effort forward to get to know him."

"Oh, okay." She pursed her lips together, feeling rather deflated.

James pulled her close to him. "Emma, this will all work out."

"I know. I just wish we could skip the middle process."

James kissed her softly until Rick walked up and handed James his extra .357.

"Want to take Emma back first or just go check this out?" Rick asked James.

James looked at Emma to see what she wanted to do.

"I'm going with you." She stood up. "You're not taking me back. I'm tired of being afraid. Which way are we going?"

James looked at Rick with a grin.

"South, along the beach," Rick stated.

Emma took off walking south with James and Rick behind her. At least her feet were more content on the sand than the road.

James spoke from behind. "You know, since you're not packing, perhaps you should walk in between us."

"No." Her jaw was set when she answered. "I'm not hiding behind you anymore."

James glanced at Rick with a grin, as she reminded him of Tess in a small way.

A few minutes later, they came across a body. By the dark features of the man, it was easy to tell that he was someone related to the Markenna clan. James watched Emma walk to the other side of the body and pick up the rifle.

"I'm packing now." She cocked her head at James.

"Check your rounds," he told her as Rick rolled the body over. "You're going to have to fight Smith for that Saum."

"What?" She didn't understand.

"That rifle you're holding is a 6.5 Saum." James grinned. "It's about six thousand. Smith knew what type of rifle that was before he even took out this man."

"Oh." She nodded, clueless about these types of things. "So, this is kind of like his prize for hitting the bull's-eye."

James smiled. "Yes, ma'am."

"I'll give it to him. Is that okay?"

"Perfectly fine."

"So, call it in or dump the body?" Rick looked up at James.

"Let's dump the body." James shrugged, noting the perfect hole in the middle of the dead man's forehead. "I don't feel like dealing with the local PD today. Let's do a fingerprint ID on him first."

Rick got on the cell and called Jack to bring the boat over. They would dump the body at sea.

"Emma, do you want to go back to the house or dump the body with Jack?" James inquired.

"Would he mind?"

"No, Jack won't mind." James shook his head.

## Chapter 17

J ack navigated the boat out of the harbor with Emma and a dead
body—but not until Emma put on a life jacket at James's insistence.
This wasn't the first time he dumped a body for James, and he was
certain it wouldn't be the last. They had about two hours before the sun
would set, but what worried him a bit more was the storm that was setting
up in the eastern skies. Jack hoped it would hold off until they were done.

When they were a few miles off the coastline, Jack stopped the boat
and turned off the engine. Looking over at Emma, he grinned, wondering
if she really knew what she was getting into with James.

"What?" she asked.

"Nothing." He waved her over to the body at the back of the boat.
"Have you ever dumped a body before?"

"No." She shook her head. "I always called the police."

Jack grinned. "Well, get used to this. James seems to attract dead bodies."

"As long as it's someone else's dead body and not ours, I'm good with that."

"Me too." He nodded. "Let's take off all his jewelry and pull his wallet."

"Why?" she asked as she followed his instructions.

"Identification purposes," he stated. "We'll toss the body in one place
and the jewelry in another, and I'll take the wallet back to the house and
burn it."

"Why not dump the wallet?" She was curious.

"It may float," Jack explained. "I like to make sure it's destroyed,
untraceable."

"Okay." She nodded as she finished taking off the man's necklace
and rings.

Jack pulled the wallet and checked the rest of the body for any other
items. When he was certain the body was clean, he stood up.

"Grab his feet," Jack told her as he scooped up the man from under his shoulders.

Together, they tossed the body off the back of the boat. Jack pulled out his .357, aimed, and then reconsidered. Looking at Emma, he handed the gun over to her. "Shoot his belly," he told her.

Emma aimed. "Why?"

"Blood will attract the sharks," he simply stated as she pulled a shot off perfectly in the center of the stomach. "Good."

Handing the gun back to Jack, she looked at him. "Wouldn't the shot to his head attract the sharks?"

"I like to be thorough." Jack grinned with a quick raise of his eyebrows. "Besides that, I wanted to see how you handle a handgun."

"And how did I do? Did I meet your expectations?"

"I can tell you've held a gun in your hand. And it's simple to deduct that you're not afraid of dead bodies or weapons. Both are good things. Especially if you're going to be in James's life."

"You approve of me?"

Jack shook his head with a sly grin. "I'm not the one that needed to approve of you."

Emma's face went straight. "Who has to approve of me?"

"Carina." Jack raised his brows, knowing Emma was nervous.

"And? Don't leave me hanging, please."

Jack laughed at how worried she was. "You're still here, so you did something right."

"My gosh, you had me thinking I was going to get dumped out here with the dead man."

"You have a crazy imagination." Jack chuckled some more as he watched the dead man's body floating.

"Now what?"

"We wait until his body is taken under," Jack replied as he stood with his arms crossed, watching the body drift away from the boat.

Emma noted how calm and reserved he was. His mannerism was similar to James's, but his look was not. Jack had dark hair with a skin tone to match, with dusky brown eyes, full lips, and a very fit body. She imagined he made love like the other men around there. Rolling her eyes, she wondered why that thought even popped into her mind.

"Emma, you're staring," he noted, not taking his eyes from the body.

"I'm sorry." Embarrassed, she looked down for a moment.

"What's on your mind?" He asked glancing at her momentarily.

"Why do you call me Emma and not Jesse? You've never called me Jesse."

Jack turned his head to look at her. With a sigh and shrug, he said, "It's your real name. When you're with us, meaning the family, you don't have to be anyone else. You don't have to hide. You can be you. All of us work under an alias, but we are ourselves with each other. By the way, sorry about the other night."

"You scared the hell out of me. Then I remembered seeing you that night at the bar. I didn't know all of you were related."

"Ah, yes, the intricate weavings of the McGowans and the Cordellos."

"Cordellos? I thought James was the only one." Emma was confused.

"Gran's last name is Cordello. James's father wouldn't let his mom put his name on the birth certificate. The only thing James knows about his father is his first name, Stephen. Cordello is the family name."

"Oh." Emma thought it was strange that James didn't find out more about his father once he started in the business. He had full access to do that. Looking over at Jack, Emma gave him a slight smile. "Can I ask you something else?"

"Of course."

"Am I enough for a man like James?" she asked.

Jack looked out at the vast sea as he thought about her question. Thinking about James and how he was with her put a slight smile on his lips. "We may have different parents, but James is my brother. I know him very well, and I know he doesn't let women get close to him. Tess is the only one I know of in the last twenty years that he loved, until you. The way he looks at you, talks about you, tells me how much he loves you—it's not a matter of you being enough for him, because you're plenty. The question is can you handle a life and man like James?"

"What do you mean?"

"He goes all the time," he started. "But when he comes home, he is home for weeks or months on end. Either here or his house in Chicago. The things he has done and seen in his career require him to step back after a job and remember why he does what he does. If he didn't, he'd be messed up in the head. There were a few times when I had to go find him and level him out again. If he shuts down, it takes months to get him back. Usually, it's myself or Matthew who brings him back. Don't ever let him shut down. If he does, you call me immediately."

Emma took a deep breath, turning away from Jack, and looked out at the floating body. Could she handle a man like that? Or should she walk away and not get in any deeper? As she thought of her life without him, a tear slipped from her eyes, and she quickly wiped it away but knew Jack saw.

Jack clapped his hands loudly as a shark came up and snagged the body, taking it down into the depth of the dark sea. "Come on." He motioned her over to the front of the boat where the controls were.

"Where are we going now?"

"Dump the jewelry," he stated, starting the boat as he felt a raindrop. "We need to hurry. Storm's coming in quickly."

Emma looked up at the sky, feeling a little anxious, as the thought of being stuck out at sea during a storm didn't appeal to her.

Jack navigated the boat a couple of miles north before slowing. "Do you have the jewelry?" he asked, and she nodded. "Chuck the necklace here."

Emma went to the back of the boat and threw the necklace as far as she could. Turning back around, she gave Jack a thumbs-up, and he pushed the lever to move again. With Jack focused on navigating the boat, Emma slipped the bank card from her back pocket. Taking one last look, she flipped it into the ocean.

As the boat picked up speed, Jack looked up at the sky. Rain began to pelt down, and darkness began to cover them quickly. With a sigh, he looked back at Emma to see if she was okay, but she was gone. Instantly, his heart dropped as he stopped the boat to look for her. Yelling her name, he got no response and couldn't see her anywhere around the boat. Thinking she must have slipped and fell overboard when he took off again, he turned the boat around to go find her.

Jack called the house on his radio as he turned on the spotlight with the boat. He could still see but didn't want to take the chance of missing her. Knowing this water was close to freezing temperature, he needed to find her fast.

The moment Jack called James, instant dread sank deep within as the memory of his mother's death flashed vividly through his mind.

It was late September, and James had just started his last year in graduate school. Two years before, he had transferred back to the East Coast to finish school and work on his training. With his mother and Carina living only three hours away, he managed to carve out one weekend a month to visit. On this particular weekend, he was tasked to set up a presentation in his economics class. Knowing this would be a vital grade in this class, he declined his mother's invite to go on a yacht with her and her new boyfriend.

Vividly he recalled his grandmother coming into the kitchen in the afternoon, sitting at the table with him. James knew she had been crying, so he stopped what he was working on. "What's wrong, Gran?"

"That was the local police at the door." Carina wiped away a tear. "There was an accident on the boat. Your mother and Todd were killed."

As Carina sobbed, James stared at her in disbelief. This wasn't possible. He had breakfast with her just a couple of hours before. They were going out to dinner tonight. "Impossible," James said, standing up. "We're having dinner tonight after they get back. Gran, this can't be happening!"

Carina had no words to console her grandson as he processed the reality of the horrific event. James paced the kitchen for a few minutes before walking out of the house. The undeniable pain in his heart was inconsolable.

He dropped that semester of college and never went back. He learned that the yacht had a small gas leak in the galley. As soon as someone lit the stove, it blew up the boat and everyone on it into an unrecognizable, charred mess. His cousin Harrison insisted on being the one to identify the body, as he didn't want James or his grandmother to be left with that image of Sofia. James did nothing for a few months except grieve. There were days when he never even got out of bed.

On New Year's Eve, Carina told James she needed his assistance in traveling to Chicago to see Harrison. James knew she could do it on her own, but she was trying to engage him somehow to get him back into life. Knowing his Gran had been gracious the last four months in letting him just be his depressed self in her home, he decided to do this for her.

Driving as opposed to flying, they broke it up over two days and stopped often to enjoy the sites. At the halfway point, they stopped to stretch their legs. It was then that Carina gave James a little bit of advice.

Carina began speaking in her all-knowing voice. "Now, James, I have allowed you to grieve for the last three and a half months, but it is time for it to end. You can still grieve if you must, but you must function as an adult at the same time. You lost your mother. I lost my daughter. Our pain is real and very painful, but we must carry on. Sofia would knock you upside the head if she knew how long you've been down. She wanted you to live and be happy and thrive, not do what you've been doing."

"I have no parents, Gran." James's voice was soft as a lump formed in his throat.

"I know," she agreed. "But you have me, and I will never leave you, and I will never abandon you. Figure out if you want to go back to school or work, but you need to do one or the other."

"I'm done with school. I don't want to finish the graduate program. I want to continue my training with Brian and go into a specialized type of career. I know I've been moping around, but I have been thinking about my future." James gave his grandmother a slight grin.

"Brian has been calling me once a week to check on you. He'll be happy to hear this." Carina hugged him tightly. "I want you to be happy."

"Eventually, I will be. Thank you for all your patience with me since she passed away. I'm very grateful to have you."

"You're going to have me for a while. And do know I'm going to keep it straight up with you just like I do with Harrison and Jack. You three boys are all I have left of my family, and it's very important that we remain close with each other."

Jolting back to the present, James stood staring out at the bay, waiting to hear from Jack. It felt like hours had gone by, but it was only a mere five minutes. Carina walked up, patting him on the shoulder.

"He'll find her." Carina spoke with full confidence. "That young lady is meant to be a part of our family."

James looked at his gran as tears filled his eyes and he nodded.

"I know you're thinking about your mother, and trust me when I tell you that she is out there with Emma right now, making sure Jack finds her."

Moving the boat slowly and still calling her name, Jack was a bit relieved when he came upon her floating in the sea, although she was unconscious.

"Fuck!" Jack yelled. Turning the boat off, he jumped in the water to grab her body before a shark did. The instant icy water stunned him briefly. Pushing the coldness out of his mind, he swam to her body and could see where she hit her head, as blood was gushing. It was a little bit of a struggle to get her back on the boat, but he managed and began CPR, as she wasn't breathing.

"Come on, Emma!" he said. "Breathe, damn it."

Jack did several chest compressions, then gave her a breath, and she coughed up the water and was breathing again. Slowly her eyes opened.

"Thank you, God." Jack scooped her up in his arms, hugging her tightly as her body began to shiver uncontrollably. Knowing she was probably going into shock, he stripped off her cold, wet clothes and wrapped her up in a blanket, tucking her beside him at the controls.

The adrenaline kept Jack going. He knew once it subsided, he would be in the same state as Emma. With the steady rain coming down, he navigated the boat back to the boathouse as quickly as possible.

"I've got her," Jack said over the radio. "Be down at the boathouse. We both have hypothermia. Be prepared."

Jack sighed, relieved, when he pulled into the boathouse about fifteen minutes later. Someone tied the boat off as James and a couple of men hopped on the boat to help them. And that was the last thing Jack remembered.

# Chapter 18

James walked into Jack's room a few hours later. Harper had him cleaned up and tucked in the bed with an electric blanket on. She sat in a chair beside the bed, waiting. James walked over and kissed the top of her head. "How are you doing?" James asked her.

"Fine," she stated softly. "I don't know why he didn't take off those wet clothes, like he did with Emma, and wrap himself in a dry blanket. That's medicine 101. You have to take care of yourself before you can help anyone else."

"He was probably trying to get them back here as soon as possible," James stated, giving her shoulder a slight squeeze.

"I called Gina to make sure we were doing everything right, and we are. We just have to watch their temperatures and wait."

"He'll be fine, Harp. I promise you." James ran a soothing hand on her back.

Harper nodded as her eyes filled. James pulled her out of the chair, hugging her tightly. Harper was the sweetest woman he had ever met. He was happy that Jack and she had fallen in love with each other.

"I'm not dead," Jack said in a groggy voice. "Don't get any ideas."

Harper turned to Jack with tears in her eyes but a grin on her lips. Hugging him tightly, she didn't notice when James left the room.

"Baby, don't cry," Jack said softly, holding her.

"You scared me," she admitted as she pulled back a little.

"I'm sorry." He scooted over so she could lay beside him. "I needed to get Emma back here."

"What if you had passed out at sea and didn't make it back?"

"Harp." He kissed her temple. "I knew what I was doing. Besides, we don't do what ifs."

James walked back to his room to check on Emma. To his surprise, she was lying in bed awake. Lying beside her, he ran his finger over her cheek. "How are you feeling?"

Emma didn't respond at first but jumped out of the bed and ran to the bathroom to get sick. Grinning to himself, James followed her. He found her leaning over the toilet, vomiting. Grabbing a big clip from the counter, he waded her hair up, putting the clip in to hold it back as he had seen her do many times before. He didn't speak, just ran a warm hand over her back. Sitting back, he handed her a towel to wipe her mouth when she was done.

"Come here," he said, pulling her onto his lap as they sat on the floor.

"I don't feel so good. And my head is pounding."

"Do you remember what happened on the boat?" he asked.

Thinking back, everything pieced itself back together. "I slipped as Jack started to go again. I hit my head." Touching her head gently, she felt the bandage and the bump.

"You fell overboard." He kissed her temple. "Knocked out. Both of you have hypothermia. He got you out of your wet clothes and wrapped you up but didn't do that for himself."

Emma looked up at him, worried. "Is he okay?"

"His core temperature was two degrees lower than yours," James stated. "But he'll be fine."

"Oh, thank goodness." She sighed, relieved.

"Feel better now?"

"No." She furrowed her brow a little.

James kissed her cheek. "You knocked your head really good. You'll feel better in a day or so. I'll have Harper give you something for your headache."

Emma's eyes carefully searched his expression, as something was bothering him. "What's going on in that head of yours?"

"When Jack called over the radio ..." He closed his eyes for a moment, remembering the empty feeling. "And said that you were overboard and he was searching for you, everything in my life stopped functioning. It took me back to when my mom died. I couldn't imagine my life without you at this point. It was the longest ten minutes of my life waiting for Jack to come back on the radio to say he had you."

Emma had tears in her eyes as he continued to speak.

"I want to wake up beside you every day." He kissed her temple again. "I don't want my life to be just mine. I want it to be ours. I want to love you every day until I die."

A small smile crossed her lips as the tears slipped out. "I feel the same way. You don't think it's strange that we met and feel this way so soon?"

"No." James shook his head. "I've always gone off my gut feeling. It knows. Why waste time? If you know you've fallen in love with someone, I believe in telling them. And I've told you."

Emma grinned. "I love it that you are straight up, no bullshit. I love you too."

James went to kiss her, but she stopped him, shaking her head.

"I just threw up. Let me brush my teeth."

"Oh, yes, I forgot." And he kissed her cheek instead.

Emma stood up and brushed her teeth as James rose to his feet. Looking in the mirror, there was a big bruise on the right side of her forehead close to the hairline. No wonder her head hurt, she thought. Noticing she was wearing one of his button-up shirts, she turned and smiled. "You dressed me," she stated, and he nodded. "And Jack saw me naked."

James nodded again, noting the mortified look in her eyes. "But he saved your life."

"I love you." Her arms slipped around his waist as she stood on her toes.

James leaned down, kissing her deeply. As they kissed, James picked her up and carried her to his bed.

# Chapter 19

Emma woke sometime in the middle of the night. The room was dark, and she could hear the wind howling against the windows as the rain pelted the glass. Being extremely hungry, she slipped quietly out of bed and went downstairs. With everyone asleep, she turned on a light above the range and began to sift through the fridge for some leftovers. Finding some roast beef and mashed potatoes, she made herself a plate, heated it up, and sat at the kitchen table to eat. Sitting in the barely lit room, she jumped when someone walked into the kitchen.

"Freakin' a." She shook her head, realizing it was only Jack. "You scared me."

"I'd say we're even—but not even close." He got a glass of water and made himself a plate of food like she did. Once he finished heating his plate, he sat at the table with Emma. They both ate in silence for about five minutes before Emma sat back and smiled at Jack.

"Thank you for saving me," she said softly.

"You're welcome, Emma." He covered her hand with his. "You scared the hell out of me. I just kept thinking, how would I ever look James in the eyes if I killed you?"

"I slipped. My own clumsiness. You weren't even going fast. I just wasn't paying attention because I was looking up at those clouds, thinking how scary it would be to fall over and get abandoned in the middle of the ocean."

Jack laughed as he shook his head. "You have quite an imagination, and it seems to make weird things come true. Let's put some good thoughts in that head of yours."

Emma grinned. "It's kind of sad that I don't have very many good thoughts in my head. Life's been kind of shitty until I met James."

"I know you've had a rough go of it," Jack agreed. "But I can see how

131

much my cousin loves you and in such a short amount of time. I think when you know who that person is that you want to spend your life with and create a family, it's clear as a sunny day."

"Did you know that with Harper?" Emma was curious.

"Not until I did an overseas mission with her." Jack grinned, remembering a moment when Harper was helping a sick little boy, and she looked over at him with a bright smile. "Harper has this special heart that wants to find the good in people no matter how bad they are. I was trained to not trust anyone and to kill if necessary. When it's just her and me, it's simple, relaxing, safe, and we have a lot of fun together."

"Wasn't it that way with Tess?"

"No," Jack answered with a shake of his head. "There was this intense … love that her and I shared. Training her and working together on the jobs we did made what we had very intense and very … almost painfully passionate. I can't explain it properly. Any man who has loved her but has not been able to keep her understands what I'm talking about. Maybe it's because I knew I couldn't keep and build a life with her. I don't know. Don't get me wrong. Tess and I had a lot of fun together, traveled all over the world, and did some crazy jobs that nearly killed us. But she and I weren't meant to spend our lives together."

"Was it difficult?"

"At first, yes," he answered. "It's God's will, not mine. I will be with whomever He chooses for me. And Harper is everything to me. I love her in a way that I've never loved any other woman. That is why I know she is the one."

"I've watched you two together," Emma admitted. "The way both of you look at each other is full of love and respect. It's very cool to see."

Taking her hand, he leaned close. "You deserve to be happy. And if James makes you happy, embrace it and don't let it go. I watched him with you, and it is the same way. He's happier than I've seen him in my entire life."

Tears slipped from the corner of her eyes. "Thank you."

They both ate a little bit more before Emma looked up at Jack.

"What?" he asked, since she had a strange look on her face.

"After I fell." She pushed the tears back. "I felt like I floated in the sky and was looking down at myself. I was facedown, but I watched something bump me and flip me over. Then it was like hearing a mother's voice telling me it was okay. There was a comfort in her voice. It was weird because I should have been scared to death. Then I woke up in bed."

"You were unconscious when I found you. I had to do CPR on the boat to bring you back." Jack raised his brows.

"Are you saying I died? And what I saw and felt was a dream sort of thing?"

"Usually when a person is not breathing and has no pulse, they're considered dead."

"Oh, how weird." Emma replayed the event over in her mind and vividly remembered waking up in the middle of the sea. "I was so scared," she confided. "But I wasn't alone. How strange is that?"

"With Harper being as eclectic as she is, nothing like that surprises me. I was scared for you, and I wasn't even in the water. But I found you, and here we are where we're supposed to be. There's something else that you need to know, and it has nothing to do with the events of today."

Emma looked at Jack wide-eyed, curious.

"I've noticed a tension between you and Tess."

With a deep sigh, Emma raised her brows with a fake smile. "She's not nice, and she doesn't like me."

Jack grinned. "Tess doesn't like anybody, and she is very protective of her family. You are still an outsider in her eyes. You're intimidated by her, and she feeds off it. My advice to you is to relax when your around her. You want Tess to like you because she and James are close. She will always be a part of his life because of the work they've done and the bond they share. Have confidence in yourself, Emma. There's no reason not to. You are a street-savvy, smart woman. You've survived the Markennas. That alone is damn amazing. Don't be intimidated by her."

"That's so much easier to say than do. I'll try." Emma shrugged, not showing much confidence.

"There you are," James said as he walked into the kitchen. Seeing Emma and Jack engaged in a deep conversation, he almost wished he hadn't interrupted. "Everything okay?"

"We were just talking about the boat accident." Jack eyed James, hoping he would realize that they needed to have a conversation about it later.

James caught Jack's look and gave him a simple nod as he placed his hands on Emma's shoulders and kissed her head. "How are both of you feeling?"

"Fine," Jack replied, and Emma simply nodded, as there was a lump in her throat. "I'm going to head back up to bed before Harper wakes up and freaks because I'm not there." Jack rose, picked up his plate with one hand, and covered Emma's with the other. After giving it a slight squeeze, he walked over to the sink and put his dish away and left the room.

Emma stood up, embracing James tightly as she cried. James held her for a long time. There was no rush, as he could stay like this for however long necessary. With the house silent inside, the sound of the storm was evident on the outside.

"Come on, Em." Pulling back a little, he took her hand.

Together, they walked into the library on the other side of the house. After sitting her down on the oversized sofa in front of the fireplace, he started a fire. Then he took a blanket from another chair and wrapped her up in his arms as he sat beside her. Both could feel the warmth of the fire on their faces as the glow softly lit the room.

"This is cozy." Emma glanced at him.

"Yes, it is." He kissed her temple. "Talk to me, Em."

Emma sighed, resting her head on his shoulder. Her eyes were mesmerized by the fire. "It scared me," she finally said with her voice barely above a whisper. "It was weird. It was like someone was out there with me. I kept thinking, *This is where I'm going to die.* It was like I was watching myself. There was this woman's voice speaking softly, like my mom would. It was strange."

James just held her tightly, listening.

"I'm so tired of the struggle ... to live," she admitted. "I'm constantly watching over my shoulder. Leary of every person that talks to me. I want normal." Turning to face him, she continued. "I want to know what it's like to be carefree, walk along the street without second-guessing every person that says hello. Now I'm wondering if there's a bullet that's going to be coming my way at any given time. I've been afraid since I was twelve. And now I have you, who's afraid of nothing. I want to be like you, and I don't want to disappoint you by being a pansy."

James couldn't help but smile. Running his finger over her cheek, he took a breath, releasing it slowly. "Emma, don't you know that you could never disappoint me? I just want you to let me love you and you love me. Everything else will fall into place if we have that. I love you just as you are. You're not a pansy. Even if you were, I'd still love you." He looked at his hand as Emma interlocked her fingers with his. "Em, there's a lot of love locked up inside of you, and it will take time for you to share it all, but I'm confident that you and I will have a perfect love and life together."

"There's something I need to tell you that I did before I met you." She looked down for a moment. "Well, it was more like before you showed up on that Wednesday."

James tilted her chin up because her eyes were avoiding his. "You can tell me anything."

"It has to stay between you and me—no one else, because I don't want this made into something big. You have to promise me."

"I promise you." He looked at her curiously, wondering what had her acting like this.

"I don't ever want to keep anything from you," she began. "I don't want a relationship with secrets. Those never last if there's secrets."

James was feeling a bit uncertain as to what she was wanting to tell him.

"I slept with a married man the weekend before you showed up." She watched his eyes for a reaction of some sort.

"Is that it?" he wondered, thinking it wasn't a big deal.

"Yes." She looked at him rather surprised, as he was so calm.

"Emma, I had no say in your life before we ... went on our first date. I've slept with a married woman or two myself. Just don't do that now, and we have no problem." That's when it hit him. "Did he use protection?"

Emma shook her head.

"Well, hell." There was a long, deep sigh. "Now, there's our problem. If you're pregnant, the baby could be this other guy's."

Emma nodded. "I'm so sorry. It wouldn't have happened had I known."

"Who was it?" James suddenly wanted to know.

"Just a man that I had met at the bar a few weeks before." She closed her eyes, shaking her head. "He came back just to chat, and one thing led to another. I'm sorry. I should've told you sooner."

James took a deep breath and released it slowly.

"I love you, and I don't want to lose you," she began. "But if you don't want to be doing this knowing the baby may not be yours ... I understand."

"Damn it, Emma. Of all the things to drop on me, I was not expecting this."

"I'm so sorry. I didn't expect any of this to happen. It's like my life is in a whirlwind, and I'm barely hanging on." Emma shook her head, closing her eyes.

"Em, I'm going to lay this out there so you know exactly how I feel." James intertwined their fingers.

Emma took a breath, biting the inside of her lip as the apprehension was all consuming.

"If this baby isn't mine, I will raise him or her as my own, but I won't share with the biological father. I don't want whoever it is in our lives. That only causes problems, and I won't do it."

Emma nodded slowly. "I understand." Resting her head on his shoulder, Emma knew James could never find out that it was Colin that she'd been with. That would cause problems, big problems. "I love you," she said tenderly.

"I love you too. Let's not worry about this until we have to." James tilted her chin up with his index finger and kissed her slowly.

Their kisses led to the rest of the night curled up with each other before the fire. James lay on the sofa with Emma asleep in his arms as his mind wandered in many different directions. Thinking about her falling off the boat in the emptiness of the sea bothered him. What would he have done if Jack hadn't found her? That thought alone made him hold her tighter. Then he thought of her with another man. That wasn't a thought he liked, although he knew better. Emma was thirty-four, so of course she had been with other men. But a married man? Hmm, he wanted to judge to a point but reminded himself of what he did with Tess after she was married and how he lied, straight faced, to Colin. Maybe there wasn't sex, but they still saw each other without Colin knowing. Who was he to judge her? He couldn't, but he did begin to wonder who this other man was.

Thinking back over the weekend before he went back to see her, he knew it was when they dealt with Taryn. They took her body back to Jonathan and burned the beach house. Matthew ran interference for Dominic with Connor and Tess while ... Colin ... son of a bitch. James knew he was speculating, but his gut told him he was right. Colin was the married man she slept with. Colin was the one who took off for a couple days after Taryn was killed in front of him. Colin was the one who slept with Emma. It all made sense now as to why Emma felt so comfortable around him. They slept together.

James worked on controlling his rage to end Colin McGowan's life. Experience and education made him put things into perspective. *Never make rash decisions*, he reminded himself. Rash decisions always made him have regrets, and he didn't want any more of those. With his thoughts swimming against the current in his mind, he calmed his immediate need to kill.

Emma was his. Why in the hell would Colin want Emma anyway? He had a beautiful wife and kids, everything that he wanted for years. Colin knew he was going back to see Emma. Was he just going to beat him to her? James thought back to that night at the bar. Yes, Colin knew he was going back, as he had told him he was.

At some point, all the thoughts that were running endlessly through his mind came to an abrupt halt, and he fell asleep.

## Chapter 20

The next morning, James woke up to a little girl leaning on his chest, looking at him with a bright smile. Grinning back at Savannah, he wrapped his free arm around her.

"Hi, beautiful," James said to her.

"Hi, Uncle James," Savannah replied, resting her chin on his chest.

"What trouble are you up to?"

"I'm not in trouble," she replied, smiling. "Daddy said to not wake you, but I wanted to lay with you and Aunt Emma."

"Well, it's okay." He rubbed her back.

"Savannah," Colin said softly as he quickly walked in to get her. "Sorry."

James watched Colin's eyes closely. "She's not a problem," James assured him.

Colin picked up Savannah and apologized again before walking out of the room.

James noted Colin didn't once look at Emma. Maybe he was wrong and it wasn't Colin but someone else. With doubt swirling about, he noticed Emma start to stir. But what he noticed more was how hot she was.

"James." A groggy Emma tried to open her eyes. "I don't feel so good."

James sat up so he could get a better look at her. Feeling her flushed cheeks, then forehead, he knew she had a fever. "I'll be right back," he said, getting up and putting his clothes back on.

James went to find Harper or Jack. They had the medical bags with the thermometer. Hearing voices in the kitchen, he went there first but didn't find who he wanted. Upstairs, he knocked on Jack's bedroom door softly.

"Hey," Harper answered with a wondering look. "What's up?"

"Emma has a fever," he said. "She's burning up. Would you mind checking her?"

"No, not at all," Harper said, pulling her stethoscope and thermometer from the medical bag. She followed James downstairs to the library.

James stopped her at the entry to the room. "Harper, be honest with me if she needs to go to the hospital."

"I will." Harper nodded, patting him on the arm.

Harper sat beside her and began her exam. After putting the thermometer in mouth, she listened to her heart and checked her pulse. Taking the thermometer out, she sighed a bit.

"Her temperature is 104." Harper seemed to be in thought. "Her pulse is a bit fast, but that comes from the fever. Her heart sounds good."

"Should I take her to the hospital?" The concern in his voice was evident.

"Not yet." Harper ran her hand over Emma's cheek. "Emma, do you hurt anywhere or just feel crappy?"

"I ache all over," she admitted. "My head hurts, and I'm very nauseous."

"Is she pregnant?" Harper looked at James.

James hesitated a moment before continuing. "We don't know, but we've done nothing to prevent it."

"Okay. I don't think she'd be far enough along to hear the heartbeat." Harper lifted the shirt that Jesse had on and placed her stethoscope on her lower stomach. Listening intently, she shook her head. "No, nothing yet. But that doesn't mean you're not. It's about five weeks before we can hear the heartbeat. So, here's my suggestions. First, let's move her upstairs to your room. It's cold down here. I'll bring up a cold cloth and have Carina make her some hot brew."

"Hot brew?" James looked at her curiously.

Harper smiled. "Trust me."

"Okay, Harper." James grinned and scooped up Emma.

James put Emma in their bed, and Harper came up with a very cold cloth and put it on her forehead. A little later, Carina came up with a hot cup of something. James had no idea what it was but trusted his grandmother and Harper to do right by Emma.

James sat quietly in his sitting room working as Emma slept. With Adam working from Jonathan's home in Savannah, they conversed online through a direct, private chat program that Adam developed. Pulling up all information, financial and personal, on Emma, James scoured the data to see if something stood out. There had to be something that was input incorrectly that would allow Markenna to find her so easily. For the life of him, he couldn't figure it out. His work was interrupted when a call came through his phone from a private, secure line. There were only a handful of people he knew whose calls came through like that.

"Hello," he answered, putting the laptop down and standing up.

"This is Brian," he stated.

"I know. One moment," James replied as he walked onto the deck from his room. Standing under the cover of the roof, he stared out but saw nothing, as his thoughts were on this call. "What's up?"

"I've been funded to contract with you," he remarked with his typical calm voice.

"I'm working on this Marcos Markenna case," James replied, shaking his head. "I can't take on an outside contract right now. It will have to wait until I finish this one."

"Your case and my case are intertwined," Brian explained. "Meagan Trask was kidnapped a couple weeks ago on a Friday morning from her home by Marcos Markenna."

James rested his hand on his hip, listening.

"I was on the phone with her when it happened." Brian remained void of emotion. "I have her daughter in custody with me. But I heard Markenna ask her where his two children were, Dominic and Emiliana, which is actually Jesse Anders. Meagan was her contact at the Justice Department for the last ten or so years. She's been in protective custody since she was twelve."

James stopped hearing what Brian was saying as soon as he heard the words children and Emiliana. How did he miss this? Did Adam know? But Adam would have said something. Should he have known and Emma thought he already knew?

"James?" Brian said, knowing he lost him somewhere in the conversation.

"Sorry, what?" James came back to the conversation.

"Is Dominic still with Jonathan?" Brian asked.

"No, he is here with me," James answered. "You said Emiliana?"

"Emma Grace Anderson, or as her father calls her, Emiliana Graca Markenna," Brian said. "Her biological father is Marcos. She testified against him. That is how he ended up in prison for the murder of her stepfather. Meagan had her in witness protection all her life, but he kept finding her somehow and sent his dead son to beat her a few times."

"I know the story," James admitted, turning to look back in his room at her sleeping in his bed. There was a Markenna sleeping in his bed. "Wait. I thought she testified against him for the murder of her mother, also?

"This is confidential, between you and me." Brian's voice was firm. "She did testify for her mother, but it was attempted murder. Her mother is alive, in protective custody."

"Brian, that girl has struggled for years alone. Don't you think she could've used her mother?" James was a little aggravated.

"There's more to it than I can tell you." Brian sighed, knowing James was right. "It's a conversation for another day."

"I have Emma too," James told him.

"What? How?" Brian asked.

"I met her at a bar in the shitty little town Meagan put her in." James shook his head again, trying to comprehend this turn of events. "When we did the background on her, I thought her stepfather, Seth Anderson, was her father. I didn't go back to birth records."

"You won't find Markenna on her birth records. I had it altered for her protection. Are you sleeping with her?" Brian asked, already knowing the answer.

"I was," James answered.

"Oh." Brian was a bit surprised, given James's dislike for the Markenna family. "Want the case? You're the best one to find Meagan, and I don't care what you do to Marcos. And I was wanting to contract you to keep Emma and Dominic safe until Markenna is found."

"I'll take care of it," James answered. "Send the Markenna files to Adam. I still need whatever Meagan has on that family."

"Consider it done," he replied. "I'll check back in with you in twenty-four hours."

"Brian, when this is over, you can either tell me where her mother is or I will find her." James ended the call and stood on his deck staring at Emma sleeping in his bed.

It seemed like he stood outside looking in for hours, but it was only twenty minutes or so. How could he miss such a vital piece of information? This woman he had fallen in love with was a damn Markenna! Dominic was her brother. That explained why they looked so much alike. *Does either one of them know this?* Emma had to know, but he didn't think Dominic knew. What was she thinking? Did she have an underlying motive for being with him? Or was she being her true self with him? All the conversations they'd had since he met her ran through his mind. He wanted to believe she was honest with him, but his guard was now up. Why didn't he catch this when Colin put her under hypnosis? And now he found out that her mother was alive.

With a deep sigh, he walked back into his room and over to where she slept. Running a soft hand over her forehead, she was still warm but not as bad as before. Slowly, her eyes blinked open with his touch, and she smiled.

"You have me worried," he said, sitting on the bed, holding her hand.

"I'm sorry." She yawned. "What's wrong with me?"

"You're very sick." He leaned over, kissing her forehead. "Falling in the water and the cold ride back got you."

"I feel better than this morning." She looked at him, feeling an odd sense of insecurity. "What's wrong?"

"Remember when I told you I would always be honest with you unless it was to keep you safe?" She nodded. "Did you know Marcos Markenna was your biological father?"

"Yes," she stated softly.

"I didn't," he replied.

Emma felt everything in her body sink to a deathly low. Tears slipped from her eyes, and she realized that everything between them could be gone in just a few more words. Sitting up, she wiped her eyes dry.

"You told me you did a thorough background." Her eyes filled again. "I just assumed you knew."

James shook his head.

"Does it really matter? My dad is Seth Anderson." She shook her head, wishing the tears would stop. "He raised me from the time I was born. I never knew the other man until ... that night."

"Does Dominic know who you are?" James wondered.

"I don't think so," she said. "It's not like I kept it a secret. I don't talk about it because he ... he isn't my dad." Emma got out of the bed, looking for her clothes. She didn't have much there, but she wanted to leave, as the terrible feeling wouldn't go away.

"What are you doing?" James asked, watching her look around the room.

"I want my clothes," she told him, going into the closet. "I'm leaving. You clearly don't want me here since Markenna is in my blood."

"Emma, you can't leave. I've been contracted to keep you and Dominic safe."

"Great." She shook her head, walking by him. "So I'm a fucking job to you now."

James grinned, as she was so … spirited—that was the word he would use for her. "Emma, will you stop?" James followed her out the bedroom and down the hallway.

"No," she answered, going down the stairs.

Everyone seemed to be in the great room when they came down the stairs.

"Emma!" James raised his voice a little to get her attention and make her stop.

"What?" She turned to him by the front door, knowing everyone was watching. She didn't care.

"Stop running," he told her.

Emma sucked in her bottom lip, feeling a bit lightheaded as the tears streamed from her eyes.

"All you do is run." He shook his head. "It's your first reaction to every problem that comes up. I will not chase you. So stop fucking running away. This caught me a little bit off guard, but it doesn't change how I feel. You just have to let me process this for a few because up to ten minutes ago, I was ready to take out the entire Markenna family, with Dominic sitting on the fence."

"That man has ruined my life since he killed my mom and dad." Her voice was soft. "And now he's trying to kill me—again. My own father, flesh and blood. Maybe it's in my blood too."

"Stop it." James's eyes were wide with irritation.

"Look what's happened. Having me in your life is bringing ruin. You were shot because of me. It's really no surprise that this is happening because nothing ever works out for me, not that I want anyone's pity. I told you I don't love because he always takes it from me."

"Em, he's not taking me away from you." He reached his hand out to her shoulder. "I love you."

"I feel like you felt I was keeping this from you." Her hands began to tremble. "I wasn't. I honestly thought you knew. I asked you how thorough of a background you did."

"I know." He nodded once more. "There was no mention of Markenna in your history, except with the testimony."

"James!" Harper was on her feet, running over to him.

"What?" He looked irritated as Harper interrupted them.

"Grab her!" Harper reached for Emma just as he caught her from falling on the floor.

"Shit," he mumbled under his breath, with Emma passed out in his arms.

"Can we take her back upstairs?" Harper asked James.

"Yes, of course." James sighed, heading for the stairs. He looked at Harper. "Maybe we should take her to the hospital?"

"If you want." She nodded in agreement.

"I do. I won't have peace of mind until I know she's okay."

"Okay." Harper nodded. "I'll come with you."

"Jack, are you good enough to come with us?" James asked, looking over into the great room.

"Yep." Jack stood up.

# Chapter 21

J ames sat in a private room with Emma, waiting for the doctor to return with her test results. She was sleeping, so his mind was spinning. He needed to talk to Adam and see if he received the documents from Brian. To simplify the thoughts, he pulled out his phone and just called him.

Fifteen minutes later, Jack and Harper walked into the room to see how things were going.

"Doctor been back yet?" Jack asked.

"No." He shook his head, standing as he stretched a little.

"What the hell was going on with you two?" Jack asked.

"Ready for this?" James gave a slight grin. "Emma's biological father is Marcos Markenna."

"Seriously?" Jack was surprised.

James told him about the long conversation he had with Brian earlier.

"I'm going to put four of my men on security at the house." James laid out his thoughts. "I would like you and the rest of my team to go deal with Markenna once we find him."

"Are you sure you don't want me to stay here with Emma and the family?" Jack asked.

"Remember who Matthew is underneath that Italian suit he wears?"

"Oh, yeah. I forget every now and then. Why don't you take him? Not that I don't want to go, but what is your reasoning?"

"He doesn't like to get his hands dirty anymore." James shrugged. "I respect his decision to step away from this arena."

"Is Emma going to try and leave if you're not around?" Harper asked, concerned.

"I hope not." James ran his hand over her head as the doctor walked in.

"Well, James." The doctor smiled, as she had known him for years. "Congratulations. She's pregnant. Not far enough along to detect a heartbeat but enough for the test to be positive. She has a slight concussion from the fall on the boat, but it's not severe enough to cause the lightheadedness and fainting spells. I believe that is from her being pregnant. The fever is from the bitter-cold water. That will get better in the next day or two. I'm not putting her on any medication. Keep giving her Carina's magic tea, and she should be feeling much better tomorrow. She needs to stay in bed for a few days. If she gets worse at any point, come back, but I don't think she will."

"Thank you, Doctor." James shook her hand.

"I'll get the discharge papers ready." The doctor left the room.

"Handcuff her to the bed," Harper told James. "Then you can leave. I'm not chasing her down if she takes off."

"I won't try and leave," Emma said with a yawn.

"Did you hear what the doctor said?" James leaned over as Jack and Harper left the room.

"No." She shook her head.

"We're having a baby." He kissed her lips softly. "She thinks that is why you keep fainting."

Tears filled her eyes as she turned away from him. She didn't want this baby to be Colin's. Deep down, she knew it was. "Can we not say anything to anyone yet?" Emma asked as she wiped away some tears.

"I won't say anything until you're ready." James caressed the top of her head. "You have to stay in bed a few days to get rid of this fever that you have."

Emma nodded as she sucked in her lower lip to keep from crying more. This was not what she envisioned with being pregnant.

# Chapter 22

Matthew walked down the stairs with his bag flung over his shoulder as he talked on the phone with his assistant. He dropped the bag by the door as he finished his conversation and ended the call. Walking into the living room, he found Tess laying on the couch as both the children played quietly on floor before the fire.

Kneeling before Tess, he spoke. "I have to go back to Chicago. There is a man that wants information on one of my clients, and he's giving my assistant a very difficult time."

"Take someone with you?" she requested, sitting up.

"I'm fine." He brushed the idea off. "I've dealt with difficult people before, and this won't be the first or the last time."

Her hand caressed his cheek. "Dominic's father is out there loose. Please take someone with you. One of James's men. Please."

"Hey, what's going on?" Colin walked into the room.

"Colin." Tess reached her hand out to him, and he took it, sitting beside her. "Matthew's going back to Chicago. Please send someone with him."

"You want me to tell Matthew what to do?" Grinning, he looked at her and shook his head.

"Yes!" The insistence in her voice was extremely evident. "Then I will go with you."

"I don't need anyone with me," Matthew told his brother, then glanced at Tess. "And you're not coming with me. The kids need you more than I."

"You seriously said that?" Tess laughed curtly.

Colin chuckled at the entire conversation, as Tess obviously didn't know Matthew's past.

"What the hell are you three conspiring about?" James asked, standing over them.

"Matthew has to go to Chicago," Tess told him. "Please send one of your men with him."

James glanced curiously at Matthew and then Tess and sighed. "I need a couple things from my house." He shrugged, taking a deep breath. "As long as we come back tonight, you can ride with me. You two watch out for Emma please? She needs to stay in bed another day. Her fever finally broke a couple hours ago."

"Of course. Thank you." Tess nodded.

"Tess, don't be mean to her either." James eyed her with brows raised.

"I won't," she said. "Who knows. Maybe I'll go and strike up a decent conversation with her."

"Just remember, she's not like you. Doesn't have your training or attitude. Don't make her feel like an idiot because she's not."

"You think I'm going to go up there and quiz her on qualitative versus quantitative data measures? The only one who can keep up with me on that is Matthew. Colin doesn't even hit the mark. Trust me, James. I'll play nice. I promise you."

"Tess." Matthew shook his head, irritated. "I don't need a damn babysitter."

"Forgive me for wanting you alive." She stood with her hands on her hips. "Don't be an ass."

Matthew shook his head at her and looked at Colin. "This is ridiculous. Don't think this is going to become the normal."

"What?" Tess cocked her head sideways.

"The only woman who gets a say in my life will be my wife," Matthew snapped with a sharp look at her. Then he looked at his brother. "Apparently, you haven't told her who I used to be."

Colin grinned, shaking his head, and when Tess looked at him, he simply pointed to James.

"What about James?" she asked, irritated.

"Matthew used to be just like him." Colin shrugged. "And he can still be that way if you piss him off like you're doing."

Tess sighed and glimpsed at Matthew. "Sorry."

"Ouch." Matthew's orneriness surfaced as he looked at her. "I felt your pain when you said that."

Colin laughed as her face went straight.

"I'm starting to see the brother resemblance," she stated. "And I'm not talking about your looks."

"Love ya." Matthew leaned over, kissing her forehead. "Stop being a pain in the ass." Then he walked over to Savannah, kneeling to her level. "Sav, can I have a hug? I have to go back to Chicago." She stood and went into his waiting arms.

"Are you coming back?" she asked, playing with the button on his shirt, as she always did.

"Tonight, just to see you." He kissed her cheek and smiled. "I love you."

"Love you too, Daddy," she said, giving him a tight squeeze around his neck.

After Savannah let him go, Connor stood up, wanting his hug from Matthew too.

"Bye, Daddy," Connor said, making Matthew's mouth gape.

Putting the child back down, he turned to Tess and Colin to defend himself. "For the record, that is the first time that's happened with Connor, and I didn't tell him to call me that. Savannah started that a couple days ago, and I didn't encourage that either."

Colin's gaze went from Matthew to Tess, and he smiled, cocking his head sideways. "We didn't talk about how that was going to play out with the kids," he told her. "Raise them as twins, but Savannah calls Matthew dad, and we expect Connor not to?"

"I guess we're going to have to be honest with them when they get older about all of this," Tess stated, looking from Colin to Matthew.

Colin sighed. "I am confident enough in my fathering skills to not be concerned about this. It's all new for Connor. As long as he's happy, I'm happy. And if you get to share that title with me with Connor, so be it. He'll know as he gets older, just as Sav will."

"Let's roll," James said, coming back into the room and taking notice of the tense demeanor between the three adults in the room. "What the hell is going on now?"

"Nothing you'd care about." Matthew patted him on the shoulder. "Let's go."

James gave all of them an odd look and headed out the door with Matthew.

Tess took Colin's hand, placing it on her belly. "They're moving like they're running on a track."

He smiled, kissing her softly. "These two boys, I will not share the title with anyone."

"Boys?" She looked at him curiously.

"Carina said you're carrying boys." He smiled. "Although, to be honest, boy or girl, I don't care because they're ours."

Tess shifted herself onto his lap. "They're all ours."

"I know." He sighed. "I can't believe how many children we're going to have. Four is more than I ever planned. But I like it. Our home will be full. I do have this feeling that you are going to want one more."

"I want another little girl." Tess's voice was low as she rested her head on his shoulder.

"I know." Colin kissed her forehead. "And my wife always gets what she wants because she never really asks for anything."

Tess glanced at him with a smile. "You should be glad I'm that way."

"I am to a degree." He kissed her lips. "But I would like a little input on this house we're buying."

"I don't care where we live as long as it's clean and has a nice big bathtub. And you know I don't like that fancy crap. I loved the way you remodeled your house in Atlanta."

"Our house," Colin reminded her.

"You had it before us," Tess stated. "I always look at it as yours. Regardless, I like the old craftsman style with all the modern conveniences."

"Me too." He kissed her again. "I've been talking with a Realtor the last few weeks. She has some places for us to look at when we get home."

"I think you should just buy the home you think is right for us and surprise me." Tess smiled. "You know me and what I like. Besides, you have more requirements for a home than I, so you find your family a home."

"Okay." With a finger, he tilted her head slightly to kiss her deeper. "Isn't there someone around here who could watch the kids so I can take you upstairs?"

"No," she stated. "I'm going to go talk with Emma. I'll try and play nice."

\*\*\*\*\*\*\*\*\*\*\*\*\*\*

Matthew looked at James with a grin after they closed the door behind them and walked to the car.

James simply shook his head and laughed a little. "Why didn't you tell them this was already planned?"

"Tess is not my wife." Matthew looked at him coolly. "She doesn't get to know everything that I'm doing all the time."

"And here I thought she could get you to do anything she wanted." It was James's turn to smile as they got in the SUV.

Matthew slipped in behind the driver's seat. "My last name may be Taylor, but I am a McGowan. And if you think Colin is an arrogant ass, you obviously don't recall that other side of me."

"Let me ask you this." James looked at him as Matthew drove. "Would you ever go for full custody of Savannah if you and Tess started fighting all the time?"

"Tess would have to be really, really bad for me to do something like that." Matthew thought for a moment. "She's a really good mom. But if I had to, you know Harrison would have Savannah in my custody before Tess even realized what was happening."

James nodded. "True, very true. And don't think for a moment that I've forgotten who you truly are."

# Chapter 23

Tess walked quietly up the stairs, as she didn't want to wake Emma if she was sleeping. Although she knew she needed to give Emma a chance, Tess found herself instantly at odds with her. What she didn't understand was why. With the door open to James's room, Tess walked in cautiously. Looking around, she smiled, remembering the night she and James sat on his sofa talking. His kindness would always be remembered, as its value was unmeasurable.

"Are you lost?" Emma asked as she saw Tess staring at the sitting area.

Slightly startled out of her thoughts, Tess turned to Emma. "No, not lost. Just remembering. The day Jack and I broke up, I was here. James was very good to me, as he usually is. We sat and talked right over there until I fell asleep."

Emma sat up in the bed.

"That was also the night I lost the baby." Tess stared blankly at the bed Emma was in as she remembered each and every detail of that horrible but brief time.

"I'm sorry. I didn't know." Emma was sincere.

"Not exactly something I go around sharing with everyone." Tess gave her a slight grin, knowing Emma would think she was more approachable this way. Walking over to the bed, Tess put on her mother hat to check Emma's temperature. "James said your fever broke?" Tess placed the back of her hand on Emma's forehead, then cheek.

"It did." Emma nodded. "I feel better than yesterday."

"Good." Tess took the half-filled water glass and went to the bathroom to rinse and refill. After she set it back on the nightstand, she looked at Emma and smiled.

"What? Why are you being nice?" Emma knew Tess was up to something.

"My extent of dealing with women is Harper, Gina, and Carina. I find most women to be caddy, bitchy, and very manipulative. Gina told me, not too long ago, that I needed to find a way to get along better with some women, as the men in my life would be getting girlfriends and getting married. You know, all that good stuff. Men are much easier to deal with than women."

"Am I the first one?" Emma asked.

"Pretty much." Tess ran her hands over her stomach, as the babies were moving.

"I like to think I'm a decent person. I'm not using James for his money or anything like that. I really do love him."

Tess held her eyes to see if she would break, but she didn't. Damn it. Maybe Emma was telling her the truth. "He's my best friend. I know that's a little odd, as most women have another woman as their best friend, and mine is a guy who's a mercenary."

"I would never try and take that from you. I promise you." Emma took a breath.

"I'm learning." Tess gave a half smile. "You know how we feel about promises around here?"

Emma nodded.

"Did he tell you about his mother and how close they were?" Tess sat on the bed.

"Yes. Actually, Carina told me how she died and the grief James went through."

"There's a sense of abandonment that he feels from time to time. With his father leaving when he was young and then his mother dying, he felt alone, left behind. You can't keep walking away from him when things get difficult or scary. That's a terrible thing to do, especially to him, given his past."

"I always had to run or they would have beaten me more. It's a built-in instinct with my past. James knows this and knows that I'm working on the whole trust thing."

"I know it's not easy. It took years after Jonathan got us to teach me to trust him and Gina. And then, when I met Colin …" Tess shook her head. "It took him a very long time to get me to trust him enough to even kiss him. I knew his reputation, and I wasn't going to be another notch."

"You can see how much he loves you." Emma felt like she was walking over quicksand and just another notch.

"Can you?" Tess asked.

"Yes." Emma nodded.

"Hmm." Tess shrugged. "I guess. We, like most couples, have our ups and downs."

"It's certainly a learning curve for me." Emma yawned. "Are there leftovers?"

Tess smiled with a nod. "Of course. With Carina in the house, there's always food."

"My grandmother was killed when I was eighteen by someone in that family. Carina reminds me of her." Emma gave a simple smile.

Tess grinned with a nod. "I think she's everyone's grandmother. She's the only one I know. I used to come here years ago and spend weeks at a time. She was one of the people who taught me how to cook and can food. I learned a lot of things I probably wouldn't have learned otherwise."

"I've only been here a few weeks." Emma got out of bed to put on some sweats. "I've already learned things from her." Once dressed, Emma walked a bit closer to Tess, who was leaning against the bed. "Can I ... I know this is kind of weird ... but can I touch your stomach?"

Tess laughed a little. "Of course." Taking Emma's hand, she placed it on the side where she could feel the babies moving the most.

Emma grinned. "Does the idea of twins make you nervous at all?"

"No," Tess answered honestly. "We really only planned on two children. But with the way things happened, we'll be having four. And if these two are boys, I want to try for one more. I want another girl."

"Five?" Emma shook her head. "I'm mortified about having one."

"Financially, we can afford it easily. And I think we're good parents. At home, we have a good routine. I can't wait until we can go back to Portland."

"I'm pregnant," Emma said softly.

Tess's eyes hooked with Emma's, rather shocked. "Does James know?"

Emma nodded just as the tears started.

"Don't you want this baby?"

Emma shook her head. "Isn't that terrible? Thinking that way, I shouldn't even be allowed to be a mother."

"No, no." Tess ran a soft hand over Emma's shoulder. "You probably just didn't expect this. It'll be okay. And if it's not, we'll make it okay."

"I don't know if it's James's baby." Emma's voice was barely a whisper.

Tess raised her eyebrows, as this was surprising. Finally, she wasn't the only one in the family who had this issue. Maybe Emma wasn't so bad after all. "Does James know this?"

"Yes." Emma nodded again. "I made a huge mistake. A moment of weakness after years of holding myself back. I didn't know James was coming to see me or it would've never happened. I'd been alone for so long. I craved that touch of a man."

"I understand that." Tess gave her a long hug. "If James knows, trust that it will work out just fine. Do you know this other man?"

"Not really." Emma shrugged. "He was just a passerby at the bar. We got along easily. The chatting between us led to a few beers at my house and then a couple nights with him. Just sex. I've never regretted something so much in my life."

"Never regret sex. That's the animalistic side of humans that needs to be fulfilled. I never regret it. Hell, look at my past." Tess smiled, making Emma laugh a little.

"Thank you." Emma gave her one more hug before they headed downstairs.

# Chapter 24

Matthew walked up to his assistant, Anna. He was dressed in his suit and tie and was ready for whoever this man was that wanted to see him. Generally, he didn't give in to strange people and their demands, but this one made Anna nervous, and she openly shared that with Matthew.

"I'm sorry I had you fly back for this." Her voice was soft as she looked up at Matthew from her desk. "This man was … he looked … almost violent. It was very unsettling. I was hoping your friend James would've come with you."

"He did." Matthew smiled. "After all these years, have you ever known me to not be well prepared?"

"Oh good." She sighed, relieved. "Will you leave your door open please? I will have a security officer or two on the floor also, just in case."

"He really spooked you," Matthew noted. "Just one security officer at the main lobby on this floor. James has taken care of the rest. Don't worry. It will be fine. What time did you tell him to come back?"

"Three," she told him.

Matthew looked at his watch and nodded.

"Call me when he comes in, like you do with all visitors," he requested.

"Yes, sir," she said, breathing out slowly.

Matthew walked into his office and immediately pulled out his phone.

"How's your view?" he asked James.

"Perfect," James responded. "I have Grey and Thomas with clear sight lines. I will be in the office next to yours listening. Are you good?"

"Yep." Matthew nodded. "Oddly enough, I'm not even nervous."

"No reason to be," James stated as he headed into Matthew's building. "Besides, I've never known you to be nervous."

"Maybe this will turn out to be nothing at all." "Rather be safe than sorry," James reminded him.

Matthew ended the call, taking a seat at his desk. He began to thumb through his messages from the last few days. He became engrossed in his work and didn't realize how quickly the time was going by. When his phone buzzed, he looked at his watch, and it was three.

"Yes?" he simply said, pressing the intercom.

"I have your three o'clock, Mr. Antoine Markenna for you," she said.

"Please show him in," Matthew replied, standing up from his desk to greet this stranger that was somehow related to his brother.

"Mr. Taylor." Antoine held out his hand as he walked into Matthew's office. "I do apologize for the urgency of this visit. And I do hope I didn't interrupt anything of great importance."

"Mr. Markenna." Matthew shook his hand and gestured for him to sit. "Is it a pleasure to meet you?"

Matthew sized the man up quickly. He was his height and weight, with the same dark hair and green eyes as Dominic. He wore an expensive Italian suit, as Matthew recognized the material and design from a couple that he had at home. He wore a gold wedding band and had an attitude like his brother, Colin, arrogant yet seemingly reasonable.

"Probably not," he stated honestly. "My uncle has requested that I find his son, Dominic. I have a record of him investing with your company a few years back. I was wanting to know if you might have any information on how to reach him that I don't. His home is empty, his phone disconnected. We're very concerned."

"All of my client's information is confidential," Matthew stated.

"And I completely understand that." Antione was very courteous. "I was hoping you could make an exception this one time? His father is willing to compensate you very nicely for any information that you may have."

"As you can see, I don't have a need for compensation. And I would be happy to help you." Matthew sat back. "As soon as you bring me a warrant."

Antoine smiled with a sigh, knowing he was going to have to do this the hard way. "Mr. Taylor, you didn't exist fourteen years ago." He stared directly into Matthew's eyes as he pulled out a small envelope and slid it over to him. "I'm certain you wouldn't want anything to happen to that beautiful little girl, would you?"

Matthew opened the envelope and smiled. James had quietly walked into the room and had his glock pointed at Antoine's head.

"I'm certain nothing will happen to this beautiful little girl." Matthew was calm, level headed, and unaffected by his threats. "Because I can guarantee you will have a bullet in your head faster than you could blink."

James cocked his gun to make him aware of his presence.

Antoine grinned, shaking his head. "How did you know?"

Matthew chuckled, clearly amused. "You obviously don't know who I am. Which is fine. That just means my background that we placed out there in the public was done thoroughly. I know who the Markenna family is and the reputation that goes along with the name. They've touched my life one too many times. I have no problem playing adversary in a game with the Markennas."

"You are a brave man, Mr. Taylor." Antoine grinned, liking this man for some unknown reason.

"I don't negotiate," Matthew stated, weary of this conversation already. "You will not get any information on my client."

Antoine nodded in amusement. "And here I am considered the negotiator in the Markenna family. We are at odds, Mr. Taylor. Is there anything I can do to persuade you?"

"No. I will never hand over my brother to that monster. Tell him to go fuck himself."

Antoine smiled with a nod. "You have Isobelle's features. She was a beautiful woman. I should've known when I walked in here. I don't want problems. I would prefer Dominic remain in hiding or whatever he is doing. Marcos only wants him dead."

"Why are you doing this?"

"He has threatened the life of my son Lucas. I will do anything for my children."

"You say children, but you only spoke of one being threatened."

"Lucas is my son from my mistress. He's only three. You're a father; you know there are no limits to protect our children."

Matthew wanted to disagree but couldn't. "Where's Markenna?"

"Georgia," he answered honestly again. "He wants to speak with his son and his daughter. But I think there will be bloodshed."

"Of course there will be—his." James walked to the side of Antoine.

Antoine cocked his head to look at this man who had a gun pointed at his temple. "You're the one with that woman, his daughter. I told him she disappeared after she was released from the hospital. He wants her dead."

"I'm very aware of that with the bullet that was dug out of my shoulder." James didn't move from his position. "It seems Markenna didn't believe you because there was a sniper at my home. Take note, past tense."

Antoine directed his attention back to Matthew. "Look, I don't want to be here. I don't want any of this. But my family will be hurt if Marcos doesn't get what he wants. And if he finds out I've betrayed him, they will die."

"What's your relation?" Matthew asked.

"He's my uncle," he stated.

"'Tis true, we don't get to choose our family." Matthew grinned, thinking about his brother, Colin.

"Where is he right now?" James asked.

"I told you—Georgia."

"Where in Georgia?" James asked again.

"That little house that his daughter lives in," he replied.

"Is he waiting for you to come back?" Matthew asked.

"No." He shook his head. "I have to call him, and we'll meet up wherever he wants."

"Does he have Meagan?" James asked.

"Yes," he answered, closing his eyes momentarily. "He's beaten her pretty bad, and I'm almost certain he's … done other things."

James looked at Matthew and shook his head. "It can't be this easy." James pressed the sensor for the radio to his men. "Six, copy?"

"Copy six," Rick answered.

James spoke as he stared blankly at Antoine. "I need you to detain our new friend."

"There in five. Six out."

"Stand up," James told him. "Are you carrying?" he asked as he patted him down.

"Inside right ankle," he answered.

James found the small handgun, tossed it to Matthew, and motioned for Antoine to stand in front of the east-facing window.

"Don't move," James warned him. "There are two snipers on you as we speak."

Antoine nodded. "He does bad things to women. I tried to get him to let me trade her, but he wouldn't. I'm sorry."

James was silent, as he knew the bad things Marcos did. *Meagan was well trained*, he thought, *and she should be able to handle this.*

Antoine sighed, looking nearly bored. Matthew opened his door for Rick when he knocked softly, and James motioned him over.

"Where's your family?" James asked him.

Antoine cocked his head sideways but didn't answer.

James grinned at the lack of cooperation. "Here's the way I see this: you can tell me where they are, and I will extract and put them in a safe house until I beat Marcos to death, or we can just leave them at the mercy of your uncle and that fucked-up Markenna family. Your choice."

"How do I know you won't kill them?" he asked.

"You don't," James simply stated. "The key is to pick the lesser of the two evils, which, at the moment, is myself. I don't harm women and children. Well, that's not entirely true. I have killed some women but never a child."

"I do hope you have your wife and mistress set up nicely with finances," Matthew chimed in. "Because chances of your survival at this moment are somewhere down in the low percentages. I don't know who you thought you were coming to strong-arm, but that doesn't work with me."

James looked up at Matthew and grinned, as he loved this side of him.

Antoine didn't speak, as there was nothing left for him to say.

"Shoot him if he even looks at you weird," James told Rick.

"Yes, sir." Rick stood with his gun firmly placed in his hand and watched Antoine while James and Matthew stepped outside the office.

"How do you want to play this out?" Matthew asked James as they stood in front of Anna's desk, speaking softly.

"He's not getting Dominic, and Emma can't go home," James said. "It can't be this easy. Something's not right."

"I know," Matthew agreed. "Let's put a tracker in him and let him go. Have Adam get into his phone and record everything. I think he can make it be a microphone as well. Let's touch base with Dominic and see what he knows about his cousin."

James nodded in agreement. "Don't you miss doing this work?"

Matthew thought for a moment, then shook his head. "No."

"Hey, gorgeous." James smiled at Anna with a flirty little grin. "Would you mind handing me my bag?"

Anna pulled out James's black duffel from under her desk and handed it to him. "Am I going to have to clean up anything?"

"No, ma'am." James gave her a kiss on the cheek. "I clean up my own messes."

"I knew there was a reason I liked you." She grinned.

James placed the duffel on her back counter and opened it up. He took a syringe, filled it with a clear liquid, and handed it to Matthew. Then he pulled out a small lock box and opened it up. Inside was another needle with a larger head and a nearly microscopic tracking device. James prepared that needle with a clear solution with the small device and turned back to Matthew.

"I'll knock him out, then hit him with this. I don't want him to know about it."

"Okay." Matthew nodded.

James walked back into the room, standing before this man. "I'm going to let you go. Tell Marcos Markenna that I'm going to hunt him down and beat him until he's dead. I will not use a bullet. I will use my hands. I want him to feel the pain that Emma felt every single time his filthy son beat her." James was within inches of him and quickly pierced his thigh with the needle. "Now you're going to sleep, and when you wake up, you can go back to whatever hole you came out of."

Antoine's eyes stared coldly at James as they slowly began to droop. "I have something that used to belong to you." Antoine looked at Matthew and smiled. "Sarah." With that said, Antoine slumped to the floor, out cold.

"What the fuck?" Matthew was stunned to hear that name come from his mouth.

"One job at a time, Matt." James glanced at him. "We're putting a tracking device in him. Let's get Meagan, kill Marcos, then I can focus on finding Sarah. And now I have a starting point."

Matthew shook his head, still shocked.

James and Rick picked Antoine up and placed him on the couch.

Taking the other needle, James pierced his chest just to the right side of his heart and pressed the plunger. Taking out his phone, he called Adam.

"What's up?" Adam answered.

"Can you start tracing chip 876, and I'm going to plug in a phone to mine and pull the data from it as well." James held the phone between his ear and shoulder as he pulled the wire to connect the two devices. Once plugged in, he sat at Matthew's desk and put Adam on speaker.

"Okay." Adam sighed as his fingers flew across his keyboard. "I have the chip in Chicago … at … Matthew's business … in his office. Is that correct?"

"Yes," James answered.

"Okay, computer is set to track, and I sent that to your phone as well," he told him. "As for the phone … okay, all the data is coming through right now. Let me put on my program to hear all his calls and utilize the microphone. Then you can give it back. Okay, done. I'll analyze and get back to you."

"Perfect, thank you," James said, ending the call and disconnecting the phones. He put Antione's back in the same pocket he took it from. "Let's go put his body in his car and head back."

Matthew nodded and looked over at Anna, who had watched the whole thing. "Will you be okay here if I head out of town?"

"Of course." She shrugged, unaffected by what she had witnessed. "Business as usual. You know me. I would suggest waiting until after five before moving his body anywhere. Let the staff get out here first."

Matthew glanced at his watch and nodded. "It's only an hour out."

James took a seat on the couch and closed his eyes.

"Great." Anna looked at Matthew. "There's some items I need you to address now that you have some time."

"Very well." He sat back down at his desk. "Just bring it in here."

After they dropped Antoine in his rental car, James and Matthew headed to his home on the outskirts of the city. He needed to pick up a couple of items from his basement and one thing from his safe. Grey, Rick, and Thomas went ahead to James's private airstrip to prepare the jet.

"Matthew," James said as he walked back into the kitchen from the basement. "You've known me for a very long time, so tell me, honestly, what you think of Emma."

"She's wife material," Matthew simply stated.

James smiled. "That's all I get?"

Matthew grinned. "That's all you need. Let me put it to you this way. If you don't stay with her, I'm going to call her up, charm her, marry her, and have a few kids. Can you imagine what our children would look like with her eyes and my features? Beautiful children just like Savannah."

James furrowed his brow, looking at him sideways. "I'm starting to see a little bit of Colin in you."

Matthew smiled with a soft laugh.

"I know the McGowan's design and buy million-dollar rings." James paused, thinking of Tess's wedding ring from Colin. It was as stunning as she was. "Do you think Emma would like this?"

James slipped a small ring box across the counter to Matthew. When he opened it, he found a simple yet elegant diamond on a gold band.

"Where did you get this?" Matthew asked.

"It was Gran's. She gave it to me years ago. It was her original engagement ring from a man name Richard. He was killed in the war in the mid-forties just after they were engaged. She said he was her true love."

"That's depressing yet romantic." Matthew eyed him. "This is a beautiful ring. Tess would love it, so I imagine that Emma would love it even more."

"Do you say that because Tess grew up with money and Emma didn't?" James wondered.

Matthew nodded. "So, you're going to ask her to marry you?"

James nodded. "Other than Tess, I've never loved … shit!"

"You just messed up, brother." Matthew laughed.

"No one really knows but Jack and your damn brother." James shook his head, irritated with himself.

"Well, you're still alive. My brother has definitely changed over the years."

"I lied to him a while ago." James thought back to their conversation in the parking lot. "I saw his wife after they were married. I don't know. Not my smartest moment, I guess."

Matthew laughed, shaking his head.

"What?" James knew there was something that Matthew wanted to tell him but was pulling the reserved card.

"The night Taryn was killed and Colin took off …" Matthew thought back.

It was close to midnight when Matthew heard his door open. Leaning over, he turned on the lamp to see Tess walking in. Without a word, she closed and locked the door behind her, then went to the other side of the bed, lifted the covers, and climbed in beside him. After turning the lamp back off, he rolled over, wrapping her up in his arms. Time passed slowly, and Matthew couldn't resist kissing her exposed neckline. They were simple, soft kisses that led to an incredible night of deep, passionate love.

"Tess woke up just before sunrise and went to her room, so no one would find her in mine," Matthew confided.

"Interesting. She's keeping you a secret. I saw her come out of Taryn's room with Dominic, and I thought she had done something with him. You know you're the only one she would leave Colin for?" James shook his head, wondering why Tess would lie to him.

"I know. She told me about Dominic. And we talked about us. It was a very emotional night."

"She going to stay with him?" James asked.

Matthew nodded. "She's trying. She doesn't want to leave him because of the kids. I get it."

"Yes, but one of those kids is yours," James reminded him.

"Yes, but the other three aren't." Matthew sighed. "I'm not raising all of his kids. I would if I had to. But he needs to get his shit together and be a good husband. I know he's a good father."

"What the hell are you doing, man?" James asked his friend.

"I don't know." Matthew shook his head. "I'm still in love with a woman that's married to my brother but had my daughter. It's messed up any way you look at it."

"Has it happened since then?"

Matthew sighed with a guilty grin.

"We need to find you another woman," James stated. "Tess and Colin … I don't even know how to describe them except perfectly fucked up together."

"I know." Matthew nodded in agreement. "You know, with you, Colin, and Jack settling down, my father is going to be all over my ass about it too."

"Is there anyone?"

"Nope." Matthew didn't even hesitate with his answer. "Sarah and Tess, that's it. Nothing else is worth getting serious about."

"How do you think Sarah knows Antoine? Any ideas?"

"No." Matthew shook his head. "I can't even imagine how Sarah would know any of the Markennas."

"I know Gina's worried, as she hasn't heard from her in over six months. When this is over, I told Gina that I would start looking for her. When I find her, I'm bringing her home, with or without her cooperation."

Matthew was going to say no but changed his mind and simply nodded his head.

"Let's get out of here." James motioned to the door.

# Chapter 25

J ames and Matthew flew back to Maine. Jack picked them up with Dominic in tow. It was nearly eight, and James had Jack drive them to a restaurant first where they could talk in private. Sitting in a corner booth, the four men talked without interruptions.

After James shared the day's events with Antoine, he looked at Dominic for some information.

"I haven't seen Antoine since we were teenagers." Dominic shrugged. "He couldn't stand his father any more than I could stand mine. I don't know. He was going to come with me when I left but changed his mind last minute. It doesn't make sense that he would be helping my father."

"Would his family really threaten the life of his son?" Matthew asked.

"Yes," Dominic answered without hesitation. "Business comes before blood in that family."

James had his phone out, watching the tracking device that he put in Antoine. The red dot was heading south. Looking up at Dominic, he sighed. "You hate this. I get it—not your thing. But this is your father that's trying to kill off my girlfriend, your sister. I'm asking for your help in figuring this out before he succeeds."

"What do you mean *my sister*?" Dominic inquired.

"I forgot you didn't know." James realized he just gave away something that Emma may have been keeping a secret. "Shit. Emma probably wanted to tell you, but yes, she is your sister. She's known all her life."

"Why didn't she say something?" Dominic wasn't sure if he was angry or happy about this information.

"This is something the two of you need to talk about. I just found out a couple days ago from speaking with Brian. Emma doesn't think of him that way. To her, her father is Seth Anderson. Marcos is a bad nightmare."

"Holy shit," Dominic muttered. "If you know where he's at right now, why don't you go do your thing now?"

James looked at Jack, who shrugged.

"We can go now," Jack told him. "We've got three of your men here. You know the layout of Emma's place. Matthew and Dominic can go back to Gran's and take care of them until we get back. You're tracking that other guy. We go in, take him out, move on. Emma's free, Dominic's free, and I can get married."

"Is that all that's on your mind?" James asked his cousin.

"It takes up a great deal of it." Jack grinned.

James pulled out his phone and called Grey. As he spoke, Matthew and Jack talked.

"I have to go back and tell Harper before I leave," Jack told him.

"She's going to want to go with you." Matthew smiled.

Jack gave a small laugh. "It's kind of crazy when I think of how our lives will be after all this is over. Settling into a normal day-to-day life with Harper will be very different than what I'm used to."

"When Sarah and I lived together those last three years, it felt good, right." Matthew thought back. "Our only problem was that we both worked too much. But I liked having her to come home to. I miss that."

"I'm sorry." Jack's forehead furrowed. "I forget what you've been through. I don't mean …"

Matthew stopped him. "Jack, don't. You can talk about Harper with me. I'm glad you make her happy. And as her brother, I know you won't mess that up."

"She makes me happy too."

"I know. Did you set a date?"

Jack shook his head. "I haven't asked her to marry me yet. I need to find a ring. I want to do this in all the traditional ways. I wouldn't have even slept with her if she hadn't ambushed me. Harper may be quiet compared to her siblings, but when she wants something, she's going to get it."

Matthew laughed. "Who does that remind you of?"

"Her damn brother." Jack gave a nod. "It's interesting if you watch Colin and Harper. They share many characteristics that I never noticed until recently. You can tell those two take after their father."

Matthew nodded, understanding. "Did you know she graduated

summa cum laude from college and graduate school? I only pulled that in college. Graduate school was a little bit more challenging. Harper's just a sponge with education."

"Sometimes I think she's too smart for me," Jack confided.

Matthew shook his head. "No, you're book smart and street-smart. Never discount yourself. Do you really think I would have told you how Harper felt if I thought you were an idiot?"

Jack grinned. "I guess not."

"And that concludes this conversation."

Less than thirty minutes later, they were walking into Carina's home. James was on his phone planning as Jack's eyes scanned the living room for Harper.

"Harp, come here," he said, spotting her on the couch.

Harper took his hand, and they walked out of the room, down the hall to the library.

Jack placed his hands on her cheeks and kissed her slowly and deeply. "I love you," he said softly.

"I love you too, Jack." Her hands rested on his shoulders. "What's going on?"

"I'm going with James and his men back to Savannah, or rather where Emma lives." His finger ran over her lower lip. "Marcos Markenna is there."

"Is James going to kill him so we can be done with this?"

Jack grinned. "That's the intent. We should be back in the morning as long as it all goes well."

"Am I allowed to say be careful?" She bit the inside of her lip.

"No." Jack kissed her again. "I miss you already." Jack hugged her tightly.

James walked into the kitchen as he finished the checklist on the phone with Grey. His jet would be ready to fly out in forty-five minutes. That gave him fifteen minutes to tell Emma. When he finished the call with Grey, he grabbed a bottle of water from the fridge. When he turned around, Emma was quietly standing by the counter. "Hey," he said softly. "I thought you'd be sleeping. How are you feeling?"

"Fine," she answered. "You're leaving again?"

James nodded, walking over to her. "Markenna is at your house."

"My house?" Tears filled her eyes. "I tried to call Meagan again, after you left this morning, but there was no answer."

"Emma." James hesitated a moment. "You're not going to reach her. Marcos kidnapped her a couple weeks ago."

Emma turned a lighter shade of pale as an unsettling feeling crept through her entire body, making her a little lightheaded.

"The call with Brian other day was to contract with me to find Meagan and dispose of Markenna."

"You didn't tell me." Emma shook her head as tears silently fell over her cheeks.

"We got a bit sidetracked. But I know where he's at," James reminded her. "My team and I will go get her and take care of him. Em, this is what I do."

"This makes me so nervous." Emma nodded, wiping the tears away. "I don't want you to leave me alone. What if it's a trick just to take you away from me?"

James smiled, having a weird sense of déjà vu. "You'll be safe here with Matthew and Colin, and three of my men are staying here patrolling around the house."

"Just don't …" She placed her hands on his chest and pushed back the tears. "Just don't forget to come back to me."

James tilted up her chin and kissed her lips softly. "Every path I choose will bring me back to you." He kissed her softly. "I love you."

"I love you too," she said, wrapping her arms around him as Tess walked in.

"Would you mind?" James gestured at Emma in his arms.

Tess sighed. James knew she wasn't one who could console a weepy woman. "Hey, Emma." Tess put her hand on her shoulder. "Let him go do what he does best, and you can come hang out with Harper and me."

Emma turned to Tess, wiping her tears away, and nodded. "Sorry I'm being such a baby."

"It's okay. Just don't make it a habit." Tess took her hand.

"I've got to go," James told Emma. He gave her a quick kiss on the lips, then leaned over to Tess kissing her forehead. "Thank you, little mama."

Tess nodded, shooing him away. "Come on, Em. Sit with me?"

# Chapter 26

Emma sat in the great room with Colin, Tess, and Dominic. Tess was sleeping as she leaned against Colin's shoulder while he worked on his computer. Dominic had a book in hand, just like Emma. The two children had been put to bed a couple of hours before, and Carina had retired to her room about an hour ago. Harper had been sleeping for a few hours already. Emma looked up when Matthew walked back into the room after his shower.

"Do you guys hear that?" Matthew asked, looking across the room at the floor-to-ceiling windows. It was dark, but with the full moon being the night before, the outside was illuminated just enough to see the reflection on the water and the tree line around the property.

Colin stopped typing to listen. "It's a helicopter," Colin stated, looking over at his brother. "Maybe there was an accident somewhere nearby, and they're doing a life flight."

"Hmm, maybe," Matthew said as he walked across the room to look out the windows. The sound became closer, prompting him to stop halfway. "Colin." Matthew glanced over at him. "Got a bad gut feeling about this."

"Tess, wake up." Colin nudged her.

"What?" With a yawn, she opened her eyes.

Matthew saw the helicopter drop down to window level. "Everybody, down!" Matthew yelled, pulling Emma out of the chair and on to the floor.

Colin, Tess, and Dominic followed suit just as a spray of bullets flew across the room. The sound was piercingly loud and lasted a solid five minutes. When the helicopter ducked away, they shuffled out of the great room and into the foyer.

"The kids," Tess said, eyes wide, and headed up the stairs.

"I'll get Carina," Matthew said, heading down the hallway past the library.

Dominic, Colin, and Emma followed Tess up the stairs to get the children and weapons. Tess filled her backpack with a few items of necessity, put her 9 mm in her waistband, and picked up Savannah as Colin picked up Connor. Harper came out of her room just as Colin was going to get her.

"What's going on?" she asked, still sleepy.

"How the hell did you sleep through that?" Colin asked.

"Well, something loud woke me up," she explained.

"Bad people outside, Harp," Colin told her. "Grab your coat and shoes. We have to leave, now."

"Oh my gosh." Harper pushed back the tears as fear began to rule her emotions.

Dominic went up to Tess and took Savannah from her arms. "I'll take her. I can't shoot a gun like you do."

"Okay." She let him take her and pulled her gun from her waistband. "Go between Colin and me. Harper, follow Dominic."

"Emma." Colin looked at her in the hallway. "Take Connor and stay behind me." Colin looked at Tess, now that they both had free hands. "Ready?"

"Yep." Tess nodded, pulling up the rear as everyone filed down the stairs.

Colin stopped on the last step, shielding everyone from the next round of bullets that were being sprayed. Matthew and Carina were across the hall, and Matthew was talking on the radio to James's men that were outside firing back. Matthew held up his hand to tell them to duck down, which they did. Matthew wrapped Carina in his arms, kneeling just as a large explosion outside the great room sounded. Then the whirl of the helicopter losing altitude and drifting away was very evident. And when it crashed into the bay, they knew James's men had taken out the chopper.

Matthew put up his hand to Colin to round up everyone and head out the front door. Rick and Thomas met them under the stoop. Carefully, they filed into the SUV that was by the car port. Colin drove, Matthew rode shotgun, and everyone was piled in the back seat and third row. Taking out his phone, Matthew called James.

"Hey," James said. "What's up?"

"We were just attacked at your house." Matthew's voice was eerily calm. "Everyone is out and safe, but we need a ride out of here."

"You can fly. I don't understand."

"I've been shot … twice." The words were nonchalant as he glanced at Colin, knowing he heard him.

"Give me that fucking phone!" Colin took the phone from his brother. "Get me a pilot and call me back on this line." Looking at Matthew, he calmed his voice. "Where are you hit?"

"My leg and my arm," Matthew answered, feeling a need to sleep.

Colin pulled over to a secluded spot. Looking in the rearview mirror, he caught his sister's eyes. "Harp, you're up."

Harper climbed from the third-row seat and hopped out. Opening Matthew's door, she could see the blood stain on his leg and more blood trickling down his arm.

"Damn it, Matthew." Colin was agitated. "Why didn't you say something sooner?"

"Because we needed to move," he answered, then heard his phone ring. "Answer it."

"I'm going to!" Colin was still irritated. "Well?"

"Two of my men are headed there now." James took a deep breath. "Thomas can fly the jet. They are about five minutes behind you. Pull over and let them pass so they can secure the area. Does Matthew need to go to the hospital?"

"Not sure." Colin eyed his brother, making sure he was still awake. "I'm stopped on a side road. Let me check him out. If it's not too bad, we'll fly him down to Savannah. But if it is life threatening, I'm taking him to the hospital."

"Okay," James agreed. "Keep me posted. Thomas will call this cell when the airstrip is secure."

"Got it," Colin stated, ending the call. "Well, Harp, how's your brother?"

"My brother? Are you not claiming him anymore?" Harper asked as she looked at the wound on Matthew's arm.

"Not at the moment."

"Matthew." Harper turned his face to look at her. "Pain level on a one-to-ten scale?"

"Twenty." He gave her a half smile. "My thigh hurts worse than my arm. And I think I'm going to pass out."

"Your color isn't good," she stated, looking at Colin. "We should take him to the hospital."

"No," Matthew stated firmly, shaking his head. "Get me to the plane and knock me out. Let Gina fix me up. We don't need to be dealing with the local PD right now. Let's just go home."

Harper looked at Colin, unsure of what to do.

"Damn it, Matthew! Let's do what he wants." Colin finally made the decision, knowing if something bad happened to Matthew, it was on him. "You can check him out on the plane. Matthew, you can pass out, but don't you dare code on us."

"I'll try not to." Matthew's eyes drooped and finally closed.

# Chapter 27

When the jet finally landed at the private airstrip two hours later, James and Jack were waiting with Grey. They boarded the plane as soon as the stairs came down.

James went to Emma and Carina first, as they were in the front seats. "Are you both okay?"

Both nodded.

"Emma." James took her hand, kissing it softly. "Can you help Carina off? I'm going to help them with Matthew."

"Of course." Emma nodded and did as he asked.

"Harper." Jack went straight to her in the back. She was beside Matthew, who was sleeping. "Baby, come here."

Harper stood so Jack could hold her tightly. There were no tears in her eyes, as she was too tired to produce any.

After hugging her tightly, Jack held her back slightly to make sure she wasn't hurt at all. "You're okay?"

"I'm fine," she said. "We need to get Matthew to Gina. A bullet grazed his arm, which left a deep gash. I cleaned and wrapped it up. I don't think it's a bullet in his thigh. It's more like a ricochet from a bullet. I didn't have my medical bag, so I didn't have the right tools to remove whatever it is, but I did get the bleeding to stop. He's asleep of his own accord. I didn't give him anything."

Jack kissed her softly and gave her another hug. "I'll have James and Grey help me get him off the plane," he told her.

Even though the plane stopped, Colin remained sitting with Tess curled up to him, and the two children were sleeping soundly across from them. He didn't want to move.

"Are we going to get off the plane?" Tess asked, sitting up a bit.

"I wish we could get everyone off, then take the kids and go home," he said, kissing her cheek.

"Wouldn't that be nice?" Tess smiled.

"How are the babies?" he asked, resting his hand on her stomach.

"Good. Still moving around a bit."

"Good." His hand slipped under the curve of her jaw, and he kissed her softly, slowly. "I love you." Colin's voice was barely above a whisper.

"I know." She nodded, kissing him again.

James passed by Colin and Tess, not interrupting, as it looked like a moment between them, and he respected that.

It didn't take long to get everyone to the house. Gina and Jack removed a piece of river rock from Matthew's leg, patched up his arm, and put him to bed. When finished, Gina went to check on Carina as Jack walked into the kitchen where James and Grey were sitting with Jonathan and Dominic at the table, talking softly.

"Where's Emma and Carina?" Harper asked James as she walked in the room.

"Gina is setting Gran up in Taryn's old room," he answered. "Can one of you tell us what happened? I got Grady's version, but you were inside."

Dominic shrugged. "It all happened really fast after Matthew walked in the room saying her heard something. Next thing I know, we're all on the floor as bullets are flying above us."

"I was in bed asleep." Harper shook her head, remembering the sound of the glass breaking. "It was so loud, and I was upstairs."

"The glass on those windows shouldn't have shattered," James stated. "They're bulletproof, weatherproof. Top of the line. It makes no sense unless those were massive powered bullets."

"Sense or not, your home is messed up," Harper told him. "You should buzz your local PD friend and have it blocked off so no one steals anything."

"Two of my men are still there," James stated. "I'll get a contractor out there in the morning to start working on it."

Harper looked at him wide-eyed. "James, there's big bullets sprayed all over inside from that helicopter. You're going to need like five contractors."

"Harp, it's a house. It can be fixed. You guys can't. All I care about is that you're all okay."

"Did you find my father?" Dominic asked, as he had heard nothing about that.

James shook his head as he pulled out his phone to see where the little red dot was headed. Antoine must have been driving because it was taking him a long time to get anywhere. The dot turned east, heading into Virginia. "Aren't you from Virginia?" James asked Dominic.

"Yes. I still have a house there."

"I think your cousin is headed there," James noted. "We'll find out in a bit. When we showed up, the place was empty. It was the same way Emma and I left it. I don't think anyone was there. Someone's information was wrong, or they went to another house."

Emma walked in the room as James was talking. "It was another house they were in, a few doors down from mine. Meagan and I kept it looking like I lived there for instances like this."

"You didn't think to tell me?" James was a little irritated.

"I completely forget," she said. "I'm sorry."

"Well, there was nothing suspicious on your road. I'm assuming they were gone before we showed up." James shrugged. "We'll keep an eye on Antoine."

Dominic sat back in thought. The only image that kept occupying his mind was Meagan smiling during a skiing vacation they took. They had been on the slopes all day. When they arrived back to their suite, they ordered room service and soaked in an oversized jet tub together. It was very romantic. What he would give to be back in that moment again.

# Chapter 28

J ames closed his door after walking into his room. He was tired, and Emma certainly looked exhausted. Sleep would come as soon as his head hit the pillow. As he sat in a chair at the far corner, he took off his boots and looked over at her. With her head down, she leaned against the bed.

"What is it, Em?" he asked, walking over to her. He went to put his hands on her shoulders, and she shook him off.

"Don't," she said, softly shaking her head.

James was irritated. With his hands on his hips, he stood before her. "What? I can't touch you anymore? You need to explain that. Because that pisses me off."

"This is all my fault." She brought her head up, looking at him. "You should have just let me go. I should have never gone with you. I knew this would happen. He hurts or kills everyone who gets close to me—everyone, James." Emma walked away from him to the other side of the room.

"So just stay alone, no friends, no family, for the rest of your life?"

"Yes." She looked at him. "If I don't, this is what happens. You should see your house; they destroyed it. Matthew was shot, and thank God nothing happened to Tess and the babies. I can't live with something like that, James."

"I don't give a damn about the house." He raised his hands and voice in frustration. "Matthew will be fine. No one blames you."

"You said you would take me home whenever I wanted." She looked at him as tears filled her eyes. "I want to go home."

James didn't speak, as he knew he had promised her that. Taking her home meant she was leaving him. "That's like leading a lamb to slaughter." He eyed her.

"I don't care." She wiped her eyes dry. "It's me leaving this family so they don't get hurt anymore."

"No." He shook his head. "This is you leaving me."

James sat down in the chair and put his boots back on. When done, he stood, put on his shoulder holster, and slipped his gun in it. "Let's go," he said, walking out of the room.

Emma followed him down the stairs to the foyer. Walking into the kitchen, he was thankful Jack was at the counter doing something on his computer.

"Hey," Jack said, looking at them. "What's going on?"

"I'm taking her home." James looked at him, void of emotion.

"Now?"

"Yes." He took a deep breath. "I made a promise."

Jack knew what that meant, and he stood looking at them, rather surprised. "I'll come with you."

"Not this time." James shook his head. "I wanted you to know it's about an hour or so there. I'll check in with you if I'm not back by three."

"Could I have a moment with Emma?" he asked James.

With a nod, James left the room.

Jack looked at Emma, shaking his head. "What the hell do you think you're doing? You can't use one of his promises against him like this. This will destroy him, and he doesn't deserve this."

"This family doesn't deserve to have what happened to them. It's their association with me, and I can't live with something even worse happening than what has already happened."

"The family will be fine! I take care of the family, and they have been through a hell of a lot worse than this." Jack was firm. "James will not. Do you not understand what I am saying? Fuck! You make these decisions based on what? Emotion? Come on, Emma, don't be so naïve. Matthew was shot. So what? Tess was shot four times in the last month. I don't see her running away from anything." Jack's voice had raised enough that Jonathan came from his room. "Run away, and you'll want to be far away when Tess hears what you've done to him. You must be a much stronger woman to be in this family than you are, so go. I thought you were different than this. You were warned, Emma. Goodbye."

Emma ran from the room, down the hallway past James, and out the front door.

Jonathan walked up to Jack and put his hand on his shoulder. "Son, she's just scared. And you can't compare her to Tess because Tess is in a class of her own."

"James loves her," Jack told him. "This will close him off and shut him down. I don't want him that way. *You* know how many times Matthew and I have pulled him from that dark place he goes."

"I know. Let me go be a father. Because I'm certain she needs a parent of some sort. Give me the radio for the front gate."

Jack handed him the radio and went to the kitchen for a glass of water.

"Greyson, this is Jonathan. Emma is on foot, and I am thinking she is heading to the gate. Find her, detain, and I will be there in a few minutes." Jonathan walked out the front door, only to find James leaning against the post as he watched Emma walk down the driveway.

"I don't know where she thinks she's going," James said, not taking his eyes off Emma. "Grey won't let her out the gates."

Jonathan chuckled, after patting James on the shoulder he began his stroll down the driveway. Not even a minute later, James saw a jeep stop down the driveway, detaining her. Jonathan caught up, and then James turned and went back into the house.

"Thank you, Greyson." Jonathan shook his hand. "Would you mind coming with us? I'm taking her off the grounds, and you know ... safety."

"Yes, sir." Grey hopped in the back seat.

Emma looked at Jonathan. "Are you taking me home?"

"I'm taking you to have a chat," he said, getting in the driver's side. "Hop in, please."

Knowing it wasn't really a request, Emma did as he asked.

Jonathan turned the jeep around and headed out the main gate. As he drove, he talked with his southern accent. "I grew up here in Savannah," he began. "Then I moved to Atlanta for college. I met my first wife, Dominic and Matthew's mother, there. Her name was Isobelle, and she was from a small town in Peru. Isobelle Taylor. Her mother was Portuguese, and her father English, hence the Taylor name Matthew took after he and Colin had their disagreement. She had a zest for life like no other. The boy's features are that of their mother, the dark hair, skin tone. I see their mother every time I look at them. She taught them Portuguese up until she died. Matthew was almost three. He still has her accent that just rolls off his tongue at times. I didn't have much time with her, given how long I have lived so far, but life still happens. I thought Dominic died in the car accident with her, but it seems his biological father murdered Isobelle and kidnapped him." Jonathan pulled in front of a twenty-four-hour diner and looked at her. "Come on." He opened his door. "Let's go eat."

"It's two in the morning." She looked sideways at him.

"So? We're adults, and we can eat whenever we want. Besides, they make the best crepes in town. Come on, Grey."

The three of them went in. Grey sat up at the counter as Jonathan took a booth with Emma, and the waitress was with them quickly.

"Jonathan." The waitress smiled as she acknowledged him. "How are you and the family?"

"Very well, thank you." Jonathan's voice was sincere. "How's Martin and the kids?"

"Good," she replied. "Kids are growing like weeds. What can I get for you two?"

They ordered, and the waitress left, allowing Jonathan's full focus on Emma.

"After Isobelle died, I met Adalyn a year or so later. One thing led to another, and we were married, and Colin was born. After about three years, she up and left, saying only that this wasn't the life she wanted. So, it was just the boys and I, and let me tell you, it's be a hell of a life. We had our ups and downs, but it all worked out eventually. I think the girls coming into our lives was the most challenging thing Gina and I ever did. Two sixteen-year-olds and a twelve-year-old from a life of drugs, alcohol, and corruption, and I was simply used to my boys. The girls had a very bad life, but the two left have persevered."

"They've had the stability of a father and mother to help them persevere. That makes a huge difference," Emma commented.

"It does," Jonathan agreed. "But they had to be willing to accept and incorporate good parents into their lives. Harper was easy, still kind of young. Tess was quiet, but she knew no one would hurt her here, and Taryn wasn't interested. As soon as she could, she was out the door and on her own."

"She's the one that died," Emma noted as the waitress brought them food.

"Yes." He nodded. "Tess is my special one. To come through what Robert did to her and be the woman she is now is remarkable. I will give credit to my son for Tess being who she is today. He gave her confidence and skills to protect herself. And she will protect her family until her last dying breath. I know you were the one my son was with when he disappeared for a couple days a few weeks back."

Emma froze as she stared at Jonathan. He could take her out and have her killed tonight after they ate crepes. That's why he brought Grey with them. He was going to kill her.

Jonathan let her stew in her own thoughts for a few minutes as he took a few bites of his food. "Now that you've let every horrible scenario run through your mind, let's talk about it."

"I … I didn't …" Emma couldn't form any words.

"You knew he was married?" Jonathan asked, taking a sip of his coffee.

Ashamed, she nodded. "I didn't plan on ever seeing him again. I didn't know James was coming back. I didn't know. And now he won't let it go. He keeps saying it isn't over. He wants me again and he always gets what he wants. I told him no, but he's manipulative. I don't want James to know, but Colin doesn't take no for an answer. And I can't talk to anyone about this because you know what problems this would cause. That is one of the reasons why I think I should just go home. It would save a lot of problems."

"I'll deal with my son." Jonathan's voice was firm.

"I don't want your family hurt or killed because of me and my past." She looked at him.

"My sons, which includes Jack and James, excel at their professions, whichever it may be. Colin and Matthew run multimillion-dollar companies, and they are the best at what they do. Jack runs all my security because that is what he excels at. Dominic sold his company and could stay retired at his young age, should he choose to. James is the mercenary. According to damn near everyone, he is the best of the best. He must be the best, as his portfolio is outstanding. You don't make the money he's made by being half-ass. If there is someone that has been harassing you or threatening you, he will take care of it. Tess's life was marked. There were three sets of men trying to take her out. James eliminated all of them. Then there was her twin sister, Taryn, who put the bounty on her head, and James—well, Greyson—took care of that one. Tess and her children can now live freely without the threat of a mark on her because of James. Do you understand where I am going with this?"

Emma nodded as a tear escaped. "James can take care of this is what you're trying to tell me."

"You have two choices." He set his fork down, as this conversation commanded full attention. "You can either run away and be in the constant fear Marcos has seemed to instill in you, or you can come home with me. In my home, with my family, you get a father, mother, crazy siblings, and a man that loves you. And my son won't touch you again. That is my promise to you."

**************

Emma pushed the bedroom door open slowly. She didn't want to wake him, but she needed to. Walking over to the side of the bed, she looked down at James. His head turned to look at her as he held his hand out. When she slipped her hand in his, he scooted over in the bed so she could lie beside him. She took off her shoes and jeans and lay down. His arms wrapped her up close to his body.

"I'm sorry," she whispered.

"Don't do things that you have to be sorry for with me." He kissed her shoulder.

"I told you I didn't know how to do this," she reminded him.

"Well, here's what I know." He rolled her on her back so he could see her. "If you love someone, you don't walk away when things get tough. You go through it together."

"I'm learning," she said, bringing her hand up to his bare shoulder.

"Damn it, Emma, I love you." He closed his eyes momentarily. "I don't easily love."

"I know," she replied. "I don't love easily either, and you know that. I just don't want anyone else hurt because of me."

"I understand. For the last time, will you please just let me do what I do? You need to understand that I can't do my work if I'm not 100 percent focused. I don't like errors in my work. Errors mean someone gets killed. But I can't focus if I keep worrying about you wanting to take off because you're afraid. Trust in my process. It's called blind faith, and it's usually with God, but you need to have it with me."

Tears slipped from her eyes as she nodded, understanding. "You do realize the only person I've been able to trust in my life is Meagan?"

"I do understand. But we will have nothing if you don't start trusting me."

"I do trust you."

James shook his head. "You don't, or you wouldn't keep trying to leave."

Emma thought about what he was saying. "It's hard to just turn the trust back on when it's been shut off nearly all my life. I've never loved any one the way I love you. I keep trying to pull myself back because I'm afraid of losing you. I know the pain of loss too well. I wouldn't survive something happening to you or being blamed if something happened to someone in this family or your team. That isn't a burden I can bear."

"That wouldn't happen." James cupped her cheek. "Jonathan once told me, not too long ago, that everything is a circumstance of events, because I blamed myself for Tess being shot in the head. Nothing will happen to the family. This is the safest place anybody could be right now. You need to stop worrying about that and trust in my process."

James held her eyes for a moment before Emma nodded in agreement. "One more thing. I will leave you here when I go do this job. This family will make sure you are safe when I'm not around."

"Okay," Emma agreed, not wanting to fight with him anymore.

# Chapter 29

James was up early the next morning. With maybe three hours of sleep, he needed a good workout to clear his head and refocus. Everyone was still asleep when he went over to the gym. Beginning with a quick warmup, he began lifting weights first. Markenna kept popping into his mind. What he didn't tell everyone last night was that they knew about the safe house. Knowing Emma's place was empty, they went to the safe house first. There were a few blood spots on the porch. Even though he wasn't positive who that belonged to, his gut told him it was Meagan's. His mind reviewed the scene over and over, coming up with nothing—absolutely nothing except the blood. Knowing he wasn't 100 percent focused, he sighed, closing his eyes. Lying on the bench in silence, he thought of Tess then Emma.

"How is it that I do not hear you until you're two feet from me?" he asked, not moving nor opening his eyes.

"I'm just that good." Tess smiled, looking down at him. "What's on your mind? You have that look."

"Markenna, you, and Emma," he answered honestly. "And in that order."

"Hmm." Tess cocked her head. "I don't know if I like being in between those people. No offense to Emma, but I usually like to be a man's first thought."

James smiled, shaking his head as he sat up and took her hand in his. "I still love you."

Tess nodded, biting the inside of her lip. Her hand ran through his hair, and then she straddled the bench, facing him and taking both his hands. She didn't speak, only touched his fingers, then palms. James watched her eyes watch her fingers touching him.

"I want to kiss you," he said softly, and her eyes met up with his. "But your husband is probably watching you on one of these damn cameras because you know and I know that he thinks something is still going on between us."

"Whatever." Tess shrugged it off. "I don't care if he has an insecurity here or there with me." Her eyes dropped back down to her fingers touching his hands.

"Baby, are you going to be able to get through this? You need to or end it."

"I know." Tess pursed her lips, shaking her head. "It's hard."

"I don't get the two of you." James shook his head, watching her eyes for reaction.

Tess smiled, taking a deep breath. "We'll be fine. We just need to go home. We've been here too long, and we need our life back."

"So, go. What are you waiting around for?" James didn't understand.

"I couldn't fly for a month after I got out of the hospital. And there was no way that we weren't helping you and Emma. We'll get home in the next week or so. Tell me—does she make you happy?"

"Does he make you happy?" he asked her.

"Yes, but so did you." Tess slowly looked up at him.

"Remember our conversation in the hotel room on the beach just before we ..." James grinned, and she nodded. "Well, I said you were carrying a McGowan baby, and it didn't matter if you loved Colin or Matthew because you were going to be with one of them regardless because of the baby."

Tess smiled, knowing exactly where he was going with this.

His finger slowly ran down the back of her hand to her fingertip. "Three years later, same rules apply."

"I know." She grinned. "Good thing I love the son of a bitch."

James smiled with a nod. "Yes, it is. I never understood how you could love him and say that you loved me. But now I know. I love you, but I love Emma too. And I will marry her, and I only hope that we can continue to have our strange conversations at seven in the morning because you understand a part of me that no one else does."

"And you don't think Emma will understand that part of you?"

"No, it's something you have to live through, breathe through the moments to understand. The very moment you pull the trigger on that

185

mark, or you snap that neck with your bare hands, you understand. Part of me likes the fact that she doesn't know that feeling; she's a virgin in that world where we are masters."

"You carry it with you where you didn't before," she stated. "I think the list you worked on messed with your head. The only thing I carry with me is Dominic. All the other jobs are memories—not good nor bad, just memories."

"It was the children," he said softly. "What they did to those children was and is devastating."

Tess covered his hands with hers. "I hope that doesn't keep you from having children of your own. You will be a wonderful father who loves and protects as he should."

"I don't know." He shrugged. "Emma is pregnant."

"I know. She told me."

"I think I can handle being a father," he began. "But the kicker with this is that she was with someone else the weekend before she and I started seeing each other."

"She told me that too. I have no words of wisdom for you." Tess shook her head. "Except for this. Colin was in the same situation with me, remember? He was very admirable for stepping up and taking on the responsibility for another man's child. He wanted Savannah to be his so bad, and when he found out she wasn't, he was devastated. But he picked up this tiny little baby, cradled her in his arms, and said he didn't care that he wasn't biologically her father, he was going to love her as if she was."

"Colin said that? That husband of yours constantly surprises me."

"Me too." She sighed. "Not always in a good way."

James grinned, understanding.

Tess moved her hands to her stomach, smiling slightly.

"What?"

"The babies are moving." She moved her hands around. "I love that feeling. It's like butterflies fluttering about."

James rested his hands on her tiny, round stomach and smiled at her. "I'm sorry about last night."

"It worked out fine," she assured him. "No one died. The kids are good. Matthew might be a little agitated when he wakes up."

"That poor guy." James grinned. "Three bullets now in the past month or two. He has a right to be pissed. I'll make it better."

"I know you will." Tess stood up.

"I'm not going to shoot him," he confided in a soft voice. "I'm going to beat him to death."

"As you should." She gave a nod of approval and walked away.

Colin lay in bed watching the security monitors on his tablet. Seeing his wife with James was becoming a common occurrence that he could do without. There was a connection between Tess and James that he thought had disappeared when he was absent from their lives for a couple years, but now he watched her fight off this desire that he knew she wanted to give into.

"Hey," she said, walking into the room, seeing that he was awake and watching her on the monitors. "Been awake long?"

"No." He shook his head, putting the tablet on the nightstand. "Just looking for you. I worry."

Tess lay down beside him, running her hand over his bare chest. "No reason to worry."

"Feeling better than last night?" he asked, running his hand over her shoulder, down her back.

"Yes." She nodded, staring into his blue eyes. "You need not worry about him."

Colin smiled. "But I do."

"It's not like you're thinking." She kissed his shoulder.

"Mmm." He shifted his body, lying on his side. Slowly, his hand moved over the curve of her hip. "Perhaps you need to explain it to me then."

Tess's fingers moved to his chest and over his shoulder. He watched her eyes that watched her own hand move freely over his body.

"It's letting him talk about his work." Her eyes moved to his. "And him knowing that I understand and won't judge, as I know what he is feeling."

"He feels?" Colin was surprised that James felt anything, given how long he'd been doing contract work. "He should know the balance by now."

"You're different. You don't care about anyone else except your family, whether you're doing a contract job or going into the office. That's why you've had eleven assistants in the past five years."

"They've not been what I wanted for an assistant. They're too emotional.

I need someone who can handle my snappy arrogance and not take it so personally." Colin's hand slipped under her shorts and rounded her hip, moving over her thigh. "You deal with me very well. I want someone like you."

"When you find that assistant, are you going to sleep with her too?" Her hand moved over his hip.

"You've never been my assistant. Besides, you drain me of every ounce." He caught her lower lip with his teeth softly, then kissed her. "There's nothing left of me to put in anyone else."

"That was good." She laughed a little.

"I don't want any other woman." His eyes caught hers, knowing she was still a bit insecure about his indiscretion. "I'm in love with my wife, and I will kill anyone who tries to take you from me … in any capacity."

"It's the list." Her breath caught when he slipped his fingers between her legs.

"It's just a list of second-rate humans." He nipped her lower lip as her eyes closed. Slowly, he rubbed the perfect spot, making her moan softly.

"Yes … that's not …" Her breath held for a moment. "The problem … it's the … oh my gosh, Colin."

He applied just enough pressure to take her close to the edge. Then he stopped. "It's what?"

"It's … a …" Her breath held, knowing he liked to hold her on the edge. "Just do it … please."

Colin kissed her deeply, allowing his tongue to seek and explore hers as if for the first time. "Are you ready?" he whispered between kisses.

"Yes." she breathed out as her hand reached down and stroked him.

"Promise me something?" He rubbed once. "You will never fuck him as long as I'm alive."

"I promise you I will not fuck James." Tess opened her eyes, looking at him, knowing she didn't promise to not fuck his brother.

Colin kissed her again and took her over the edge. As she came down from the moment, she watched him put his finger into his mouth, enjoying the taste of her.

"When are you going to realize that I only want to be with you? Kiss you? Make love to just you?" she asked him.

He shrugged.

"No reason to be jealous." She pushed him onto his back and straddled him. "It's not very becoming with you. The only man who puts his fingers between my legs is my husband."

"My own insecurities." He caressed her cheek. "You're beautiful and mine."

"Don't fuck up again, and I'll remain yours. Otherwise, your father won't even know where to find your body." Tess pursed her lips in a smile. "You know who my friends are."

"My little badass wife. Your friends are my friends." Colin placed his hands on her round stomach, unaffected by her threat.

"Yes." She smiled. "But I slept with them."

"True," Colin admitted. "But all of them know I'm a little bit crazy when it comes to you and my kids. They won't mess with me. Just like they won't mess with you because they know that we are on a dangerous ledge. You and I are the only ones who play on that ledge because everyone else is afraid."

"That is true."

"I like this cocky side of you. It turns me on." Colin repositioned himself to slide his hardness inside of her. "Damn, I love you. I don't know what the hell I was thinking."

"You weren't thinking; your dick was." Tess's voice was soft as her eyes closed to enjoy the feeling of him.

"I love my children growing inside of you." Colin pulled her down for another kiss. "You never finished telling me what it was."

"Oh, yes." She sat back up. "It's the children. The list has been difficult because of what these people did to the children."

# Chapter 30

Dominic stood before the French doors in Matthew's room just staring out. His mind was deep in thought yet again. The unfortunate event that his father was free and roaming about made him extremely nervous. *Emma thought she had problems with Marcos.* He laughed to himself, knowing the two times that he went to the parole board and spoke on her behalf, without her even knowing, solidified the bullet that his father had for him. The look his father gave him each time reminded him of the vicious man he was.

"Aw hell," Matthew grumbled as he woke. He winced in pain as he tried to move his leg. "Damn it again."

Turning toward his brother, Dominic grinned, walking closer. "Good morning," he said, looking down as Matthew turned to sit up on the edge of the bed. "Would you like some help?"

"I'd like to not get shot." Matthew smirked.

"Here." Dominic leaned over, giving him a hand standing up. "Where do you want to go?"

"I would like a shower." Matthew looked at Dominic, then smiled when Tess walked in the room. "Ah, little Mama T, help me shower?"

Tess looked at him and cocked her head sideways. "You think I should help you?"

"Better you than him," Matthew stated. "You've seen the goods anyway."

"Oh my gosh." She shook her head as she walked into his bathroom and turned on the shower. "Dominic, can you bring him in please?"

Dominic helped Matthew hobble into the bathroom and leaned him against the counter.

"Anything else?" Dominic asked her as she turned to face them once the water was the right temperature.

Tess sighed as she eyed the two men. "I cannot believe how much you two look alike. It's weird."

"Mother had dominating genes." Matthew reminded her. "Look at Sav. Then go look at my baby picture."

"I know. I was looking at those pictures in your dad's office. It's crazy how much she looks like you, but then everyone says how much she looks like me. She's our little chameleon."

"Is there a party in here or what?" Colin walked in with two kids in tow.

"I just want to take a shower." Matthew shrugged.

"With both? I didn't know you had that in you." Colin grinned.

"Smartass." Matthew curved his lip up.

"I will help him," Tess told Colin as she watched Dominic pick up Savannah.

"This should bother me," Colin said, shaking his head.

"Yes, it should." Matthew nodded at him. "Because I so have the energy to seduce your wife. Would you get Gina for me please? I need something for pain."

"I'll take the kids." Dominic reached down, picking up Connor with his other arm, and carried them both out of the bathroom.

"I'll get Gina." Colin looked at Tess. "Baby, get his ass in the shower. Then we all need to sit down and talk about this Marcos character."

Colin left the room, leaving Tess staring at Matthew. Reaching over, she caressed his cheek and gave a soft smile.

"If you could just unwrap my leg, I can do the rest," he told her.

"I don't mind helping you." She knelt and began unwrapping the bandage around his thigh as Matthew pulled off his shirt. "Is there a lot of pain?"

"Yes, a fair amount." He watched her as she lifted the gauze off the wound. "Not as bad as the ones last month. Last thing I remember was them getting me on the plane and lying down. Everything else is a blur."

"You didn't miss anything." She tossed the bandages into the trash and stood back up.

"How are you doing?" he asked, taking her hand in his.

"Fine." She smiled and held his eyes as she placed her hands on his hips and slid his underwear off slowly.

As he stood naked before her, he shook his head as she smiled. "You're a dangerous woman," he remarked.

"I know." Tess looked at Matthew, touching his face softly. It was easy to remember her time with him, as he was the only man she would have stayed with had Colin not picked her up.

Matthew slipped his hands behind her neck, resting his forehead on hers. "What I would give to have you as my wife," he whispered.

Tess brought her arms around his shoulders. "You deserve better than me. You're a damn good man. I'm damaged, and Colin is very good at dealing with me."

"You're not damaged." His hand caressed her cheek.

"I am." She grinned and kissed him softly.

"Do you know how awkward this is standing here naked?" He smiled.

"Awkward or not ..." She stepped back with a smile as her eyes slowly scanned his body. "I miss my time with you ... naked."

Matthew reached over, shutting the door. His hands slipped behind her neck, and he pulled her lips to his. The kiss was slow and lingering with undeniable passion.

After a long couple of minutes, Tess pulled back. "This is dangerous," she whispered. "He's in the house."

"Yep," Matthew replied as he traded spots and picked up Tess, putting her on the edge of the counter.

Their lips met back up with a needing desire. Matthew pushed her dress up, moved her panties aside, and slipped into her without hesitation. Tess stopped breathing as the feel of him was intense. With her arms tightly around his shoulders, Matthew kept a firm, quick rhythm.

"Damn, baby," he breathed out.

Tess brought his lips to hers as she was close, and she knew he was to. When she came, her legs locked tightly around his waist, prompting him to come just moments after.

"Damn," he whispered under his breath, kissing her again. "I'm sure we shouldn't have done that. Besides, that has to be record timing."

Tess smiled as he stepped back, and she slipped off the counter to straighten up. "Just like we shouldn't have done it those couple other times?" She readjusted her clothes. "I don't care."

"Why?" Matthew was curious as he hobbled over to the shower.

"Because I know Colin fucked some other woman while he was gone for three days," she stated, looking in the mirror. "I just haven't figured out who yet."

Matthew stopped just before getting in the shower and turned back toward her.

"Do you know?" she asked him.

"No, I don't know who." He shook his head, easily lying for his brother. "He told you he did that?"

Tess shrugged. "Yes. He admitted to it once I told him I knew."

"So, what we've been doing, is it simply payback?"

Tess walked over to him, and with a soft hand, she caressed his cheek and then leaned up and kissed him softly. "No."

"That night he didn't come home and you came into my room, did you know what he was doing?"

"Yes. He's not a difficult one to read," Tess admitted.

"I'm sorry he did that to you." Matthew ran his hand over her shoulder.

"It's okay. I will have my revenge, just like I did with Taryn. You think he would've learned with that one." Tess flashed a wicked grin.

"Don't ever let me piss you off." Matthew kissed her one more time before she left the room.

# Chapter 31

Dominic took the two children into the family room and sat them down to play. After pouring himself another cup of coffee, he mindlessly watched them as his thoughts were still on his father. Admittedly, he thought about leaving, taking off, in hopes of his father not finding him. But he wasn't keen on the idea of being on the run the rest of his life. No, he was ready to settle down, have a family of his own. Having to avoid his father the rest of his life wasn't an option. Perhaps he needed to just go confront him.

"Good morning," a soft voice sounded behind him.

"Good morning," Dominic replied to Emma as she poured herself a cup of coffee.

"You seemed deep in thought," she said, sitting across from him. "I didn't mean to impose."

"Impose, please." He gave her an easy smile. "I was just thinking about my father—or should I say *our* father."

Emma grinned with a slight nod of her head. "I'm sorry I didn't say something sooner. I'd already had one brother beat me. So you can understand I was afraid."

"I'm sorry for what they did to you." Dominic's forehead furrowed. "I had no idea, or I would have helped you before it got as bad as it did."

Emma shrugged. "I'd never been hit before Dimitri. I'm assuming Marcos never told him that I was his half sister."

Dominic sat back, thinking.

"I'm glad you're not too chatty, as that would be awkward."

"I'm sorry. It's just very surreal that I have a sister. Did Meagan know?"

"Yes." Emma nodded.

"Wow." He wondered how much more there was that she withheld from him.

"It's kind of strange," she admitted. "I've had no family since he killed my parents, and now, almost instantly, I have James and a brother and this McGowan family. It's weird."

"How did James take it when he found out you were a Markenna?" Dominic was very curious, as he knew James didn't care for him.

"That fight we had the other day coming down the stairs was from him just finding out."

"He doesn't trust me," Dominic noted.

"He doesn't know you. And neither do I, so I hope we can change that."

"Of course we can." He smiled with a nod. "Absolutely."

"Was he mean to you?" Emma asked.

"I don't know if mean is the right word." Dominic thought for a moment. "When I was a kid, he was okay. As I got older, he didn't shield Dimitri and I from any of the bad things that he did. You know, like beating people, women included. In our teens, we started seeing him kill people. That was when I started stashing any money I could get my hands on, because I knew one day he would come after me."

"Did he?" She wondered.

"Yes." He nodded and proceeded to tell her the same story he told Matthew about growing up and getting out.

"You certainly didn't take after him in any way."

"Thank goodness. I got all my mother's traits in looks and personality." Dominic looked past Emma and saw James standing quietly in the hallway to the kitchen, just listening. "May I ask how many times did he get to you before I saw you at the courthouse?"

"When you saw me …" Emma thought back. "That was the third time. Every time he beat me, his intent was also to rape me. But he had performance issues, and all that ever did was make him hit me more. Sometimes I wonder if I hadn't fought him off and had just given him what he wanted, would he have hit me less? Or would it have been the same, regardless?"

"It would have been the same," Dominic told her honestly.

"Well, I'm glad I stopped him and endured the beatings."

"Glad you're a fighter." Dominic smiled, then hesitated before speaking again. "There's something I should tell you, something I did a long time ago for you without even knowing you. Maggie wouldn't let me talk to you or anything. She said it would have only scared you more knowing there was another brother. And she wanted you to get a break from my family and try to live a normal life after everything you went through."

Emma listened, unsure of what he was going to say. Feeling her heart pound loudly in her chest made her a little bit nervous.

"The house you've been living in all these years is yours. You own it."

"How?" she asked, extremely curious.

"When I saw you that day, I was so disgusted by what my brother did that I wanted to do something good for you. I knew it wouldn't take away everything they'd done, but as I told Mags, I wanted you to feel safe somewhere. I let her find the home, and she never told me where, but she said it was perfect for you. I paid for it, and there's a trust set up in your name that pays all the expenses."

Emma looked at him, uncertain as to what to say. "Meagan said the government took care of all the expenses."

"No." Dominic shook his head. "I know you can get angry with this or take it for what it is, but what they did was so wrong, and this was the only way I could do something right for you."

"But they were the ones who did wrong, not you." Her hand reached out, covering his. "You shouldn't have to pay for what they did."

"Neither should you," he replied. "Wait for it. There's more."

Emma grinned. "Should I worry?"

"I hope not, and I hope you don't get mad either." He shrugged a little. "Your trust is available to you when you turn thirty-five, which we know is in a few months. Matthew holds the trust with his company and has been investing the money."

"How much money are you talking about? Because I know that Matthew doesn't deal with small accounts."

"Well, when Dimitri was killed, I took his money … all of it and put it in the account. And when my father was incarcerated …" He smiled at the memory. "I took about 90 percent of his money, that I could find, and threw it in the account as well. I considered it restitution for what they had done to you. There's a fair amount in the trust. Managed carefully, you shouldn't have to work again, unless you want to."

Emma went to speak but couldn't, as nothing would come out. She was shocked.

"I'm hoping you will do some good with it," he admitted. "I know you could refuse it all together, but you have a good heart despite them trying to break you. If you don't want the money, maybe you can find a cause and put it to good use."

"Dominic, I'm beyond words. My first instinct is to refuse it. I don't want anything to do with them and that money. I wish it could buy my dad back his life."

"I'm sorry." He shook his head. "I know having Markenna blood run through your veins is a difficult concept, but one trait that isn't horrible is the strength and perseverance that comes by being one of them. You're a strong, independent woman. You've been through hell and still persevere. Very admirable, sister."

Emma smiled. "You're my brother. I've wanted a decent one for a long time."

"There are some weird family dynamics with the Markennas and McGowans." Dominic smiled.

"I completely agree. You know my real name is Emma Grace?"

"That's the American version. The real way to say your name is Emiliana Graca." The accent rolled off his tongue easily. "Are you ready to start being you? You don't need to hide behind an alias, as you are part of this family of … assassins. Hell, your boyfriend is the world's top mercenary."

"Isn't that weird? I never thought I'd end up with a man like him. But I can't imagine my life without him. It's all very new and good and scary."

"I know he doesn't care for me, which is fine." Dominic glanced at James, who was still listening. "But I can see how much he loves you."

"I know he does. I have these moments of complete self-doubt. And I don't feel like I'm good enough for him. I don't know how he can be with me after being with a woman like Tess. She is stunning and educated and very intimidating."

Dominic looked at James, who simply shook his head as he walked up behind Emma. Softly, he put his hands on her shoulders and kissed her head. "I wish you wouldn't talk like that."

Emma closed her eyes, taking in a breath. "I know. They're just moments. They come and go."

There was an awkward silence between the three of them for a moment.

"Dominic, you said the name Mags, Maggie?" Emma cocked her head. "Do you know her outside of the court thing?"

"Yes." It was an easy admission for him. "We met that day I saw you at the courthouse and were together for over a year before she was promoted and moved. We tried the long-distance relationship, but that didn't work for us. I loved her deeply."

"I'm sorry." Emma covered his hand with hers. "Why didn't you go with her?"

"My company." He shrugged. "The hazard of being work orientated. My mistake, always."

Emma nodded slightly, and then a thought popped into her mind. "Oh my gosh!"

James already knew the thought that hit her.

"What?" Dominic looked at her oddly.

"Baby Aria is yours," she stated.

"Excuse me?" Dominic shook his head. "We didn't have children. I would be in my child's life if I had one."

"That's why she never told me." Emma was more talking to herself than him. "She didn't want me to be afraid."

Dominic leaned toward her. "Emma, when did she have a baby?"

"Less than a year after she got the transfer," she told him.

Dominic sat back, processing Emma's words. How could Maggie do this to him? Was this child really his or was she with someone else while she was with him? No. He shook his head. Mags wasn't like that. *Oh my gosh*, he thought, standing up. Running his hands through his hair, he looked at the two children playing in the family room. He could have a child older than them.

"Dominic," James said. "I know we don't see eye to eye, but if this is true, I can find out for you, and I already know where the child is." James didn't have it in him to tell him that Marcos kidnapped Meagan.

"Isn't the child with Maggie?" Dominic shot a piercing glance at James, knowing something was wrong.

James sighed, not wanting to tell him the truth. "Meagan was taken by your father a couple weeks ago."

Dominic turned a shade lighter. Flashes of what his father was doing to her sped through his mind. "Do you know what he's doing to her? He will beat and rape her. Why haven't you found him yet?"

"We're trying."

"Try harder … please." Dominic would have dropped to his knees and begged if it would help. "I will give you every dime I have. Just please save her from him."

"I don't want your money. I want your father's head." James didn't finish the rest of his sentence—that he wanted to send it to Marcos's brothers to let them know he was coming after them next.

"Why wouldn't she have told me?" He was speaking more to himself. "Maggie wasn't like that. I don't understand. My choice in women is shit."

Tess walked into the kitchen just in time to hear Dominic's last words. She stood silently, as she knew Dominic was upset about something. She just hoped it wasn't something she had done.

Dominic's eyes caught Tess's for a moment. "I can't …" His hand ran over his hair. "I can't even do this anymore." Without any more words, he walked over to the two kids playing and knelt. "Hey." His voice was kind. "Mommy is in the kitchen. I'm going to go. So I will see you both later."

"Bye, Daddy." Connor stood up, giving him a hug. Then Savannah followed suit.

Dominic kissed each one on the head, and as his eyes filled, he got up and walked out the door.

"Did I do something?" Tess asked, walking over to James.

"No." James shook his head as his eyes went from Emma to Tess. "Not directly."

"Should I go talk to him?"

"No," James stated firmly. "Give him some time to process what just happened."

"Are you going to tell me what just happened?" Tess asked.

"No." James shook his head. "It's not my place. Just hang with your kids, and Jonathan can deal with him."

Emma looked at James and shook her head. "I didn't mean to upset him. I shouldn't have said that. It wasn't my place. It was between him and Meagan. I feel so bad."

"He has a right to know about his kid." James took her hand and kissed the top of it. "I need to go talk with Jonathan."

# Chapter 32

Dominic's gaze focused on the distinct line where the water met the sky. His heart felt broken. Women were a devilish hell in his life, from the time his father kidnapped him. The thought of leaving crossed his mind again. There was plenty of money in the bank. He would need a passport under a different name. Would James do that for him? It would be a win for James. The man didn't like him, and this way he would be getting rid of him. With a solid desire to keep Meagan off his mind, he failed. Every thought kept going back to their time together. Did she try to tell him about the baby and he just didn't listen, or did he miss a sign? Was she not wanting to raise a child with a Markenna? That was certainly a possibility, given the family reputation. Did she know before they broke it off, or was it after? And why wouldn't she call him when she found out? He had a million questions and no answers. Frustrated, he closed his eyes, remembering the first time they spoke.

Dominic stood outside the courtroom, contemplating how to make his next move work. His brother had just received four years in prison, which meant he would probably only do two years. So, how could he help this woman that Dimitri kept beating? And would she even trust him enough to let him help her?

"Mr. Markenna." Meagan Trask stood before another one of the Markenna men. "Why are you trying to reach me?"

"Ms. Trask." Dominic stood, holding his hand out.

Meagan looked at his hand and finally shook it.

"I know what my father and brother have done to that poor girl," he began. "Please know that I'm not like them at all. I left my father when I was seventeen and have worked like hell to make a good name for myself."

"So?"

"I would like to help Emma," he said. "I can't take away anything that's happened to her, but I can make her future better, I think."

"You can't help her. She's going back into witness protection." Meagan shrugged.

"I can," he said optimistically. "I know the government gives them a couple thousand dollars and a shitty little place to live in until she can get a job or whatever. You find her a home, a nice home, and I will give you the money to buy it for her. You don't have to tell me where or anything like that. But she deserves something nice for a change, and I have the money to do this for her. And you can set up a trust to pay for the expenses so she doesn't have to worry about money at least. You can't tell me that wouldn't be nice for her."

"Mr. Markenna," Meagan began.

"Please, call me Dominic," he said.

"Dominic." She grinned, shaking her head. "I don't … let me think about it. I'm not sure how the coordination will work. Call me in a couple of days. You already have my number."

Dominic smiled with a nod. "Thank you for considering this."

Meagan nodded as Emma walked out of the courtroom with two government guards.

"I have to go." Meagan shook his hand again.

"I'll call you in a day or two," Dominic stated as she walked away.

Dominic called her the next day, and she answered her phone this time. He smiled, thinking he might have a chance to help Emma. That was his goal, to help the girl, but Meagan Trask was constantly on his mind. She was very beautiful with her dark hair, nearly black, that fell to her shoulders. Pretty green eyes dominated her facial features, along with her full lips. She probably stood five inches shorter than him, but that didn't matter; he liked her confidence.

"Mr. Markenna." Meagan smiled as she answered the call.

"Please, call me Dominic," he reminded her. "Only clients call me Mr. Markenna, and you're not a client."

"No, I'm not." She took a seat at her desk.

"Would you like to have dinner with me tonight?" he asked.

Meagan didn't answer. She didn't even speak. Was he asking because of how he wanted to help Emma or was this like a date?

"Hello?" he said to the silence.

"I'm sorry." She buzzed back to reality. "I'm here. Why dinner?"

"Well, I would like to talk about Emma," he stated. "But honestly, I'm very attracted to you, and I want to see you."

"You are not one to beat around the bush," she replied.

"No, I'm not." He sighed. "I don't play games. I'm honest, and if I like someone, I tell them. And I like you, and I want to take you out to dinner if you will let me."

"You are so different from your family." Meagan smiled.

"I hope so," he replied. "I like to think I took after my mother."

"I don't know her, but I'm beginning to think you did." She took a deep breath. "Meet me at Stella's on the riverfront at seven."

"Yes, ma'am." Dominic was pleased.

"And you better not turn out to be like them," she warned. "Or I will ruin you."

"I promise I am not like them at all," he stated firmly.

Maggie turned out to be the first woman that he fell in love with. When she got her promotion, he didn't want to be the one to hold her back, as he knew how much she had worked for it. They tried the long-distance relationship, but it wasn't enough. He wanted more, but she was tied to her job in another state.

Dominic vividly remembered the last time her saw her. It was very much like his last days with Tess. Very intimate, very passionate, very emotional. And when he left her to fly back to Virginia, he knew he wouldn't see her again.

Feeling a hand on his shoulder, he didn't even flinch. At this point, he didn't even care if his father found him. Death would feel better than what he was currently feeling.

"Son." Jonathan took a seat beside him.

"I've worked all my life to not be like my father," Dominic began, staring out at the ocean. "I don't really have it in me to be the way he is with women, people in general. I wanted to make a name for myself, away from the worldly reputation that he put on the Markenna name. I just seem to keep getting fucked every time I turn around, with my company, women, family. I'm so … done."

"When Tess came into my life, I was happy again." Dominic shrugged.

"That was short-lived. Getting played like I was … it was tough to overcome, but I did with Tar. Taryn was very independent, and it was so hard to get her to trust me and let me love her, but when she did, it was amazing. We could've had a great life together if she hadn't been so obsessed with revenge."

"As a father, I'm glad she had you the last couple of years. She needed a man that loved her, just her, and I'm sorry you lost her."

Dominic shrugged. "Doesn't matter anymore. She's dead, and Tess is married. And Mags, well, I can't even process this one. If she had our baby, she's got to be six. Six years and she couldn't call me? I don't understand? I know I'm not a bad man. I was going to propose, but she got a big promotion, and I didn't want her to turn it down because of me. She'd worked so hard and deserved it."

"I'm going to tell you the same thing I tell the other kids." Jonathan rested a hand on his shoulder and looked at him. "Work is important. It is what supports you and your family and puts that roof over your head. But none of that matters without love. God is the foundation, and love holds it all together. One doesn't work without the other. You don't know the circumstances surrounding Meagan and the child. And you need to give her a chance to talk to you and explain her side."

Dominic looked away from Jonathan and stared blankly at nothing. "I feel like such a failure in all aspects of my life," he stated.

"Not a failure." Jonathan grinned. "You've had some detours in your road, but you're not a failure. You will work through this and persevere."

"And if I don't?"

"You will," Jonathan assured him. "You may not be my son by blood, but you are your mother's. And no matter how difficult things were for her, she never gave up, and I won't let you either. It may not be an easy road ahead, but you have family, and we love you and are on this journey with you, whether you like it or not."

Dominic's eyes filled, and Jonathan hugged him tightly, just as he would his other sons.

# Chapter 33

J ames was on his phone standing inside the hangar. His jet was off to
the left, and Jonathan's was beside him. Four of his men were lying
on the ground under the wing of his plane with their duffel bags used
as pillows. It was easy for them to sleep wherever they were. With some of
the jobs they've had, they could be up for three days straight. They learned
to sleep whenever and wherever they could, and today it was under the
wing of his jet.

He'd been on the phone with Adam trying to track Markenna and his
possible next move. While on the phone, they both noticed Antoine was
heading south from Virginia. James knew he was headed there and would
be ready for him. He just hoped that Marcos was with him. Hearing a car
to the right, he glanced outside the hangar only to see Jonathan driving
up with Dominic. With a sigh, he walked out to greet them.

"James." Jonathan got out of the car and walked over to him, with
Dominic following. "How's it going?"

"Okay," he replied but not feeling that way. "What's up?"

"I know you're working on this Marcos thing, but would you mind
working on two things?"

James smiled. "I'm actually working on four things right now, and one
them is Meagan Trask."

"Thank you," Dominic finally said.

"Here's what I know so far. Her house was broken into, and the little
girl is in protective custody with Brian. Adam is working on getting the
video footage from a neighbor's camera to confirm who broke in and how
many men were there."

"If he took her, he will use her to get to me if he knows we were
together in the past."

"Nobody is using anybody here. That isn't how I work. One sec." James put up a finger to give him a moment to look at the video that Adam sent to his phone. After about thirty seconds, his eyes went from the screen to Dominic.

"Marcos, as I already knew, and my new friend Antoine and four other armed men," James told them.

"He's going to kill her before I even get a chance to talk to her." Dominic turned around, walking away.

James looked at Jonathan and shrugged. "He has no faith in my work. I've only lost one client, and that was because I shot her."

"That will make him feel better." Jonathan grinned.

"I'll get her for him," James said, glancing at Dominic as he walked away, then back to Jonathan. "And I'll bring his little girl to him as well. Jonathan, this is what I need from you. Can you just get him and Emma to leave me to my work? I know what needs to happen, and they need to trust me to do it. I've tried talking with Emma, but her actions still show that she doesn't trust me. And Dominic ... I don't even know what to say there."

"I'll talk with him. Do you want me to talk with Emma too?"

"I don't care, but I don't think it will do any good." James shrugged. "I'm not fully focused, and I need to be. I don't want to worry about either one of them taking off. I need that piece of mind that Emma is safe. Then I can work."

"Well, then, let me do what I do best." Jonathan gave James a grin and a pat on his shoulder.

"Thanks." James gave a nod just as another car showed up. "What the hell?" Cocking his head sideways, James wondered why Tess was here. After getting out of her car, she walked over to Jonathan and James.

"Darling." Jonathan caressed her shoulder. "Why are you here?"

"I don't like this uncomfortable feeling I have about Dominic," she told him honestly. "I need to speak with him."

"Tess, you should really leave him alone," James told her.

"Don't tell me what to do." She shook her head, looking around for Dominic.

"Where's Colin?" James eyed her. "He's supposed to keep you on a short leash."

Tess's eyes went wide, and on pure instinct, she balled her fist and hit him in the jaw.

"Tess!" Jonathan snapped her name like a whip.

James's face set firm as he shook his head. Pulling out his phone, he called Colin. "Get your wife out of here—now," James demanded to Colin when he picked up his phone. "Or I'm going to tie her up and gag her."

"Where is she?" Colin asked.

"Airstrip," he told him and ended the call.

"That was mean, James," she grumbled between gritted teeth.

Grabbing her by the arm, he walked her into the hangar and pressed her against the wall with his hand at the base of her neck, when they were out of eyesight. "I can't have you here and work," he explained with his face inches from hers. "I don't want anything to happen to you or the babies."

"Fine," she stated. "But you don't have to be such an ass."

"I'm sorry." His eyes were wide and irritated. "Dominic is not in a good place right now. I really don't think you should be alone with him. Please?"

"Will you tell me why?"

"Before he met you, he was with a woman named Meagan and just found out he has a daughter with her. He's very upset about the whole situation. And Marcos kidnapped Meagan a couple weeks ago."

"Oh my." Tess sucked in her bottom lip.

"Yes, so now you understand why you should just give him some space," James advised. "He's not had great luck with women, and you were one of them."

"Okay. You could've just told me." With irritation, she eyed him as Colin drove up.

"I can't work with you around, being pregnant, or Emma," he told her as Colin walked over. "Please, just stay at the house with her where it's safe."

"She will," Colin affirmed with his arms crossed, looking at Tess.

"Good." James took a deep breath and turned to Colin, handing her over. "Leave Dominic alone too. If he comes to you, fine; otherwise, leave him be. Let Jonathan deal with him. It's not your place."

Colin took her hand in his, having no idea what was going on.

"Tess, you married Colin. There are boundaries within your life now when it comes to being 'friends' with the men you've been with in your past. Learn them; otherwise your husband is going to start shooting them in the head." James glanced at Colin and shrugged as Colin's brow furrowed. "Take her, please. I have to work."

Colin put her in his jeep and asked his father to bring her car back to the house when he came. Driving off the airstrip, he turned right and headed into town. Pulling out his phone, he called Harper and asked her to watch the kids for a bit so he could spend some time with Tess. He noted Tess hadn't spoken since he drove up and decided to let her be until he pulled up to a restaurant in town. After putting the jeep in park, he turned to her, and she slowly glanced at him.

"Am I not supposed to be friends with men I've been with?" she asked him.

"I'm not friends with any of the women I've been with," he stated. "You just kind of kept it all in the family."

"I had no idea all of them would end up being related one way or another." She sighed in frustration. "I want to go home. You, me, and the kids. I just want to go home. I'm done with all of this."

"We're scheduled to leave tomorrow," he reminded her.

# Chapter 34

J onathan walked into his home. It had been a long day, and it wasn't over yet. James was sending Emma and Dominic home with Colin, Tess, and the children and one of his men. Knowing the tension between Tess and Colin, he hoped distance from Georgia would put them on the right track again. But first, he needed to speak with his son.

Walking down the hallway to the kitchen, he smelled some great southern cooking. Gina and Tess were making dinner as the kids played in the family room with Harper.

"Smells wonderful," Jonathan commented, giving Gina a kiss.

"It'll be about another twenty minutes before supper," Gina told him.

"Perfect. That's gives me enough time to speak with my son." Jonathan gave Tess a kiss on her forehead. "Honey, where's Colin?"

"In your study with Matthew," Tess answered. "They're working out numbers for this merge."

"Thank you." Jonathan gave her an easy smile, then walked to his study.

"Father," Matthew said, noticing him first before Colin looked up.

"Dad," Colin acknowledged him as he was jotting down some numbers.

"How's it going?" Jonathan asked his sons.

"Good," Matthew answered. "Keeping it simple, straightforward. Combining the companies, but I will continue to manage my side. I will move the buy/sale to your side, as Colin is going to move large investors to my side."

"Why only the large investors?" Jonathan asked, knowing the answer but wanting to see if his sons were thinking like he was.

"Matthew's company has returns up .0879 percent more than ours.

Our clients will make more money, and when they make money, we make money." Colin understood the business inside out, as did Matthew.

Jonathan grinned with a nod, knowing his sons were excellent in their profession. "Sounds great. Not to sound condescending to any degree, but I'm proud of you both. Working together to merge the companies in a peaceful manner is refreshing. I've seen many hostile takeovers, and I'm glad that this is not the case here."

"It's easy for us because it's not about the money." Colin glanced at Matthew, then his father. "It's about a very special little girl who needs her father as much as he needs her. I will do almost anything to make sure this co-parenting works out for all of us."

Matthew nodded in agreement. For the slightest moment, guilt crossed his mind for his indiscretion with Tess. It was then that he realized how much his brother loved his wife and their children.

"Matthew, would you mind giving us a few minutes?" Jonathan asked.

Standing, Matthew glanced at Colin, then patted his shoulder. Both knew that when their father wanted to speak with them in private, they were in trouble of some sort. "Good luck, brother."

"Thanks." Colin gave a half grin, watching Matthew leave the room and close the door behind him.

Jonathan took a seat behind the desk, facing his son.

"What have I done now?" Colin asked.

"Emma."

"I was wondering how long it would take you to put that together." Colin sat back, waiting for the reprimand.

"As soon as I met her and heard her name, I knew. She's a beautiful woman. And you knew James was going back to see her. Why did you do it?"

Colin shook his head. "It was just to talk, nothing more. And now she's pregnant and has no idea if it's his or mine."

"Let it be his, even if it isn't. This will ruin your life and your marriage. I'm certain that's not what you want to hear, but trust me, son, Tess finds out it's her, there will be hell on earth."

"I know. There will be hell, but Tess won't leave me."

"How are you so certain about that?" Jonathan was curious.

"A promise we made to each other before we decided to have children of our own. We didn't want our kids growing up in a broken home. We wanted them to have a mother and father under the same roof. Kids need both parents. They learn different things from a mom and a dad. With Tess being brought up in that toxic environment, we wanted to make sure it didn't happen to our children, and it won't. I will never leave her, and she will never leave me."

"Would you have preferred having a mother while growing up?" Jonathan wondered.

"Dad, you did great with us. I don't even remember my mother. You were the rare exception in the world of single parenting. I have no complaints."

Jonathan gave a slight grin. "I did my best, given our circumstances. Emma said you told her it would happen again."

Colin grinned. "It's not going to happen again. I made a promise to Tess and Harper, and I can't go back on that. Besides, it was just a mind game. Emma is really easy to mess with in the head. When I told her that, I was only trying to drop her guard so I could put her under and hop in her head for James. It was no big deal."

"That girl is not used to being around people like us. Play nice, Colin."

Colin laughed a little and shrugged. "Yes, Father."

"How do you feel about all these kids you're having?" Jonathan sat back.

"I love it. It's easy with Tess. We have similar thoughts on how to raise them and try to be the best parents we can be. If the twins are boys, Tess will want one more. She wants another girl. And I would never deny my wife something she wants."

"I don't know how you got so lucky in that respect. Be good to her, Colin. You know her past; make her future wonderful. She deserves nothing less."

# Chapter 35

Emma stood by James in the hangar as he was talking on the phone. Everyone else was getting on the plane for their flight to Portland. Emma struggled with leaving, as she really didn't want to. The idea of being with Tess gave her mixed feelings. They seemed to get along better, but there was still something that Emma wasn't comfortable with. Maybe it was her own guilt for her indiscretion with Colin. At some point, Emma needed to tell James. This wasn't a secret she wanted to keep from him. With a quiet sigh, she patiently waited for James to finish his call.

James wrapped up the call with Adam and turned to Emma after he slipped his phone in his pocket. Gently, he placed his hand on her shoulders, knowing she was nervous about leaving him. "You'll be safe with Colin," he reminded her.

"I know." She gave a half grin. "I would rather be here with you."

"I know, but I can't focus properly with you here. And I will not have something happen to you because I'm distracted."

Emma nodded, understanding.

"The next couple days will go fast," he assured her. "Then I will come pick you up, and we can go anywhere you want in the world. Just pick your place."

"I just want to go home," she said softly. "My little home with you. I want to walk on the beach. Share another sandwich in that little café. Make love all night."

James grinned as he leaned down, kissing her softly. "I'm offering to take you anywhere in the world, and you want to go home." He tilted his head as she nodded slowly. "Then that is exactly what we'll do. I love you, Em."

Emma's eyes filled as she pursed her lips together to keep them from quivering. James wrapped her up in his arms, kissing the top of her head. He didn't want to let her go. He didn't want to send her away, but that was what was safe.

"We're ready to roll," Grey announced, walking up to them.

James took a deep breath as he nodded. Then Four came over his radio.

"Incoming from the east," Four stated.

"Copy," James replied. "I'm thinking it's our new friend Antoine. Can you confirm?"

"Nope, not yet," he answered.

James moved Emma behind him as the car came in fast, only stopping when three AKs were pointed at him.

"Stay behind me, Em," James told her, pulling his 9 mm.

Emma did as he directed without hesitation.

"Out of the car," Grey told this man with his weapon pointed at his face.

The man slowly stepped out of the vehicle with his hands in the air.

James sighed, recognizing Antoine immediately. He'd hoped that everyone would have been on the plane in the air before he showed up. Just another glitch in the plan. Keeping Emma behind him, he let Grey do his thing.

"I'm not carrying a weapon," Antoine said as Grey patted him down. "I'm just here to tell you that Emma has a tracking device in her. That is how he knows where she is. It was implanted years ago when Dimitri broke her shoulder. I don't want trouble. I just want out."

Emma stepped out from behind James and slowly walked over to Antoine. James grabbed her arm to stop her, but she shrugged him off. "I'm fine," she tried to assure him, unsuccessfully.

"Grey." James's voice was soft but firm. "Bullet in his head if he moves in the slightest."

"You got it," Grey said, not moving his eyes from Antoine.

"You're my cousin," Emma said cautiously to him.

"What?" Antoine didn't understand. "How is that possible?"

"Dominic is my brother." She watched him carefully. "Marcos is our biological father."

"I guess that would make you my cousin. You look so much like Marcos. I'm sure you don't want to hear that, but you do." Antoine's brow furrowed. "He talks about you often."

"Uh huh," Emma said softly. "Why are you with him?"

"I didn't get a choice." Antoine didn't take his eyes from hers. "My father told me I had to come help Marcos, then bring him home. Marcos threatened the life of my youngest son."

"How old is your son?" she asked.

"He just turned three. Lucas." Antoine smiled, thinking of his blond-haired little boy.

"He's just a baby," she stated. "How many children do you have—and why only threaten one of them?"

"I have three children. Lucas is my son with my mistress."

James just listened. Most people freely gave away information without realizing what they were doing, and Antoine was no different. James was happy that Matthew was on the plane with the children.

"Oh, I see. Don't you love your wife?" Emma was curious.

Antoine grinned. "No, it was an arranged marriage for the business. My wife is a real bitch. I do what I must for my children. They are all that matters to me."

"Why don't you leave?"

"It's a little difficult to just leave the Markenna family." He gave her a half grin, amazed at her ignorance about her own blood. "As you should know."

Emma nodded, understanding. "Are you here to hurt me?"

"No." He shook his head. "Marcos wants me to take you back to him. But let's face it. I know that's not going to happen. Get the tracker out of you, put it on me, and I will tell your boyfriend where he can find him."

"What about your son?" she wondered.

Antoine took a deep breath. "If everything is timed right, he should be fine."

Emma turned to James. "I'm almost afraid to ask." She closed her eyes momentarily. "How do we remove this tracking thing?"

"Is it metal?" James looked at Antoine.

"I don't know." Antoine pulled out the small device that tracked Emma and handed it to James. "This is what he has to follow her with. He has two. Maybe there is something on this to tell you what it is."

James took the device and Emma's hand. Together they walked into the hangar. Taking out his cell, he called Adam and gave him all the information on the device, then waited. Pulling Emma close, he kissed her forehead as he listened to Adam's finger type on a keyboard.

"I don't want his child hurt because of me," Emma said, looking at James.

"I know." He nodded. "We'll come up with a plan to avoid that somehow. Let's focus on getting this thing out of you because you can't leave until it's out."

James was quiet as Adam began speaking. After about five minutes, James ended the call and looked at Emma. Colin and Tess had come off the plane to find out what was taking so long. With all of them standing around, James began to explain.

"Adam said it's a metal device about the size of an almond." James took a deep breath. "He said if we know where it is on her body, we open her up and take it out, or we can use a magnet to draw it to the surface, but it will hurt."

"Just do the magnet thing," Emma simply stated.

"Okay. Let's do this so we can get going," Tess said, walking to the back of the hangar to look for a magnet amongst the tools, with Colin following.

James cupped her face, bringing his close to hers. "Em, are you sure about this? This will be painful, and you know I don't want you in any pain."

"James, I have to do this. I can deal with some pain to get this thing out of me."

James closed his eyes, knowing she didn't realize the pain that this was going to cause.

"Found one," Tess announced, holding up a five-pound magnet.

Colin looked at her. "Tess, that's kind of big."

"So? If it will do the job, does it matter?"

Colin glanced over at James to get his take.

"It's fine," Emma stated, walking over to Tess and Colin.

"I've never done this before," Tess told Emma.

"Me either." She shrugged. "Just do whatever you have to do."

Emma closed her eyes as Tess ran the magnet over her shoulder, then slowly in front of her collarbone. An instant pain ripped through her chest as the magnet pulled the device to the surface of her skin right below the collarbone. Without thought, her hand reached out, grabbing Colin's arm, as he was the closest.

Jack ran over with the medical bag, dropping it to the ground. Jack looked at the magnet that had the device attached, with Emma's skin pinched in between. "Tess, why didn't you wait for me? I could've numbed the area ahead of time."

"Maybe next time." Tess shrugged him off.

"James, can you hand me the needle with the red tip?" Jack asked him as James zipped open the medical bag to get what Jack needed.

"Here." James handed him the needle.

"Emma." Jack made her open her eyes and look at him. "This is going to hurt at first for a couple seconds, but it will numb this area a bit. Problem is the magnet is very large and strong. If I can't get the device to separate from the magnet, I will make an incision all the way around, and you will have a scar."

Emma's eyes went from Jack to James as she sucked in her bottom lip. The pain was intense. With her hands slightly shaking, she still held Colin's arm tightly.

"It's just a scar, baby." James looked up at her as he knelt by the medical bag. "We all have them."

As Emma was listening to James, Jack numbed the area and began the incision. As he predicted, the device wouldn't separate from the magnet. Carefully, he cut the skin around the device. Colin stood behind Emma, as they were afraid she was going to faint. Once Jack separated the skin and the device, he had Tess took it over to the workbench as he went to work on repairing the one-inch open wound that was left in front of her collarbone.

Emma leaned back, resting her head back on Colin's chest as Jack stitched her up. She could feel the pull of the suture as Jack put in each stitch, but the pain had subsided a great deal. James assisted Jack and focused on that because when he saw Emma leaning back against Colin, with her hands in his, a rage began to surface. The two of them looked entirely too comfortable that close to each other.

"James, could you hand me another piece of gauze and a couple pieces of the tape?" Jack asked him. "Emma, I'm almost done."

"I want to sleep." Her voice was very soft as her body began to relax more, prompting Colin to slip his arm around her waist to hold her up.

"Just another minute," Jack told her as he finished bandaging the wound. "Done."

Emma turned into Colin's shoulder, crying. Instinctively, he wrapped his arms around her as he would with Tess and his children.

"Colin." Tess yawned. "I'm going to go check on the kids. See how Harper and Matthew are doing with them."

"Okay." He nodded. "We'll wrap this up and head out soon."

Tess walked away as James zipped up the medical bag. Jack picked up the used medical supplies and went to dispose of them properly.

"It was you," James said to Colin as he stood upright, his voice low.

"What are you talking about?" Colin asked, with Emma still in his arms.

"You are the man that Emma was with the weekend before I went down there." James eyed him.

Colin took in a deep breath, releasing it slowly, wondering where James was going to take this conversation.

"You slept with her," James said with gritted teeth, not wanting anyone else to hear this conversation.

"You slept with my wife. I think it would be in your best interest to let this go," Colin advised.

"I'm sure you do." James nodded.

"Emma." Colin looked at James for a moment before tilting her head up to look at him. "Are you okay? Do you need to go lie down?"

"I just want to sleep," she said as her eyes struggled to stay open. Without thought, she hooked her arms around Colin's waist, just letting him hold her upright.

With Colin's daring eyes on James, he tilted his head just enough to kiss Emma on her head, knowing it would enrage James.

"Game on." James swiftly pulled Emma from Colin, then focused his full attention on Colin.

With a fast, strong fist, he hit Colin hard in the jaw. Colin only took one step back before he charged him. James wasn't the only one who knew hand-to-hand combat. Colin had learned long ago how to defend himself and anyone else that he deemed worthy of his defense. Both men went round after round, evenly matched and equally bleeding.

"What the hell?" Jack stated as he walked back into the hangar.

By then, a few of James's men had filtered in and were watching the fight. It wasn't until Grey came in that Jack, with his help, was able to break them up.

Grey held James back as Jack had his hand on Colin's chest, daring him to make another lunge at James.

"Are you two done here?" Jack asked as they were catching their breath.

"Yes," Colin stated first, eyeing James.

"James?" Jack looked at him.

"Fine, done," he answered, shrugging Grey's hands off him.

Jack looked from one to the other, then Grey.

"Let me get the medical bag again," Jack told Grey, who would keep an eye on them.

When he came back a few minutes later, Colin was leaning against a counter with his head tilted forward over a trash can, as his nose wouldn't stop bleeding. Above his brow, there was another inch-long cut that was bleeding down his face. James was sitting in a chair rolling his jaw, swearing that Colin broke it. His lip was bleeding, as was the gash to the side of his eye. His hand pressed slightly on his ribs, as he was certain one or two were cracked. To Jack, Colin was in worse shape, so he went to him first.

"Move your hand," Jack told him as he pulled out his cell. "Harper, I need your help." Jack ended the call, knowing Harper was on her way from the jet.

When she got to the hangar, shock was evident on her face. Then he pointed over to James.

"Can you help him?" Jack asked. "I'm having a hard time getting the bleeding to stop with Colin."

"Yep." Harper went over to James without asking any questions as to why they were both beat up.

"Colin!" Tess ran over to him with fear in her voice. "What the hell? Jack, is he okay?"

"I don't know yet, T." Jack grabbed more gauze from the medical bag. "Just let me get the bleeding to stop. Call Gina and have her come over here please."

Tess pulled out her phone and did as she was told, then took Colin's hand and held it tightly.

"Damn it, Colin," Jack muttered under his breath as the bleeding continued. "Tess, hold pressure on the cut above his eye. Maybe that one will stop bleeding. We may have to take him to the hospital to cauterize whatever is bleeding."

Doing as she was told, Tess pressed gauze on the cut above his eye. By the time Gina showed up, the bleeding had stopped there, but his nose was still a consistent stream.

"Jack, pinch at the bridge of his nose," she directed. "Colin, lean forward a little bit. I'm going to put your nose back in place, and let's hope that slows up the bleeding. It's going to hurt."

"I know." Colin nodded slightly. "I've been through this before. Just do it—and do it quick."

Gina repositioned his nose quickly and pressed gauze on his nose, hoping the bleeding would ease up. After about five minutes, she removed the gauze and was happy to see the bleeding stopped.

"Don't touch your face yet," she warned. "I know you'll want to clean up, but give yourself a few minutes. I'm going to go check on James."

Colin closed his eyes, trying to control the pain as Tess stood by his side with his hand still in hers.

"How is he, Harper?" Gina asked, walking over to James.

"His jaw hurts, but it's not broken or he wouldn't be moving it." Harper rested her hand on his shoulder. "I stopped the bleeding on his cuts, and as long as he doesn't get into another fight, they shouldn't require any stitches. He may have a cracked rib or two. In short, he's good."

"Okay." Gina nodded, then looked from James to Colin and spoke to both. "I don't know what caused this, but I'm strongly suggesting that you two resolve your issues in a more productive way. Beating the hell out of each other isn't the answer. We will not have fighting amongst the family ever again. We've been through too many years with that, and we're not repeating history."

Gina went over to the jet to check on the children and left the adults to sort out their issues and hopefully not kill each other in the process.

"What caused this?" Tess asked Colin, and when he didn't answer, she looked at James.

"It's just a guy thing," James told her, glancing at Colin. Looking over to his right, he saw Emma standing on the side, quietly watching them. "Emma."

Emma shook her head slowly and walked out of the hangar.

"Emma, please." James went after her.

Emma walked away from the hangar, the jet, everyone. Tears fell from her eyes, and she wanted to vomit from the stress of what she just witnessed. With a quick pace, she had no idea the direction in which she was heading. All she knew was that she was walking away from all of that. There had been enough violence in her life. She didn't want anymore.

James had to pick up his stride to catch up with her, as she was hustling, which made his ribs hurt even more. "Emma, please." James touched her shoulder softly when he caught up.

"What?" She abruptly stopped to face him. "What the hell was that?"

"There's this thing that has been building and building between him and me, and it was bound to come out eventually. It just happened to be today. He knows exactly what he did to provoke that. So, if you want to point the finger and blame me for what just happened, that's fine, because I would do it again."

Emma shook her head as more tears fell.

"He knew I was coming back to see you." James shook his head. "He knew, and he still went to you."

"You don't get to be mad about this." She shook her head. "I didn't know, and we've been through this before. I had no idea that you were coming back."

"I know, but he knew. And I do get to be pissed at him." James shook his head, irritated. "Do you love him?"

Emma looked through the tears, with her breath catching. "No! It was three days, not three years! I'm in love with you. And I can handle a lot of stuff, but I can't do that. I cannot do what just happened. I don't have it in me."

"What are you saying, Emma?" James had an uneasy feeling.

"I'm ..." She hesitated a moment. "I'm not sure."

"I love you, Emma." James was within inches of her face. "I don't want to lose you. I know we've dealt with a lot of things that normal couples wouldn't deal with, but please don't run away from me. This will get better, calmer, and peaceful once this Marcos thing is over."

"Yes, so we get through the Marcos thing, but we'll still have this ... thing that happened between Colin and me looming over us. He and I are friends, just like you and Tess. If I've got to be okay knowing what happened between you and her, you need to be okay with what happened between him and me. Otherwise, we might as well be done now."

James took a deep breath, closing his eyes for a moment. "I know," he admitted. "I will be okay with this, but he was such an asshole in there with you. And I know you are blissfully unaware of what he did, but trust me when I say he had it coming."

Emma touched his shoulder. "James, if you feel a need to beat someone, go beat my father. Don't hurt this family please."

James slowly nodded as he reached out, wiping her tears. He kissed her softly, knowing his lip was cut and swelling slightly. "I'm sorry I upset you with that in there." He ran his hand through her hair.

"I'm sorry too." She slipped her arms around his waist, hugging him tightly.

"He's the one that could be the father to the baby?" James stated as a fact more than a question.

Emma nodded, with more tears flowing. "I'm so sorry. If I could take it all back, I would."

"That's why Colin didn't say anything with Tess in there." James was processing several thoughts at once. "Damn it! I should have let it go."

"What are you talking about?" Emma was confused.

"I have to rework this plan for you. You won't be safe with Colin and especially not Tess. If she finds out, you're dead."

"You can't make her stop?" Emma suddenly felt faint.

"No." James took her hand, kissing her knuckles. "We've got to go rework this plan."

James walked back into the hangar with Emma's hand in his. With a deep breath, they went over to Colin. Tess had an ice pack over the bridge of his nose and another above his brow.

"How is he doing?" Emma asked Tess, hoping she didn't know.

"He'll be fine," she said, still agitated because she didn't know what had caused the fight.

"Do you mind if I have a word with him?" James asked Tess. "Alone?"

Tess stared at James without answering him for a full minute. Then, to his complete surprise, she pulled her 9 mm and aimed it at him.

"What the fuck are you doing?" James asked, knowing everything just clicked together in her brain.

"Oh wait, I had it on the wrong person." Tess sighed, moving the aim of the gun from James to Emma.

James eyed her, shaking his head slowly. In his heart, he knew Tess would never shoot him, but he wasn't too sure about Emma. Tess knew he loved Emma, but he knew Tess loved Colin. When that clicked together, he grinned. "I get it." He nodded, as if conceding. "Remember one of our many conversations when I told you I wanted to take out your husband so we could be together?"

Tess remembered but didn't answer.

"I know you remember, so I'll just continue." James's glare was hard. "But I didn't because I knew how much you loved him. You made your choice and chose him, with his multiple faults. Emma is my choice."

"Emma with her one major fault, fucking an assassin's husband." Her brows raised, straight faced. "And I don't care that you love her, and I don't care that she's had a hard life. All of us have. I told you what I was going to do when I found out who the whore was."

"He slept with her," James said with gritted teeth, pulling his gun out, aiming it at Colin.

"I know," she simply stated, with no emotion showing, "After all these years, do you still not know who I am and what I'm capable of? When the emotions are off, they're off, and I don't care about anyone. Colin's good at this stuff. Jack is good also. I've had years to watch both and you and learn. What is the one thing I protect without hesitation?"

"Your family," James stated. "Am I not your family?"

"Yes, you are, but she's not." Tess looked at Emma. "Don't think you have one over me because you fucked him for a few days. He has fucked many, and you are just another notch. Well, James, at least you know who the other man is now. Do you really think Colin will give up all custody rights if that child is his? He's a McGowan, and you just stepped into the lion's den."

Emma didn't say a word but could feel her heart pounding in her chest. Tess was a scary woman with a 9 mm in her hand and an attitude to go with it.

"He doesn't play fair when it comes to his children. Look what happened with Taryn. He would have dragged her through the pits of hell to get full custody of Connor. The bullet I had put in her head saved her from a life of misery. The only thing that balances him is me."

"Tess." James knew he had to reason with her. "I know you're pissed and hurt by this, but please, I'm begging you, put down the gun. They have a line on you. Please, put down the gun."

"Wrong." Tess held his eyes. "They have a line on Emma and you."

James glanced at Emma, seeing the red dot on her shirt, aimed at her heart. Then he saw the one on his shirt.

Colin stood up a bit, knowing he needed to control his wife somehow because that was the only way James was lowering his weapon. "Baby." Colin moved his hand down her arm that held the gun, slowly, until his hand was on the barrel. "Give me the gun. You can't shoot Emma any more than you can shoot James."

"I had my own twin sister killed." Tess stared hard at Emma. "Do you really think I can't kill her?"

"Morgan." Colin figured he would change tactics since the other way wasn't working. Calling her by her work AKA might jolt her a bit, but he was thinking maybe not. Morgan was a coldhearted woman. "Morgan could kill her, but Tess won't. I know the battle in your head right now. I've had that same battle because of you and the men you've slept with. Let it go. It was just a drunken night, and it meant nothing."

"I guess this is where I should lie and say I believe you." Her eyes shifted from Emma to James, but she was talking to Colin. "I do believe that it meant nothing, because she is nothing. I guess you have to go slumming occasionally to appreciate perfection."

"Baby, please?" Colin held firm, knowing he could sway her thoughts. Leaning down, he whispered in her ear. "I love you and you are ten times the woman that she is. Please put down the gun."

Tess held her place and gun for a long moment before sighing and putting the weapon back in her waist band. With her eyes briefly on Emma, she shifted them to James when she quickly grabbed Emma by the neck, spun her around, and put her in a headlock.

"Christ almighty, Tess!" Colin laughed a little, as his wife was so unpredictable.

"Let her fucking go, Tess!" James warned, aiming his gun back at Tess's forehead.

Tess gave him one of Morgan's deathly looks, daring him to come near her. "You may as well put the gun away, as you know and I know you're not going to use it." With her eyes on James, Tess spoke softly in Emma's ear. "It is simply by my respect and love for James that you will live." Tess kept her eyes on James. "Don't you ever look or even think about my husband again. Make sure you get on your knees and pray to God that this baby isn't his. Anything ever happens again, I will put a bullet in your head and make both watch. You don't fuck with me and what's mine." With that said, Tess released her grip and pushed her over to James, then walked away.

James holstered his 9 mm, breathing out, not realizing he had been holding his breath the entire time.

Emma looked at Colin, furious for what he told Tess. Taking a deep breath, Emma leaned over, placing her hands on her knees and dropping her head down. *That was intense*, she thought, trying to calm her nerves. Out of everything in her life, she had never stared into the barrel of a gun, knowing a simple pull of the trigger and her life would be over. The urge to vomit was sitting at the base of her throat, and she was doing her best to keep everything down.

"Emma, deep breaths." James ran his hand over her back. "She wouldn't have hurt you."

Emma didn't respond immediately, as she couldn't find any words that would come out without vomiting.

James knew this was a pivotal moment for their relationship. Glancing at Colin, he shook his head, not knowing if he should be angry or just relieved that Tess walked away.

"You're welcome. I have to go deal with my wife," Colin told James as he followed Tess out.

Tess kept a quick pace to the jet and was about to head up to get the children when she abruptly turned to face Colin. "Don't say a damn word to me! The only thing you're going to do right now is help me get the kids off the plane and put their car seats in the SUV. Don't call me. Don't track me. Leave me the hell alone."

"Tess, come on, damn it." Colin sighed, as his face was throbbing. "Don't take off and don't take off with my kids."

"You're really going to try to pull that card with me?" Tess snickered as she shook her head, turned, and walked up the stairs, with Colin following.

Matthew was occupying the children when he saw them come on the jet. He knew something was up but wasn't certain as to the details.

Tess took the two car seats that were at the front of the plane and handed them to Colin.

"Tess, you're not taking off with the kids." Colin's voice was firm.

"Fuck you!"

Matthew instantly unbuckled the children, knowing he needed to get them off the plane, as he didn't want them witnessing the fight that was close to happening.

"Change in plan." Matthew smiled at the children, who were unusually quiet as they watched their parents. Matthew walked over to them, and his voice was barely above a whisper but firm. "Both of you shut the fuck up right now. You will not fight in front of them. You let me get them off the plane and out of earshot, and then I don't give a damn what you two do to each other. But it will not be in front of the children."

Both Tess and Colin, took a deep breath and nodded. Without a word, they put the car seats in the SUV and buckled the children in. Tess had the keys in hand and went to get in the driver's seat when Colin stopped her. Pulling her to the back of the SUV, he made her look at him before speaking.

"Go and cool off. This is not ruining our marriage, our family. I made a huge mistake, and I've apologized over and over to you for it. I love you and our children, and we need to get out of this toxic environment and back to our normal."

Tears filled her eyes as she briefly looked away before speaking. "Just let me get away from all of this for a few hours. If you want me to come back, she needs to be gone."

"Okay," Colin agreed as she turned to walk away, but he grabbed her hand. "Tess, I love you, only you, and always you."

"I know." Tess nodded, taking a breath. Wrapping her arms around his shoulders, they hugged tightly as she whispered in his ear, "I love you, but I'm so angry right now, you must let me go calm down."

"I know. Just be careful, and if you start to not feel well, call me."

Tess gave him another nod before walking away from him. To her surprise, Matthew stopped her as she went to get in the SUV.

"Where are you going?" Matthew asked.

"I'm just going. I don't know where."

Matthew raised his brows. "Well, I'm coming with you. You shouldn't be alone. You're upset, pregnant, and that's my daughter in the car with you."

Tilting her head sideways, she gave a soft smile. "Do you think I'm going to run the kids and me off a cliff? You should know better than that. If I was going to kill anybody, it would have been Emma in there."

"I understand that." He nodded, taking the keys from her. "I don't care about any of them the way I care about you. I'm driving."

Tess gave him a half grin, went to the other side, and rode shotgun, leaving Colin to watch her drive off with his brother.

# Chapter 36

J ames wrapped his arms around Emma after Colin walked away. Kissing her temple, he held her quietly for a few minutes before pulling back a little. With his fingers, he pushed back the few hairs that hung beside her eyes, then softly kissed her lips. He noted her eyes filling. "What?" James asked tenderly.

"The things they said." A few tears slipped down her cheeks. "It was so mean."

"Don't let any of it bother you. Tess was angry, and Colin said whatever he had to say to calm her."

"It doesn't make me feel any better." A few more tears fell as her breath hitched.

"I know, Em." James sighed. "I know Tess very well, and she spoke out of pure anger."

"I'm not a whore," she defended.

James grinned. "I know that. I wouldn't be with you if you were. Tess knows, and she knew the word would sting."

"Don't leave me here please. Can I just come with you?"

James hesitated. "I can't just take you on a job like this."

"I'll stay on your plane. Just please don't make me stay here—or can I just go back to my house? We know Marcos isn't there."

James thought for a moment, wondering if it would be safe enough for her to go home. Doing a quick head count on how many men he would need for this job, he figured he could spare one or two of them to go with her. Dominic should probably go with her, as he was responsible for him as well.

"Let me go talk with my men. Maybe you could go back to your place while we're up there."

Emma nodded, excited that he would even consider this.

"Stay here." He parked her on a stool. "I'm going to go see what I can do."

"Okay." She nodded again.

Emma stayed put while he rounded up his men to talk. At this point, she would make a deal with the devil to avoid seeing Tess again. And heaven forbid she should ever glance at Colin. It was his words that hurt more than Tess's. Deep down, she wondered if he really felt that she was beneath Tess. Was Tess ten times the woman she was? If so, why did he stay with her for two nights, buy her a car, and give her a $50,000 bank account? Was it to keep her quiet? Hush money? Or did he lie to his wife to protect her? As Emma pondered her thoughts, she didn't see Colin walk back in the hangar.

"Emma," he said, knowing she didn't notice him.

"You need to go." She stood up, stepping backward. "I don't want your wife thinking anything is going on between us. She made me feel about two feet tall. Just leave me be."

"Emma." He put his hands out to gesture peace. "I'm sorry about all of that. I didn't mean the things I said about you. That was just to calm her."

"You hurt me," she whispered as her eyes filled again.

"I know, and I'm sorry." He reached out to touch her shoulder, and she stepped back. "Don't be afraid of me."

"I'm not. I'm afraid of your wife," Emma answered honestly.

Colin deflated, as he knew it was going to take a lot of talking to prove to her that she didn't have to be afraid of him or Tess. "Emma, let me see your hand," Colin said, holding her eyes until she raised her hand to him. Gently he held it with his. As he felt the softness of her skin, he closed his eyes briefly, absorbing the touch. "I'm sorry."

"Don't because it doesn't matter," she said softly.

"It does matter." He watched her eyes to see if she believed him. "You are kind, beautiful, and passionate. Harsh words can break a person, and you don't deserve that."

Instantly, her mind drifted back to the second night he stayed with her. The kissing started on the beach and slowly moved to the front porch swing and eventually to the bedroom. Colin was a master with a woman's body. He knew the perfect places to touch, kiss, and squeeze.

"Emma," James said as he walked into the hangar. Seeing Colin holding her hand, even though they were at arm's length, irritated him.

"It'll be okay, Emma," Colin said as James walked up, giving him an eye of distrust.

"I don't want to see her ever again." She slowly pulled her hand away from him. "If that's possible."

James looked at Colin and sighed. "I told her Tess would be fine after a while," James advised him.

Colin nodded as his head was pounding. "True."

"I'm having two of my men take Emma and Dominic to her house. They should be safe there. I don't want to deal with Tess in this state of mind. At least not tonight. I need full focus on Markenna and Meagan."

"Good. My wife won't come back until she's gone. I'm sorry, but you know where my loyalty will always lie." Colin raised his brow at James, who nodded. "I'm going to go get drugged up by Gina. I'll talk to you later. Emma, I'm sorry."

Emma didn't reply. She just let him walk away.

# Chapter 37

Colin walked over to Harper as she was sitting on the lower step of the plane. He needed a ride back to the house, and Harper had the car.

"You two will be fine." Harper stood, looking at her brother. "Matthew is the most levelheaded, reasonable man I know besides Jack. They'll be back tonight."

"I'm not reasonable?" Colin asked, leaning against the rail.

"No, brother." She smiled, shaking her head. "You're a smart man but an idiot sometimes. Stop thinking you can have it all without her finding out. Tess knows all. She reminds me of our father."

"I don't want it all," he disagreed.

Harper turned, facing him. Gently she placed her hand on his heart. "Don't lie to me. You know I see through that."

"Damn it, Harper." He shook his head. "I had a moment of weakness. I feel like I'm going to be paying for this the rest of my life."

"You, brother, don't have moments of weakness. You like to conquer." Harper looked him in the eyes. "Between you and me, Emma's going to lose this baby. That isn't something you will have to worry about."

Colin shook his head. "I feel bad, but on the other hand, it's a relief."

"Don't make that mistake again, Colin." She pursed her lips. "You will lose Tess if you do. So, behave as a husband should. How would you feel if Jack did to me like you did to Tess?"

"I got your point, Harper. Can you give me a ride back to the house? I need drugs and whatever you've got in your magic herbs to make me feel better."

* * * * * * * * * * * * * *

229

Matthew drove Tess and the children north along the coast. The drive was quiet as the children fell asleep and Tess just stared out the window at the ocean. The weather was surprisingly nice. It had rained most of the morning but cleared up when they headed to the airstrip after lunch. Reaching over, Matthew covered her hand with his, prompting Tess to glance at him.

"How are you?" Matthew asked, concerned.

Tess wiped away a tear and gave him a soft smile. "I'm fine. Where are you driving us to?"

"Nowhere in particular. Is there somewhere you would like to go?"

"Not really." She shook her head. "When the kids wake, they'll be hungry."

"Okay." He nodded. "We'll stop and eat somewhere then. Do you want to talk about it?"

Tess looked at Matthew and smiled. "I wouldn't have hurt her, but I certainly got my point across. I don't think she'll ever sleep with another married man."

"I imagine not," Matthew agreed. "How do you justify what we did yesterday morning? It was just as bad as what Colin did with Emma."

"It's different," Tess responded, even though she knew it wasn't.

"No, it's not."

"He made me feel inadequate as a wife," Tess admitted softly. "Part of me wants to walk away from him, but this bigger part won't let me. I should've stayed with you." Tess glanced at him, then back out the window.

Matthew didn't say anything. He simply gave her hand a squeeze.

"Could you imagine the nasty divorce that would happen between Colin and me?" Tess grinned with a small chuckle. "I know how he is with people, and when they're on his bad side, he's vicious. Taryn thought I was oblivious to this side of him. I'm not, never have been."

"Our father would never let him be mean to you," Matthew said with confidence.

"I really don't want to divorce him," she admitted. "I just don't want him to cheat on me again. Especially with a damn barmaid. That's degrading. He's supposed to cheat on me with someone who is better than me."

"Colin will never find anyone better than you." Matthew sighed. "I can assure you they didn't have some of the discussions like you have with him regarding finance, shareholder distribution, stock market dividends, and so on. Emma's a nice girl, but my brother would tire of her after a while. He needs mental stimulation, not just physical. But you need to remember who she is."

"Why? What do I care?" Tess didn't understand.

"Emma is a Markenna, Dominic's sister who's had a horrible life because of her father. She was only working in a bar because of her circumstances. Otherwise, think of where she would be."

"South America, working beside the other Markennas in the drug, guns, and human trafficking market," Tess answered.

"Yep." Matthew nodded. "Chances are she could've been like Dominic and gotten out, but—don't take this the wrong way—she's a woman and not a strong woman like you. She'd probably be in it with daddy if she didn't know any better."

"Am I supposed to feel sorry for her?" Tess glanced at him.

"I don't know. I don't have an answer to that."

"Do you feel sorry for her?"

"I do." He was honest. "She had no idea who Colin was, and she probably thought she would never see him again. You had no idea who I was or who Dominic was. Do you think you would have let happen what happened had you known who we were?"

"I don't know." She shook her head, thinking about that.

"I can tell you, for me, had I known you were my brother's girlfriend back then, I wouldn't have let happen what happened. But on the flipside, we wouldn't have Savannah. I love our baby girl so much. So, in having her, I wouldn't want to change anything except keeping you and having you as my wife."

Tess felt a tear slip down her cheek, realizing how much Matthew still loved her. Looking at him as he drove, she ran her hand through his hair. Matthew took her hand, bringing her palm to his lips for a soft kiss.

# Chapter 38

J ames sat on the steps of his jet, waiting for the time to tick by. As the events from earlier played through his mind over and over, he regretted confronting Colin. Maybe if he hadn't, Tess would have never found out, and Emma wouldn't have had to endure the confrontation with her. But then again, hitting Colin was satisfying. Perhaps it was years in the making. Regardless, it was well deserved. Glancing at his watch, they had another two hours before heading out. James knew he was sporting a black eye, split lip, large gash above his other eye, and a couple cracked ribs, but the pain was worth it.

Wes and Rick took Emma and Dominic to her place south of Savannah. He understood why she didn't want to stay there without him, and he certainly wouldn't take her with him. With Marcos in Virginia, Emma and Dominic would be safe at her home.

"James." Grey walked over to him. "Want some of the pizza the guys picked up?"

"No, I'm good," he replied, noting Grey wasn't leaving.

"Want to talk about it?" Grey asked.

James looked at his friend. Next to Adam, Grey was the only other man that James had known for this long in his life. Greyson Parker was a good friend, and James trusted him wholeheartedly. "I don't know what to say because I don't even know how I ended up in this position in the first place," James stated, noting headlights were coming from the west. "Expecting anyone?"

"Yes, sir." Grey nodded, eyeing the SUV that pulled up.

"Damn it," James stated, noting Matthew was driving and Tess was passenger. "You knew about this?"

Grey put his hand up when James stood. "Brother, you and Tess have been through a lot of stuff. Listen to her. She is reasonable once she's calmed down. And I'm certain Matthew wouldn't have brought her here if she wasn't calm."

James nodded, knowing Grey was right. Then his eyes shifted to Tess as she got out of the car. Grey waved Matthew over to the hangar for some pizza with the men as Tess slowly walked over to James.

Tess stood before James, taking a deep breath. As she tried to form the words in her mind, James sighed, gave in, and hugged her tightly. Feeling her arms come around his waist, he held her tighter as his eyes filled.

"I'm so sorry," James said first, holding her.

"I'm sorry too," she whispered as tears filled her eyes.

After a few minutes passed, James loosened his grip to look at her. His hands cupped her cheeks, allowing his thumbs to wipe the tears from her face. "What do we do now?" James asked as he sat back down on the stairs and motioned for Tess to sit one step below between his legs. James rubbed her shoulders gently, knowing she liked that.

"I have to go talk with my husband and, eventually, Emma."

"She's really upset, Tess." James rested his chin on the top of her head.

"I was really upset, James," Tess said. "Why am I not allowed to react to my emotions when I have them? Why do I always get in trouble? Other people do much worse things than I."

"Because you react with a 9 mm," James simply stated. "Or a head lock. Most people don't react that way. They simply yell or cry or whatever. Baby, you take your emotions to a whole other level. In watching all of us over the years, what is the one thing that remains in constant control with all of us?"

"All of who? You, Jack, Colin?" She wanted clarification.

"Yes," he answered. "Even Grey."

"Control over your emotions." She shrugged. "Just for the record, I do control my emotions on the job. This wasn't a job; this was my husband fucking your girlfriend. And I am pregnant. All I have are emotions."

"I know, I know." He sighed, wrapping his arms around her so his hands could rest on her belly. "I've wondered, if I had gone and seen her sooner, would any of this have happened?"

"That's a what if, and we aren't allowed to do that." Tess tilted her head up to look at him with a smile.

233

James grinned, nodding his head, as she was right.

"Are you going to let me marry her?" James asked.

"Yes," she grumbled with a shake of her head.

"You could still leave your husband," he reminded her.

"I could, but I'm not going to." She was resigned to that fact. "We can get through this somehow. Besides, you don't need an instant family. Four kids are a lot."

"I would take that on with you, and you know that." He kissed the top of her head. "But I also know that you and Colin will persevere through this just like you do with everything else."

"What happens if this baby she's carrying is his?" Tess asked softly.

"I'll deal with it." James wrapped his hands around her shoulders, and leaning close, he rested his chin on her head. "Do you really think he will be difficult?"

"No. I was just being a bitch. I'm sorry about that."

"Who had the line on Emma?" James was curious.

"I don't know. I just saw the red dot. Hell, I knew they were on me. There was one on you and Colin too."

James laughed a little. "You know that was my men. I can see I have men with favorites on my team."

"I don't think any of them really knew what to do." Tess looked up at James. "I don't want another one of his stray children."

"Well, I can tell you that I won't share the whole father thing like Matthew is doing. Although that situation is a little bit different. I will raise the child as my own. I won't do the bouncing the kid between him and me. Hell, we live on opposite sides of the country. I already told Emma that too."

Tess stood up abruptly. With her hands on her hips, she cocked her head sideways at him. "How long have you known about this?"

"Shit." He shook his head. "I'm so off my game. Just a few days. I found out the night after she fell overboard."

"And you couldn't tell me?"

"Hell no!" His brow furrowed. "Look at how you just reacted earlier. Emma is not you or like any of us. She doesn't do the in-your-face confrontations. She's been beaten down too many times. Do you really think I would put her in that situation with you?"

"You could've told me." Tess was irritated all over again. "It would've probably worked out a little bit better than what happened earlier."

"I didn't know it was Colin until all that shook down in the hangar. I was simply working off a gut feeling," he admitted.

"You're telling me that she told you that she had fucked someone else and you didn't ask who?" She needed clarification.

"Yes." He nodded. "In a way, I didn't really want to know. But there was just something about those two and the way they are so comfortable around each other. Everything fell into place. And when I asked him, he didn't deny."

"Whatever." Tess shook her head, aggravated.

"I'm sorry, T." James stood up. "I'd never intentionally hurt you."

Tess looked at him for a long moment before nodding. James stepped over and hugged her again as Matthew walked back.

"Is it safe to assume that you two are good?" Matthew asked with a grin.

Tess nodded, as did James at the same time.

"Come on, Mama T." Matthew motioned for her to come closer to him. "You have a couple more people to talk to. I called Father, and he said Colin was sleeping and Emma went home with Dominic."

Tess looked at James confused.

"She didn't want to stay here with you and Colin. You scared the hell out of her, Tess. What do you expect?"

"Guess I will apologize later." Tess leaned closer to Matthew, taking his hand that he held out for her. "I'd rather go kill people with James."

"If you'd stop being knocked up all the time, you could come with me." James kissed her forehead and sent her on her way. Looking at his watch, he saw there was still an hour and half before it was time to leave.

✱✱✱✱✱✱✱✱✱✱✱✱✱✱

Tess finally made it to her room. She stood quietly for a moment, looking at her husband on the bed sleeping. Colin's face was badly bruised, but in her mind, he deserved it. He was lucky he wasn't in a hospital bed recovering. Completely switching thoughts, she liked the fact that he always slept shirtless. His body was taut and sexy. Was it his body that kept her with him? she wondered. That would be a lame reason to stay with a man. She laughed at herself, knowing very well that wasn't why she was with him. Sighing, she ran her hands over her protruding belly and closed the door softly behind her. Wanting nothing more than to change her clothes and sleep, she began to strip down. Tossing her clothes into a basket, she looked for one of Colin's oversized T-shirts to put on and was startled when he came up behind her.

"What are you doing?" he asked, moving her hair aside so he could kiss her neck.

"Changing, then lying down," she told him. "Aren't you in pain or hurting or something?"

"No. Gina and Harper have great drugs," he replied, moving his hands around her body and cupping her breasts. "I want to make love to my wife."

"No." She tilted her head as his lips were on her neck. "Your lip is split, and I can't kiss you the way I like. Besides, I just want to be angry with you."

Colin's hand ran through her hair, turning her head. Then he kissed her lips. "We can do angry sex. It wouldn't be the first time."

"I shouldn't give you anything." She turned to face him. "But if I do that, are you going to go whore around again?"

Colin sighed. "No. But I won't live the rest of my life with your jabs about it. I've apologized many times already. I know I hurt you, and I'm so, so sorry. Can we please move forward?"

"I hear the words come out of my mouth, and it makes me cringe every time I say something. I don't want to be that woman, but you broke my heart, Colin. It's the only defense I know other than leaving you, and I don't want that." Tears slipped from the corners of her eyes. "I married the man I was in love with. I'm having your children. I should be so happy right now, but I'm not. And I don't like that."

"What do we need to do to fix this?" Colin kissed her forehead.

"Go home. We just need to be away from here and go home with our kids. And just do what we did so well for the last three years."

"Then we'll go tomorrow morning after we get up." He hugged her tightly. "Promise me?"

"My promise to you. No matter what happens with James and this

Markenna thing, we will go home tomorrow." Colin wiped away the tears that were sliding down her soft cheeks. "I love you."

"You're a pain in my ass," she said, kissing his bruised cheek softly. "But I love you too."

Colin stood back a moment, looking at his almost naked, pregnant wife. "You're sexy as hell."

Tess shook her head in disagreement.

Colin nodded and scooped her up, taking her to their bed.

# Chapter 39

With Emma gone and peace made with Tess, James put his full attention to the job at hand. Saving Meagan was his priority. Being able to kill Marcos was his prize. With his men and Adam, they devised their plan for that night. Antoine was his hostage for the moment. After Marcos was dead, James planned to let him go back to his family. There was one stipulation to his release: he had to get out of the family business, or James would finish the list with Antoine on it. And there would be a conversation about Sarah and where to find her. After watching Matthew drive Tess away from the airstrip, James sat down to make a few calls.

"Hello?" Harrison's voice came over the line.

"Harrison, I was just wanting to make sure you and Carina made it safely to Chicago."

"Yes." Harrison sighed, staring out the window of his apartment in downtown Chicago. "Gran is settling in. I really think she wants to go back home as soon as possible."

"I know," James agreed. "I have contractors starting tomorrow to fix the house. I asked that they just get the house enclosed first, and we'll work on the inside this winter. I have a feeling I'll be there most of it."

"Don't feel that you have to take on the full responsibility of Gran," Harrison reminded him. "Jack and I will help you. I don't have any cases going to court for another four weeks. I'm available to help."

"Thank you, Harrison." James grinned.

"At least I'll get the full benefit of having Gran here with her cooking. And if she gets her way, I'll be engaged to Elizabeth before she leaves." Harrison smiled at his grandmother, who was already in the kitchen making a shopping list.

"Yes, you will." James nodded, knowing his cousin loved Elizabeth but was afraid of the financial aspects of marriage at his age. "I need to get back to work. Stay safe and call me if anything comes up."

"Will do," Harrison replied. "I expect to have dinner with you and Emma when this is all over. Put that on your calendar."

"Yes, sir." James smiled, ending the call.

Turning around, he saw Jack walking toward him. "Hey," James said as they shook hands and hugged like brothers. "What are you doing here?"

"I'm going to do this job with you," Jack informed him. "You're down three men, having two with Emma and Dominic and one with Harrison and Gran. I thought you could use me."

James grinned with a slight nod. "Thanks, Jack. Is Harper okay with this?"

"Yep. She suggested it." Jack shrugged.

James was rather surprised, but then again, not really. "Is Harper at the house?"

"Yep."

"I need to go talk with her," James stated and saw the confused look on his face.

"Why?"

"I want to know how all of this is going to turn out," James simply stated with a grin.

"I'll let Adam catch me up on the plan." Jack smiled, walking away as James headed back to the house.

James walked up on the porch to find Harper sitting in one of the rockers. He took a seat in the other. They were quiet for a moment. It was easy for James to just be when he was in Harper's presence. There was always a calm, relaxing atmosphere emanating from her. Even when Taryn had a gun pointed at her head, she was still very calm.

"I was waiting for you," Harper began. "You know this will all work out with Marcos Markenna."

James pursed his lips with a nod.

"The problem is going to be with Emma." Her eyes shifted from the scenery to James. "She will be there when Dominic kills him."

"Dominic kills him? They're on their way to her place with Rick and Wes. My men would call me if she takes off or something. Are you sure? How do you know this?"

"I don't know how I know things." She shook her head. "I just do. There's going to be a rough patch coming for you with her. I don't know what. I just know it's coming."

"She's not going to die, is she?"

"No." Harper shook her head. "She won't, but …" Harper's voice trailed off, as she didn't want to tell him what she told Colin earlier.

"But what?" James persisted.

"She's going to lose this baby and push you away." Harper knelt before him. Taking his hands in hers, she saw his eyes fill a little. "James."

James shook his head before tilting it down, as he was unable to speak.

"James." Harper's soft hand touched his cheek, making him look at her. "This is where you have to fight for her. It will be hard for you, but fight your instinct to walk away. She is your future, but this is going to happen. You can't let the sadness and the pain of loss shut you down again."

"I love her so much," he said, wiping away an escaped tear.

"I know, and she loves you." Harper smiled. "Never give up on her, because you two have a great future together, but you have to work through this. It will be hard for you, but just remember, it will be even more difficult for her. She has suffered so many losses in her life. This will be devastating to her."

"And that's why she will push me away." James now knew what Harper was talking about.

With a simple nod, she stood up, as did James. Without a word, she hugged him tightly.

"You're the one who's having Jack come with me," James stated as he pulled back, placing his hands on his hips.

"Yes. Please don't fight it."

"For you, sweet Harper, I won't." After giving her a kiss on the cheek, he headed back to the airstrip.

# Chapter 40

Dominic and Emma sat on her porch swing getting to know each other. Emma asked Dominic about his life from as far back as he could remember. Graciously, he told her everything he could think of that mattered to that point in his life. Even though his life had been difficult at times, his only regret was Meagan. If he could do it over again, he would have sold or moved his company to be with her, as he loved her that much. And now, having a child with her confirmed his desire to reconnect.

"Meagan was truly upset when she found out she was pregnant," Emma told him. "I remember her coming to visit one week when she found out, and all she did was cry. I told her that she needed to tell the father. I had no idea it was you. Obviously, she didn't listen to me. I'm so sorry, Dominic."

"Was she upset because the baby was mine?"

"I don't think that was it. It was more of being a single parent, new job, things like that. She should've called you."

"James said getting her out alive is his main priority." Dominic looked in the direction of the ocean. "Killing Marcos would come second, but only after Meagan."

Emma nodded, knowing James would hold true to his word.

"Do you love him?" he asked, and she nodded. "Don't let it go. Love doesn't come often. Make sure you embrace it when it does."

"Umm, brother, I think you need to take some of your own advice."

There was a relaxing silence between them.

"I really wanted to be the one to kill Marcos," Emma finally said.

"You still can," Dominic told her.

"It's like an eight-hour drive from here," she reminded him.

Dominic grinned. "Let's fly."

"I can't." She shrugged. "I'm broke."

"I'm not." He smiled. "But even better, I have a brother with a plane."

Dominic pulled out his phone and called Matthew. Their conversation was brief but solid in their plan. Matthew told him if they could get to the airstrip in an hour, he would fly them to Virginia.

Emma walked into her house, and Rick followed. She needed to get her car keys from the kitchen.

"What are you planning, Emma?" Rick asked, knowing she was up to no good.

"Nothing." She tried her best to not look guilty.

"Hmm, don't believe you." Rick stood before her, arms crossed.

Emma sighed. "I want to confront my father. It's my right, and I need to go … now."

"No." Rick shook his head. "James will have all of our asses if we mess up the plan. Once he has a plan, he sticks to it, and you're not in this plan."

"Fine. Tell him I knocked you out and took off."

Rick laughed, as he was probably twice her weight and a good foot and a half taller.

"Come on, damn it. Please?" she begged. "You can either come with me or stay here. I'm going … with my brother."

"Damn women," Rick stated, heading back out the front door. "Come on, Wes. We're taking them back up to the airstrip."

Emma followed Rick onto the porch and looked over at Dominic with a grin.

## Chapter 41

J ames refrained from throwing his phone after Rick called telling him Dominic and Emma insisted on being at the strike tonight. Standing outside of his jet, he placed his hands on his hips and looked up at the sky. Why couldn't they just listen to him? Was it really that difficult to follow his request? No wonder Harper said they were going to be having problems.

"What was that call?" Jack asked, coming down the stairs, noting James's annoyance.

In one brief sentence, James told Jack what Dominic and Emma had done. Jack pulled out his phone, calling Adam for James.

"Adam's running a trace of Dominic's cell, as Emma's isn't showing up anywhere. She must've turned it off." Jack shrugged.

"No." James shook his head. "She lost it when she fell into the ocean. We just haven't replaced it yet. She said she didn't need one if she was with me. What is going on in her head? I don't understand. What is it with these damn women?"

Jack simply laughed. "Adam will tag and keep an eye on them."

"We need head out," James stated. "We have a schedule to keep."

Jack followed James up the stairs on the jet. His men were assembled, ready and waiting. They had laid out the full plan and finalized it an hour before. They weren't planning to infiltrate the home Marcos was in until the witching hour, as James always referred to it. If he was killing someone, it needed to be at that specific time. Normally, he wasn't a superstitious person, but he held true to this one ritual. Even the attack on the McGowan home was in the middle of the night.

Sitting in his seat, James looked out the window as Thomas flew the jet north. They would be landing at a private airstrip that was a mere ten minutes from Dominic's home. The fact that Marcos decided to hold up there still amazed James. Did that man really think Antoine would be able to bring Emma to him? Or was this a ploy of some sort? The thought perplexed him, but his plan was solid, and Brian would be in after to clean up.

"Adam," James said, answering his phone when it beeped.

"They're about an hour and a half behind you," Adam said. "His phone is on if you want to call him. Dominic knows what he's doing. I'm sure he's waiting for your call."

"Thanks, Adam," James replied. "Keep an eye on them."

"Will do," he answered. "I'll be in touch."

James ended that call and made another. When Dominic picked up, he sighed.

"Hey." Dominic spoke first.

"One question. You knew I'd trace your phone?" James asked.

"Yes," he answered. "There's an odd safety factor knowing I'm being tracked by a mercenary."

James laughed. "Will she talk to me?"

"I don't see why not." Dominic handed the phone to Emma.

"Emma." James looked out the small window of his jet. "What's on your mind?"

"I always imagined being the one to kill him," she mumbled.

"You're telling me that you and Dominic have conspired your own plan in the last hour just so you can kill your father?" James inquired.

"Yes," she answered.

"This wasn't in the playbook. I'm not happy with you." He wasn't going to fight her on this because she would do it anyway. "May I ask one favor?"

"You can ask me anything except to stop." Emma was firm.

"I'm not asking you to stop," he replied. "But I would like you to let me secure the area and detain Marcos for you first. Would you mind letting me do that?"

Emma thought for a moment. "That would be fine. I don't want you to be mad at me."

"I'm furious," he said, but his voice was calm. "But I will do this for you. I will pick you two up at the airstrip when you land. Be out front."

"We will be."

James swallowed the irritation in his voice. "Emma, I will let you kill him. But it is my way until the area is secure. Do you understand?"

"Yes." She nodded. "Please don't be mad at me. This is something that I have to do."

"I understand, and I would have understood had you said something before you left." James was doing his best to maintain a calm voice. "All you had to do was tell me."

"I didn't think about it until we were home." Emma sucked in her bottom lip. "James, I love you."

James closed his eyes as his leg bounced to control his anger. She was messing up a perfected plan and possibly endangering the lives of his men. "I love you too," he finally responded. "I'll see you when you land."

They ended the call, and James flipped his phone between his fingers as his mind was racing. Learning how to control his anger was the best thing his mother ever taught him. And right now it was being utilized in full force. Looking across from him, Antoine sat with his eyes closed.

"Woman troubles?" Antoine opened his eyes slowly.

James simply chuckled, not answering.

"I've had my fair share of that."

"Tell me about Sarah," James probed.

Antoine stared at James for a full minute. His gaze went from hard to soft in that time as a small grin emerged. "Beautiful Sarah."

"Yes, beautiful, pain in the ass, Sarah. I kept you away from Matthew because I'm certain he would have beat you for information on her whereabouts. How did you come upon her? She was in Africa."

Antoine shook his head, thinking James should have known the answer to that question. "My family's business in all over the world. How do you think I met her?"

"Don't fucking play games with me. I'm already irritated."

"We met in Africa. It was just a brief affair. Then I had to go back home. We said our goodbyes and went different directions." Antoine sighed, shaking his head.

"When this Marcos thing is over, I'm sending you home. I know there's more to this, but honestly, I don't want to know right now. I prefer to finish one job before starting another. But I'm going to call you when I'm ready, and you're going to tell me where to pick her up. If you help me with her, I'll leave your family alone. Betray me on anything, and I will wipe out the entire Markenna line." James sat back, needing to refocus on the present job.

# Chapter 42

James and Thomas picked up Emma and Dominic. It was almost one, and they needed to get back to their rendezvous point. Taking Emma aside once they made it back to the team, James placed both his hands on her shoulders.

"Emma, you've never taken a life before. I need you to understand that it will change you. If at any point you change your mind, it's okay. Nobody, especially the men on my team, will judge you. In that split second when you have that choice and you decide you don't want to, just look at me, and I will know. Walk away, and I will finish. Do you understand?"

Emma nodded, knowing it was one thing to think about killing someone, but it was entirely different in real life. She had certainly seen her share of dead bodies, but she'd never been responsible for taking one. "Thank you for letting me at least confront him." Her voice was soft.

"I just wish you would have said something earlier." He kissed her forehead.

"I didn't realize I wanted this until the eleventh hour." Her eyes burned from lack of sleep.

James nodded, trying to understand this thought process of hers, as he was never impulsive. Everything was planned, especially when it came to his work. He hadn't gotten to be number one in the business by being impulsive. Precision in his work was necessary, just as it was in the selection of his men. Only the best were on his team. And if he brought in anybody new, they worked with him for at least two months before taking him on a job. He wanted to know what the reaction of his men would be in any circumstance.

Emma was a loose cannon in his mind, as he had never worked with her in this capacity. And given the fact that he had only met her a month ago made him question her desire to be here for this. He hoped she was on the straight line with him; otherwise his men would put a bullet in her head if any danger were to rear up from her.

"Here." Grady handed Emma a bulletproof vest. "Put this on. It will save you from anyone except the men on the team. We don't aim for the chest; we're all head shots. Be careful."

Emma looked at James with her mouth slightly gaped. It was then that she realized they didn't trust her. How could they? They didn't know her. She hoped James didn't feel that way. "What are they thinking?" She asked James off to the side.

"We don't usually have circumstances like this on our jobs." He shrugged. "They don't know you and don't know how pure your intentions are. I can't save you if you're lying in any capacity. Do you understand what I am saying?"

"Yes." She nodded, disillusioned at the lack of trust but understanding. "I promise you I have no ulterior motive."

"Good." He nodded. "Do you want a gun?"

"No." She shook her head. "I don't need one. I need a switchblade."

James took her to the back of the SUV he had. Taking out his duffel, he pulled out a six-inch switchblade and handed it to her.

"Play with it," he told her. "Get the feel for how it opens, closes, the weight in your hand. Why a knife, not a gun?"

"Dimitri always put a knife to my side." She pulled up her shirt to show him the scars that were on her side by her liver. "He always threatened to stab me in my liver. He said I would die slowly, painfully, and no one would be able to save me."

"I noticed those scars the first night," he stated. "I figured it was from your past. And he was right. If you puncture the liver, go deep; your victim will die, and it will be painful. You know exactly where it is on a man?"

"I think so," she stated.

James took her hand with the blade held firmly and pointed to his liver. Knowing his men were watching them closely, he continued.

"You can go through the ribs if your aim is perfect and strong." He showed her with the knife. "But if you go just below the rib cage, aim upward and slice to ensure death."

"Okay." She nodded as her eyes glanced behind to see each one of his men watching them.

"You good?"

"Yes," she stated, then shook her head. "No, wait."

Emma turned to James's men to address them. "I don't have any other motive than to see Marcos killed." She hoped they believed her. "I would never hurt James or any of you. I promise. He had my brother beat me for years. I want my revenge."

"We'll have your back," Purcell said. "But anything out of line, and we'll shoot you in the head. One of us will always have a line on you."

"Are you sure you still want to do this?" Wes asked.

"James already has this all planned out," Grady stated.

"I need to confront him," she replied.

"Gentlemen." James stepped up, as that conversation was done. "Radio check, and it's almost the witching hour."

James ran through the radio check with his men. Then they got into the two SUVs and headed to the meeting point with Brian, which was a block from Dominic's house. James went up to Brian to confirm a couple of things.

"I will call you once the house is secure," James said. "One thing changed. Emma wants to confront Marcos before he expires. I'll call you in after that event happens. Do not rush in until I call you. I don't want my men's lives at risk, and we all know how the government can jump the gun sometimes."

"This is all your show," Brian reminded him. "I just want Meagan brought out alive. I don't care what happens with Markenna. Do as you please."

Within five minutes, James and his team surrounded the house. Dominic's home sat in a prestigious neighborhood on a two-acre parcel, so he wasn't worried about neighbors. They knew the layout and had on their heat sensor goggles to see where the Markenna men were posted. Four men were on the lower level, and two, who he figured were Marcos and Meagan, were on the second level, likely the master suite. The woman was on the bed with her hands bound above her head and her legs bound at the ankles. The man in the room was walking around the bed as if inspecting his prey, but then again, he may have been on his phone. The thirst in James's body to beat this man to death was at an all-time high.

Confirming position with his men, James and his team moved in quietly. He left Emma and Dominic behind one of the manicured bushes by the front door. This would be an easy maneuver for his team. Within five minutes, the four men downstairs were taken down without a single bullet being fired. James, Grady, and Purcell made their way up the stairs to the master suite, while the other men secured the downstairs. Without a word, the men quietly slipped into the room while Marcos's back was turned away from the door. The woman lay on the bed naked, with a thin sheet barely covering her body, and it was easy to ascertain how badly she had been beaten. James was hoping she was sleeping instead of unconscious.

With weapons pointed directly at Marcos, James walked in behind his two men with his assault rifle down. He stood staring at Marcos as the man turned around with a very unexpected surprise on his face.

"I knew Antoine would mess up." Marcos grinned at James.

James didn't speak because all he wanted to do was beat this man. Pulling out his switchblade, he cut the ropes that bound Meagan as she woke. Standing, she pulled the sheet around her body.

"Kill him or I will," she stated as her swollen, black, and blue eyes filled.

"Get dressed," James told her. "Dominic has clothes in his closet. Brian will be here after the area is secure to help you."

"Brian from the bureau?"

"Yes," James answered, watching Meagan's eyes spill over.

Meagan went into the walk-in closet to find clothes to put on, and when she heard the first connection of a man's fist to another man's face, she knew she would be okay. Dressing in sweats and a T-shirt, she stayed in the closet, almost afraid to come out. Her hand shook uncontrollably, her ribs hurt, her face hurt, everything on her body hurt. Sliding down the wall in the closet, she curled up in a ball and cried.

James handed Thomas his weapon and wandered over to Marcos.

"I see you like to beat women," James stated. A nasty smile emerged. "Let's see how well you do against a man, you fucking pig."

"Looks like you've already been beaten." Marcos grinned.

"Hardly."

Marcos swung first, and James simply leaned back, making him miss. With a short laugh, James balled his fist and nailed him in the jaw with a punch that spun the man around, making him hit the wall. Picking him up, James hit him again and again. The man tried to fight back, but he was no match for James. The beating continued for another five minutes before James stood back. His fist was bloody, and there were splatters all over his body, but it wasn't his own.

James motioned for Grady to watch him as he went into the bathroom and washed his hands. Knowing Meagan hadn't come back into the bedroom and wasn't in the bathroom, he walked into the closet and found her curled up in the corner.

"Hey," he said, extending a hand to her shoulder. "Emma's going to finish this. Let's get you downstairs."

"I want him to suffer like I have for the past three weeks," she cried. "He beat me, raped me, and beat me some more. I'm supposed to be stronger than this, but he broke me. That fuck broke me."

James was quiet for a moment, unsure of how to handle this woman. "No, he didn't. You're still alive. He didn't break you because you have a daughter you need to get back to and be strong for. You helped Emma get through this. Let her help you this time. She has a huge support system that will help you as well. He was a monster. So was his son, Dimitri, and now they're both dead. Well, he's almost dead."

"I heard she met a man." Meagan tried to smile, but her split and swollen lip prevented it. "You're a little beat up though."

"Compliments of Colin McGowan." James laughed a little.

"Colin McGowan worked you over?" Meagan asked in disbelief.

James grinned with a nod. "I'm bad, but he's worse. A story for another day."

"Thanks to you, I will have another day." A tear slipped from the corner of her eye.

"Many more days. I know Emma would love to see you."

"I can't believe I'm going to say this, but I'm glad you're the one she's with. You'll keep her safe."

James smiled. "I love her very much."

"Good. She needs that in her life. Help me up please?"

James helped her stand up slowly. Her body was sore and bruised, and she really needed to go to a hospital. When upright, she walked with James into the bedroom. Marcos lay on the floor bloody and nearly unconscious. She looked at him, then looked back at James.

"Nice job." Meagan gave a slight nod of approval.

"Probably beat him a little more than I should have." He stood with his hands on his hips. "Emma wants to confront him. I just want to beat him for all the times he had his daughter beaten."

Meagan looked at him through her one good eye. "After she confronts him, beat him to death. It would be a fitting way for him to die."

James grinned, motioning for Grady and Purcell to pick up Marcos and take him downstairs. Once Marcos was out of the room, James turned to Meagan after he slung his automatic weapon over his shoulder.

"I want to be fair in telling you that Dominic is here with Emma." He watched her face for some sort of reaction.

"Does he know about Aria?" Knowing James Cordello's reputation, if he was working a job, he had thorough information on all the subjects involved.

"Yes." He nodded. "He's struggling with that. He's been through a lot of shit the last couple of months. And the son of a bitch is growing on me. Be gentle. And if that is his kid, he wants to be in her life. Prepare for that."

"Okay." She nodded once, feeling the need to sleep.

"Let's get you downstairs." James scooped her up, as she wasn't looking well.

Taking her downstairs, he laid her on the couch and covered her with a blanket. He did a quick check-in with his men, then waved Emma and Dominic in the front door. James took them down a hallway to a large open area where the kitchen, dining room, and family room were all combined. Grady had put Marcos in a chair in the middle of the room.

"He's not tied up," Purcell told James.

James looked at Emma to see if this was okay with her.

"That's fine." She nodded to him. "May I?"

James nodded, allowing her to walk up to Marcos.

Dominic hung back, as he had nothing to say to this man, and he couldn't wait for him to be dead. As much as he wanted him dead, he wasn't capable of taking another human's life, even that of this man, unless his was threatened. That DNA was not in his blood.

"Marcos." Emma tilted her head slightly.

"Emiliana." Marcos grinned at his daughter.

"It's Emma," she reminded him. "I see you got back a little bit of what you gave Meagan. Did you really think you would get away with kidnapping and beating an agent? You're a damn idiot. But then I guess prison does that to people."

"Maybe, but it got you here." He eyed her with deception.

"James." Emma looked over at him, although he was only a few feet away.

"The house is secure," he assured her.

"All I wanted to do was see you." Marcos slowly stood up, and his daughter stepped back. "And I've gotten what I wanted. Actually, I got both of you here."

Dominic eyed his father but didn't say anything, as he didn't trust the man in any capacity.

Marcos looked from Emma to Dominic, then back to Emma. "Out of all my children, you two are the biggest disappointment."

"All of your children?" Dominic said. "You only have three. And one is dead."

Marcos chuckled at his son. "You are my first born, and Emiliana is my youngest. But there are six of you."

"If they're like you, they'll be dead by year's end." Dominic glanced at James, then back to his father.

"We could have been a family." Marcos ignored his son and focused on Emma. "You didn't have to live the life you've lived, Emiliana, but you chose to betray me. And you, my eldest son, supposed namesake of the family, you certainly proved to be my biggest disappointment. You could've run a great empire, but you chose to run away."

"An empire of drugs, weapons, and human trafficking." Dominic walked up to him, evidently annoyed. "What makes you think I would want anything to do with that kind of life? Always watching over my shoulder, needing constant security because someday someone will get you. No thank you. You're fucking disgusting. And what the hell were you doing having Dimitri beat his own sister? You know he tried to rape her? How is a person so fucked up in the head to let his own kid do something like that? If anybody is a disappointment, it's you. What a fucking great father you turned out to be."

"That life is in your blood," Marcos said.

"I have been lied to, cheated on, life threatened, and beat down. I've had to use my own money—that I earned legitimately—to clean up so many of your messes and Dimitri's." Dominic grinned, while shaking his head slowly. "I know you're in my blood. But the difference is I know how to control myself, my anger, my emotions. And I am so good at it James doesn't know if he should shoot me in the head or buy me a drink."

James's eyes connected with Dominic's briefly. When Dominic looked back at his father, James glanced at Rick to make sure he had a line on Dominic's head—just in case.

Dominic rolled up the cuffs on his sleeves twice. "But, Father, I must tell you that you bring out this side of me that I can't really control anymore. Or rather, I should say, I don't want to control anymore. I'm tired of everyone taking what's mine. I'm going to get my business back, the woman I'm in love with, and my children. But first I need to rid myself of the source of my issues."

Without another word, Dominic balled his fist and punched his father square in the face, hearing the bones of his nose break upon impact. When Marcos stumbled back a few steps, Dominic followed as a rage set in and he wasn't stopping. With another fist, Dominic hit him again. At some point, Dominic lost track of how many times he hit the man. It wasn't until James pulled him back that he realized what he'd done. Stepping away, Dominic took a deep breath, noting the blood all over his hands.

"You are going to die." Dominic had rage in his eyes. "After you are dead, I will make sure every other Markenna is dead, and this family's legacy will be done."

Marcos coughed up a little blood. "You're going to kill your own child?"

"My children will grow up loved and without the threat of death beside them. They will not see their father hit their mother so hard she dies. They will not see men beaten and murdered before their eyes." Beyond irritated, Dominic turned away for a moment.

Emma slowly walked up to the side of Marcos, who was on the ground beaten, bleeding, and broken but still alive. Thinking he was nearly unconscious, she didn't react fast enough when he grabbed the leg of a chair, opposite of her, swung it around, and hit her hard in the abdomen. Stumbling backward, Grady caught her before she fell to the ground.

"Emma," James whispered as the moment played out in slow motion.

"James." Her eyes were full as she tried to catch her breath, but it hurt too much as Grady handed her to James.

"Grey, radio Brian," James said on his way out of the room.

Dominic looked down at his father as he pulled out his five-inch blade from his pocket. Smiling at Marcos, he knelt beside him. "Emma was going to pierce you through the liver, give you a slow, painful death. But I, Father, will not do that. I'm going to slide this blade into your heart. Then I'm going to twist the knife a full 360 turn. This way, you can feel the pain that you've caused me all my life." With the tip of the blade just above his heart, Dominic pressed it in quickly. Marcos couldn't move and only winced with a groan as the knife went in.

"That is for Meagan," Dominic told him. "And this is for Emma and myself." Dominic twisted the knife a full circle, watching his father's eyes widen with pain. And as the last breath left Marcos's lungs, Dominic pulled his knife from his heart and wiped it clean on his father's shirt before standing back up.

"Hand it over," Wes told him before he slipped it back in his pocket.

With a slight grin, Dominic nodded as he handed the knife to Wes and noted the two weapons pointed at his head. Knowing his words currently had James's men not trusting him, he shrugged it off to find Emma. But first he went to the kitchen to wash his father's blood from his hands.

Taking Emma in the living room, James laid her on the floor by Meagan. "Emma, stay awake. Don't sleep yet, baby."

"It hurts to breathe," she said in a few short breaths.

Meagan sat up. "James, what happened?"

"He hit her with a chair across the front of her body," he relayed quickly.

"Probably has a broken rib," Meagan noted. "It might be piercing her lung."

"Emma." Meagan got on the floor opposite James as Emma began to cough up blood, the same time that Dominic and Jack walked in. "James, give me your knife. Get me a straw or tube, pen … something like that."

James did as Meagan stated, finding a ballpoint pen in the office. Coming back, he took it apart, so it could act like a tube.

"Have you done this before?" Jack asked Meagan.

"Only practiced on a dummy." Meagan shrugged.

"Here. Let's not have Emma be your first." Jack took the knife from

Meagan. First, he put his ear on her chest, closed his eyes, and listened to each lung to figure out which one was filling up. In less than twenty seconds, he knew. "It's her left lobe."

James sat above Emma, taking her hands in his as he watched Jack work his medical magic.

"Don't let her hands go," Jack told James as he looked into Emma's eyes. "If you'd pass out, this would hurt less."

"Do it," Emma muttered slightly as her eyes closed.

Jack lifted her shirt up, felt for the place between her ribs on the left side, and slid the knife in just far enough to create a small hole in her lung. With his fingers keeping the small area open, he took the tube and inserted it into her lung to drain the blood.

James watched his cousin work on Emma. It was a quick, nearly effortless task; at least Jack made it look that way. Emma squeezed James's hands when the knife first went in. Then she passed out, but he held her hands tightly anyway.

"That was smooth." Meagan grinned at Jack.

"Years in the field." Jack shrugged, then looked at Meagan from a medical perspective. "You need to lay down."

"No." She looked at James. "Is he dead?"

"Not when I came in here," James stated.

"Umm, actually he is," Dominic said.

James looked from Dominic to Jack, who nodded in confirmation.

"Don't fucking try anything," Jack told Dominic. "Wes is behind you with a perfect line on your head. And it will remain that way until James states otherwise."

James looked at Dominic. "Who's the woman you're in love with?"

Dominic glanced at Meagan, who was barely conscious. Dropping to his knees, he took her hands. "Maggie, I should have sold my company and gone with you. I'm so sorry."

"I'm sorry too." Meagan had tears in her eyes. "I thought I was too late by the time I figured out my mistake. You were with Morgan, and I couldn't compete with her. I really want to keep talking, but can you take me to the hospital?"

And Meagan passed out.

# Chapter 43

J ames sat in another uncomfortable chair in another hospital room. The only difference this time was it was Emma in the bed and not Tess. With Tess, he could always call Colin to come and sit with her, deal with the emotions, comfort her. This was so far out of his league, and he wasn't sure what to do or say. Standing up, he stared out the window, watching the sun rise.

"Hey."

James turned around to see Dominic standing in the doorway, with Wes right behind him.

"How's Emma doing?" Dominic asked, walking in.

"She's been sleeping since she came out of surgery," James told him as they both looked at her sleeping. "She lost the baby."

"I know. I'm sorry. Want to go get some coffee? I owe you an explanation, and perhaps it would get you to call your guy off."

"Yes, that sounds good right about now. And I'll let *you* buy the coffee because I'm still not sure if I should shoot you in the head or buy you a drink." James gave Wes a nod to stay with Emma.

Dominic laughed with a simple nod.

James followed Dominic out of the room and down the hall. Eventually, they found the cafeteria. After getting some coffee, they took a seat in the dining room area.

"How's the hand?" James asked, seeing it wrapped up.

"Broken," Dominic answered with a shrug. "Hurts like hell. The last time I hit a man, I was leaving my father's compound in South America. One of his guards tried to stop me. I had $50,000 in my backpack that I had stolen from my father over a period of two years. If my father had seen that, he would have killed me. I fought with his guard for a few, then shot the man."

"Why play the innocent card?" James asked.

"I don't want to be like my father. I don't want to be associated with him either." Dominic was honest.

"Why didn't you change your last name if you wanted disassociation?"

"Would it have made a difference?" Dominic asked.

"I don't know. Maybe?"

"It was hard enough navigating immigration at eighteen, much less doing a name change. Besides, my brother began communicating with our father four or five years after we got to the States. It is what it is."

"Meagan is the one you love? Not Tess?"

Dominic nodded. "Don't think I didn't love Tess because I did. Maggie and I obviously had more than what Tess and I had. I was with Maggie longer, so naturally the love was deeper, more connected."

"And the children you spoke of?" James sat back, waiting for the answer to this one.

Dominic thought for a minute. "Aria, of course. But you need understand that I was with Taryn since Connor was six months old. I raised him as mine with her for two years. I know Colin is his father, but I still want to see him, spend time with him. I love him as my own. And he still calls me daddy. I can't just walk away and turn off those emotions."

James nodded as he processed the thought of Colin sharing some sort of custody with Dominic. "You know Colin isn't going to let this happen."

"He may not, but maybe Tess will." Dominic shrugged, as that was the best he could hope for.

"Tess is pretty levelheaded when it comes to the children. I would start with her," James suggested. "Now, as for that Markenna blood that's running through your veins."

Dominic laughed. "Don't worry. I'm not like them. I'm not him. I just didn't want him to think I was a pushover."

"As soon as you said that, three of my men aimed at your head, waiting for my signal."

"Your men don't mess around," Dominic noted.

"No, they don't. It was hard enough for our plan to change when you and Emma wanted to be there, but then hearing you speak, they were ready for the unexpected. They weren't going to be taken out by any Markenna. Do you know who the other three siblings are?"

"Not a clue." Dominic sat back, thinking. "There were no other kids around except Dimitri and I when we were growing up. All I can think is that he had kids elsewhere and kept them away from the compound."

"I'm going to have Adam start working on this, as I'm very curious." James took a drink of his coffee. "How's Meagan doing?"

Dominic shook his head. "She's the one beaten, but I feel her pain. I don't know how he could hit a woman."

"Meagan is tough." James eyed him. "She'll pull through this."

"Not only did he beat her, he raped her." Dominic stared blankly. "I called Tess." Dominic looked at James for an angry reaction, but there was none. "She lived through rape and losing a baby. I was hoping she could talk with Maggie and maybe Emma."

"Emma's scared of Tess. She won't talk to her at this point." James smiled, shaking his head.

"Maybe she won't be so intimidating given the circumstances," Dominic offered.

"Maybe." James pondered his next question for a moment before asking. "You killed your father. How do you feel?"

Dominic shrugged. "If I feel anything, it's peace."

*************

Dominic walked quietly into the private hospital room. Two days had passed, and Meagan still hadn't been coherent enough to talk. If Meagan was asleep, he didn't want to wake her up. He would just take the seat by her bed that had been his since they put her in this room. But she wasn't sleeping; she was simply lying in the bed staring blankly. When she noticed Dominic, she smiled slightly.

"Hi," he said softly, pulling the chair to her bedside. "I'd ask how you are, but I know you've been through some bad things with my father, and I'm sorry."

"It's not your fault." She shook her head, trying to hold back the tears. "You don't have to apologize for him."

"That's what people keep saying, but I find I keep doing it." He shrugged.

"Besides the obvious, what else is wrong with me?"

"Concussion, broken ribs." He took her hand in his. "Physically, those are the worst problems. Mentally … you know how this works."

Meagan shook her head as tears filled her eyes again. "Damn, it even hurts to cry.".

Dominic closed his eyes, bringing her hand to his lips, kissing her palm softly.

Meagan noted his hand bandaged up and smiled. "You beat him to death?"

Dominic shook his head. "Not all the way. Knife to the heart is what killed him."

"Good," Meagan stated, feeling no remorse.

"He won't hurt anyone else ever again."

"Aria." Meagan said their daughter's name, knowing she needed to talk to him about her.

Dominic simply nodded his head.

"I should have told you." Gently, she wiped a tear from her bruised cheek. "But the promotion and the move happened so fast. You and I had tried the long-distance thing for a few months, and it wasn't working for us … and I didn't want you to be with me because I was pregnant. I wanted you with me because you loved me."

"You took that choice from me. I wasn't with you for a year just because of the sex. I loved you, Maggie."

"I know, and I was wrong. I wish I could go back and do it differently, but I can't."

Dominic nodded his head again, understanding.

"Have you met her yet?"

"I'm a few steps ahead of you on this one, given your current state. Brian released Aria to Colin and Tess McGowan until you are released and feel better to take care of her."

"Why would he do that?" Meagan was a bit surprised.

"He's my stepbrother. They have two two-year-olds and twins on the way. They are very family oriented, I promise you. Aria couldn't be in more capable hands unless she was with you."

"My daughter is living with a mercenary and an assassin," she said more to herself than him.

"At least you know she'll be safe and protected." He laughed a little.

"Have you met her yet?" Meagan asked again.

Dominic shook his head. "I was waiting for you."

Meagan grinned, happy to have Dominic here.

"I've been wanting to ask you something." Dominic looked down for a moment, just praying she would say yes to his next question.

"What?" Meagan was curious.

"I want to take you with me when they release you from here." He raised his eyebrows. "I want you to let me take care of you and Aria until you're better."

Meagan smiled. "A six-year-old can be a lot of work."

"I've been taking care of two-year-olds. I think I can handle this."

"I missed you." Meagan felt tears fall down her cheeks. "God, I missed you so much. And I'm so sorry."

Dominic stood beside her bed, running a soft hand over her head. "Mags, let me do this. I want to do this."

"Okay." She agreed easily, as there was no fight left in her. Besides, she really didn't want to fight with Dominic; she missed him too much. Reaching out, she touched his cheek as their eyes connected and held. "I don't want Aria to see me until I look a little better. It will scare her."

"Aria is in Portland. I would like to take you to Savannah where Harper ... I guess she's my stepsister, can help you heal faster. She makes weird things with herbs to speed up healing. Apparently, the things she makes work great. Jonathan's wife is a doctor. She would take great care of you also."

Two days later, Emma and Meagan were discharged. James was flying Emma, Meagan, and Dominic to Savannah. From there, James would take Emma home, her home. The trip was quiet, as Emma slept for most of it, leaving James with his own thoughts. Things weren't good between them, which brought him back to his discussion with Harper. Everything she had said was true. Now he would have to deal with this thing with Emma and their relationship. What if Harper was wrong and their relationship didn't survive this?

After the jet landed, Jonathan and Gina greeted them. James noted how quiet Emma was with everyone. She shied away, even from him. Getting the keys for the SUV that Jonathan brought over to him, they said a quick hello and goodbye, and he drove Emma home. There was very little talk on the drive.

Once they arrived at her home, James helped Emma change and lay down comfortably. He went to go in the other room so she could sleep, but she stopped him.

"You need to go home," she told him, sitting up.

James didn't speak, just looked at her as a deep pain in his heart reared up.

"I need to deal with this, all of this somehow." She bit on her lower lip to keep it from quivering.

"We deal with it together," he reminded her.

With tears surfacing, she shook her head. "No, I need to deal with this myself. You can't help me right now."

James sat beside her as tears filled his eyes. "This wasn't just your loss. It was mine too."

"Do you realize what I've been through in the last month?"

James closed his eyes, as he knew he was supposed to fight for her. "We went through the last month together."

"You may be used to this sort of life, but I'm not. I'm not built for that lifestyle."

"You think that is how I live my life day in and day out?" James sighed. "That is not my life. That is my work life, and up until this month, when I met you, it has never been taken home with me. I do a job for a couple of days, I come home, and I have a life just like everyone else. I don't have security detail at my home. I do repairs on the house, I go fishing and hunting, take my grandmother out to dinner and to visit my cousins. I don't like my home shot to hell, keeping my men there for security because we have someone who was trying to kill *you*. That whole mess was to keep you safe, keep you alive."

"Colin said bullets fly around you," she muttered.

James shook his head, standing up. Now he was irritated. "And bullets fly around you, Emiliana Graca Markenna." His eyes were wide with fury. "You're right. I should go home."

"That's not what I—" she began, but he cut her off.

"Doesn't matter," he said. "All he wants is you to be his mistress, since his last one got shot in the head. Maybe he would be a better fit for you than me."

With that said, James walked out.

# Chapter 44

A week passed by, and Dominic decided to visit his sister. The fact that he had a sister was very surreal but welcoming. He knew she was by herself, that James had left, but he wasn't sure when. Matthew had found the SUV that James borrowed in his father's hangar when he went to fly back to Chicago a few days before. Currently, neither James nor Emma were answering their phones. Worried, Dominic was going to check on his sister.

The directions Jack gave him were easy to follow, and he did remember some of it from the one time he was there before. The drive would've been easier if it wasn't pouring down rain. Dominic arrived in front of her small cottage early afternoon. Not knowing what he was going to say, he got out of the car and walked up to the porch. He was rather surprised to find her wrapped up in a blanket, laying on the porch swing.

"Emma," he said softly, and she opened her eyes. Walking to her, he knelt beside her and ran a soft hand over her cheek. "You're really hot, Em."

"I'm freezing." Her voice was barely audible. "I want to go to the doctor, but I don't have my phone. I was trying to get to my car."

With ease, Dominic picked her up and carried her into the house. Laying her on the couch, he unbundled her to get a good look. Seeing her eyes swollen and red, he knew she'd been crying, but worse than that, she was running a high fever.

"When was the last time you ate?"

Emma shook her head, not knowing and wanting to go to sleep.

"Hey, hey, little sister, stay with me." Dominic knelt back down before her pulling out his cell. He ran a soft hand over her head as he waited for Gina to pick up the phone. "Gina."

"Dominic," Gina's voice sounded over the phone. "Your calling me means something's not right."

"I found her on the porch swing wrapped up in a blanket. She is burning up. I don't know the last time she ate. She looks bad, bleach white and a little grayish. Should I take her to the hospital?"

"See if she'll talk to me."

"Emma, talk to Gina." Dominic put the phone to her ear.

"Mom." Emma was wanting to sleep.

"Emma, honey, I'm going to have your brother bring you home to me. Okay?"

"Mom," Emma repeated. "I feel my body dying."

"Not today, sweetheart." Gina shook her head. "I'll make you better."

Dominic brought the phone back to himself. "Gina, do I take her to the hospital?"

"Yes," Gina told him. "There's not really any hospitals near you. Bring her up here to the one Colin and Tess were in. We'll meet you there at the ER. I want you to wrap her up and get a cold cloth for her forehead. Get an ice pack wrapped in a towel and put it on her tummy. I'm wondering if she's septic from infection. Get moving but drive carefully in this weather."

"Okay." Dominic ended the call.

An hour and a half later, Dominic had Emma in the emergency room. Gina was with Emma as Jonathan sat with him in a waiting room full of strangers. Every half hour or so, Dominic would get up and pace around to walk off his impatience.

"Should we call James?" Dominic asked Jonathan.

"Jack and Harper are already on their way up there, as he wasn't answering his phone."

\*\*\*\*\*\*\*\*\*\*\*\*\*\*

James heard a knock on the door. Glancing over, he sighed. It was Sunday, the first day there were no construction workers inside his home. The silence was welcoming, as he wanted to sit in his own misery and do nothing. But there was another knock. Maybe if he sat there long enough, whoever it was would go away and think he wasn't home. When he heard a key slipping into the lock, he knew it was either Harrison or Jack. He didn't want to talk. He didn't want them asking if he was okay because, clearly, he wasn't. Not moving from his preferred sofa that faced the bay, James didn't acknowledge his cousin when he walked in.

"I knew it," Jack said, taking off his coat, hanging it in the hall closet. Then he helped Harper with hers and hung it beside his.

"Let me," Harper said, touching Jack's chest gently.

Jack nodded, knowing James and Harper had a weird connection between them.

Harper shyly walked over to James and sat on the couch beside him. She didn't speak; she simply took his hand and held it with hers. They both looked out at the bay in silence, together. Time slipped by sluggishly. Harper knew James would speak when he was ready, and she would wait until then.

"She hurt me," James finally said in a very soft voice. "My natural reaction is to hurt back, so I did and left. Even after you told me to fight for her, I walked away."

"Do you love her?" Harper asked.

"More than anyone else in this world," he confided. "I miss her smile and her laugh."

"Emma is a beautiful woman."

James nodded. "I want her back."

"Go get her." Harper couldn't make this any simpler.

"Maybe she's better off without me."

"No one wants to be alone. It's our human nature to love and want to be loved. The rules apply to you too."

James took his attention from the view to Harper and gave her a soft grin. "I'm very happy that Jack has you. You're an amazing woman."

"I'm pretty lucky too. Emma and you belong together. Please don't let fear keep you from a lifetime of love and happiness."

James turned from Harper to ponder her words as he gazed upon the endless ocean.

Jack was in the kitchen looking for some food, but since his gran was with Harrison in Chicago, the place was kind of bare. Disappointed, he was distracted when his phone rang. What surprised him was the caller. "Gina?" Jack said as he answered.

"Jack." Gina's voice sounded sad but urgent. "Are you with James?"

"Yes," he answered. "He's in the other room talking to Harper."

"Emma's in the hospital," she said with a calm voice. "She has severe sepsis. She's in and out of consciousness. Delusional, as she thinks I'm her mom. They're hydrating her, but her blood pressure is very low."

"Antibiotics?" Jack asked.

"Yes, they're pumping her with everything, hoping this doesn't get worse." Gina was silent for a moment. "Let me talk to James. He needs to know."

"Okay, one sec." Jack walked into the great room with his cell in hand. He looked at his cousin. "Gina wants to talk to you."

"I don't want to talk to anyone." James shook his head.

"You're going to talk to Gina." Jack stood before him with the phone extended. "You need to talk to Gina, as she's at the hospital with Emma. Talk to her before she calls you from the damn morgue."

James's eyes shifted from Jack's to the phone in his hand. There was fear crawling through his body, rendering him unable to reach out.

"James?" Harper noticed that he was paralyzed. Taking the phone from Jack, she put it on speaker before James. "Mom, it's me, Harper. He's right here, so talk to him."

"James," Gina began. "Emma has severe sepsis. It's probably from when she was in the hospital. She is really, really sick. She's being put into ICU, but she's unconscious, and I think you need to come here."

"Is she going to die?" James asked as he stared straight ahead.

"I don't know," Gina told him honestly.

"We're on our way," James said, standing up. Taking a deep breath, he released it slowly. "Let's go."

Jack and Harper looked at each other with a nod, and the three of them headed out.

# Chapter 45

atthew flew from Portland to Savannah with a quick stop in Chicago. The only thing that made another flight like this bearable was Tess. They left Colin with the kids in Portland, as this trip should only be a few days at the most. Dominic and then Gina asked Tess to come and talk with Meagan about her experiences and triumphs, being a survivor of abuse.

Stopping in Chicago first, Matthew planned to stay for the night and fly out in the morning to Savannah. If things went smoothly, they would leave Savannah tomorrow night for Portland.

Matthew stood before the floor-to-ceiling windows looking out at the city. Anna had him review all the paperwork that was waiting on his approval about an hour earlier. Everything with his company was running smoothly even though he was only there on average three days a week. Most of his work could be done from any point in the world if he had an internet connection.

The driver dropped Tess off at his apartment when they arrived. Since Matthew never packed up any of her things from years before, she was going to go through her stuff, as he was putting his apartment on the market.

"So this is what you do all day," Tess stated as she walked in unannounced. "Anna wasn't at her desk, so I took a chance to find you in a compromising position with another woman."

Matthew laughed as she walked over to him.

"I really don't like packing. The movers could've done it." She touched his cheek. "But I wanted to hang out with you for a couple days."

"The first time I kissed you was in this office," he said, looking at her enchanting eyes.

"So that is what's on your mind." She took his hands in hers. "I knew you were in deep thought somewhere."

"We had a great time together in this city." He smiled, looking around. "And in this office."

Tess smiled this time as her arms slipped around his waist. Resting her head on his shoulder, she felt Matthew kiss her forehead as he held her tightly. "I miss being with you." Tess raised her head to look at Matthew.

"I don't know how to do this for the rest of my life. I can't stand being around you and Colin when you're together. I'm sure it will change eventually, but lately, it's been very difficult."

"I'm sorry." She closed her eyes momentarily.

"Don't apologize." Matthew tilted her chin up and kissed her lips. "I need to get this merger and move over and start finding that one woman who will have the rest of my children."

Tess grinned as she nodded. "It will happen when you least expect it. Until then, can we have dinner at that steak place we used to go to all the time?"

"Anna already made us reservations," he stated, releasing her as his phone was ringing.

Tess walked over to the window and looked out at the city as Matthew had done before. It was moments like this that she regretted her decision to go with Colin instead of Matthew. Matthew would have never cheated on her, never lied to her. Her life would be completely different. But then the thought of not sleeping beside Colin every night bothered her. She missed him when he went to Savannah or Chicago without her. On impulse, Tess pulled out her phone and called Colin.

"Hey, honey," Colin answered after just one ring. "Can you come home now? I miss you."

"I haven't even been gone six hours." She smiled.

"I know." He sighed deeply. "I like you close to me. I know that is strange coming from me, but Portland has been you and I for years. It's very lonely without you beside me."

"How are the kids?" she asked, staring down at the city.

"Fine. They're building a castle on the floor in the family room. I think one will be an architect and the other a financier. And little Aria is running the whole show. Her leadership abilities are quite impressive for a six-year-old."

"Connor will be the architect," she noted, as he was always building something out of anything he could get his hands on.

"Yes, that's my thought too," he replied.

Tess smiled. "I'm glad you have time with them like this. The kids need more of this with you."

"I know," he remarked. "Did you pack your stuff?"

"Yes." She glanced at Matthew, who was still on the phone. "I finished and came over to Matthew's office. I'm starving or your boys are starving. Either way, I want to go eat."

"I'm sure Matthew won't let you starve." Colin stood up to look at the city.

"I should go. It looks like he's finishing his call," Tess noted as she glanced at Matthew.

"I love you." Colin imagined holding her in his arms. "And I miss you. Tomorrow can't come fast enough."

"I love you too," she replied. "I'll call you before I go to sleep."

"Okay. Enjoy your dinner. Talk to you in a bit." Colin ended the call and continued to stare out the window. His wife being with his brother didn't ease his irritation that they were together in the first place. Knowing he had to trust Tess, he tried to ease his anxiety and focus on his children. The kids would take his mind off this.

Matthew finished his call as Tess walked over to him. "Ready?"

"Yes."

A few hours later, they walked into Matthew's apartment. After setting his keys on the table in the entryway, he followed Tess into his bedroom. As she took off her shoes, he slipped off his suit jacket and hung it up in the closet. Then he took off his shoes. Tess walked up to him and began to unbutton his shirt. Matthew cupped her face, bringing his lips to hers. Their kisses were soft, slow, and continuous.

"Let's shower," Matthew suggested.

Tess sighed with a small grin. "My stomach is so big, Matthew. I'm kind of uncertain about you seeing me naked."

"Seriously, Tess." Matthew smiled. "I saw you naked a few weeks ago.

This doesn't bother me at all. I find you beautiful pregnant. I wish I could have seen you pregnant with Savannah."

Tess gave him a small grin.

Matthew kissed her softly as he slowly took her clothes off. The kisses were passionate, as it always was in the past. His hands gently caressed her body, including her protruding stomach. With his lips on her neck, his hands ran down the sides of her body as he felt her hands on his hips. "Come on," he whispered, taking her hand.

Guiding her into the oversized shower, they kissed again as the water ran down their bodies. Soaping his hands, Matthew lathered her up, including her stomach that was perfectly round before her. Knowing she was very self-conscious being naked at six months pregnant, he tried to ease her anxiety.

"T," he began as he massaged her back. "You're a beautiful woman."

Turning around to face him, Tess ran her hands through his hair and over his shoulders. "I miss you," she said softly as their lips met up again.

"I miss you too." He kissed her again. "I know we shouldn't be doing this, but I don't give a damn. I feel I was cheated out of us, and I want us back so bad I'm willing to risk everything."

"You can't," she said softly. "You know you can't. You know what Colin is made of and what he'll do. I won't leave him."

"This is so frustrating." Matthew sighed, turning off the water. He handed a robe to Tess.

Tess wrapped herself up in the robe and towel dried her hair in front of the bathroom mirror. An unusual sense of déjà vu washed over her as she remembered doing this every day when she lived with Matthew three years before. As she was lost in her thoughts of the past, Matthew came up behind her, wrapping his arms around her waist.

"I'm sorry." He kissed her temple. "I don't want to upset you or make this any more difficult than it already is."

"Don't apologize to me. I'm doing this with you. I'm making my own life difficult." Turning in his arms, she kissed him softly.

"Is this what we're going to do then? Sneak around?" he asked with a smile.

"Yes," she answered. "It's this or nothing."

"Damn, you make me crazy," he said and touched her lips with his in a slow, deep kiss.

"I love you." Tess cupped his stubbly chin.

"I know." He nodded as he untied her robe. "I'll take you naked whenever I can get you."

They were in Savannah by noon the next day. The home was unusually quiet when they walked in. Matthew took Tess's coat and his and hung them in the foyer closet before they walked to the kitchen.

"I wonder where everyone is," Tess said as they glanced in the family room from the kitchen.

"I don't know." Matthew took her hand, pulling her easily in his arms, nipping at her lower lip.

"Someone could walk in any moment," Tess reminded him with a kiss.

"I know." Matthew smiled, giving her another kiss.

"Hello?" a woman's voice sounded behind them.

Tess and Matthew both sighed, slowly turning, knowing they'd been caught.

"Meagan?" Tess asked knowing exactly who this woman was.

"Yes. And you are Tess McGowan, or as I know you, Morgan Kellas." Meagan grinned, knowing these two were not the ones married.

Tess curved her lip, knowing this woman knew more about her than she wanted. "Meagan Trask, Dominic's first love and Brian's friend from the Justice Department. How are you doing? And where are Jonathan and Gina?"

"Let me answer the question you didn't ask." Meagan smiled slightly, as her lip was still healing. "I know you two aren't the one's married, but I won't say anything because your husband is a mean motherfucker, so don't get caught. Next question, I'm okay. And last, your parents are at the hospital with Dominic."

"Are they okay?" Matthew said.

"They're fine. It's Emma. She got an infection after she got home. James and Emma had this big fight. She was alone, Dominic found her, and now she's in the hospital."

Matthew gave Tess's hand a squeeze. "I'm going to call my father."

Tess nodded and watched him leave the room. When he was out of earshot, she put her full attention back to Meagan. "I know you know lots of things about my professional life, which doesn't bother me. But when it comes to my personal life, I strongly suggest that you turn your head if you see something that you don't approve of."

"Don't worry about that." Meagan laughed a little. "You can be a mean motherfucker too. With that aside, between James and your little trio, you've eliminated many bad people."

"We like to think so." Tess walked into the kitchen, poured herself a glass of water, and grabbed an orange from a bowl on the counter. Taking a seat at the table, she gestured for Meagan to sit. "How was your time with Marcos Markenna?"

Meagan simply shook her head slowly as she stared mindlessly at the orange Tess was peeling.

"As a woman, I know the feeling of sickness that rolls in your stomach when you close your eyes and he is what you see. That will change with time." Tess handed her a piece of the peeled orange. "The first time you let a man touch you will be difficult. Just make sure it's the right man, with the patience of a saint."

"Who was it for you?" Meagan asked noting how sweet the orange tasted.

"Colin." Tess grinned. "Made him wait months and months until I was ready. It wasn't easy. As time goes by, it gets easier. I still have moments where I don't like to be touched by anyone."

"I feel safer at night when Dominic just holds me close." Meagan's eyes moved to Tess's, realizing what she just said. "I'm sorry."

"Why are you sorry?" Tess popped an orange in her mouth.

"You were with him. I don't mean to say things like that."

Tess took a breath, remaining void of any emotion as she finished the piece of orange. "It's fine. I made him fall in love with me knowing there was no future for us. I loved my time with him, even though it was short. Just be good to him."

Meagan grinned with a nod.

"Your daughter is beautiful. Savannah and Aria could be sisters, as they look alike. Isobelle Taylor's bloodline is strong."

"As if you don't look like a model yourself." Meagan cocked her head.

"No, I don't." Tess sat back, running her hands over her stomach, as the babies were moving a little. "You know what caught me off guard with Matthew when we met?"

Meagan shook her head.

"The accent," Tess stated. "It was just like Dominic's. I should have caught it back then, but surprisingly I didn't. I fell in love with that man just like I did with Dominic."

"Are you just having an affair, or is it more?" Meagan was curious as to how Tess McGowan's mind worked.

Tess smiled as she eyed Meagan. "You don't want to let that one go, do you?"

"Just curious."

"I love Matthew with every inch of my being," Tess confided. "Colin is in my soul. No matter how much I want to be with Matthew, I will never leave Colin. I can't. Matthew knows this."

"I won't tell anyone. I promise." Meagan knew it was rare for Tess to share any private information.

"And you know how we feel about promises around here?" Tess held her eyes firmly.

"It's the only thing you've got."

"Remember, I protect my family, the people I love. Don't mess with that." Tess smiled as Matthew walked back in.

"Everything good?" Matthew asked Tess.

Tess nodded. "I've given my subtle threat with what she saw. But I think we're good. I might like her. At least I like her more than Emma."

"You're making progress," Matthew noted, holding his hand out to her. She took it with ease as he helped her up. "I'm going to go to the hospital. Would you like to come?"

Tess stared at him for a long moment. "Why? I'm still shocked that you got me this far. I only came to meet Meagan." Tess's eyes shifted to Meagan, and then she smiled maliciously.

Matthew grinned, running his hand over her shoulder. "Emma's been very sick. She almost died. Will you please make peace? For me, if no one else."

"You know I would do anything for you." Tess closed her eyes, taking a moment. "I'm not going to do this for you. I'm going to do this for James."

Matthew kissed her cheek and hugged her tightly. "Even better. Thank you, T."

An hour later, Matthew and Tess walked into Emma's hospital room. James had been quietly sitting by the bed, watching Emma sleep. Instantly, his eyes connected with Tess's, wondering what she was doing there. Standing, he walked over to Matthew and shook his hand.

"Dad told me what was going on," Matthew stated. "I'm so sorry. Is she doing better now?"

"Yes. She was up a little bit ago. The nurses got her to eat some and walk around for a few minutes. Huge improvement from a few days ago." James was talking with Matthew but watched Tess as she walked over to Emma's bedside.

Tess looked at Emma's pale face. The woman was thinner, if that was even possible. Perhaps being near death did that to a person. Tess wondered if this was what she looked like after she'd been shot in Chicago or if she had more color. Carefully, she ran her hand over Emma's forehead as she did with her children when they slept. Her skin was warm to the touch and very soft. It was then that she wondered if Colin touched her the same way. Abruptly turning on her heel, she shook her head at Matthew as tears filled her eyes. "I'm sorry," she barely whispered as she shook her head, walking toward the door.

"Tess, wait." James caught her just as she slipped through the door.

"I thought I could do this, but I can't do it yet. I'm sorry. I know I said I would, but I look at her and wonder if Colin's hand caressed her cheek the way he does with me. That's all I keep seeing and wondering."

James wiped the tears from her cheeks, then kissed her forehead. "It's okay. You take however long you need."

"I wanted to do this for you. I really did." Tess shook her head and walked away.

Tess headed down a corridor, turned a corner, and wiped her eyes dry. Walking toward her were Gina, Jonathan, and Dominic. Without speaking a word, she walked into Gina's motherly arms.

"Why don't you two go ahead?" Gina suggested to Jonathan and Dominic.

Jonathan nodded and patted Tess on the back gently before heading off with Dominic.

"Hey there, sweetheart." Gina's voice was kind and caring as she let Tess pull back a little. "Let's go outside."

Tess nodded as Gina kept a protective arm around her, and they walked outside.

"I find it easier to work a contract than to deal with my husband and this whole marriage thing." Tess sat down on a bench outside.

Gina laughed a little. "Marriage is not easy. There are usually more good times than bad."

Tess nodded in agreement. "But when it's bad, it's really bad."

"What's got you upset?" Gina asked.

"I came here with the intent to apologize to Emma for that one day at the hangar, but when I look at her, all I see is Colin touching her. It pisses me off. I wanted to do this for James, but I can't."

"Tess, you dealt with Colin when you found out what he had done. Dealing with something like that is not easy, but you did. And now you've found out who it was. This is an entirely different set of feelings to deal with." Gina took her hand, holding it tightly. "Don't be so hard on yourself. It will take time to work through these emotions. Your intent is good. Just let your emotions catch up."

"James has been too nice about this. I don't understand. I would think he'd be angry with me, but he's not."

"James loves you," Gina said with certainty.

"I don't know why anybody loves me." Tess stood up to ward off the tears. "I manipulated them to love me. I knew what I was doing, and I didn't care because I wanted their attention and their love. This is my karma. I chose Colin over the rest. His cheating on me is my karma. I deserved it."

Gina grinned as Tess rambled on.

Instinctively, Tess ran her hands over her tummy. The babies hadn't moved around in a while.

"You need to get out of your own head." Gina sighed. "Stop overthinking all of this. Take a breath and focus on what's important in your life."

"Colin and the children," Tess answered immediately.

"Did you see how there wasn't even a moment of hesitation with your answer?" Gina smiled as Tess nodded. "Tess, you don't forgive people for their sake; you do it for yours."

Tess knew Gina was right. When her phone vibrated and she noted the caller, she was a little perplexed with the timing. Answering it, she took a few steps away from Gina.

"Hey, baby, I got this weird feeling, so I had to call you. Are you okay?"

"No," she answered as a few stray tears slipped slowly from her eyes. "Don't worry, the babies are fine. It's me getting in my own head and overthinking."

"Ah, I see." Colin watched Savannah, Connor, and Aria lay on the sofa watching a cartoon. "Come home. Just walk away and come home."

"Colin, it hasn't even been twenty-four hours." Tess smiled.

"I don't care. You belong here with me. Please come home tonight."

"We are. I've talked with Meagan. I'm trying to talk with Emma, but I'm struggling with that one. I keep having these visuals of you with her."

"Well, Tess, I have the same visuals of you with my brother, Jack, and Dominic. And let's not forget James. You know my history with women. You need to remember that I married you because you're the one I love more than anyone else. I thought I almost lost you a few times, but thankfully I haven't. We need to move on from these insecurities that both of us have with each other because neither one of us is leaving the other. We have a great life ahead of us with our brood of children. It's going to be crazy and stressful, but I know I can do this with you by my side, and I hope you feel the same way."

Tess was quiet for a moment as his words processed in her mind. He was right. Colin being right wasn't uncommon.

"I bought a house for you—well, us." Colin knew Tess was in thought, so he just kept talking. "There's a couple things I want to change before we move in. But we should still be able to move in three to four weeks. I really think you're going to like the tub in the master bath. I can't wait to show you the place."

"I love you. I've been on a very reckless path for a month or two because I was hurt. And I just want to say I'm sorry."

"It's okay, honey. Just come home. I miss the hell out of you."

"Okay. Let me find Matthew, and we'll start saying goodbye to everyone. I'll be home tonight." Tess wiped away another stray tear.

"I love you, Tess."

"I love you too." Tess ended the call and turned around in time to see Matthew walking toward her.

"Are you okay?" Matthew asked Tess, wrapping her up in his arms.

"Yes." She grinned. "It was Colin. He just randomly called, as he had this gut feeling something wasn't right with me. Isn't that strange how he just knew?"

Matthew nodded, knowing there was nothing strange about it, as his brother was connected to Tess in an unexplainable way. In a way that he would never be. Running his hands over her hair, he cupped her cheeks and kissed her forehead. "We can never do again what we've been doing. I love you, always will. But you and Colin are connected in a way that few married couples are, and I won't be the one to mess that up."

Tess soaked in his words, knowing Gina heard everything. With a nod, she agreed, knowing in her heart he was right. Giving him a soft kiss, she agreed.

"Let's go home," Matthew stated.

"I have to go speak with Emma first." Tess gave Matthew's arm a slight squeeze before she walked back into the hospital.

Matthew sat by Gina for a few minutes before speaking. "I'm sorry you had to hear that. I don't want to put you in that type of position with my brother." Matthew glanced at her.

"It's not like we didn't know." Gina gave him that parental glance.

"Who's we?"

"Your father and I."

Matthew sighed. "It was tough to not say goodbye to her years ago. I never really moved on. I always had this small hope that I would get her back. Kind of like I did with Sarah."

"I'm so sorry for what she did and the way she did all of that back then. I was proud of her for wanting to volunteer like she did, but to not come back was not right. And now she doesn't even call. I fear something bad has happened and have no way to find out. As a mother, it's eating me up."

"James might have a lead on finding her. But he was trying to get through all this Markenna crap first." Matthew wanted to give her hope.

"That's encouraging, but he needs to take care of himself and Emma first. I don't want to impose on him right now." Gina patted Matthew's leg. "She'll be back one day. I'm sure of it."

As Tess walked down the corridor, she realized she was now in the right frame to speak with Emma, providing she was awake. Turning the corner, a calm washed over her as James smiled.

"Better?" James asked.

"Yes," she answered, kissing him on the cheek. Glancing at Emma, she noticed she was awake and watching her with an odd look of uneasiness. "Relax, Emma. I'm not here to threaten or hurt you. I won't even belittle you."

Emma's eyes followed James as he came to her bedside. He gave her a kiss on the forehead. "I'll be right outside the door. You'll be fine." James noted the grip Emma had on his hand for a moment before letting go.

Tess watched James walk away. Then she turned to Emma. Giving her an easy smile, Tess took a breath and walked over to the bedside. "I know you've been really sick. Therefore, I won't drag this out. I wanted to apologize to you for that day in the hangar. I know I scared the hell out of you, and for that, I'm sorry. You should see this through my eyes. Imagine being married to James, and he and I go spend a couple of days having a little fling. How do you think you would feel?"

Emma shook her head slowly as tears slipped from her eyes. "I'm so sorry."

"I know. Time will make this better for me, but I still have the emotions, heightened, because of the babies." Tess ran her hand over her stomach. "Shit. I'm sorry. I forgot for a moment."

"It's okay." Emma wiped the tears away. "One less thing we have to deal with."

"Colin wouldn't have been an ass. I was just being mean." Tess leaned against the bed. "Your hair is driving me crazy. It's this hot mess and not in a sexy way. May I?"

Emma chuckled a little as she sat up. "I don't have a brush."

"Please, I'm a woman with this mess of a head of hair. I have a daughter with some crazy hair too. Therefore, I carry a brush and hair ties."

Emma sat in the chair by the bed as Tess brushed and braided her hair. "I remember my mom doing this when I was a kid. She kept threatening to cut it off if I didn't take better care of it. I was quite the tomboy when I was young. I'd wake up, put it all up in a hat, and go play all day. My hair was pretty gross."

"I'm going to cut some of mine off before the twins are born. Hair maintenance is a lot of work, and I'm not going to have the time with four kids in tow." Tess casually talked as she braided her hair.

"You're lucky. You have everything most women dream of." Emma's voice was soft.

"Hmmm." Tess thought for a few minutes. "I guess I do. I should appreciate it a little more, I suppose. You are very lucky to have James love you. I know his career choice isn't normal, but aside from that, he will love you fiercely, protect you, and be your best friend. You will want for nothing except his continued love. Be good to him please. And there is no threat with that. Just a simple request from his best friend that's being replaced by you."

Emma stood up as Tess finished. Turning toward her, tears slipped from her eyes again. "I promise to love him even after my last dying breath."

Tess nodded, holding back the tears. Unexpectedly, she caught her arms going around Emma, giving her a hug. "I need to go home. You need to recover, as life is waiting. Besides, you're causing me to have emotions."

"Thank you." Emma gave Tess one more hug, then watched her walk out of the room.

Turning the corner outside the room, Tess found James leaning against the wall, knowing he had listened to their entire conversation. What surprised her the most were the tears in his eyes.

"Damnit, James, don't cry or you're going to make me cry, and I'm trying really hard to not cry."

James pulled her into a tight hug. "Thank you, Mama T. I don't know if you will ever know how much that meant to me."

"I do know," Tess said, pulling back. "I meant what I said. I wasn't just letting words spill from my mouth, telling her what she wanted to hear."

"I love you." James hugged her again. "Go home, fix your marriage, and stop fucking my other best friend."

Tess looked up at him with a smile. "I'm working on it."

James watched Tess walk away. Taking a deep breath, he released it with a new calm. Knowing he hadn't been able to talk with Emma since he arrived three days before, he walked back into the room. Emma was reorganizing the IV tubes connected to her arms. Once settled back in bed, she remained sitting up and smiled as James walked in.

"Hi," she said with a soft smile.

James grinned as he sat on the bed before her. Carefully, he ran his hand over her cheek as her eyes watched his. "You feel better?"

"Yes." Emma took his hand, holding it in hers. "I'm so sorry I told you to leave. As soon as you left, I wanted you to come back. But I couldn't even call you, as I didn't have a phone."

"I remember the evening when my father left. It was my understanding that he worked all over the world, so he was never home. But when he was, it was great. He was a good father until he left and never came back." James thought back to the transitionary point in his childhood with his father.

It was two weeks after his eighth birthday when his father left. James remembered the day vividly, as if it happened last week. Typically, his father wasn't around much, as he traveled constantly for work. The few times during the month when James would see him, it was great, as if he never left. But every time his father left for another trip, James would find his mother crying softly to herself. Not really knowing what to say, he would often get his Gran to come and talk with her, as they lived in the same home.

Tonight was different. His father had come home a few hours before but seemed preoccupied. Stephen had Carina take James over to his cousin's house for a couple of hours, as he needed to speak with his mother. Everyone seemed to know something was happening, but no one would speak to him about it. Not wanting to hang out with Jack and Harrison, James sat on their couch until Gran took him home.

Standing just inside his doorway to his room, James peeked around the corner, down the long hallway, where he could see his father packing and his mother sitting on the edge of the bed crying.

"Sofia." Stephen knelt before her, placing her hands in his. "Please don't cry. You know I've stretched this out for as long as I could. I will not risk your life and our son's. I love you both too much to be that selfish."

"I know." She nodded her head. "It doesn't make it any easier. Imagining a life with never seeing you again is heartbreaking. I don't even know how to explain this to James."

"I will speak with him." Stephen kissed her softly before standing.

James saw his father stand up, so he backed away from the door and hopped on his bed, knowing his father was walking toward his room.

"James." His father walked in quietly, making his way to the bed. Sitting down beside his son, he turned on the lamp beside the bed.

"Where are you going, Father?" James asked.

"It's not safe for you and your mom if I stay." Stephen's voice was soft.

"I don't want you to think that I don't love you or your mother, because I love both of you more than anyone else in this world. Which is why I must leave, so both of you are safe. I know this is hard to understand right now, but as you get older, hopefully you will understand."

Tears filled James's eyes.

"I'm going to give you a key." Stephen took a key that was on a silver chain and handed it to James. "Never lose this. Put it in a safe place. When you are older, you will receive a letter telling you what the key is for. Until then, keep it safe and know that I will always keep an eye on you even though you won't be able to see me. Always know your surroundings. Never trust strangers. Be good for your mom and Carina and know that I love you very much, my son."

Stephen hugged James tightly for a long time before letting him go. He knew he would probably never get the opportunity to hug him again and wanted to embed the memory deep in his mind.

"I love you, Dad," James said through a few tears as he tried to put on a brave face.

Stephen kissed him on his head before leaving.

James managed a half smile toward Emma as he finished sharing his memory.

"Did you ever get a letter explaining the key?" Emma asked.

"Yes," James answered with a short nod. "I never opened it. I wasn't there yet in my mind. I have it in the safe with the key at Carina's."

Emma looked at his hand holding hers. "Now I understand. You don't let yourself get close because people leave, or at least that's how you feel." Pulling him closer, James rested his head on her lap as her hands held him.

"After my father left, Brian came around more to check on my mom and me. My father and Brian went to college together, and I know they worked together in some capacity, but I never asked for more information. You would think I would want to know more, but I find I don't."

"Why?"

"I have this image of my father, and I don't want it changed. I think if I dive into his life, I will find out things that will change my idea of the type of man he was." James gazed into her green eyes. "I love you, Em."

"I will never leave you, and I will never ask you to leave, ever again. I love you, James."

# Chapter 46

Two days later, Brain walked into Emma's hospital room. Seeing James lying beside her didn't surprise him. They were awake and simply chatting.

"Brian." James glanced oddly at him as he stood. "What brings you here? This is a bit out of your norm."

Brian nodded, taking a deep breath before he spoke. "Do you remember our conversation when I contracted with you to keep Emma and Dominic safe?"

"Yes." James knew this was a conversation about Emma's mother.

"Well, with Marcos Markenna dead, I found no reason to keep Mia in protective custody anymore." Brian gave a slight grin.

"Are you talking about my mom?" Emma sat up straight.

"Yes," Brian answered and gave her a nod.

"She's alive?"

Brian nodded. "Yes, and before James went on his search, I wanted to come and tell you about her, for a lack of a better word, condition."

"I saw him shoot her in the head," Emma stated.

Brian agreed. "You did. But what you didn't see were the paramedics finding her still breathing. Mia suffered brain damage from the gunshot wound to her head. Sometimes she's coherent enough to know who people are. Other times, she will just stare, as if lost in a sea of strangers."

Emma nodded, understanding as the scene played over in her mind.

"I was going to bring her to see you today, but she wasn't in her right mind to take her away from her home. Her surroundings are key to keeping her anxiety at bay. She gets very worked up if she isn't in familiar surroundings with the people she knows."

"Does she remember me?" Emma's eyes were full.

"Sometimes, yes. I won't lie to you, Emma. She's not the same mother you knew. She had multiple surgeries after that night to restore her to who she is today. I've personally made sure she had the best care possible. I remain her legal guardian, and I don't plan on relinquishing that ever. Please don't think I'm doing this to be an ass or to have control. I do it to maintain Mia's lifestyle the way it is."

"Is she in a hospital or institution?" Emma asked.

"No. She's in a private home with twenty-four-hour care. There's only one other resident like her. The owner of the home is my cousin Kathryn, and she's also a psychologist. I wouldn't let Mia be in anything less than a home like she's in."

"Why are you just now telling me?" Emma held on to James's hand.

Brian's eyes shifted from Emma to James and then back. "I wouldn't be telling you at all, but James found out about Mia and said I could either tell you or he would find her himself. Mia will not add any value of significance to your life except heartbreak and, perhaps, despair. Knowing your life has already been hellish, I wasn't wanting to contribute to that."

"You knew?" Emma asked James.

With a nod, his eyes shifted from Brian to Emma. "The same day I found out Marcos was your father, I learned of Mia."

"I will send James the information for where Mia is living." Brian stared out the window for a moment before directing his attention back to Emma. "You can visit her, but don't be disappointed if she doesn't recognize you. Don't think about taking her from her home either. You can't give her better care than she is already receiving."

"Are you saying I can't even have her home for Thanksgiving or Christmas?" Emma asked.

"No, I'm sorry." Brian took a breath, needing to wrap this up. "Emma, I know this isn't what you wanted to hear, and don't think James can fix this, because he can't. And if you have him forcibly take her, I will find her and prosecute both of you. James is only the best in his profession because of me."

James grinned with a slight laugh.

"Is that true?" Emma turned to James.

"My skills are mine, but the jobs I do come from Brian for the most part. Every now and then, I will contract outside of his work. Brian deals will all the legal aspects if I get into tangles with the law stateside and abroad. He has very long reaches globally. Let's just say it's better to keep Brian on your good side than the alternative."

"Why do you care about my mother? Why have you been the one to take care of her like family?" Emma needed to know his motive.

Brian didn't answer her right away. This was an arena he really didn't want to jump into, but he knew Emma was a persistent woman. Knowing her history in detail, Brian needed to decide at this moment to tell the truth or lie. "Emma, I've been dealing with Markenna issues most of my career. Mia was a good person who got caught up in a bad situation with a bad family. You've never been in a position to help her, and someone had to or she would have been put in the system. A slight moment of compassion on my part. It doesn't happen often."

James caught Brian's eyes, knowing he was lying.

Brian shrugged. "With Marcos dead, he can't hurt her anymore."

"I don't know if I should be mad at you or thank you," Emma said.

"Mia got into the drug scene and rode a slippery slope for a couple of years until Marcos found her working in a bar in Louisiana. He married her. Few years later, she became pregnant with you, and she wanted out but she didn't tell Marcos. She just left. Seth Anderson met Mia when she was about six months along, and he helped her at first because, financially, she was struggling, and he was falling in love with her. Just before you were born, she annulled her marriage to Marcos and married Seth, moved to a small town an hour out of the city, and was happy until Marcos showed up. You know the story from there."

"I know Mama's story, not yours." Emma raised a brow.

"And you will never know my story. The Markennas are filtered throughout the world. My professional life is separate from my personal life. The two will never mix. I've known James since he was a kid, and even he doesn't know my story." Brian took a deep breath, glancing at James. "I've done my best to keep you safe over the years, and that is why you had Meagan as your contact. She has been my most trusted friend and confidante for years."

Emma closed her eyes as she absorbed the information.

"I will continue to take care of Mia until she dies. Emma, this information must stay in this room, between the three of us. I'm sorry, but it has to remain that way."

Emma gave a slight nod.

James wrapped his arms around Emma's shoulders, holding her close to his chest as he looked at Brian. "I'll explain to her the importance of why it has to be like this. I understand. Emma's been through hell the last couple of months, so give her some time."

"I know she has, and the only reason I'm not worried about her is because …" Brian grinned. "Is because she's with you. I know you will take exceptional care of her, and she will have a very happy life from here on out. As shocked as I was to hear about you being with her, it was also a relief."

James nodded with a slight grin.

Emma shrugged James's arms off her and walked over to Brian. "You promise me that my mother is receiving the best care with the kindest people and there is no abuse of any sort?"

"I promise you." Brian gave her a nod.

"Is he good for his promises?" Emma looked back at James.

"Yes, he is." James gave Brian a nod.

Brian headed out of the room, and James walked with him.

"What stopped you from telling her the truth?" James asked as they walked down the corridor.

Brian shook his head and shrugged. "Maybe if she wasn't with you, I would've told her. She doesn't need me in any capacity as long as she has you, Carina, and your cousins. Hell, lest we not forget the McGowan family. Emma will never be alone again. I can live with that."

"You could be a father figure for me but not your own blood?" James didn't understand the reasoning behind the secret.

"Sorry you have to bear this secret." Brian gave a half grin, not sorry at all.

"Well, it's not like I don't have many secrets already." James looked down at the ground as his hand ran over his stubbled chin. "Brian, if I lose her because I keep your secret …"

"You won't," Brian said with full confidence. "You are the best at what you do. You and Matthew are the only ones that know. My wife doesn't even know. You two will be fine. Are you going to finish the list?"

James looked up at him with a grin and nodded. "Once I finish the list, the only jobs I want are the ones involving Markenna descendants. I want that family wiped from this earth."

"Not all of them please. There's a few I would prefer continued to breath. You really need to speak with Meagan about the Markennas. She knows everything."

"I was trying to leave her alone, given what Marcos did to her. She needs to heal."

"Meagan's tough. She'll bounce back quickly."

"You know her and Dominic are—"

Brian cut him off. "I know they're going to get back together. Maggie doesn't know everything about him though. Keep an eye on him."

"You told me, not too long ago, that he was clean and to leave him alone. Something change?"

"He has that place down in Peru. Just makes me wonder. Dominic is a great manipulator. I don't think he would ever hurt the McGowans, but there's something he's not sharing. Call it a gut feeling."

James's mind began to spin.

"Anyway, I need to go. Take care of Emma for me. Keep your inner loop with the McGowans to keep them safe. There's a lot of people who would like that family dead."

"I've already got five of my men working security at the McGowans'. It's a hefty payroll," James stated.

"And I reimburse you quite nicely. Does everyone think you still only work with twelve men?"

James laughed. "Yes. Even Tess doesn't know it's eighteen."

"Matthew knows, right?"

"Of course. I really wish he would go active again. He won't do it with a kid now."

Brian nodded, understanding Matthew's position. "Ask him anyway. Think Tess will work again after having these babies?"

"Yes," James answered without doubt. "She's restless."

Brian smiled with a nod. "Good. Take care. Your father would be proud."

James pursed his lips together as he watched Brian walk away.

## Chapter 47

J ames stood barefoot on the sandy beach. The sun kept popping through the intermittent clouds, so he was glad he wore his sunglasses. When he thought back about how his life changed drastically in the past three months since the ordeal with Tess began, he realized he wouldn't have altered any of it. Knowing his actions shaped the events in all their lives, how could he want to do it differently? Getting to pop Colin McGowan in the face was probably the most satisfying event that took place. Tess was happy with that man and his faults. Although Tess wasn't without a few faults of her own. Which made him realize those two were perfect together, just like Jack and Harper. Sweet, sweet Harper. Just her name brought a smile to his lips. She was a special woman, and Jack knew that. Hell, everyone knew that.

What surprised him the most was the relationship between Dominic and Meagan. Once she was released from the hospital, they were rarely apart from each other. Meagan seemed to be doing well after being held captive by Marcos Markenna for a few weeks. She was a strong woman, and from the rumors, she and Tess were becoming good friends.

"What's that grin for?" Emma walked up to him with a seashell in her hand.

"Just thinking about Dominic and Meagan," he answered as she slipped her hand around his waist and his circled her shoulders, bringing her in for a hug. Softly, he kissed her head.

Emma looked up at him with a smile of her own. After being in the hospital for seven days, she had been released with a nearly perfect bill of health. The time they spent together in the hospital was needed for their relationship to grow. Emma learned of his childhood in graphic detail. It was through their conversations that she learned how Brian and James became the kind of friends they were. And learning her mother was still alive was of the utmost surprise. Although she had memory issues, Emma was thankful to just have her. Since leaving the hospital, she had visited her twice and planned trips once a month to see her. Mia was in an excellent home with the best care. She knew she couldn't match that.

"I wish we didn't have to go yet," she told him, looking at the waves rolling in.

"I know." James stood behind her with his arms wrapped around her shoulders.

Emma brought her left hand up, resting it on his arm.

James looked at the wedding ring on her finger and realized how thoroughly happy he was. Truly happy.

"This was a perfect honeymoon." Emma smiled as she turned to him again.

"Yes, it was, Mrs. Cordello." James kissed her softly.

"This is our honeymoon shell." Emma held up the white shell in her hand.

"Is this going to be one of those collection things you're going to start?"

"Yep," she stated.

"Are you feeling okay?" he asked, as she was perkier than earlier in the week.

"I am." Emma looked out at the horizon. "Better than last week and better than the week before and so on. Don't worry so much. My kidneys were functioning at 95 percent when we left. The doctor was pleased with my progress and optimistic about a full recovery, and so am I."

"I know." He slipped his hands behind her neck and kissed her full lips.

"Besides, I want the okay from the doctor to have a baby," Emma told him as he rested his forehead on hers. "I want to give you a family, our family."

James leaned back to look her in the eyes. "I know you do, and just so we're clear on this, whether we have kids or not, I'm perfectly happy with it just being us."

Emma grinned, as he made her happier than she'd ever been in her life. "I love you."

"I love you too." James kissed her again, then held her tightly in his arms.

# Epilogue

J ames walked into Matthew's office since the door was open, and Anna simply smiled at him. Knowing they hadn't spoken in a few weeks, he just wanted to stop by and check in, like they'd done with each other for years. To his unwanted surprise, Colin was standing before the large windows, looking out at the lake with his hands in his pockets. James could tell something was different with him.

"James," Matthew said, standing from his desk to shake his hand.

"Matt, how the hell have you been?" James asked, noting Colin turned around.

"Good. Just working on the merge and move. Want a drink?" Matthew offered, walking over to the small bar.

"Water's good." James took a bottle from Matthew's offered hand. "What are you two up to?"

Matthew glanced at his brother with raised brows.

"I'm here to speak with you," Colin fessed up. "I was just talking with Matthew first. Then I was going to call you."

"Should I be concerned? Tell me this has nothing to do with Emma." James waited for his response.

"I'm going to step out for a few minutes," Matthew stated. "Don't kill each other. I would prefer to keep blood out of my office."

Colin gave him a sideways glance, as that was not his intention. Once Matthew left the room, Colin sighed.

"Get on with it," James stated.

Colin laughed a little, knowing James expected the worst. "I wanted to apologize to you for everything that happened with Emma. I was ..." Colin took a breath. "I was out of line. She was not just someone to conquer, and

I don't want you to think that. Emma is an exceptional woman, and I took advantage of an opportunity, and I'm … sorry."

James grinned. "This is a rare, humbling moment for you."

"If you only knew." Colin chuckled.

"Did Tess put you up to this?"

"No." Colin shook his head. "Tess didn't know that I wanted to talk with you. Matt and I are working some numbers for this move. Apologizing to you was something that I needed to do."

"Apology accepted." James reached out, shaking his hand. "How's Tess doing?"

"My wife is uncomfortable already. There's no possible way she can carry to term. Jo was talking about a C-section, but Tess does not want that. She rather be induced early to deliver naturally." Colin leaned against Matthew's desk. "May I ask how Emma is?"

James raised his brows as he contemplated answering. "She's fine. Her kidney function just reached normal levels. She's insistent about having a family."

"You understand why, don't you?"

"I'm thinking it's because she didn't have one," James answered, shrugging his shoulders.

"Yes." Colin moved to the couch. "It's almost like she's not complete until she has a family."

"I told her I'm happy with just her and I. I don't need kids to complete my life. She completes it." James sat opposite Colin.

With a grin, Colin explained, "With Emma having a very tough life, to her, having a husband and children is what will complete her. You've already given her something she never thought she would have."

"All I do is love her." James shrugged.

"And that is what she was longing for. Before you, when I saw her, I knew she wanted more in her life, and …" Colin's voice trailed off, as he didn't want to finish this conversation.

"Say it." James stared at him.

"No."

"Say it or there will be blood spilled in Matthew's office. Then he will kill both of us and take your wife." James gave a slight grin.

"I knew I could give Emma a baby at least. She couldn't have me, but she could have a child. And I knew I would support her and a baby, just as I apparently did with Taryn. Tess would never know, and that was arrogant of me. My father came to me the night before I flew my family home. He reminded me of that night when Tess had been shot in Chicago and was in surgery. Remember, it was touch and go for a few hours?"

James nodded, remembering that night very well.

It was late. James didn't even know how late it was. Colin called him from the hospital. Knowing it had been a hit on her life, Tess needed protection, and he could provide it. They sat together in the surgery waiting room for hours. James slowly watched Colin fall apart minute by minute. Not knowing Colin well enough to help him, James called his father, Jonathan McGowan. It would have been easier to call Matthew, but James knew they hadn't spoken in years.

"How long is this going to take?" Colin stood, pacing.

"Well, it just means she hasn't coded on the table. This is a good sign in a way," James said trying to be optimistic.

Colin took a seat again before James. With red, bloodshot eyes, he leaned forward with his elbows on his knees. "I can't live without her."

James glanced oddly at Colin, for he wasn't speaking like the egotistical ass that he was used to.

"Tess and I have been through a lot with each other, but I can't imagine my life without her. Promise me that you will put a bullet in my head if she dies?" Colin had tears running down his cheeks.

"Hey, man, she'll pull through this. Tess is a tough girl. Stop talking like this. You're just … everything is emotional right now. Tess will be fine. You'll be fine. None of us are living without her. Besides, I haven't gotten to work with her yet. I've been waiting to do that for a long time."

"This is probably from the work we've done. We should've stopped those jobs a long time ago. I got her into that business, and now it's going to kill her. The feeling of the bullet pushing her in my arms will never go away. I knew she was suffering because she couldn't breathe with the blood filling her lung." Colin broke down again. "I can't live with those being my last images. Please?"

James didn't know what to say. This was not the Colin McGowan that he knew. This man before him was broken and needed someone other than himself to help him. Never would he end his life as he asked. Never. "She'll be fine. I'm not killing you."

Colin shook his head and leaned back, closing his eyes.

Watching his breathing, James knew when he fell asleep. That was when James stood, stretching. Four or five hours had passed by already, and James was thankful when Jonathan McGowan finally walked into the waiting room.

Seeing his son asleep, Jonathan walked over to James and shook his hand. "Thank you for calling me. Have you heard anything?"

"Not yet. They haven't come out and told us she died, so I think that's a good sign. Your son's not doing well. He'd rather have a bullet in the head than live without her," James said as they turned to glance at Colin sleeping.

Jonathan patted James on the shoulder with a nod. "When Colin first met her, I didn't want them together. It took years of therapy to get her to trust and work through the damage her stepfather caused. Everyone knew my son was a player with the women. I didn't want Tess to be played by him."

"I think they are a good balance for each other."

"They are." Jonathan grinned. "I've seen changes in both that are for the good. They make each other very happy."

Colin sighed deeply as he woke. Tears slipped from the corner of his eyes as he thought of Tess. He didn't notice his father until he sat up. Seeing him sitting beside James made his despair more apparent as more tears surfaced. "Dad."

"I'm going to check in with my men that I brought." James politely excused himself, hoping Jonathan could help his son.

"Dad, I can't do this. I don't want any of it without her. I need her. She's part of my soul." Colin leaned forward again with his elbows on his knees as he cried.

Jonathan sat by his son, putting a reassuring hand on his back. "You can do this whether she lives or not. She's made it this far, and that's a good sign. The two of you have come a long way and have an even longer future together."

James turned around at the entrance of the waiting room to observe the comfort that Jonathan gave his son. The interaction made James think of his own father. Did he ever think about him or wonder how his son was doing? Did he watch him and James didn't realize it? There were many unanswered questions he had about his own father, and watching the bond between Jonathan and Colin made him wish his father was still around.

James's memory made him stand, needing to walk. "I remember walking out of the waiting room that night, when you were having a breakdown and your father showed up. Jonathan was ... he was the kind of father I wish I had. I had been thinking how lucky you were to have him. I was envious of you but only for a moment. You were this spoiled, rich asshole. The only reason I ever tolerated you was because of Jack and then Tess. She is an amazing woman. I can't believe all the bullshit you've put her through, and she stays with you. Blows my mind."

Colin smiled. "Yes, but you also know the shit she's put me through. The men she's fucked before and after we were married."

"For the record, we never had sex after you two were married. Never. I would visit, but we never slept together."

"Do you know who it was?" Colin asked.

James stared, knowing he would never tell. "I won't lie to you, but I won't tell you either. Don't ask."

"It's my brother or Dominic. And I can't get pissed off at her because of what I did with Emma. I have to let it go."

"Tess has to let go of what you did to her too. I know it has not been easy for her. I think the two of you need to call it a draw and move on. You've got way too many kids to have problems like this between you."

"I know. We're doing much better since we left Georgia. Something about that place brings out the worst in us. Things are almost back to normal. We moved into the new place a week ago. Things are good." Colin poured himself another drink.

"I love her," James said out of the blue, surprised he said it aloud.

"I know you do," Colin acknowledged without surprise. "I just hope you love Emma more than my wife."

James glanced at him and grinned. "It's a different love."

Colin nodded. "You need to know that I don't love Emma. I care what happens to her and that she's happy, but I don't love her."

"I know." James shook his head with a deep breath. "You seem to forget what I do for a living."

"I do. I've never seen that side of you. I don't associate you with that sort of work. Even the night when Taryn's little army invaded, I was knocked out before you came in."

James nodded slowly. "I shot her hand, and the gun fired, shooting Jack in the shoulder, lodging the bullet in Tess's skull. Not exactly my best work. I should have shot her in the head."

"Why didn't you?" Colin was curious.

"I don't know." James shook his head. "I think personal involvement put me off my game. I was hoping she would ... just fucking stop so she didn't have to die. I didn't want to kill Tess's twin. And look, I didn't have to."

Colin shook his head slowly, remembering when the bullet hit her head in front of him.

"I see you still struggle with that one," James noted with the lack of response from Colin. "I know you loved her even though you won't admit it."

"I did." Colin nodded. "I cared about her. We had fun, but it's not like it is with Tess. You know how there's that one person that is meant for you and only you. That is Tess for me, and nothing will change that. Now I've told you entirely too much."

James grinned. "As if I didn't already know. Did you sleep with Emma because Tess was with Dominic? How did you make the connection?"

"No. I don't do that payback bullshit. It was just a moment with alcohol and a beautiful woman. Emma told me Marcos Markenna was her biological father that night. I didn't even think of the relation she had to Dominic. I never told her that Jack and I killed Dimitri or any of the other involvement with the Markenna family." Colin stood, as did James.

"She still doesn't know. I think it's irrelevant at this point."

Matthew walked back in the room. Looking at each one for a sign of peace, he was content that neither was bleeding. "Everything good?"

James nodded, as did Colin.

"I need to go." James shook Colin's hand and walked over to Matthew. "Talked to Brian. He wants you back."

"Are you sure it's Brian and not you?" Matthew laughed, shaking his head, knowing James wanted to work with him again. "Not going to happen at this point in my life. And certainly not with Savannah."

"That's what I told him." James grinned.

"Thanks for coming by." Matthew shook his hand. "Will you and Emma be around next week? Thinking we could have dinner."

"Yes, we'll be around. I'll call you. I'm going to start looking for Sarah. Just wanted you to be aware."

Matthew had no words. He just nodded with a shrug of his shoulder.

"I want no issues between you and me when I start to do this. So, if there's a problem, speak your mind with me."

Another nod.

James looked back at Colin just before walking out the door. "Thank you."

Colin gave a half grin with a slight tilt of his head.

# Book III

*Boundaries Within; The Series*

Preview

# *Unlimited Boundaries*

Seven Weeks Ago

A s her heart pounded in fear, she closed her eyes, trying to go to that peaceful place deep in her mind. Slowly, the screams eased with every shot that was fired. Her body jolted every time a shot rang out, and the sound got closer and closer. *Close your mind*, she told herself. *Remember the perfect, peaceful times.* Then another shot sounded. A smile came to her lips as she remembered her son giggling as he played on the beach with his father. And another shot rang out. Unexpectedly, Matthew came to mind. Easily, she remembered the night he asked her to move in with him. He put his apartment key on a diamond bracelet and gave it to her at dinner one evening. They'd only been dating for few months in Chicago, but both knew they were in love with each other. What she would give to go back in time and choose to go home when she was given the choice. Nope, this was the life she chose, to be with the other man she fell in love with in a ravaged country. Was this how her life was supposed to end?

Feeling the barrel of a gun on her forehead, she opened her eyes as the man spoke to her. Speaking fluent Portuguese, he told her this mass killing was because of her, and her son would be persecuted because of her as well. As soon as they pried her son from her arms, she died inside, knowing his future was not to be. *Fight and survive*, she thought, *or give up and die.* That was her choice. Without her son, she wanted to die, but a little voice in her head told her no, she had to survive.

The man laughed and pulled the trigger. Sarah flinched, but nothing

297

happened. He began cursing, as he was out of bullets. As he reloaded, she knew this was her opportunity to survive. Without any hesitation, she turned and ran, as humanly possible, into the jungle. Knowing the others in the lineup ran when she did, Sarah prayed some would make it as the sound of the automatic weapons ripped through the jungle.

✳✳✳✳✳✳✳✳✳✳✳✳✳✳

Present Day

Matthew paced his office as he reviewed the moving schedule with his assistant, Anna. Everything needed to be timed out perfectly to avoid any inconveniences to his clients. The new office would be set up and ready to go in six weeks. All the employees that were transferring to Portland—surprisingly, nearly 65 percent of the staff wanted to relocate and continue working for him—had to be ready in the six-week time frame. There was to be no lag time in availability for his clients. Thus far, everything and everyone was on schedule.

"Anna." Matthew stopped pacing to look at her. "Thank you for doing this move with me."

"Well, you gave me quite an incentive." Anna grinned, raising her brows.

"Worth every dime," he told her. "You make my life in the office simple. I love coming to work every day."

"You love your company, as you should. But the difference with you, compared to others, is that you value your hardworking employees. And it shows with the way you treat them, and that makes all the difference. Besides, you pay them what they're worth. You are the most respected employer in the district. I'm very proud to be your assistant and work for your company." Anna pursed her lips as she stood. "Everything is on track. Your Realtor called, and there's an offer for your apartment. I told her it needed to be a six-week escrow."

"Perfect."

"Harrison called earlier." Anna grinned, knowing Matthew and Harrison got along very well. "He will be here at two, as he wants you to meet the attorney that will be going to Portland to take care of your division once the merge with MGI is complete."

Matthew glanced at her oddly. "Harrison doesn't have an office in Portland. What's he up to?"

"Well, rumor in the cubicles is that he is starting a division in Portland. You've inspired him." Anna grinned, heading back to her desk.

A few hours passed quickly as Matthew dove into his work. When he left tonight for a four-day weekend, he wanted nothing pending on his desk.

"Matthew." Anna was at his door. "Harrison is here with his associate. Can I send them in?"

"Sure." He nodded, thankful for the interruption. Standing up, he walked over to Harrison as he and a beautiful woman walked in. He was a little lost for words at first. She was a few inches shorter than him with long, wavy brown hair and striking green eyes. There was this radiance of confidence and respectability that emanated from her. Instinctively looking at her hand, he noticed she didn't wear a wedding ring.

"Matthew." Harrison gave him a knowing grin, noting how taken his friend was with Ella. "Thanks for taking the time."

"Like you have to ask." Matthew shook his hand, then went to the woman and put his hand out for hers. "Hello. I'm Matthew."

"Hello, Mr. Taylor. I'm Ella MacCabe." Ella shook his hand with a grin. Oddly, she felt her cheeks flush a bit.

"Please call me Matthew. Full Irish decent?" Matthew asked.

"About 75 percent." Her smile wouldn't tame. "My father is 100 percent, and my mother is only 50 percent. The other half is actually Finnish. And I can tell that you are at least half Portuguese. Am I correct?"

"Yes." He nodded, impressed. "How can you tell?"

"Your eyes and that little accent you have along with your skin tone. You know, I'm probably overstepping my boundaries right now. I apologize." Ella looked down for a moment, pulling herself together. Why did this man make her feel giddy, like a schoolgirl?

"Please don't apologize." Matthew gestured for them to take a seat on the sofa. "I find you very refreshing compared to what I've been dealing with. It takes quite a bit more to overstep any boundaries with me."

Harrison sat quietly, watching the exchange between Matthew and his colleague, which pleased him very much. He had a feeling these two would hit it off, and that's exactly what he wanted for Matthew ... and Ella.

"So, what brings you to my office?" Matthew asked them.

Harrison spoke first. "I wanted you to meet Ms. MacCabe, as she is your Portland attorney with my firm. She's been working on all your business dealings for about four years. Therefore, she knows the ins and outs of your company and the merger with McGowan Industries. Admittedly, she is the one doing all the work."

"This means you will be in Portland … physically?" Matthew asked her, not giving a damn about the merger.

"Yes," she answered. "I'm originally from there. I only moved here to work for Mr. Keene, as he has a stellar reputation. Although I've come to love living here in Chicago, I'm excited to move home and run this division."

Matthew gave Harrison a look. It was the look that told him he was highly aware of what Harrison's motive was.

"I heard a rumor about you opening another division. Where's the office located?" Matthew asked Harrison.

"I've acquired a floor in the building you're in."

"A whole floor?" Matthew cocked his head sideways.

"You're a big client, Mr. Taylor." Harrison grinned. "Besides, if MGI can have two offices, so can I."

"Indeed, you can." Matthew nodded in agreement.

Harrison looked at his phone. "Well, I do apologize, as I must be going. I have another client waiting."

Ella went to stand and leave with him, but he put his hand up.

"Please stay," Harrison told her. "Get to know each other because Matthew can be very demanding at times. I will see you back at the office later."

Matthew stood, extending his hand to Harrison.

"Matthew." Harrison smiled. "A pleasure as always. Call me later."

"Oh, I will." He nodded, opening the door for Harrison. After walking back over to Ella, they both sat back down. "Did Harrison tell you why I was moving my company?"

"Yes." She nodded. "For your daughter. Which is very respectable. Not many men or women would do that for their child."

"No, I guess they wouldn't. Being in her life is the most important thing to me." He smiled and looked at his watch. "Have you had lunch yet? You probably have, given how late it is."

"No, I haven't. The day just seemed to get away from me."

"Great. Let's go have a late lunch, early dinner." Matthew could tell she was as attracted to him as he was to her.

"I don't want to impose."

"Please, you're not." He stood up, putting his hand out to assist her up. "One thing you need to learn about me, if I don't want to do something or be around someone, I won't, and I certainly wouldn't offer to take them to lunch … or possibly dinner."

Ella caught his eyes on that last comment and felt her cheeks flush again. With a simple nod, she agreed. "I just don't want to overstep any boundaries in our professional working relationship."

Matthew smiled. "Don't worry. There aren't any boundaries in my life that can't be adjusted if necessary."

Ella took a slow, deep breath and released it. Years ago, Harrison had told her she needed to meet Matthew Taylor, but she just blew him off, not fond of blind dates or being set up. But now she wished she had listened to him sooner. Butterflies swirled in her stomach as he extended his arm to her, and they headed out the door together.